DEAR RETROSPECT
A NOTTINGHAMSHIRE FANTASY

DEAR RETROSPECT
A NOTTINGHAMSHIRE FANTASY

by

Joan Stephenson

ASHRIDGE PRESS

Published and distributed by
Ashridge Press
A subsidiary of Country Books

ISBN 1 901214 04 4

Design, typesetting and production:
Country Books, Little Longstone,
Bakewell, Derbyshire DE45 INN

Tel/Fax: 01629 640670
e-mail: dickrichardson@country-books.co.uk

Printed and bound by: Antony Rowe Ltd, Chippenham, Wiltshire

Some of the eighteenth century characters are based on real people. The Davison, the Knight and the Fletcher families of that time and all the modern characters are fictitious and any resemblance to real persons, living or dead, is accidental.

ACKNOWLEDGEMENTS

I thank my family, my many friends and East Midland Arts for their valuable help and encouragement.

Thanks are also due to Tom Errington of Screveton for designing the book cover so well.

I acknowledge information from the following sources:

Illustrated Social History: G. M. Trevelyan
England Under Queen Anne: G. M. Trevelyan
Annals of Nottinghamshire: Thomas Bailey
Memoirs: Lord Hervey
Transactions of the Thoroton Society

PROLOGUE

I was the youngest of a large family. Father worked abroad for a French oil company and Mother ran off with his best friend before I started school. I don't remember much about her except her arms were warm and her voice soft. The others said she had the most remarkable blue-grey eyes. Speaking eyes, they called them and I used to fantasize a lot. The upshot was our Great Aunt Jane Shaw came down from Yorkshire to look after us here in Newent St. Leonards. She rolled up to our front door with the smallest of bags, a floppy young labrador called Fred plus a ginger cat with broken whiskers and bad breath.

Our lives improved from that moment and, best of all, she wouldn't let us forget our runaway mother.

"Flibbertigibbet", said Great Aunt Jane. "Let her heart rule her head, she did. She never would have gone, though, if your father had kept that good job at Simmo's instead of going off to such a rum place to make pots of money for that French lot. She'll be back, don't fret."

I hung on to those words like a lifeline.

Great Aunt Jane took to Newent as much as she took to us. She said it was a grand place to live and what more did we want? She didn't even turn her nose up at Newent's smells and reckoned our market place brewed a scent all its own; a stir-fry of wet fish, ripe fruits, cut flowers and factory new fabrics with more than a hint of roasting coffee beans, baking bread and smoking bacon. She even relished the strong odour of malting that stuck in our throats and the smell of cooked sugar beet when the campaign was on. She didn't even blench at the stink off the sugar factory's waste lagoon, nor the glue factory neither. Nowdays she could add baked potato take-aways but not then, back in the sixties.

I can still feel her strong hand tight round my own as she dragged me over those toe-stubbing market place cobbles.

"Keep your eyes up, you", she'd shout, "and listen to me."

I would squint into sunshine bouncing off weather cock and steeple and duck my head as shoppers gawped at the sound of her alien voice.

"It represents Time, this square, my lad. Just like a scotch kilt. Now work that one out, you."

"Pleats?" I asked hopefully.

"On the right track. But there's summat else as well. It'll come when you're ready for it."

What really got her going was Webster's Place just beyond the Parish Church. She was potty about that street, was Great Aunt Jane. It gave me the creeps with its tall three storied walls blocking both light and air, its peeling paint and shutters askew. I would hold my breath for fear of catching a fever while she carried herself off to catch glimpses of long skirts, clean pinnies and mob caps. I didn't put it past her to see sedan chairs down there as well.

I just kept my mouth shut and let her rattle on.

"No need to lift your head up here," she said. "This street's intact from top to bottom since the day it was built in seventeen hundred and summat. And if we shut our eyes, like as not, we'll see somebody wearing a wig at one of these windows."

My lids dropped like roller blinds but I daren't let on neither somebody nor wig materialized. Her eyes caressed every brick while my lungs were near bursting.

Nothing would induce me to open my mouth in that street.

We'd be turning into the old graveyard on our way home before I'd feel safe enough to breathe again. It was the same ritual every time. She'd swing round and point to the Webster's Place roofline.

2

"Look at that, my lad. You'll never see a finer townscape than that."

She was right.

That double row of high chimneys with its sharp pattern of rectangular stacks and curved pots dark against writhing smoke and changing sky made us both gasp. She'd be thinking of the man that built it. I was always glad to be safely out of it.

That street haunted me.

To cap it all, as if she hadn't got enough to do, she found herself a part-time job in Newent's municipal offices. I don't think she did much more than answer the phone, make pots of tea and direct people to whichever rooms they were due for various meetings. But I'm pretty sure she'd not miss the chance to squint at minutes and notes. And I bet any money she went through waste paper baskets as well.

These offices had once been a fine mansion built by the same chap who'd built Webster's Place. Great Aunt Jane said they had an atmosphere and no amount of electric light could shift the gloom of the place. She was positive Webster's unhouselled ghost roamed its warren of rooms and labyrinth of passages. It never occurred to her as she licked her lips over her ghostly tales she was sending me off to nightmarish dreams. Being her top favourite was not always pleasant.

She was an odd mixture of disciplinarian and free spirit was Great Aunt Jane. Trespassers will be prosecuted notices begged her to ignore them, gates cried out to be opened and fences positively demanded to be climbed over. If ever a day promised to be dry and sunny after a miserable wet spell and as long as it didn't fall on one of her working days we'd catch her Yorkshire voice leaping up the stairs.

"No school uniforms today. Get your old clothes on, you lot. We're off for a bit of exercise. That'll do you more good than a stuffy classroom."

We knew our Dad wouldn't approve but he wasn't here to object, was he? Off we'd trek to fields and woods with dog

3

and picnic and she'd find jolly tree-climbing, stream-damming places, all within a stone's throw of Newent. She never showed the slightest compunction as she dashed off our separate excuse notes next morning.

"Take your pick," she'd shout. "Do you want snuffles and sneezes, diarrhoea or convenient headaches"?

The novelty soon wore off for the others. By the time I was well past eight the eldest had left school while the rest had got themselves into various sports teams and weren't so ready to play truant.

I was different.

About eleven o'clock of a fine morning, in early April '68 not long before my ninth birthday, she and I were off on another illicit jaunt. This one started with a tedious walk through dull streets where Fred strained at his leash eager to get his pads off hard pavements on to something more comfortable.

"It's a mystery trip, is this," said Great Aunt Jane.

She led the way up Clay lane, over the railway bridge, past a rubbish tip on the right with an odd unsavoury character lurking about which added a certain frisson to the expedition. To the left was a large playing field with swings and a solitary mountain slide, but no children. We crossed this bleak expanse of rising ground to climb over a fence into a scene so unexpected I was dumfounded. We slipped Fred's leash and he nosed around in glorious freedom.

"Eeh lad, look at this," said Great Aunt Jane.

She had discovered a copse I never knew existed. Tight budded trees let sunshine dapple its quilted floor. We looked at each other and both knew we had breached a secret garden. There were too many exotic fronds unfurling, soft clumps of primroses, all shades of pink and on through butter to cream, violets too bold to be wild and, besides, there were echoes of paths, crumbling low walls and gold splashed ivied banks. Scents were heady and dangerous.

Rabbits scattered, birds sang their hearts out and Fred

4

circled ever more madly, nose down, tail high. Great Aunt Jane caught hold of my hand. We pushed on further uphill and for the second time stopped dead in our tracks. We'd stumbled across the ruin of two or three old stone columns.

"It's a folly," she whispered, too overcome to shout. "An eighteenth century garden folly."

She let go my hand, walked all round the columns, then stood, pressing her back against cold stone, gazing up the slope through the trees. I knew she was off where Webster's Place so often took her. Ladies in silken gowns and ribbony caps gentlemen in knee beeches and long fancy waistcoats had once strolled here along neat terraced paths. And she could see every one of them. Together we walked between the columns, not speaking, hardly daring to look at each other.

It was a magical place.

There must have been some odd trick of bright sunshine and shadows of leaves, a pretty shimmer of light and shade. The columns looked different. More slender. A kind of domed canopy linked them together above our heads and a figure, no more than a wraith, appeared between them.

We stopped, all three; the hairs on Fred's back rose in a ridge. His ears pricked, his tail stiffened. A shiver ran down my back like a stream of iced water. I heard Great Aunt Jane's intake of breath.

The sun shone fiercer. The figure crystallized to that of a young girl as clear cut as the trees and the columns. I saw her face as plain as day till a sudden light breeze ruffled my vision. Small leaves fluttered. The quality of light changed and she slipped away.

"Did you see what I saw, lad? An old fashioned lass with a white wig and a long green silk dress? We'd best get home and say nowt. Nobody in this world would believe us," Great Aunt Jane's voice was still no more than a whisper. And all this from somebody who said she felt more at home in a wood than anywhere else.

5

I had bad dreams that night. Nothing would induce me to tell Great Aunt Jane that I, too, had seen a girl. But my girl showed no sign of a wig and I didn't notice her clothes either. I was too much taken up with the most remarkable blue-grey eyes looking directly into my own. Neither one of us ever mentioned that girl or that place again.

When things got on top of her, as they did now and then, our Dad always away, and there being so many of us, she would threaten to build herself a bungalow on a favourite wild patch in our large garden.

That was how she met Mr. Beresford, the architect.

They were both local history buffs and she came home from her Beresford sessions chockful of nostalgia, an excited sheen on her face, that mole over her left eyebrow fairly bristling and not so much as a faint outline of her threatened project. But she did bring back tales of the Beresford family, nearly as large as our own. I didn't expect to meet them. Their boys went to private school and I got the notion their mother was a snob. But there was a girl I took a fancy to, though she was nearly twice my age. Great Aunt Jane said she had eyes just like our mother's and I was cursed with this imagination too lively by half.

When our Dad sent the birthday money for my very first bran-new bike I had the nerve to ask for a cricket match party as well.

"It's too early for cricket" said the others.

"He can have a cricket match in December, if he wants one" said Great Aunt Jane and I watched the others bite their tongues.

"I mean a proper cricket match with eleven on each side in whites and two reserves."

"Oh, aye."

I don't know how she managed it. We didn't even know twenty two nine year old boys plus two ready to come for nothing more than the off-chance and a jolly good tea. She was on the phone for days.

6

After her Yorkshire tea party – 'we don't want any shop muck in this house' was one of her expressions – the Beresford twins said it was the best party they'd ever been to. I couldn't take my eyes off their big sister when she came to collect them for home. She strode onto our lawn with legs right up to her bottom in fancy tights and the shortest of short skirts in her granny print shift. She tossed back her glossy brown hair and reminded the twins – 'the Nibs' she called them – to say their thankyous. She made a pretty speech to me, wished me many happy returns of the day and my heart was quite lost.

I stood at our gate to see them off while Great Aunt Jane was pouring sherry for parents come to pick up their sons. Lucy Beresford turned round, her lovely blue-grey eyes looking straight into mine.

I had seen her before and, more than anything else in the world, I wanted to see her again.

1968

CHAPTER 1

The mid-morning racket from Number Ten Fair Promise Road confirmed the beginning of Easter holidays for Sam and Flo Beresford's five children. Trying to contain the row inside gave Flo more headaches than the row itself and no wonder she longed for a house without neighbours. A tiny woman, with the energy of half a dozen twice her size, even she was harassed this morning, her dark curly hair going its own way, taking her last dab of face powder with it, her eyes showing a tangle of trouble: Beacon House, food, Sam's Ashfield job, Music Club minutes . . .

The small whine of her polisher skimming the hall floor was all but snuffed out by the larger sounds in the house.

Talentless thumps of piano keys clamoured from the music room upstairs. That was Emily, sixteen and the eldest by twenty minutes, enjoying her own composition. Flo winced at the discords of a grand finale and could not, for the life of her, think how that girl came by the soubriquet, Silent Em, whenever the boys wanted to tease.

Now Emily's din was replaced by clash of pot and pan above hiccup and whirr of an ancient washing machine. That must be Lucy, Emily's twin, though nothing like her in looks or ways, and Flo often said that was why they got on together so well. She recognised the cacophony of Lucy scuttling through kitchen chaos, picking up this, cleaning that, putting away the other, muttering fierce epithets about everything in sight. There was no mystery why the boys dubbed her Madam Dragon. They'd all been scorched by her fiery tongue. Crash. A dish must have slipped in the hubbub. Hell, Damn and Blast and Hell again and Heaven knows what under her breath. Flo didn't know where Lucy got the words from. Sam and she never swore. Sam's office doorbell, his desk bell and the telephones rang incessantly.

"Bells, bells, bells, bells, bells," rang out from the kitchen. "How I love to hear the ringing of the bells."

"And so you should, my girl. Bells might mean money in this house," countered Flo, forgetting her own complaint that their whole lives were being lived through those tiresome chimes. Thank goodness Sam would set up an office in the town as soon as they, moved house.

The hall floor now had a gloss high enough to break a leg and she switched off the polisher just as the long case clock struck eleven. Good. She wasn't so far behind after all.

"Lucy, darling," as she looked into the kitchen. "You've cleared up beautifully. Will you see what the Nibs are doing please? They're being rather too quiet for my liking though why that should bother us, Heaven knows. Make them clear up those cuttings in the bottom garden and then we'll have coffee."

"If those lazy little devils . . ." The rest was lost in fierce slam of back door.

Flo put her hands to her ears as she tried to sort out what she ought to do next. The tired washer switched itself off with a rickety click and final judder. Emily's dissonance changed to the clatter and stop of a decrepit sewing machine as she now struggled with over ambitious dressmaking. Well, a girl's, as well as a man's, reach must exceed her grasp, Flo supposed, though dreading the messy mistakes she'd have to sort out before Emily's grasp got anywhere near reach.

The sound of new pop music twisted down from another bedroom.

That must be Robert, fourteen, and the lone wolf of the

9

family. Younger, he had been like a triplet with the girls but now he had grown up and away from them, his sudden gangling height and cracked voice embarrassments they mocked unfeelingly. Really, if that boy had been spending any more money on those rubbishy records. It was unhealthy music anyway. She loathed it. Sam must speak to him. Though she'd have to nag till blue in the face first. It was always the same. She'd even had to tell Robert the facts of life herself. Men . . .

The back door burst open. Lucy blazed into the kitchen swinging a blackened saucepan in each furious hand.

"What is it now?" asked Flo.

"Those hooligans you call boys, those devilish fiends . . ."

"Lucy, Lucy." It was only a mild reproof. She felt nearly as worn out as the old washer this morning.

"Well, look at what they've done. Look at your new copper pans."

"What on earth . . . ?"

"They've been making toffee in the summerhouse. You never saw such a mess. Sugar all over the place, the new tin of golden syrup all gone. And who's going to clean these, I'd like to know?"

She dashed the saucepans together and bits of burned toffee flew about the newly cleaned kitchen.

"Now then, now then. They'll soon come all right. Pop them into the sink and I'll soak them in vinegar." Flo's voice was calm against Lucy's distress.

"If we'd done that you'd have murdered us."

"Yes. I know. I'm getting old. What are Henry and Edward doing now?"

"I don't know." Lucy's voice had a little catch in it. "I banged their heads together and booted their behinds."

"Well, they can clean up the summerhouse and get on with the bottom garden. I'll go and tell them. Flick a duster round the snuggery for me, there's a good girl. Double pocket money this week for helping so much."

The fear of Lucy in tears drove her quickly outside, across a little paved courtyard, through a small orchard and into the summerhouse where Henry and Edward, nine year old identical twins, were hastily clearing up. Good Grief, people said, two sets of twins in one family, however do you cope? And no wonder, she thought, putting on her set look.

"Mum, Mum, it wasn't our fault. It was Lucy. She . . . "

"Yes, I know, and you deserved it."

She looked round the summerhouse. It wasn't as bad as she had expected. Lucy always piled everything on with a shovel. Tense lines in her face relaxed and colour returned to the Nibs' pale faces. She wasn't cross but she noticed the sticky state of their clothing as they rushed to defend themselves.

"We've got our old things on."

"And a good job too," she returned rather more sharply than she felt. "Now be useful for the rest of the morning and I might let you have a bonfire this afternoon."

"Good-o. Can we roast potatoes?" They pressed round her. She looked down into their upturned, freckled faces and loved them. She felt she ought to be angry with them for Lucy's sake. Poor Lucy.

"I don't know. We'll see." She kept her voice deliberately stern. "It depends." They ran off, leaping over flowerbeds, scattering daffodil heads this way and that, doing more damage than last night's gale. Sam would be furious. They fell headlong over the rockery and Flo gritted her teeth as she glanced at her watch and turned back to the house.

She sank into a deep armchair in the little snuggery and put up her feet. Ten minutes' rest. Then coffee. She closed her eyes but unseasonably hot sunshine bored through the leaded lights till she was forced to open them again. Lovely day, the first in over a month. High winds in the night had certainly cleared the air. She made up her mind there and then. No bonfire. Not here anyway. They would go to

Beacon House this afternoon and get some work done up there while Sam did his site visit in Ashfield. The beginning of three weeks' holiday. They must all help. And why on earth Sam was wasting a precious morning on batty old Jane Shaw she couldn't think. There wasn't the remotest chance of a job from that quarter. He was too kind, that was his trouble. Sorry for the old girl because she'd come from Lord knows where to take on that unruly brood belonging to that no good nephew of hers. No wonder his wife had . . .

She closed her eyes again.

Thank Heavens they would soon have room enough to spare and noise wouldn't matter. Beacon House. The Ashfield job. Music Club minutes. Why the dickens had she agreed to be secretary again this year? Poor Sam. Worried about Ashfield, but never saying.

The front door bell jangled.

"I'll go, Lucy," she called.

A quick look in the glass. What a sight. She wished her hair would be like other women' s and stay tidy, and was nonplussed to find herself facing a clergyman on the front doorstep. She wrenched her eyes from the blatant dog collar to the handsome face, vaguely familiar. She hoped there was some money somewhere. in the house, remembering an earlier scrape through three handbags before she could pay the milkman. Record player and sewing machine still belted out their hideous concert. She could hardly hear herself think. The man raised an old fashioned black homburg.

"Good morning, Mrs Beresford." An attractive, deep voice.

"Do you remember . . . ?"

"Good moming. I'm afraid I . . . "

"John Clements, the Rector of St, Wilfred's at Edgington. We met at the Appleby's party last Christmas. I thought you might . . ."

"Of course. Good morning, Rector. Yes, I do remember

you." Her face relaxed to a welcome as she led the way to the snuggery. "This is my daughter, Lucy. Lucy this is Mr. Clements, the Rector of Edgington."

"How do you do, Lucy?"

Flo noticed the man's gaze at Lucy's short skirt and she thought Lucy needn't smile so prettily in reply.

"Sit down, Rector," she said. "Lucy, would you like to make some coffee? Daddy will be ready in five minutes or so." And if he had dared breathe a whisper to that old Shaw woman about their move to Beacon House, she'd murder him.

She looked at the Rector. What a handsome man but . . . and did not know why she added that qualifying 'but'. He was a big man she saw now they were on level ground together; not as big as Sam but looser limbed and more agile as he lowered himself comfortably into a deep armchair, placing his hat on a little wine table nearby. Thirty eight? Forty perhaps. Not more. His dark hair had started to grey at the sides but was still thick, not like Sam' s that grew everywhere but the top of his head. It was a strong face, though, well-tanned, firm jawline, good teeth. Now she knew. It was the eyes she wasn't happy about. Who had once said the eyes are the mirror of the soul?

"What a beautiful spring day it is," she said brightly.

"Yes." He coughed, nervously, she thought. "And how is the work at Beacon House coming along Mrs. Beresford?"

"Oh, very slowly, I'm afraid," she laughed ruefully.

"H'm," the Rector cleared his throat again. "The previous owners, old Mr. and Mrs. Newton, always came to evensong at St. Wilfred's in Edgington whenever they could. I got to know them rather well, in fact. And I've always been interested in the house. I was just passing and thought I would enquire. You won't be moving yet awhile, I suppose. You have five children, I believe . . .

His voice trailed off. It was an arresting voice, though, apart from that cough, seductive almost. But she could not think of a suitable reply. I wonder what he really wants, she

13

thought, and wished Emily and Robert would stop their din.

"Of course, you know it has been a most unhappy house." The Rector frowned. "Not only in the Newton's time but long before that, I believe."

"How do you mean 'an unhappy house'? Can a house be unhappy?

"Mrs Newton died there most miserably, you know." He lowered his lids before Flo' s direct gaze and shifted uncomfortably in his seat. "I did what I could . . ."

"I know she was ill for some time, poor woman. It' s an old house. Before 1700 we think. Obviously people have died there – some of them unhappily, no doubt. Some of us might die there if we stay long enough."

Her voice was brisk and she flung out the last like a challenge. She sat upright on the edge of her chair, alert as though on her guard. She looked straight into the Rector's eyes but could not put a name to what she found there. She wished Sam would come and the noise upstairs would stop. Suddenly her unexpected caller gave a sidelong look from under thick brows and his voice had new warmth in it.

"Mrs. Beresford, I strongly advise you to have that house exorcised before you move into it."

"Exorcised?" Her tone was incredulous, the word obliterating both sewing machine and record player. She heard neither from that moment. "Do you want to take us back to the Middle Ages?"

"You know what I mean, of course?"

"Exorcism? Witchcraft, I suppose."

"No, no, no. Not witchcraft, Mrs. Beresford. Not exactly. Evil spirits. Bad influences."

"Evil spirits." She laughed derisively. She could not help it. "Really, Mr. Clements, it's no use talking to this family about such things. We have our feet planted very firmly on the ground, I assure you."

"Do you mean to tell me, Mrs. Beresford, that none of you has ever noticed an – an atmosphere in that house?" He sounded serious and insistent.

"Good Heavens, no." She laughed again. I certainly wouldn't notice anything for I don't believe in such stuff – do you?" She shot the question straight at him, aiming well below the belt she thought.

"Well, I expect you've heard all about the Newtons and how unhappy Mrs Newton was."

"Of course. Everybody knew. How could she have been anything else with that mad husband and his daft experiments?"

"I don't know. She was a sweet woman but very bitter at her husband's apparent neglect. She was lonely up there, needed company. Her husband was engrossed in so many different projects, you see. If it wasn't one idea it was another. Always tinkering. Nothing successful. There was a deal of hate in that house. It's a strong emotion and contagious I think. Certainly I never liked the atmosphere. Sometimes the hate was so strong you could almost smell it like – like an unwashed blanket."

"But, Rector, as a churchman you don't meddle in such things, do you?" Flo was shocked at the idea and revolted by the simile.

"No, no, no. Not meddle. But I have read a lot and have a wide experience, and I do believe there are supernatural powers, good and evil, that we know very little of. After all, what do we really know of the mysteries of the human spirit? I can only warn you."

"Ah, here's Lucy with the coffee." Flo stood up in relief. "Put it down there, darling. Do you take sugar, Rector? She busied herself with the mugs. "Lucy, be a good help and put the soup on for lunch. And make a quick lemon mousse for pudding. There's a packet somewhere."

Lucy shuddered inwardly at 'the packet'. She picked up her coffee and smiled even more prettily.

"Will you excuse me, Mr Clements?"

The Rector nodded and Flo knew he had noticed that

smile as well as the shudder. His gaze was still following Lucy when her father appeared.

Sam Beresford paused in the doorway, a big man with a vigorous, jolly face, gold rimmed glasses, a shiny bald head whose crinkly brown hair still grew thickly at the back of his neck, his big rough hands, unlike those of any other architect they knew, coaxing the bowl of a pipe to life. Even now, after eighteen years, Flo knew why she had married him. She introduced the Rector, her large eyes flashing frantic but incomprehensible messages till she could contain herself no longer.

"Sam, the Rector wants us to have Beacon House exorcised!"

She dropped her bombshell and could hardly believe either eyes or ears when Sam calmly helped himself to four spoonsful of sugar and smiled pleasantly.

"Well, Rector, if that's what you think, as soon as there's a room fit enough to hold a service we'll let you know."

Flo's pink cheeks turned bright crimson. She was speechless.

"Of course, there' s so much still to be done," Sam went on even more pleasantly. "All that junk of the Newton's lying about. I wish the executors would put their skates on and get rid of it." He turned to Flo. "Such a nice day, my dear, pity to waste it. I think I'll give that Ashfield site visit a miss, the others can manage, and we'll go up Beacon Hill straight after lunch and get some work done there."

She was still astounded and could find only a very small voice to ask if their visitor wanted more coffee. The row from upstairs started to bang inside her head again as the Rector picked up his hat.

"No, no, my dear. You're very busy. I'm sure your husband is right. I'll be getting along. It's a fascinating house. There is quite a story about the family who built it. When you've more time you might be interested." He fished in his coat pocket and pulled out a tube of sweets. "You won't mind if I take one of these? Seem to have a permanent tickle. Most annoying but these are very good."

"No, of course not." She could hardly get the meaningless words out but no sooner had she closed the front door than she ran back to the little room, tears of anger starting up in her eyes.

"Sam, how could you acquiesce to such stuff and nonsense? Just by agreeing to have that stupid service we admit we believe in such rubbish. How could you?"

She shook with indignation and stamped a small foot at her large husband. Her head ached fit to burst and she would go mad if that perishing row didn't stop. Sam drained his mug at one gulp and looked down at her shamefacedly, head on one side.

"Well, I don't know, my dear. What else could I say if the silly chap wants to hold his blessed service? Of course you know I don't believe in such stuff." Then defiantly, "Well, I got rid of him, didn't I? You'd have had him here all day arguing the toss."

He laughed good-humouredly, his sharp eyes teasing her as Lucy burst into the room, bowl in one hand, egg beater in the other.

"Mummy, Daddy, I heard all that. What a hoot. Mum, you'll have to finish lunch; I'm going to tell Em and Robert."

She threw the utensils on to an antique settle near the door and Flo watched a glutinous mixture drip off the seat on to a fine Shirvan rug.

"Lucy," she wailed, but Lucy was dashing up the stairs two at a time.

"Em. Emmee. Rob. Robert. Whaddyaknow? Ghosts at Beacon House. Beacon House is haunted."

Sewing machine and record player ceased their rowdy duet and Flo turned on Sam in vexation. Anything to break the now ghastly silence.

"It's all very well you wasting a whole morning on old Jane Shaw. I don't suppose her plans for that mythical cottage she's always on about are one brick further on, are they?"

"She's not always on about that. She happens to be very knowledgeable about Newent's history and, what's more, you didn't object when she invited the Nibs to that boys' cricket match, did you?"

Flo didn't reply.

Remembering how that match had given her a blissfully clear day at Beacon House to measure up for curtains and fittings, she set about cleaning the mess left by Lucy to stifle her conscience.

CHAPTER 2

Flo tried to shut her ears against family bickering as, squashed into Sam's big old car, they turned up Beacon Hill Road but it was impossible to ignore Lucy breathing fire and brimstone all over the Nibs as they bandied the word 'ghost' about.

"Shuddup, you two, if you can't talk sense. And if you don't shuddup, I'll thump you."

"Huh. There's a law against it, is there?"

"What?"

"Against speaking, that's what. It's a wonder Henry and me don't have tongues that shrivel up through not using 'em. Well, let me tell you there's a law about free speech in this country. Only this rotten family's never heard of it." Edward was in full spate. "It's a wonder to me we ever learned to speak at all. I know what you'd like. You'd like us two to've been born deaf and dumb, wouldn't you?"

"Yes."

"Mum, did you hear what Lucy said? She said . . ."

Lucy promptly carried out her threat that left Henry and Edward quietly thumping each other. Fighting always cleared the air quicker than argument.

"And that' s quite enough," said Flo, turning to fix them with one of her looks. "I don't want to hear the word ghost again. There isn't such a thing and I'm tired of the whole subject." She wondered at her own vehemence. "We've come out here to get some work done. Robert, you can chop down that sapling near the odd room at the back. Nibs, you can get rid of the ivy on the coach house walls. And don't

19

leave it lying about any old how. Put it in a tidy heap . . ."

"Can we light a bonfire? You promised."

"No, I didn't. And don't interrupt. Girls, you can . . ."

"Oh, Mummy," pleaded Lucy. "Can we choose our rooms today?"

"Yes, you two can make lists and then help Robert."

The car purred its comfortable way to the top of the hill and turned right into a concealed drive that continued on level ground where the crown of the hill had once been levelled to a fair-sized plateau.

"If anybody's mad," said Robert, "I should think that Rector . . ."

"Enough," said Flo shortly. "He' s obviously a most unintelligent man."

"Handsome, though," murmured Lucy.

"No more!" thundered Flo. When roused, she had a powerful voice for such a small body.

"Don't get het up, old girl. It's not worth it," said Sam, steering between pothole and ridge. "Let's look at our house."

Feeling hard done by, Flo kept a tight rein on herself. From the back a frantic unwinding of windows, poking of heads and kicking of shins set off a fight for the view. She ignored them. Sam was right for once.

Ahead straggled the rest of an unkempt drive, patchy with moss, encroached by rank grass, in its turn smothered by nettle and bramble and on each side dark evergreen walls draped with last season's wild clematis. Not a single Beresford saw any of that. They saw only the old house that was to be their new home.

Standing in romantic isolation, that house soared into the April sky. Its vertical lines drew their looks straight up to the magic of a balustraded hipped roof with fairy-tale cupola and graceful chimney stacks. The roof with its high dormers sloped down to the rose-red walls. Reluctantly their gaze turned from the perfectly balanced windows to the handsomely pillared doorway crowned with the prettiest fan light they had ever seen and on past wide stone steps to weedy drive and cruel reality.

The cupola vanished, the balustrade hung like a broken fence; tiles slipped; rose red bricks showed like open wounds through scabby skin of peeling stucco.

"Look how beautiful that cedar tree is in the sunlight," said Flo tucking her mouth into a smug little Mona Lisa smile. Oh, yes, it's a jewel of a house, she thought, not another like it so close to Newent.

Together they scrambled out of the car to the strain of workmen's harsh voices and a wireless at full blast drowning their family banter. Sam and Flo were left in the forecourt still transfixed with admiration for their new property.

"Darling, look how badly the stucco is peeling. I can't wait to see it all off. The bricks will be beautiful," enthused Flo. "Can that be the next job now the roof is done?"

"We'll see. There are more important things than that. Let's go inside."

"Oh, Sam, look. Those damp stains are getting bigger." Flo groaned as they stood in the high wide hall, larger than any room at Fair Promise Road.

"Yes, my dear, your map of Europe up there will soon be a map of the world."

They turned their backs on the offending wall and Flo regained her cheer.

"Every autumn, as soon as the weather turns cool, we'll have blazing log fires in here. Nobody else we know has a hall with a fireplace. Not even the Applebys." She tapped the chequered flags with her small feet. "These can be cleaned till they come up like new. That' s what the Applebys did with theirs. They'll look beautiful with our old rugs. They made do with repro but we . . ." She regarded the ceiling and walls again. "Two shades of green we'll have in here. And lots of off white. Or would blues be better?" She was thinking of the rugs. "Aren't the cornices beautiful and aren't we lucky?"

"I'm not sure about that, my dear. We haven't got there yet."

"Cold feet, Sam?" she quizzed.

"Blocks of ice," he returned, looking at the daunting staircase.

She knew immediately that the one difficulty had attracted another. He had too much conscience for his own good. What difference could one missed site visit possibly make? She refused to let the Ashfield job dampen her own enthusiasm, whatever it might do to Sam's.

Oh, those curves, she thought. What silken skirts had once swept down these wide shallow stairs and whose half-mittened hands had once stroked these oaken rails? It's beautiful. At least it had once been beautiful. Now the rounded nosing had been knocked off the lower steps. Some of the lyre-shaped balusters were broken and the whole staircase was caked with flaking plaster. But wait till she and Sam got down to it. She closed her eyes and the oak gleamed richly brown, the balusters repaired and gilded.

"Kitchen stinks," shouted Lucy. "A pigeon must have died in the chimney unless it's dead rats." Her disgusted shrieks made Flo wince.

"Take no notice," said Sam leading her into the drawing room.

"Large enough to have a dance in," Flo was determined to see the bright side of the lofty walls, carved cornices and graciously shuttered windows. "It's the most handsome room I've ever seen. Think, Sam, five twenty firsts and two weddings." She squeezed his arm. "Yes, it's worth it."

"Won't take you long to strip this lot, my dear," Sam indicated the sagging wallpaper that hung in bedraggled strips, showing the mould-spotted plaster behind. He grinned at the flicker of dismay in his wife's large eyes and took her arm. "Come on. No more time wasting. You suss out the kitchens while I have a word with the men."

Beyond the stairs the drawing room opened into a smaller

22

sitting room that Flo had earmarked for their new snuggery, to be called 'the little parlour', though 'little' was a bit of a misnomer considering the rooms they were used to at Fair Promise Road. Still, she liked the phrase and repeated it often, since it was the room they were likely to tackle first. Opposite the drawing room was the dining room of similarly elegant proportions and, leading off it, another smaller room to be called the study. Behind them all was a conglomeration of kitchens, pantry, scullery; each dour and forbidding. But just wait till she got her hands on them. Just wait.

"Em. Emmee. Emily. Where the dickens are you?" Lucy was still shouting her head off.

Flo frowned. That child's voice. She decided to give the kitchen a miss and go straight to the odd room, her steps echoing through the servantless passages.

Here was so obviously an unaccountable addition to the back of the house, not at all in keeping with the rest. The ceiling so high and plain. The dreary windows of the meanest methodist kind. Whatever had it been used for in the first place? Was it a chapel? Had a family of dissenters once lived in the house? And whatever could they do with it now? It would cost a fortune to heat. The sheer size of it. She shivered in the chill of its musty air, remembering the Rector's hideous simile. Well, there was certainly a bit of a smell, but as for his talk of hate – what rot! She did not dislike the room. It had a peaceful feeling and only needed an open window and a roaring fire in the great fireplace to freshen it up. She felt calm in this room, probably because Sam had put his foot down – he could sometimes – and said it must stay as it is for the time being. It would certainly be the only room in the house not being turned upside down and inside out.

She looked with distaste at the untidy crates of Newton paraphernalia stored in one corner. If it were true what Meg Appleby had said on the phone this lunchtime, that the

Rector fellow was a beneficiary, then she hoped to High Heaven he would not be involved in clearing things out. He was the last person they needed at Beacon House. Great Scott, was that a squeak she heard? They must put down some traps.

She wondered if the children were getting on with their jobs.

Emily, she knew, would be poking about the bedrooms choosing the one with the best view and most space. Well, it was time they all had rooms of their own. No more squeezing gallons of clothes into pint-sized cupboards. No more non-stop chat from one when the other wanted to sleep. She could hear Lucy now, still shouting from somewhere or other. Where on earth had she got to?

She struggled to push open a window overlooking the back of the house. Directly below there was Robert battling with a stubborn sycamore root. She supposed she should send the girls to help. She ought to get back to Sam but she'd rather stay here and dream dreams.

Past the weedy courtyard, bound by the odd room on one side and coach houses on the other, a paved terrace stepped down to an overgrown rose garden enclosed by the narrow red brick of an earlier century. Beyond that, through an arched gateway, lay a neglected shrubbery, almost a dwarf forest. She could hear the Nibs' voices, faint and far away. It looked as though they had abandoned the ivy job. She saw Lucy streak out of the yard, straight down the terrace, hair flying, lungs yelling. She must have heard the Nibs and was racing to tell them off. Bang through the iron gate, Flo watched Lucy striding into the rose garden, leaping over the tangled growth of wild greenery as if she'd grown wings, and out through the opposite gate, by the sound of it, to be lost in a brown-green jungle. Madam Dragon to a T.

Flo turned back to her dreams, while outside Lucy listened for the Nibs. She could still hear them but where were they?

Afternoon sun shone warm and bright; young spring green

showed everywhere through winter brown. Again, the Nibs' voices floated from somewhere beyond this riotous mass of scrub twisted about by briar and bramble. She would never get through it without cutting herself to ribbons. She pressed on, pushing herself along the outer edge of the low rose garden wall to the left of the gate till she came to the high boundary wall skirting the gardens on that side. Here the bushes did not quite reach the old brick and there was room, only just, for her to squeeze past.

Somebody had preceded her by the look of the herbage. It must be the Nibs. Where the dickens were they?

She edged herself along the narrow way, on one side scratched by sharp thorns, on the other scraped by old bricks, till she reached the formidably high fence that ended their property. Two or three boards had been dislodged by last night's furious wind and a little help from the Nibs, no doubt. Though they'd been warned on pain of a good hiding to keep well away from it, she chuntered, as she scrambled over the fallen pales to squeeze through the gap.

The ground dropped away beneath her feet and she was conscious of going steeply down hill, until she stopped dead in surprise at the dramatic end of the shrubbery into an enormous ivy-clad hole on her right, surely dozens of feet deep and wide – well, big enough to swallow Beacon House, at least.

Pushing the sweaty tangle of hair back from her face she could hear the Nibs' voices, loud and clear.

"Hey! Look at me!"

"Land ahoy!"

There was not a cowardly bone in Lucy's body but she peered timidly enough over the edge of that great pit and caught her breath at the chilling sight of Edward swinging like a miniature Henry Morgan from a bent sapling wrapped in old man's beard.

"Land ahoy! Watch out!"

He swung through the air towards her and back again.

25

"Hi! Look at me!"

She jumped at another yell as Henry hurtled down the ivy-covered slope like a bobsleigh and landed with a dishevelled crash and blood curdling scream at the bottom. She half expected to see him in separate pieces but he gathered himself together, picked himself up, waved a rusty tin tray aloft and started the perilous ascent at a back-sliding pace.

Lucy was too taken aback to tell them off. This was their first warm sunny day at Beacon House. Always before it had been cold and wet and they had never fully explored the shrubbery which terminated their new property. She looked with some curiosity at the stream of red marl with here and there a crumbling-looking white rock that showed through the torn ivy of Henry's slide, like a gash cut deep to the bone. Whatever would Em and Robert say? She didn't care. She wanted to follow the little path clinging to the old wall on one side and dropping away into the abyss below on the other. Ignoring the Nibs, rather taking it for granted that boys spent their lives on the brink of sudden and violent death, she inched along the little path, her path, praying not to fall down the slope, trying not to hear Edward's shouts. She could do without his company, thank you very much, forgetting that beyond the fence they were all trespassing.

"Hey! Lucy! Lucy! Wait for me!"

She reached the far edge of the pit and for the second time stopped dead in her tracks. Before her and to the right of the wall, which still continued down hill, was a wood in all its springtime loveliness and a sight so wonderful, so unexpected that she cried out with surprised delight. She could not help it.

The trees were not too close and still tight-budded enough to let sunlight stipple the floor of bright fresh greenery, huge purple violets, the last few faded celandines, and clumps of pale primroses. Her excitement quickened as a closer look showed the softer ferny leaves of wood anemones and here and there the large coarse rosettes of last year's foxgloves. A rabbit scuttled, a pigeon cooed and the clear monotonous notes of a chiff-chaff said spring is here and, amazingly, not a sign of last night's gale.

She was conscious that among this wild growth were a few trees, an odd bush, an unknown creeping plant that had once been cultivated. And she knew, was certain, the gardens of Beacon House had once reached down as far as this, beautiful, orderly, tended. The continuation of the old wall proved it. And people had once walked down here along clean terraced paths, uninterrupted by that ugly old fence.

Head full of ideas she dare hardly give tongue to, she picked her way over the embossed floor further and further into the spinney and for the third time came to a halt. Well, things always went in threes, didn't they? Good things as well as bad, and here was her third joy in one day.

Here, in the middle of this wood she had stumbled upon a decaying ruin. But what was it? What had it once been? Folly? Gazebo? Rotunda? No, she decided emphatically, not any of these, but a garden house. Yes. It had surely once been an elegant Georgian garden house. Now only one of its columned sides remained and its roof was completely gone. The columns were the same as those at the front of the house. They had been fashioned by the same hands.

She would never be able to explain the light-headed feeling that swept over her at the sight of that ruin. She stood in ripples of sun and shade and their effect was intoxicating. Nothing must interfere with her perception of this place and nobody must know of this new springing joy in her heart.

She ran round the missing sides of her discovery and, beneath the grass and ivy, stubbed her toes against the concealed edge of what had once been the raised floor of her garden house. In the middle of this platform, like some old forgotten tombstone in a country churchyard, was a big hexagonal hunk of stone, now covered with green creeper. She piggled away at the verdant overcoat and swore she found the bas relief of Grecian figures crumbled by weather and ivy tentacles.

She stared at the dense green block. Surely it was just the right height for sitting. How that stone beckoned her to sit.

The ivy tickled her legs like horsehair upholstery as she settled herself to face that huge mysterious pit beyond the trees. The vanished roof had once been domed. she was sure. The remains of a sculpted frieze linked the columns high above her head. The sun shone bright, the chiff-chaff went on as loud as a preacher for ever and ever, Amen. Oh, yes, it was beautiful and only she had found it. It must be her own secret and private place. She would bring her things down here and paint the scene from each of its several sides.

She was alone and happy and very much aware of the feeling that some longed for excitement, even danger, awaited her in this magical place.

She closed her eyes and had the curious sensation her spine was supported by some rounded niche that was not there. A shiver ran through her body as cold as stone. She tried to open her eyes and could not. The chiff-chaff sounded further away and her ears were filled with a swishing sound she could not identify, a sound she had never heard in her life before. Yet she knew what it was. No she didn't. What was it?

She pressed back her head and could have sworn it touched cold hard stone. She breathed deeply to drown that troublesome sound. Shish sh. Swish sh. The sunlight pricked at her eyelids, yet it was dark, pitch dark and with the darkness there came a smell. A smell as mysterious as that sound. Not the bosky smell of a springtime wood. Not earth. Not flowers. Not a feminine something out of a bottle. What then?

She filled her lungs and suddenly her bewildered brain sprang to life. It was surely a smell like pot-pourri from Mama's great blue and white bowl, with stronger hints of the apothecary shop. Immediately she was on her guard. Where had these unfamiliar words sprung from? She sniffed again. Somebody was sucking a scented cachou and that somebody was close at hand. Swish sh. Swish sh. Both sound and smell together shut out all other sensation. They filled her head like the effects of hay fever till she felt too heavy to move, stifled and afraid.

"Hey! Wait for me!"

"Boh! Lucy, wake up!"

"Ey-oop! What's this place?"

She opened her eyes and there stood Edward panting and grinning. Both sound and smell were gone. He moved closer and stared at her ruined columns and creeping evergreens.

"Isn't it lovely?" she said and noticed then, in spite of his running, that his eyes were coal black in a chalk white face, the colour even gone from his freckles.

"I don't like it," he said. "Let's go back." And his face was still white all the way back to the house.

But Lucy's cheeks were flushed, and her eyes bright, for excitement had over-ruled danger and she knew she had opened a forbidden door. Let the rest of the family rattle on as much as it pleased. She hugged the ghosts of Beacon House to herself. Whoever they were, they were not the recent dead.

CHAPTER 3

Lucy and Flo faced each other in the hall of Beacon House after clearing up picnic debris. Flo was impatient to be off.

"It's too bad," she complained, "where have they all got to? It will soon be dark and there's supper to get. Edward was here with you a few minutes ago. Where . . .?"

Lucy was listening, but not to her mother. Swish sh. Swish sh. She cupped her hands round her mouth and shouted up the stairs to blot out that terrible sound.

"Daddy. Em. Emily. You lot. We're ready for off. Come on!"

"I'll look in the garden," said Flo in exasperation. "You look upstairs."

Swish sh. Swish sh. Lucy's ears were filled with that sound, louder and clearer and closer. She sniffed. A different smell hung in the stuffy air of the panelled hall, a vital ingredient missing. This was no more than the floral scent of verbena and lavender from Mama's blue and white pot-pourri bowl on the great oaken chest. But the swish sh, that was the same sound she had heard before and whatever was it? She turned suddenly and in a flash she knew the rustle of silk.

With knowledge came relief.

Her mother paced the hall impatiently, long skirts rippling in agitation. She was dressed for outdoors in a loose hooded cloak of a soft grey colour and, as she moved, Lucy caught sight of a watered silk lavender gown divided to show off a sprigged under petticoat of light green. It was a very pretty outfit, she thought, but why did Mummy look so much older,

30

head enveloped in hood, face stippled with little holes she had never noticed before?

"The carriage is late," her mother was saying. "It is always late. Hobbs is getting too old or too careless, Lord knows which. Drusilla, straighten your back."

"Yes, Mama." The expression slipped off her tongue as though a key had been turned inside one of those new mechanical toys from Germany. She was neither afraid nor excited at this moment, though she remembered that alien word 'apothecary' of half an hour ago and the effect it had had upon her then. And that was it; that was the missing ingredient of the smell in the hall; something from the apothecary shop.

So there was nobody here sucking a scented cough sweet as there had been in the spinney.

Her mother turned her back. Lucy stretched to peer into the ornamental glass above the great fireplace and was conscious she was not as tall as she should be. I wonder how old I am, she thought, but it was an idle thought with no depth to it. Events had overtaken her. She was not her own mistress and without surprise she identified the rattle of iron-shod wheels on stone flags and the slithering of hooves outside.

"The carriage is here now, Mama," she said in a childish voice unlike her own.

"Tish!" Her mother showed her impatience and swept past the manservant by the front door, on between the handsome columns, down the wide stone steps and into the front courtyard where Lucy followed like a little automatum. What she saw outside was a peep show, yet so familiar she barely understood her interest.

Sunshine flooded the paved court in front of the house showing the bold black outline of a graceful young cedar. Pigeons strutted over flagstones and flapped suddenly in a whirring cloud at the noisy stop of a carriage. Restive horses stamped and snickered. Strong light bounced off the many paned windows of the great house, fading its narrow red brick to a rosy hue where lanthom holders of wrought iron showed up like black Spanish lace against its velvety walls. She recognised a child in the yard as the grand-daughter of coachman Hobbs and her only playmate in this grand new house on top of the hill.

Mama was helped up to her seat and there was a flutter of servants, both men and women, bowing and scraping. Mama hardly noticed the attention, concerned only with the arranging of skirts, cloak and hood. Lucy hesitated and Drusilla felt herself lifted up high beside Mama, for Past was so ravelled with Present she could scarce disentangle the two.

"Thankyou Nellie," she said to the smiling mob-capped face that bent over her own, for she knew the solicitous hands tucking a mantle round her lap belonged to Nellie the housekeeper.

"Goodbye May. Goodbye May," to the girl in the yard.

"Straighten your skirts underneath that lap-mantle," Mama's voice was colder than ever today.

Drusilla pressed her small hands on her outstretched knees and looked down at her white-stockinged ankles and shiny black-buckled shoes. Her feet would not touch the floor and still she did not know how old she was. She parted the neck of her cherry red cloak, pure merino, as light and warm as swansdown. She stroked the bodice of her blue and green dress, new soosey and as pretty as Mama's.

She was conscious of a door closing, softer than a car door, the crack of a whip and a giddy-up. Then away sprang the carriage to roll down a neat gravel drive, scattering a gaggle of geese, hissing and honking, to a stiffly cut evergreen hedge with never a trace of old man's beard. Between a pair of wonderfully wrought iron gates Drusilla caught the flash of their gilded spikes. A soft flick from the coachman, down Beacon Hill towards Newent turned the carriage, quite new and well sprung, with a curious swaying and rolling gait she was not used to.

"I hope you're not going to be sick, child," said Mama severely.

"No, Mama." But she did feel sick. She always felt sick when they came into Newent. Mama said it was the roll of this new-fangled carriage but Nellie, who knew everything, said it was the bustle and excitement after the quiet at home. And it was quiet at home, and lonely too, in spite of Nellie and May and all the others. Mama, whose attention she craved more than anybody's, spent all her time at the desk in the little parlour with so many cares that made her as cross as two sticks. Don't interrupt. Why don't you write a long letter to Papa or to your Aunt Peabody? Take up your sampler and hush, child. Help Nellie to tack up the pieces for the new quilt and don't plague me. Tomorrow, if you are good, I will hear you read.

Always tomorrow.

How different everything looked now; Beacon Hill steeper than she remembered it and not much more than a cart track through pleasant greenery. She could not see the town below for the trees, but she could see the tall, pale steeple of St Leonard's Church and she could hear the solemn peal of its passing bell, too familiar a sound to question. She held on to the lap-mantle and wished the gripe in her stomach would lessen. Perhaps Mama would be kinder when the next packet came from Papa. She usually was. Drusilla sighed. Oh, to have a Mama that was never cross. Better still, to have a Papa who stayed at home instead of sailing thousands of miles to the Americas, even though he did make fortunes.

They splashed through the Goat Stream at the foot of the hill and slackened pace as the ground rose again. Drusilla pushed her face to the window. All she saw now was a huddled conglomeration of mud-walled thatched cabins, a mean ale house or two, with here and there a patch of green and a cow, a mill and a maltkiln; all of it through the distorted greenish hue of carriage glass. She watched a cart with a steaming load of goodness knows what turn into a yard. An unpleasant stench churned up her stomach worse than ever. Only the strongest curiosity forced her to open her mouth.

"Mama, what . . . ?"

"Please don't stare so, child. You've eyes as big as saucers. We simply must not see these things. Do you want to be sick?"

"No, Mama."

"You shall have a drink at Uncle Peter's. Better safe than sorry."

The horses pulled easily up the slow rise through Northgate towards Bargate, where humble cabins gave way to large fashionable houses for gentlemen, all quite new. The coachman reined in outside the finest.

"You look so pale, child," said Mama, making it sound like a sin, pushing Drusilla past a little blackamoor through the handsome portico of Mulberry House.

A fine looking man, a complete stranger, for Lucy was trying to ease her way back, advanced towards them, arms outstretched in welcome. The child stared at his blue coat, his immaculate white ruffles all but hiding the gold chain on his chest that along with his grey full-bottomed wig showed him to be both physician and surgeon. Yet she could not tell how she knew that. He is rather like Mama, she thought, but taller and not at all crabbed.

"And how is my poppet today?" A pair of the merriest blue eyes twinkled down at her.

"She feels sick," said Mama. "Can she have a drink?"

"Ho! Ho!" laughed Uncle Peter, for he was a stranger no longer, looking down from his great height. "What makes her feel sick, eh?"

"It's that carriage," said Mama, letting down the hood of her cloak. Drusilla flinched. The words were said with some sound of satisfaction.

They had walked the length of a long passage which now widened into a big room at the back of the house where a settle, a few handsome chairs and small tables had been scattered about with a studied carelessness.

"Do sit down, my dears," said Uncle Peter, indicating the seats with one hand, thrusting the other into a waistcoat pocket to bring out a small gold box. Drusilla stared yet again as he helped himself loudly to snuff and blew his relief into a bright yellow handkerchief. He lifted the full skirts of his blue coat to sit down, looking hard at Drusilla who tried to count how many tiny blue covered buttons there were about him.

"It is not that carriage that makes her sick, my dear Dorothy," he said decisively. "It's the lack of company at Beacon House. You're too melancholick up there, sister, the pair of you. What Drusilla needs is a companion or a dozen companions of her own age, if you can supply 'em. You mark my words. A little sociability is an invigorating medicine. Your physician recommends it." He gave his sister a sly look. "When can we expect Anthony home, eh?"

Drusilla caught the hurt in her mother's eye and wondered, unhappily, what had caused it, but Uncle Peter slapped his thigh and laughed. He pinched Drusilla's pale cheek till the blood came and she looked quite pretty, though as he and Mama settled themselves so comfortably tête à tête, she felt the cold draught of a door shut in her face. Ah. If only her cheeks were rosier and her hair less red, would that make Mama better pleased? Still, Papa's hair was the same colour and Mama never chafed about that.

Anthony. She mulled over the name. That must be Papa. And Dorothy. That must be Mama. Such a pretty name compared to. . . She could not remember what. She struggled to clear her brain till a sound cut through the mist like a blade of light. Mama's voice, sharp and clear.

"What is the news brother?"

"You heard the passing bell, no doubt? It comes to us all,

35

Lords and Ladies and us plain folk alike. Margaret Hatton
has died in Vienna. Robert Hatton will be done up. He doted
on her – whatever they say about him making the match for
money. Sad to think she was still in her prime and three
children left motherless. We must do what we can when they
come back to Park Lodge."

"I'm sorry, " said Dorothy. "I wondered who the bell was
for, but I meant your own news, dear brother."

"I ride to London tomorrow, as you know, my dear. Spend
a few days with old colleagues, listen to the latest remedies,
come home and make a fortune as the foremost medical man
in the shire. I won't stay long. The season gets shorter.
Everybody will be back in the country by the first week in
June. They tell me our new Queen Anne is sick with the gout
and a dropsy. Who knows? She might hear of my success
with Lady Reville."

He laughed good humouredly at himself while Drusilla
stared over the rim of a little delft mug put into her hands by
the smiling blackamoor. She sipped at the small beer laced
with Uncle Peter's Gold Drops Guaranteed to Cure All
Gripes and Megrams and wondered why Mama was bent on
being so sour today. And poor Biddy and Anne and William
Hatton to have lost their Mama. Whatever would they do?
And here was her own Mama shrugging her shoulders and
moving on to things of no consequence.

"Our Papa would turn in his grave to hear you," said
Dorothy. "All this place produces is fairground quacks. You
should have set up in Bath when brother-in-law Peabody
offered."

Dorothy sniffed as Drusilla remembered the family tale of
her young Mama pleading with Uncle Peter to stay on in
Newent after her first lying-in. She was not surprised at his
raised eyebrow as Mama rattled on.

"Bath would have given you some standing. Money is all
very well, Peter, but standing is. . ."

"Pooh, sister! I want for neither. Dr. Peter Fletcher of

Newent St. Leonard's suits me well enough. You have no conception of the world at all. We're on the brink of a new age, my dear. It's where our family back in Somerset, bogged down with its rents and nothing more, made its mistake. Money, in other words trade, as your Anthony very well knows, is the lingua franca of the day. But not forever, my dear. Knowledge will count for more soon enough. And not a parson's knowledge neither, you will see. And I intend to have my share of both while old-fashioned standing can go to the devil. The Bible already has a rival in the ledger, my dear Dorothy, and journals and newspapers are catching up fast now we're well into Anno Domini 1702.

"Which reminds me, my poppet," turning to Drusilla and ignoring his sister's look of impatience, "persevere with your reading, dear child, and since there is nobody else, make use of little May Hobbs. She is bright enough. Teach her and you will teach yourself. Remember, knowledge should be free to all of us, well, most of us, at least," with a significant look at the blackamoor, "I will hear the both of you next time I visit."

He leaned forward, settling his hands on his knees, while Drusilla drank up his words along with his physick and Dorothy tished.

"Yes. We've come a long way since the days of the old alchemists, my dears. Science is becoming more separate and exact, and physicking is a science, in spite of your fairground quacks. Important people recognise it as such. Why, in London . . ."

"You will have some spare time, of course" interrupted Dorothy, having no time at all for her brother's hobbyhorses.

"I think so," the doctor's eyes twinkled. "What commissions have you for me this time eh?"

"Can you bring me a bolt of blue holland for the servants from Edgar's? Eighteen yards of duck's wing green silk and twenty yards of white dimity. I have the patterns for you here." She fished in the pocket under her voluminous skirts.

37

"Certainly, my dear, but why go to London for the servants? Whatever is wrong with Webster's here in Newent?"

"They're hopeless and they get worse. There is hardly a reliable draper in the town nowadays." She placed the patterns on a small table.

"Yes, I hear the Websters have fallen on hard times."

"It's that spendthrift wife, I dare say. She dresses like one of the quality."

"His first did have some kinship with our friends, the Hattons, my dear." The doctor smiled mildly.

"A mere case of her family cat was caught by their tom," came the coarse reply.

"That's what you think, is it? I expect they are in Sir George Markham's company a great deal, as well. Webster does most of his electioneering for him, you know."

"And I expect his second wife is as bad as the first. Everybody in Newent knows what she did for Sir George Markham," said Dorothy with a significant look Drusilla could not fathom.

This gossip of people who were nothing but names whirled inside the child's head as she finished her physick. She gave a little cough, hoping Uncle Peter would notice, but instead he seemed determined to rattle Mama.

"Not to mention Matthew Jenison," the doctor smiled. "Though as rich as Croesus, he don't seem to scorn Draper Webster' s company no more than Markham."

"And we all know how the both of them, Markham and Jenison alike, procured their elections, plying the innkeepers with money to slop out free ale willy nilly to voters crackpot enough to give them their pledge. And not all of 'em franchised either."

Drusilla's ears pricked. She could not put a face to the name Markham but Matthew Jenison's old face loomed in her mind's eye most horridly. Desperate for attention, she gave a louder cough.

"Dorothy, my dear, I do believe you're a Tory at heart."

"I remember how our own family lost lands and money in Somerset," Dorothy's eyes were like ice. "Jenison! The old devil! As rich as Croesus you say? Everybody knows how the Jenisons got their wealth while others lost it. Nothing but robbers of loyal royalists, were they not? And it's not only gold they got away with either. Were there not title deeds besides bones dug up from their cellars and vaults after the War?"

Drusilla's eyes bulged over the rim of her mug. Was old Mr Jenison truly a devil? He had once proffered her a bag of sugarplums and his powdery old face had crinkled horribly and his breath stank like a privy as he extracted payment of three kisses. She had needed to spit into a handkerchief to clean out her mouth. The sweetmeats she had passed on to May Hobbs. They were too dear at that price.

"That's as maybe, my dear Dorothy. That big old house of his was the safest in Newent at the time and half the country people as well as townsfolk dragged their treasures up there to hide from the rascally Roundheads. Was it his fault that most of 'em didn't survive to claim back their own?"

"His family made no great effort, so poor Margaret Hatton told me, to seek out their heirs."

"You will soon change your tune, my dear Dorothy. Your devil has been promoted to archfiend. He is now Sir Matthew Jenison on account of that loyal address he gave to the new Queen, and next time you meet him you'll be bobbing a curtsey and calling him Sir. And what's more, he has staying from Yorkshire a young niece called Elizabeth who might make a useful companion to this little poppet here."

The dropping of Dorothy's jaw gave the poppet the chance of more desperate coughing.

"Well, it's a pity about the Websters," Dr. Peter continued. "They were good drapers once and they have a very clever son. Pride of the Free School, so I'm told and, if there's any justice in the world, somebody will do something to help him." He had noted the cough and turned to his niece. "And what would you like me to find for you in the big bad city, Little One?"

Drusilla blushed with delight, wriggled and smiled but did not speak till Mama tished her irritation and Uncle Peter twinkled encouragement.

"Come on, my poppet, tell me all the playthings you like best."

"Well, shuttlecock and battledore, a peep show, a chap book . . ." the strangely familiar words tumbled out.

"What plebeian tastes you have, little maid. Your Mama can get any of those things any day from the old pedlar man." He leaned further forward to pinch both her cheeks. "Let me tell you what Lady Reville's daughter, Arabella, showed me at Shefford yesterday. She had a miniature tea set, perfect models of all the party things you can think of in shining silver and all the way from Amsterdam in Holland. I'll lay a silver toy, Drusilla, for every book you can read to the end on my return."

"Thank you. Thank you." She lifted her face to be kissed for Uncle Peter was no man-devil like Mr. Matthew Jenison. Now *Sir* Matthew.

"That's settled then. The child will have something to show the young Arabella for a change." Drusilla watched her Mama's mouth curl into a tart smile while pulling up hood and drawing on mittens as Uncle Peter rose from his chair.

"Think on what I've said, Dorothy. You're as melancholick as sick parrots on top of that hill, the both of you. Medecine don't only wage war on a pox or a fever, my girl. We want you to enjoy health and vigour of mind, don't you know?"

"I know I am grown sick of being a woman alone, left to cope with house and servants, to say nothing of Anthony's brick kilns, woodyard and plaster pit, no matter how good an overseer we have. And now my tease of a brother is off on another jaunt and I am left feeling as low as the Trent Valley itself which I very much blame, by the way, for my own melancholicks, the aches and pains of the servants and Jove knows what, not to mention Drusilla's pale cheeks.

She took her walking cane from a hovering servant and Drusilla felt none too gentle a prod.

"Come, Drusilla, we have to call at Webster' s for bonnet ribbons. If by any chance they have the holland or the dimity we'll let you know, Peter, and we wish you a safe journey."

"Might prove to be an exciting one," smiled the doctor. "They say the roads are as full of highwaymen as a buck's back with fleas!"

"Take care then and don't come back with your ruffles as black as coal as you usually do," she presented her bitter pock-marked face to be kissed and her brother did his duty while Drusilla hopped from one dainty foot to the other, knowing the pleasure to come.

Kind hands fixed round her waist and she felt herself lifted high in the air and whirled round and around, gripes and megrams forgotten, till she landed in a heap of giggles and squeals and flashes of white teeth from the blackamoor.

"Heigh-ho, Drusilla! Who knows, my dear poppet, the world is moving so fast, before you're a grown woman we'll be flying to London and highwaymen will have gone to the devil?"

And before Drusilla could ask the whys and wherefores of that there was an opening of doors, a command to the coach-man, the wave of a hand, the crack of a whip and off they wheeled.

CHAPTER 4

"What nonsense the man spouts," said Dorothy. "And don't you go asking if we are all to sprut wings," as Drusilla opened her mouth which she now shut tight to ponder the question until they rolled into the market square alive with milkmaids and wights, pack horses and drovers, a man in the stocks . . .

Lucy nudged at her elbow as she jumped at yet another poke from Mama.

"For Heaven's sake, Drusilla, don't stare so. I noticed how boldly you stared at Uncle Peter's. It is the most unladylike thing. Never do it. Though his crack-brained ideas are enough to make a blind man stare, a deaf mute's ears prick and his tongue wag, not to mention that ridiculous new coat he was wearing. Now let's see if that wretch Webster can help us. Whatever is happening here today?" pushing her way through the crowd with Drusilla in tow.

The scene inside the shop was chaotic.

"Bailiffs!" scoffed Dorothy, as a hectoring bully flung his arms one way and his stentorian voice the other so that the two or three underlings hardly knew what they were about.

Fine silks and brocades spilled everywhere as Draper Webster's half-wound bales were shouldered from shelves to a waiting wagon without. Drusilla was carried away outside herself by the brilliant confusion while Dorothy remained fixed to the ground in vexation.

The hapless draper looked on with a useless wringing of hands. An equally ineffectual moaning and wailing from beneath a shawl-covered figure that rocked back and forth on a high stool brought Drusilla back from Heaven knows where. This must be the extravagant second wife, she thought, noting the quality of the shawl. And that must be the clever son, as her eyes met those of a boy at the back of the shop. Quite forgetting Mama's lecture about staring, she took in his good bearing and the cut of his clothes. He was not expected to be a draper like his father then, this pride of the Free School. Peeping from behind the boy were other younger children, girls, she thought.

She jumped as Mama rapped the floor with her cane, her haughty voice ringing out above the shop chaos so that even the wailing woman hushed and lowered her shawl and the little girls shrank further into the shadows.

"Webster, be so good as to tell me what is happening. Drusilla and I have driven in especially for bonnet ribbons."

The wretched draper cringed at the voice, bowing and shaking his miserable head.

"Ah! Mrs. Davison, you see . . ."

"I see well enough. Your extravagant ways have led you where I always thought they would – the bailiffs." Her words stung the man to a spirited reply, for he ceased his cringing and drew himself up to his full height. He was a tall man, Drusilla noted, and handsome.

"Not my extravagant ways, madam, but those of the quality," he snatched at a roll of bills from the confusion. "See . . ."

"Sue them," snapped Dorothy while the poor man's shoulders sagged again as his best bales trailed on the floor.

"It is not for myself I mind so much, Madam. My poor wife . . .", indicating the shawl screened figure still moaning softly. Dorothy did not even turn her head. Drusilla knew she would have no opinion whatever of Draper Webster's poor wife and she shrank at her Mama's look of disapproval, her own eyes now big as best blue dinner plates staring out of her small white face.

"It's my son Bernard, as well", whined the unhappy

Webster, he is doing so fine at the Free School. They tell me he should go to Westminster and on to Cambridge but now . . ."

Drusilla almost saw Dorothy's ears prick as her formidable Mama swung round to dodge the bailiffs' activity.

"Where is he? Let me see him." Dorothy studied the handsome boy in his suit of good clothes, "H'm. You have more dignity than your stepmother or your father, either."

Drusilla blushed and hoped nobody else had caught the added whisper, 'if he is your father.' She felt rather than understood the slight to the boy.

Webster's poor wife increased her rocking and wailing. Dorothy's face wore its calculating look.

"Set your mind at rest on that score, Webster. Your son shall come with me. We need a companion for Drusilla and he will not miss his chance to go to Cambridge when the time comes," while Drusilla marvelled at her Mama's impetuosity.

Webster's wife re-hid her face in the costly shawl and wailed louder than ever; the little girls whimpered; the bailiffs carried on with their miserable task; the obsequious draper took up his cringing again.

"Mrs. Davison, madam, however can we thank you? Such munificence. You will not regret it madam. Bernard . . ."

"I give you half an hour to get his box ready. And now, are there any bonnet ribbons among this confusion?"

Tish! The dolt of a man, surrounded by allapoons, bunts, tammies, sooseys and scotch cloths, yet no bonnet ribbons nor dimities nor hollands neither! Was there any wonder such a fool should be broken? Great Jupiter, with the new Queen having lived as a Princess in Nottingham, the whole county had gone wild at her accession. He should be sold out of banners and streamers this past month. There'd been enough coronation favours flying through Newent and all the villages to keep a dozen drapers going. The man was a fool to neglect his own business for Markham's politics – if Peter

44

be right. And if he grovelled any lower his hair would soon be sweeping the floor along with his bales. Again Drusilla shrank at her Mama's testy muttering.

Exactly the half hour later young Bernard's box was loaded on to the Davison carriage, only Drusilla marking the tearful farewells.

She wondered if he had noticed the carriage. Nobody else had carriages like the Davison family. Papa and Uncle Peter and Nuthall, the old coach builder, had put their heads together to design a vehicle that would make light work of Beacon Hill. "And you'll have to have hosses according," the coach builder had warned, "only the most sure footeds'll do. The coming down'll be wuss than the gooing up."

Everybody remarked on the Davison carriages and horses too, but this boy took his seat opposite Drusilla and said nothing. Dorothy turned her face to the window, ignoring the two children who watched each other covertly. The boy ceased his snivelling.

They were rolling down Appletongate and just passing the Friary. Drusilla willed herself not to look. Mr. Jenison – Sir Matthew Jenison – lived in that big old grey stone house. Did the niece, Elizabeth, have to suffer that old man's wet kisses, she wondered? The boy's eyes snapped and she noticed his changed expression of face and figure. So he knew where the Jenisons lived as well as she. And if there were also connexions with the Hattons and Markhams, then he was not so low born after all. No matter what Mama might say about somebody's cat being caught by somebody's Tom. She was not aware they knew a Tom. So who, in the world, was he?

The boy leaned forward.

"How old are you?" He asked and his eyes glittered.

Ugh, Drusilla recoiled. His breath smelled, though not as bad as that man-devil Jenison's. She snuggled into her corner and smiled. Nellie would soon be after him with Uncle Peter's sulphur tablets. But she warmed to him nevertheless. He was not perfect and bound to come in for his fair share of

Mama's carping. There'll be less of it for me, she thought.

"I'm eight," she tilted her head and with those emphatic words moved a little further down that dangerous path as the forbidden door almost closed behind her.

"Two years younger than I," said the boy and regarded her boldly the rest of the way.

She, for her part, stared at her Mama. Dorothy's hood had slipped. How brightly fair was Mummy's hair today. Now that was the oddest thing. Was Mama wearing one of the new-fashioned wigs that she had always sworn she never would? And why had she not noticed the change before? There was a confusion in her mind she could not fathom. The complexity, like an unusual dream, was too much for her.

The carriage strained to a standstill outside Beacon House. There was a bustle of strange people and noise in the courtyard. The rose-red brick was scabbed with peeling stucco. The plush of the carriage seat had become peculiarly cold and smooth. She looked down to find she was now seated on red leather and showing a pair of bare knees below a short-skirted dress. She shivered.

"Come on, day-dreamer," said Edward, "hutch up."

"Day-dreamer yourself," said Flo tartly. "Lucy and I have been kept waiting at least half an hour."

"Home, James, and don't spare the horses," said Sam starting the engine.

"Oh Dad," from Henry. "You say that every time. Give it a rest."

"Don't be rude," said Flo.

'I'm back,' thought Lucy and was unusually quiet all the way home. She had a problem. How could she get herself up to the Rectory at Edgington without the others noticing?

She now knew there was more to Beacon House than met the eye, more than she had ever dreamed of, in fact. And she now knew she was ready to cross boundaries.

CHAPTER 5

By eight o'clock that same evening the Beresfords were sitting down to supper at number fourteen Fair Promise Road. It was their usual lively gathering.

"Lovely curry, Mum," Henry smacked his lips, helping himself to more from a variety of dishes.

"What do you mean 'lovely curry, Mum'? Emily and I did it all," snapped Lucy.

"Lucy, don't slouch so," Flo deflected the argument.

"Huh. It's all right for you and Daddy. Here we sit like serfs on these old benches while you Lord and Lady it on. . ."

"Wait till we get to Beacon House," said Flo grandly. "We won't have deal there. All this can go to the sale room. We'll have walnut and mahogany and you'll rest your backs on. . ."

"And our bottoms on blue bombazine," cut in Edward.

"Or what about bums on purple plush?" said Henry, giggling at his own wit.

"Or arses on . . . ," came sotto voce from somewhere.

"Shuddup!" exploded Lucy, glaring at the Nibs, then rounding on Flo in a passion. "If we'd used words like that you'd have murdered us. Why do these two always get away with it? This is the most awful vulgar family I've ever known."

"You've never known any other family," smiled Flo. She usually frowned at any form of vulgarity.

"Oh yes, I have. What about the Applebys? When I stayed with them their boys didn't. . ."

"They weren't a family while you were there, were they?"

"Oh come on," Sam laughed refilling the glasses. "We're

47

all drunk tonight. It must be the cider."

"I think it's the excitement," said Emily quietly.

"I don't know what there is to get excited about, my dear. We have already told you our property only extends to the end of the shrubbery. We'll replace that old fence as soon as we can afford to. Beyond is nothing to do with us at all. We didn't even get the option to buy it. And we've told you to keep well away from it."

"Yes, but it was all part of Beacon House once, wasn't it?" chipped in Lucy, choosing to ignore the latter remark.

"Of course, but what on earth could we do with it if we had it, which we haven't, and even if we wanted it, which we don't?"

"We do. We do. We do want it," Lucy's voice was passionate. She looked at her father. "The people who built Beacon House must have been awfully rich mustn't they?"

"Um. Quite up to horse and carriage standard I should think – though Lord knows how they managed that hill. It would have been much steeper then."

"I think they had some famous man to landscape the garden. That great hole was once a lake. And there would have been grottoes and artificially pumped little streams with bridges and waterfalls ...."

"No. No. No. You're letting your imagination run away with you, Lucy. That great hole is nowhere near as old as the house. I shouldn't think so, anyway. It was obviously once a gypsum quarry. A previous owner must have sold the mineral rights ... ."

"Well, what about my garden house?" Lucy's tone was belligerent.

"Those old columns in the middle of the spinney? Oh, Lucy, I don't think they were once a garden house – I . . ."

"They were! They were! They were! One of the family must have done the grand tour and come back with the idea of reproducing a palladian . . ."

"Yes, my dear. I think you might be right there,"

interrupted Flo briskly, "And if you'll clear away the curry dishes I'11 reproduce the puddings left over from . . ."

"Last time we had any," laughed Sam.

There was an immediate shuffle by all five, the boys' slowness furiously chided by Lucy. "Get a move on, you lot."

"Get a move on yourself, Madam Dragon. You're a better foreman than a worker." But they got a move on, just the same, and within five minutes were scraping their plates again, all except Lucy who slipped her share to Robert.

As soon as they'd finished Henry and Edward engaged in a hideous face-pulling contest, doubling with laughter at each new grimace.

"Now we've chosen our rooms, I want to cover my walls with murals of the right period," said Lucy, averting her eyes as far as she could from the Nibs' antics.

Sam leaned back and Flo frowned at both the creak in his chair and the Nibs' behaviour.

"That was very nice, my dears." He lit up a pipe and puffed contentedly.

"You're going to be busy, Lucy. Any prep these holidays?" looking at Robert.

"Not much," came the answering croak. "Bit of French, that's all."

"You'll have time for elocution lessons, then," said Lucy cruelly.

"Your wit!" squeaked Robert with as much scorn as he could muster.

"Ha! Ha! Give her a clap," chorused the Nibs, brandishing their sarcasm in Robert's defence and redirecting their face-pulling efforts at Lucy.

"What about you girls?" asked Flo.

"Environmental Study," said Lucy.

"Whassat?" The Nibs' eyes popped.

"Morons! Work it out."

"Look it up," said Sam and straightaway a pocket Oxford

was flung across the room.

"Who threw that?" Flo frowned. "How many times have I told you we don't throw things in this house? And we don't study books in the middle of a meal either."

"Are we still in the middle of a meal?" Henry's eye brightened. "Good. What's next? Bring on the boar's head – I'm ravenous."

Lucy shuddered. The lingering smell of curry sickened her. And the thought of these boys feeding their faces at every meal for the next three weeks didn't help either. She noticed her mother's crestfallen look at the dishevelled table. Not another spoonful of anything left on it. Poor Mummy. She glared at her father.

"Don't get despondent girls. We'll see if we can manage the Chinese once a week." Sam caught her eye and grinned.

"There'd be more point if you set to and showed these layabouts how to cook," muttered Lucy as she flicked over the dictionary pages and thrust the open book into the Nibs' faces. "Here you are, cretins."

"Environment," read Edward obediently. "Surrounding objects or circumstances. That's us. Have you got to write about the family?"

"God forbid !" said Lucy with feeling.

"No, no, no." said Sam. "I expect they've got to study some aspect of Newent and district."

"That's right. Now give us some ideas. What would you do?"

"The Civil War?" Sam puffed out a cloud of blue smoke and both girls turned down their mouths while Flo started to clear the table.

"Um. You could do nonconformism, I suppose. Suss out why it's so strong in Newent. Take a walk down Miller's Street. You can see those arched windows of our first methodist chapel quite clearly."

"Doesn't mean a thing," said Lucy, "Lots of old buildings have windows like that, even factories. What about the odd

50

room at Beacon House? That wasn't a chapel, surely?" She automatically stacked a few plates. "Or perhaps it was. What do you reckon? And were they dissenters or Roman Catholics? Anybody want to bet on it?

"Well done, Lucy," said Flo, coming for another tray load of used dishes "We'll have you joining the Civic Trust next. Which reminds me, Sam, you didn't see the post this morning. There was a letter from the Local History Society, something about a public meeting to stop the Borough Council pulling down Webster's Place."

"Now that is an interesting street and absolutely unique to Newent," said Sam. "Why don't you dig up what you can about that?"

Webster's Place. Lucy's ears pricked though she hid her excitement at those words in noisy help for her mother.

"Old Jane Shaw probably knows more about that street than anybody," continued Sam, making sure Flo was safe in the kitchen but forgetting to keep his voice down so she was back in a trice with one of her looks while he assumed an air of inane innocence.

Their dumbshow was lost on the others but Lucys' sharp eye took in every nuance. Webster's Place. Bernard Webster. Was Webster's Place anything to do with that boy? She could not ask but she burned to know.

"I hate Webster's Place," said Edward. "It gives me the creeps and I'll be glad if they do pull it down." Lucy remembered his chalk-white face at the garden house and shrugged when Flo asked what she would be doing.

"Haven't thought about it?" She lied. "We've got until next term." She diverted the question. "How old is Beacon House? Do we know, exactly?"

"No", said Sam. "The deeds belong to the bank. Seventeen hundred or thereabouts most likely".

"Just imagine being stuck on the top of that hill with nothing but horse and carriage to get about in," Said Robert and Lucy, whose moods changed with the weather, felt a sisterly relief his vocal cords were behaving themselves for once.

"It's not only travel" Robert went on "Everything must have been so slow. It must have affected their minds, don't you think? They must have been sort of closed in."

"I don't know about that," said Sam. "Industry, agriculture, trade philosophy, they were all on the move. There was a phrase they had. 'Into the bonfire with dogma and superstition and let's go forward into Newton's light.' We shouldn't under-estimate our forebears."

Lucy let fall the used cutlery she was collecting and hardly noticed yet another dirty mark on the soiled table cloth. She looked across at her father and was taken aback to see the kind, handsome face of a medical man under a full bottomed silky grey wig, ruffles of creamy linen all but hiding the gleam of gold on his chest. She struggled to find a name.

"I wonder what Beacon House was like when it was new?" Robert's voice was now starting to crack, harsh to her ear.

She deliberately pushed the handsome face away and, strangest of all, noticed this horrible curry smell over-whelmed by the waft of pot-pourri from Mama's blue and white bowl on the great oaken chest in the panelled hall.

Edward left off his antics with Henry. "What would we have looked like in those days?" he said.

"A nine year old schoolboy? You'd have looked like a miniature adult. Ram's horn buckles on your black shoes, white roll over stockings, blue knee breeches, fine white shirt and muslin cravat with long ends tied round twice, blue coat with big cuffs, lots of buttons and two or three vents in the skirt. Hair a bit longer, three cornered hat and you'd have looked quite a popinjay."

Edward stared as Lucy fell silent. She had just described that Bernard Webster. As she remembered he was ten, not nine, and as she wondered how easily yet another alien word had rolled off her tongue, she took one more small step down that unknown road.

She caught her mother staring at her. She felt disturbed and knew it must show on her face. She looked at the others. Robert tired out. Edward white as a sheet Perhaps they were all sickening for something. It was a relief when Flo said she'd finish the clearing up.

"Off you go, children."

There were groans all round but they went obediently enough, arguing the toss for first bath.

"It's definitely my turn," from Emily.

"Silent Em's found her tongue, ha-ha."

"And Silent Em might find the ghost ha-ha," from the Nibs, one after the other.

"And no she won't ha-ha," from Flo on her way from kitchen to snuggery.

Only Lucy was quiet. She was planning an early bike ride to Edgington. Very early, if only she could get out without waking Emily. There were things she needed to know and the Rector might be a safer bet than old Jane Shaw.

Flo piled up the pudding plates and looked across at Sam settled comfortably in his favourite chair.

"Oh Sam! I hope we've not bitten off . . ."

"Nonsense, my dear." He turned his paper to the back page for the crossword puzzle and reached for a pen. "Here's an easy one for you. What are crackers for redheads?"

But Flo had abandoned the dishes for the local paper. An item on the front page caught her eye. 'Latest Wills. Rector Benefits'. Meg Appleby was right then. That wretch was a beneficiary. He had been left the contents. The rest to charity. No relatives, obviously. I should think he nearly frightened that poor old woman to death with his daft ideas. Funny that he'd never mentioned the contents this morning.

"Yes, Sam," she murmured. "You're quite right, he must be crackers."

Her preoccupation was not noticed for, in spite of his apparent cheerfulness, Sam had his own problem. He wished to Hell the Ashfield project was not so dodgy. There was too

53

much subsidence for comfort in that area. He had a gut feeling that all was not well on that site, though dammit, he'd taken every precaution, obeyed every rule in the book and he'd employed a damned good structural engineer. He'd been more than pleased to get the contract and now here he was wishing it in anybody's hand but his own.

CHAPTER 6

The following afternoon found both Flo and Lucy back at
Beacon House while the others were clearing out cupboards
at home. From the drawing room Flo sifted ideas and plans.
She knew she was wasting time but could not help it. After
all, she deserved a few dreams.

From the neglected courtyard, among mounds of sand and
cement, dented buckets and ladders of all sizes, Lucy looked
up at the front doorway. If it were up to her they would move
in today. They could work twice as hard if they lived on the
spot. Picnic meals. Everybody helping. She couldn't wait.
Why on earth didn't Mummy and Daddy . . . ?

She shielded her eyes against the strong sunlight and,
softly, the peeling stucco faded away; wrought iron lampholders showed up like delicate lace against the wine-red of
new brick; windows glittered; sunlight glanced off the
pretty cupola, the tall chimney stacks and white painted
balustrade. Fantails whirred over the rooftop and settled to
strut and peck at her feet, with scarcely a weed between well-
laid flags.

The front door of the dark panelled hall opened to the light
and she was irresistibly drawn towards it, hardly questioning
its manner of opening. A heightened excitement hanging in
the air like the scent of newly stirred pot-pourri wrestled
with fear. The only noise, apart from her own muffled heartbeats, was the soft coo of doves in the yard, drowned by the
harsh clang of a harpsichord from the drawing room. She did
not question these sounds. She was prepared for them.
Lifting a foot to the topmost step between the handsome

55

columns, she caught the sound of a name, faint and far away.

"Dru-sill-a!" That name filtered through the budding trees. "Dru-sill-a!" Her foot stayed on the step. Her head cocked. The three clear notes sounded now so bold and piercing she could all but see them like flashes of light in the dark hall. 'Dru-sill-a!" Again, her thrill of fear was lost in excitement. Those haunting sounds conjured up such pictures of beautiful men and women, such flutterings of pretty fans and rustlings of lace at elegant wrists, such thudding hooves, jangling harnesses and rolling carriages, such promises of silver toys all the way from Amsterdam and such a snap in a boy's eyes her heart was quite lost. 'Dru-sill-a!"

She knew that name and the voice that called it.

"I'm coming," she cried, and Lucy was snuffed out like a candle as she scuttled away with clatter of buckled shoes over flags and whisk of blue damask round the far corner of the house. Past coach houses and stables she flew on to the back terrace.

"Dru-sill-a! Dru-sill-a!" The call was still far off as she leapt through the iron gateway into the rose garden.

"Wait for me. I'm coming," she shouted, keeping straight as an arrow down the centre path, through the far gate and into the shrubbery where clipped bushes were laid out in the severest symmetrical patterns, their different shapes arranged to suit a perverse and puckish mind. The bushes had been planted on a downward slope, set and cut to give the illusion of level ground. Strangers were surprised how the earth dropped unexpectedly beneath their feet. It had been Papa's delight when he was home to catch his guests' discomforture as they realised the illusion. She stopped running, pushing the tangles of long hair out of her eyes.

"Where are you?" she called on the same three clear notes.

"Come find me!"

She hesitated. She knew her way through this shrubby maze like the back of her own hand but, if one had sight of one's pursuer, it was an excellent place to hide. Pressing oneself against smooth clipped bushes, turning quickly and silently round grassy corners, one could play cat and mouse all day long and never be caught. And if Bernard were already hiding here he would have seen her for sure.

"Give a sign," she shouted.

"Tu whit whoo!" and in a flash she knew he was in the woods beyond. Zig-zagging like blue streak lightning along close-cropped paths, out through the far gate she half stumbled into the spinney.

"Tu whit whoo!" A swoop and a pounce from an overhead branch nearly knocked her to the ground, scaring her stiff. He laughed wickedly at her embarrassment and she laughed with him.

"You're a tease, Bernard," she smiled. "Come back with me to the paddock. Hobbs says we can help with the ponies and May will be there." She held out her hands.

"No. Let's stay here. By ourselves."

He pulled her towards him and his voice was compelling, but discretion made her falter. This was Papa's shoot, a copse carefully tended for the culling of pheasants – even though Mama complained he was never here to do the shooting and would have to watch the game laws if he were. Besides, May would be disappointed.

"But what about Capel? He doesn't like people disturbing the woods at nesting time and there's May . . ."

"What a goose you are, Drusilla. Do the woods belong to the keeper? And who cares about stupid May Hobbs?"

He tugged again at her hands and her resistance was lost. He led. She followed and the forbidden door shut fast behind them.

She watched his straight back and the proud set of his handsome head. How tall he was, how agile, how fearless. He had cut himself a hazel switch and was lashing out at herbage with a passion she was not used to. He had all the confidence in the world, as though he were king-emperor of the place, plaster pit, brick kilns, woodyard and all. As though he were Papa come home from the Americas. Out of the blue she recalled the disdainful look her own Mama had cast at his weeping stepmother on their first meeting. He must have hated that look. Her heart went out to him, no matter how much hope was tempered by apprehension. Bernhard might have taken on the mantle of an emperor but she felt as far from an empress as little May Hobbs.

So she tagged behind, eyes as big as millponds, terrified lest the woodkeeper. appear. A disturbed pigeon flew out of the branches above their heads and she started aloud. A squirrel chattered to itself among the trees. Rabbits ran this way and that, white scuts bobbing. A pheasant called and another of its kind called in reply. At every sound she clapped a hand to her mouth and looked round in fear. Capel was a bad-tempered man and sure to complain to Mama.

Suddenly, where the wood thinned into a flat glade like a great green shelf in the slope, Bernard stopped short, making her start worse than ever.

"Whew!" he whistled, "Look at this."

Drusilla peered from behind. She saw the remains of a fire where a few stones had been strewn about. And was that a rabbit's head, a head with no body? Surely not – but it was – and that bundle of rags hanging from a low branch was certainly a pair of dead crows with a jay suspended like some awful warning.

"Have a care," she whispered. "Capel might have been laying traps. Let's go back."

"This isn't woodkeeper's work. Not on your life."

"Gypsies, then? Please let's go back."

"Witches," his voice quickened and a strange expression crossed his face. "There was a full moon last night and a coven met here, I'll swear it."

She nodded and between them a frightened look of knowledge passed. Drusilla shrank back, anxious to return to the safety of paddock and ponies and little May Hobbs. But

58

Bernard cast off his fear, which was a weak thing anyway, and looked about him.

"Beacon House. Beacon Hill. It's an old site, Drusilla. The Ancients could have used this place. And look. Look at this." He crouched on the trampled grass, snapping his fingers to urge her closer, pulling her down to her knees beside a large flat stone.

"This could have been their altar. Depend on it. Witches make sacrifices, do they not?"

"Sacrifices?" She squeezed the words out of a tightening throat.

"Sacrifices to their God, the Devil." He laughed at her fears and that light in his eyes flicked more wickedly than ever. "Come on. Let's look for blood."

But Drusilla was fixed and could not, dare not, move. She watched in horror as the boy searched grass and stones and, though he found nothing, his excitement did not abate.

"I can feel them, can you not, Drusilla? And hark! We might hear them if we're sharp enough."

"Witches! Did they make spells here, do you think?" She could feel and hear nothing but her own heartbeats and still she could not move.

"Spells!" The boy's voice was scornful. "Witches have more important things to do than make spells. Killing Farmer Stray's cow, giving Capel the bellyache, making cream turn sour – that's fairy stuff. Witches do all manner of strange and dangerous things."

"What things?"

"Meeting with Spirits. Making Time stand still or turn topsy-turvy. Elevating their bodies."

"Do you mean flying?"

"Yes." He gloated over the alarm on her face. "Flying. Racing through the air as they please. Diving, climbing, floating, speeding." He stretched out his arms and dipped and swooped towards and around her, his face contorted like the Devil himself.

Good Heavens. It was only the other day Uncle Peter had talked of men flying to London. Did Uncle Peter believe in witches? If Uncle Peter believed in witches then . . . Bernard caught hold of her hand and she could not resist.

"Shut your eyes. Open your mouth and see what God will send you."

And before she understood the command he pulled at her lower jaw to stuff her mouth with sugarplums that stuck to her teeth and sent a drool of saliva down her chin. The boy was smiling at her and very handsome. Her body regained its mobility. She swallowed with a great gulp, took up the hem of her dress to mop up her dribbles and settled herself beside that flat stone as Bernard raised himself up to tower above her. She abandoned herself to the game, giggling nervously, pushing away her fears of Capel and Mama.

"I am the Prince of Darkness, Drusilla, and you are my slave." Again she giggled and mopped her dribbles. "And while I was hiding up in that tree, I had the strongest sensation of wanting to fly. If only I dared to spread out my arms and let go I would have flown like a bird. And one day, I will. On my mother's death, I will."

He dropped down beside her and she looked him boldly, full in the face.

"You will never do it," her voice was decisive, not like her own voice at all, and now it was his turn to stare. Words tumbled out of her mouth. She could not stop them for they seemed to fall of their own accord. "Men will never fly that way. Uncle Peter told me. Icarus tried and got his feathers burnt. But one day somebody will build a carriage with wings that will lift off the ground, no horses needed, and sail through the air like our ships sail on the sea."

"What else? What else? Go on. Go on." He pressed himself closer till she caught that peculiar scent of his breath.

"Oh, the sky will be full of the strangest of things. Like giant dragonflies. They will fly round and round the earth just for sport, like our maids skip round the maypole."

Together they looked up at the far away patch of clear blue and fleecy white allowed by the clearing. "Perhaps they'll be like Papa and find new kingdoms, miles and miles and miles away, but up in the air instead of over the sea."

"Drusilla, you must be half a witch yourself. Even your red hair is a witch colour. Tell me some more. Go on."

"They won't only sail faster and further. Everything will be different. Their thoughts and minds will . . ." She bit her bottom lip as she searched for the right word. "Will be different," she said lamely. Her face puckered for she had not sounds enough to tell all she knew and felt.

"Well, what about us? What can you tell about us?" Bernard gripped her shoulders to snatch back her fading mood.

"Us?" she said, archly, for the mood had fled and could not be recalled. "Oh, we girls will dress like boys and go to the same schools and beat you at all your lessons." She clapped her hands at the merry thought till he caught tight hold of her again.

"This is a good game, Drusilla. Let's call this our own place and come here again. There are books I've seen, and a month from now will be the first of May. Think of it, Drusilla. A full moon and May Day. There's no knowing what we'll see if we're game enough." He squeezed her all the tighter. "Promise we'll come here again a month from now."

She shivered in her thin clothes. The sun, penetrating the copse in patches, now hid behind cloud. The smell of damp earth and crushed herbage was strong. Bernard released his hold and stirred at the grey ash and blackened wood with the little hazel switch. Drusilla sat cold and forlorn till a bitter-sweet smell of pungent herbs and charred sticks tickled her nostrils. She sneezed and in a flash her glimpse of fore knowledge was gone. With it her apprehension went too and she was left, like Bernard, trembling with elation.

"Yes," she whispered. It's a good game. We'll play it again."

"And nobody else," he ordered. "We won't tell May Hobbs or Nellie or your Mama, and especially not Dr. Peter. Cross your heart and hope to die." And again there was that spark in his eye that affected her so.

They puffed their way back to the house as the harpsichord still jangled from the white and gold drawing room. Drusilla was only too grateful she would not have to suffer her Mama's inquisition.

She need not have troubled herself. Dorothy's thoughts were elsewhere. If only she had not fallen sick of the small pox all those years ago. If only the boy babies had not died as soon as born. If only Anthony had not had such a wander-lust.

Her hands rested on the keys. Tish! Show the world some bottom, Dorothy, she told herself. Drusilla is brighter looking than she's ever been, thanks to the Webster boy, no matter what the Newent prattlers clacked about his parentage. The child must have a new dress, green damask with a gold-yaller pinner. And Bernard a new coat, snuff coloured with plenty of frogging. Anthony would approve. Nobody could ever call him a skinflint.

Her fingers quickened to a lively jig. If the Devil himself had bounded into the room she would not have noticed him.

CHAPTER 7

Bernard was insistent, Drusilla besotted. Exactly one month later the two children had kept their secret meeting in the little copse and there were thrills enough without any sign of a coven meet.

Drusilla had alarmed herself as the nightmarish pictures tumbled out of her mouth for, again, they seemed to fall of their own accord. She had gabbled of strange women with hair cropped like old fashioned levellers or hanging straight and long half way down backs, skirts cut above knees in outlandish mode. And she had. actually seen such women moving about as freely and easily as men, as strong and as tough as men. In fact it was a puzzle to sort who were the men or who were the women and it was not so much a question of dress as of attitudes. These women were no respecters of persons. They chipped in, they argued, they stamped feet and did as they pleased.

She had been bewildered and frightened by what she had seen, for she felt reality had invaded her dreams and her dreams had become realities. And Bernard had kept her there in the copse, forcing her to see more than she cared to, making her describe the women over and over again till she was exhausted and could scarce climb the steep hill back to the house, terrified in the moonlit air of Nellie's stern figure on the steps. She felt her thin shoulders folded none too tenderly into the warmth of Mama's pink cashmere shawl and sensed, rather than saw, for she kept her head down, the housekeeper's mouth stiff with disapproval.

"Lord above, Miss Drusilla. There you be. And the night

air coming on enough to give us all a fever." Nellie shot a fierce look under drawn brows at Bernard and whisked Drusilla upstairs, muttering threats of possets and potions.

Thereafter, the children played that game but seldom, and then only at Bernard's insistence. For Drusilla the excitement was sharpened by apprehension. Yet it was all a game and pretend was it not? She could not truly see into another century like the gypsy fortune tellers could see into next week; it was not really true that her nightmare world could push its way into this. And yet, and yet . . .

When mice scuttled in the wainscot she strained her ears to catch sounds of girlish whispers; or when her own face shone back at her from the reflected night of an unshuttered window, for one fleeting moment, she thought that face belonged to another; and once, when teetering on a stool to peer into Mama's glass, she had seen, over her shoulder, a girl with eyes as startled as her own. That it was not herself she could swear, for the girl's shoulder length straight brown hair had swung in the breeze from an open window as Mama's new fangled curtains billowed softly.

"Stay. Oh, stay." She had longed to cry.

As for Dorothy, she noticed nothing other than the child's bright eyes and flushed cheeks had changed her daughter into a promising beauty. Thank the Lord, Drusilla would grow up to be a belle after all. A little powder, when she was old enough, would soon tone down that high colour and if Nellie carried on with the juniper rinses at new moon then her hair would be as bright as Anthony's, more gold than red. Yes, Dorothy found it suited her well enough these days to glimpse no more of her daughter than a flash of gold pinner and flying green ribbons as the once quiet house filled with scuffles and laughter, let Nellie protest as she would.

"He'm a sly child Miss Dor'thy and will take advantage, you do mark my words."

But Dorothy had no time for advice that did not suit her, wherever it came from. God be thanked for small mercies,

64

Drusilla was no longer a nagging reproach now that her pasty looks had improved. Why, her once lack-lustre spirits were now as light as Anthony's own and that was saying something. Well, she had listened to Peter, had she not? And he was a physician, was he not? And an important one at that, spending near as much time in London and Amsterdam as in Newent ever since the curing of Lady Reville's gout. Well, his remedies worked for his niece as well as for Lady Reville.

Dorothy's mouth crimped into a self-satisfied smile. For the first time since Anthony's wanderlust had taken him away she was enjoying herself and her addiction to pleasure increased daily. There were far more interesting things to do than play at dolls' house or visit brick kilns, or plaster pits, or wood yards either for that matter. Whyever she had not made Bolland the overseer earn his keep before this she could not imagine and she had to admit that, given a free hand, his figures were a deal better than hers. Anthony should be pleased. How the fellow did it she never thought to question. It was all she could do to find time to counter-sign the accounts, let alone ask the whys and wherefores.

So the two children were left to amuse themselves when-ever Bernard was not at school and Drusilla waited in a fever of impatience for each homecoming.

Together they tended their ponies and rode with the grooms through the lanes and over the moor to Edgington and beyond. They followed old trails flanked shoulder high with bright yellow goss. They played hide and seek in the shrubbery, climbed trees in the copse and tumbled head over heels on soft turf. They chased each other round the big house, outside and in, from down in the huge vaulted cellars up the great staircase, through the many passages from one room to another, down the back stairs, through kitchens and offices and out on to the terrace between pots, urns, seats and stone statues. Only the small door on the top landing leading out to the roof was denied them and the household wondered whoever would have thought such a mealy-mouthed miss could have become such a tomboy.

"H'm. 'Tis easy to see who do lead and who do follow," fumed Nellie, noticing the wistful looks of little May Hobbs.

But the coachman's granddaughter knew her place and was thankful enough to wear Drusilla's cast offs, to eat up any sweetmeat thrown her way, and if ever they remembered her skill with the battledore, or her sharp eye for a bird's nest then that was bliss indeed.

For Drusilla, her once safe, dull world as placid as the slow moving River Trent, its currents deep and well hidden, was suddenly dappled with a golden light that lit up her life. And if highlights showed up the shadows of her green-gold world, well then, she must do as Mama counselled about offal carts, the brickies coming home from the kilns or the white dust from the plaster pit: 'my dear Drusilla, you simply must not see these things'. But there was a difference because shadows were not only fearful, they were as exhilarating as the first strawberry snatched from under the sharp nose of the head gardener.

And besides, there were so many things one needed to know, and Mama was busy with a different busyness these days, while Uncle Peter was still too full of what Mama called hobby-horses. And Nellie, well Nellie was kind and wise, but there was a watchful look in her eye nowadays that was not always pleasant. Still, Bernard was clever and from him she could learn many things. Did Mama and Papa really do that? Will I have to do it? Have you ever done it? Oh yes, Bernard brought home many tales from the Free School and luckily he was home so often these days which was the most wonderful thing in this world.

"One pretext after another," fumed Nellie. "'Tis a wonder how Mr. Twells the master do stand it," working out her disapproval on Dorothy's hair one morning at her mistress's toilette.

"Ouch, Nellie! Please don't pull so," from Dorothy only

made Nellie tug the harder and jab the pins in more fiercely. The time had come for a little plain speaking about young Bernard and she did mean to let Miss Dor'thy have it.

"The tales they do tell in the town, Miss Dor'thy ...."

"I remember well enough Dr. Peter telling us Bernard was the pride of the Free School."

"That was nearly a year back, Miss Dor'thy, and things done have changed." Nellie's Somerset accent was never more strong than when she was delivering a piece of her mind. "You should y'ear what old Grandpa John Twentyman do say about him."

"The innkeeper's father," scoffed Dorothy.

"Innkeeper or no, the Twentyman's is highly respected in Newent. One of the oldest families, Miss Dor'thy. Didn't old Grandmam Twentyman, Great, Great Grandmam to this y'ere old John, didn't she get out the old family drum and make her grandson to beat it all round the town when Cromwell were coming? And didn't everybody rally round with . . . ?"

"That was a long time ago, Nellie, a good seventy years or more."

"That's as maybe. I don't know about that and maybe I done got mixed up with the greats. But what I'm saying now happened no further back nor last week!" She pushed Dorothy back in her chair. "There's been a spate of lewd talk at the school and some shameful bullying such as they never did have there before. Well, old John's grandson got his share of this y'ere. And no other than young Bernard at the bottom of it. And old John's been to the school to see Master Twells and he's pressing the corporation for an inquiry, Miss Dor'thy. Don't look too good, do it, our protegé the subject of an inquiry? Mr. Anthony wouldn't like it, Miss Dor'thy, for sure he wouldn't. And it isn't only the Twentymans neither, Miss Dor'thy. 'Tis the Warburtoons complaining of him bullying their young one and .

"Pass me my cap, Nellie. No, not that one. The one with

67

blue ribbons, if you please." Dorothy pressed her lips together.

Just when things were going so well, Nellie had to come up with this tittle-tattle. Well, she would soon put a stop to any inquiry nonsense. My Goodness, but servants were the most provoking creatures - though the Lord knows what one would do without them. She noted the hurt look in Nellie's eye and her voice softened. She knew there was a loyalty in Nellie and Hobbs and Capel and the rest that money could not buy; and a lone woman was vulnerable and dependent. And husbands in Virginia were no help at all.

"Tie up my cap, Nellie, and I promise I will speak to the schoolmaster myself."

Master Twells, a kindly disposed scholarly man, was no match for the formidable Mrs Anthony Davison. She was a woman of influence and besides, the Webster boy's godfather was Sir George Markham, member of parliament for Newent and a friend of the almighty Duke of Newcastle, while the complainant's family were no more than local innkeepers – though they did boast a mayor or two in the family. The schoolmaster did the usual bowings and scrapings as he helped the lady back into her carriage.

As it was, he was pleased enough to mollify the Twentymans, and others too, by turning a blind eye to Bernard's frequent absences. That way there was less trouble all round and, by Jupiter, a schoolmaster's life was hard enough without looking for mischief and the last thing he needed was an inquiry.

Dorothy might 'tish' as much as she pleased but that did not stop Nellie's prattle.

"Must be nigh on a year, Miss Dor'thy, since Draper Webster be broken. And everybody in Newent do know who 'tis keeps his household in victuals. That miserable lodging house over the old shop don't do it. And we all know whose carriage 'tis for ever waiting outside. Sir George Markham do leap up they stairs like a jack rabbit after a doe. Webster's second wife must be as bad as his first."

She rearranged glass bottles and china boxes on Dorothy's dressing table with enough clatter to waken the dead but not enough to rouse her mistress who was mulling over the guest list for her next party.

"And to think of that shop empty as a begging bowl when it used to be full as a rich man's plate – though most of it not paid for."

Nellie's teeth shut tight as a trap.

No wonder that with collusion from school Bernard became more and more at home at Beacon House, more and more used to the ways of the quality, more and more indispensable to the Davison family and less and less a part of his own. And if he missed his little stepsisters he put the thought to the back of his mind, as he put so many other things these days, and kept it safe.

Summer days shortened to winter and, if anything, the excitement of living at Beacon House increased. Huge fires crackled and flamed in vast fireplaces; servants staggered under great dishes of boiled and baked meats; beeswax candles and plenty of them were lighted long before nightfall; fine horses whinnied from the stables and visiting carriages filled up the courtyard, for Dorothy was gayer than ever and used every excuse to fill the big house with company. She prided herself that nobody yet had refused an invitation on account of the hill.

Drusilla and Bernard were allowed brief peeps into the drawing room for glimpses of the quality and from every corner, it seemed, rang out sounds of fiddling, piping, laughing, drinking, shouting, dancing. Even the servants were caught up in the flurry of runnings hither and thither, sweepings of elegant hats from white powdered heads, curtseyings of beautiful gowns and flutterings of pretty fans. Lord! How the gossips busied themselves and buzzed and buzzed and buzzed again. Little May Hobbs was run off her feet and even Nellie, who could turn a hand to anything, had enough to do to keep up with it all. And Miss Drusilla, she noticed, was getting away with murder nowadays.

There was a curious mixture of behaviour at Beacon House introduced by Dorothy's new friends, a kind of free and easy formality the children were not slow to pick up. They hummed under their breath, whistled the new gay tunes, sat down in one armchair with their feet upon another, leaping on to the nearest stools with the straightest of straight backs, all folded hands and sweet decorum at the first sound of Nellie's approach, and remembering always their deference to elders and betters, no matter what might be whispered behind hands in dark corners.

Dorothy had copied her brother and taken up the new fashion for scattering furniture about a room instead of having it stand stiffly with backs up to walls until needed. All the old ways were pushed out in the cold and the new welcomed in with open arms.

Drusilla herself became aware of lace on petticoats, silk-made hose, silver buckles on shoes, pots of face paint on Mama's dressing table, rose water and sweet oil of lavender.

"My, my, little poppet! How tall you are grown!" Uncle Peter would say. "You will soon be a young lady and able to come to the ball with no time at all for the little silver toy collection, I'll wager."

He would chuck her under the chin and pull at her ear while she smiled and preened, hugging herself for sheer joy. She no longer needed to climb on to a stool to look in Mama's glass; a little stretching on tiptoe showed her almost a half-length, and a little manoeuvring of handkerchieves gave her bodice a bulge. And if only the shades of her red gold hair would either darken or lighten then she would be content.

On quieter evenings, when windows were tight-shuttered and doors barred, then from the drawing room came the soft hum of conversation from Dorothy's select card parties, the tinkle of glass and the swish of silk as players toasted one partner and moved on to another. Ladies and gentlemen played hazard, basset and swobbers for golden guineas and amused themselves still further with wicked tales of mutual friends.

"Ha!" Dr. Peter chuckled as he shuffled the cards. "This house is the giddy limit. Our newspapers are full of a fight on the High Seas to settle the fate of a whole nation, and all we care about is the mighty battle waging twixt Matthew Jenison and Tom Belcher over half a hectare of land off Northgate!"

"And why not, sir?" was his partner's reply, cutting the cards with a snap. "I'll wager every mortal in this room thinks more of his own than any amount of ships full of foreigners! "

The children stayed in the little parlour that had never lost its unassuming homeliness to play dominoes or beggar my neighbour for brass farthings. Their supper was brought in on trays and they enjoyed a delicious intimacy, especially on the rare occasions they played their old game. The flickering light from fire and candle heightened their senses as they continued those dark speculations that excited Bernard and frightened Drusilla. On nights such as these, Drusilla lay in her high canopied bed, trembling with fear and blaming the rich colour of her hair for such fancies, as the strange people of that other world danced inside her head.

Sometimes her old childish dream returned when she could scarcely breathe for the press of an old powdered face and a mouth stuffed full with sugarplums. Always on the point of suffocating to death, that old man-devil's face receded to become the handsome features of Bernard Webster, as the sugarplum juices oozed out of her mouth and on to her chin.

But for all that she would not have changed places with any of Mama's friends, be they as rich as the Revilles or as high born as the Hattons. Life was lovely at last and she prayed that nothing would ever change. Mama should never

71

grow old, she and Bernard should never part, Beacon House should always be home and Papa . . . Oh my goodness, what about Papa? Dear Papa, there should be packages coming soon and one day perhaps . . . She snuggled into lavender scented sheets and was asleep most nights before Nellie came to snuff out the candle.

CHAPTER 8

Succeeding years tumbled from one highlight to another. Drusilla would have been hard pushed to settle the order of any of them as she struggled out of her childhood but was not yet a woman.

Her memories were always brought on by the ringing of bells. All through her growing up, the bells of St. Leonard's in Newent, of St. Wilfred's in Edgington, of St. Saviour's in North Heskham, and of every other village round about, sounded their chimes for the county's joys and sorrows. Dorothy said, often enough at the time, that she thought the church bells would never stop clanging. What had once seemed a delight had become 'that din that gives me a headache!'

"If they're not pealing a pleasure they're tolling a trouble till one don't tell one from t'other," she complained to her brother. "And they do nothing for one's concentration," rearranging her playing cards.

"Why can't you rejoice with the one and give thanks the other is nothing to do with us, my dear?"

"Tish! You're like Anthony. You've an answer for everything," slapping her hand face down. "I'll call you a guinea."

Drusilla and Bernard heeded neither the bells nor her complaint. They lived in a separate world, going about their own important business, leaving elders and betters to dabble in their own trivia. The two children were fed and clothed to a surfeit but thereafter met with a welcome indifference that handed them a freedom unfettered by correction. The gardens, the stables, the woods were their own domain where servants were fellow conspirators or mortal enemies. They hugged themselves in their own minds, thankful that Dorothy and her set spent most of their time stuffily indoors. True, at breakfast in the little parlour and at dinner in the great dining room, they were required to present themselves washed, clean and tidy, tethered and quiet. Then, as their elders clacked miles over their heads of this or that social or political consequence, they would eat silently, their feet touching under the table in a delicious conspiracy, mouths full of food, heads full of secrets and plots.

What did they care if Queen Anne had dropsy? If the Queen was breeding? If the Queen was not breeding? If the Queen was breeding again? What could the phrase 'protestant succession' possibly mean to them when they half-heard on all sides 'we don't care a fig who rules as long as they let us and our money alone'?

And whatever was meant by 'into the bonfire with superstition and dogma and let us go forward into Newton's light'? They knew what a bonfire was right enough and pricked up their ears at that word like a couple of pyromaniacs, but as for the rest, it might as well have been the Latin and Greek Bernard had flogged into him at the Free School, whenever he was there, and of which Drusilla knew not a syllable.

So the news, national and local, with its bell-ringing accompaniment, clanged through the house, keeping tongues on the wag and Dorothy's eyebrows set in a perpetual arch.

The little parlour was cosier than ever as it hummed most evenings with card playing friends. And, as Dr. Peter said, his sleeve ruffles all of a quiver, as he redealt the pack, "Marlborough's wars are one thing and Newent's wars are another. We're more interested in which of us will win the free-for-all at Edgington Moor than which army will win the race to get to some unknown village on the Danube. For, though we cared not a fig that a thousand Fritzes lay dead as mutton, we felt it mightily when we heard the same of our own young Tommy Footit, naught but a sixteen year old drummer boy, who'll ne'er see his family in Northgate again."

"And thank the Lord for that, Sir," laughed his new partner, sweeping his hand to a neat pile. "Let the state look after itself and we'll take care of our own. I'll bid you ten, Sir."

"Plus c'est la même chose," muttered the doctor as he fanned out his cards and wondered how the deuce to make the best of a duff hand.

A great flood of water between Newent and Buckford showed rather more promise. 'A veritable sea of water, you never saw the like,' made the children lift up their heads, since it was the nearest they were ever likely to get to a sea. They left off their secrets for a moment to hear how Dr. Peter had visited his patients at North Heskham by boat, for it seemed only the occasional holiday or calamity could ripple the surface of the satisfactory state of their affairs.

There was no shortage of calamities and once they had the excitement of both.

The spring floods had subsided as searing winds sucked up the moisture from the sodden ground with rather more speed than a thirsty labourer guzzles his ale. There followed a hot dry summer and corn had been piled into barns more quickly and easily than anybody ever remembered. Farmers were as pleased as ever they allowed themselves to be. If ears were thin, at least they were safe, but a fine harvest time was a two-edged sword. Dry pastures had the look of bare stubble. Animals would have to be killed off earlier than usual this year and rumour had it that salt was to be taxed to help pay for Marlborough's War.

The land was as dry as snuff, the Trent low and the Devon reduced to a trickle.

Drusilla's tenth birthday at summer's end dawned as bright and hot as the months before. The children were crotchety, the servants bad tempered, their betters exhausted and all of them longed for rain and a breath of cool air.

Drusilla had pleaded for fireworks and showed herself in a pet when her Mama demurred. The mere thought made Dorothy feel faint. And Drusilla's wheedling, turned into coaxing for Uncle Peter, had been in vain. She resorted to sulks. No, as she stamped her small foot in a pique, the two golden guineas he pulled out of his purse would not make up for no fireworks. The usual birthday picnic with hide and seek and treasure hunts and racing back to the lawns for cricket and bowls could not take the place of the rockets and crackers she had so set her heart on. She tossed her head. She pushed out her lips to a pout. Biddy Hatton had had fireworks on her birthday. Besides, she had unwisely boasted to Bernard of lights and bangs and catherine wheels, and her failure to get what she wanted had spoiled the whole day, especially since Bernard did nothing to ease the pain of her lost face.

The disappointment of the day, the heat, Drusilla's sulks and Bernard's needling turned them all the more tired and fractious. Dorothy insisted the party was at an end and ordered the playthings to be put away. In any case the sun was already sinking; it was late enough.

She dabbed at the moisture running down her cheek so that her ruffles hung limp. Jove. How she wished Anthony was home.

"May! May!" turning to Nellie. "Why is it that girl is never here when needed?"

"And about time, too," as May came running from the house, cap flying by the strings round her neck, pinafore skew-whiff as her skirts flew behind in the light, hot, east wind, feet half-leaping out of her shoes.

"Whatever in the world . . . ?"

"Miss Dorothy! Miss Dorothy!" The girl flung herself at her mistress and the garbled tale they got out of her they could make no sense of. But whatever it was sent them all racing up to the top of the house to the maids' attic window and what they saw from up there made Dr. Peter look reproachfully down at Drusilla.

"You shall have your firework show, after all, my dear. You can smile at last and let us hope we're not all crying before the night is through."

But Drusilla could not see a thing as they crowded against the small dormer lights and, before she could push her way between Mama and Nellie, Uncle Peter was out of the room, lighting a lantern and unbolting the low door on the uppermost landing that had always been locked against them.

"Follow me up. And have a care," he commanded.

One behind the other, they stumbled up the little top staircase. Drusilla had never been there in her life before and felt she never wanted to be there again, where feet tripped over skirts and blundered through cobwebby shadows cast by the lanthorn. Thankfully, they all blinked their way through the cupola door and spilled out on the leads to the bright light of day. A great flapping and whirring of wings sent a cloud of white fantails to settle on balustrade and chimney stacks.

"There!" Dr. Peter pointed to a huge red glow in the northern sky, more glorious than all the rich harvest sunsets they had seen this year.

May was still tearful. Drusilla and Bernard giggled shamelessly between excitement and fright.

"Lord, Miss Dor'thy, like Black Jack, the preacher, says, the end of the world be at hand!"

"Tish, Nellie!" Dorothy's voice was scornful but she looked to her brother for reassurance.

"No, Nellie. It is not the end of the world in spite of your Black Jack and his prophecies. That is one of the villages off the Great North Road going up in flames. We should be on our knees to thank God for our new tiled roofs. And now, miss," looking down at a chastened Drusilla, "you know why

77

you were not allowed your crackers and rockets today."

Drusilla shrank at her uncle's reproof while the doctor's kind heart got the better of him. She felt the loving hands lift her up for a grander view of that horrid glow and everything, the sulks and stamps and pouts, was now over and all quite right, though not the far off sky, for that was very wrong indeed. They watched in silence. The distant air raged with a red madness and they were affected by it. Drusilla sensed the crackle and roar as of a gigantic party to celebrate the night of Guy Fawkes. Her fertile imagination added the stench and screams of calamity.

Dorothy and Peter could only guess at the spitting hiss of water tossed from every ineffectual bucketful and the effort of dragging the vessels up the high bank of the low-lying river.

Drusilla's heart was pierced. Were people burning inside their houses? How could they get out? Would everything burn? Their beds? Their books? Their cats? Their dogs? Their hair? Their babies, even?

"Oh, surely not their babies, Mama?"

Dorothy's mouth tightened. She thanked the Lord for Newent's Mayor and Corporation who were banning the repair of worn out thatch. Her kilns had never been busier. They were turning out clay pantiles by the thousand. Her eyes glinted as she forced down the guilty thought, but it was, after all, an ill wind. She licked the salty moisture from her upper lip and mopped at her face with a handkerchief. Phew! It was hot. Her damp hair clung with the weight of a wet towel.

Bernard, too, licked his lips. He saw only the spectacle a hundred times grander than the few crackers and rockets Drusilla had promised him, till the doctor said they had seen enough, so putting a stop to the bright end of such a miserable day. Bernard had thought of little else but his own birthday the month before. Though May had given him a nosegay and Drusilla had stitched him a silk handkerchief, nobody else had made any kind of fuss. There had not been picnics and games for him and, after so long with the Davisons, he was already taking his new birthday clothes for granted.

"There, Miss Drusilla," said Nellie, never one to miss a trick, "now you do know why I do make you to wear your prettiest cap and go to bed tidy – 'tis in case of a fire. And there'll be sulphur tablets for you my lad," casting a black look in Bernard's direction.

Next morning a pall of smoke still hung over the ruined village and the passing bells of all the churches within earshot tolled all that day for the disaster at Buckford. And yes, Uncle Peter thought Drusilla quite right to donate her birthday guineas to the survivors and if she could do that then he and her Mama could each quadruple the sum. Dorothy thought so too, calculating how many bricks and tiles might be needed to rebuild a whole village.

Drusilla could not get the disaster out of her head but no, she was told, she could not go with Uncle Peter to look at all the poor people with their hair burned clean off. They would not be a pretty sight. And yes, most likely their eyebrows and lashes would be gone too and Bernard could make himself useful for once.

"Come here, my lad, and let us see you earn your keep. Hang this lanthorn back on its hook."

The boy's gorge rose as he found a great slight where none was intended. Again, it was only Nellie who noticed the angry cheek and the set of his teeth.

In any case, in the way of all nine day wonders, one smartly followed another and by the close of November Dorothy was soon chafing for news of the great storm that had crashed on the country from the western seas, screaming its fury across the southern counties from Devon to Kent. She nagged at her brother to seek out the newspapers that still gave only the bare bones of the tale. She harried him to ride off to Sir George Markham of Sedgebrook who owned a house in Bath and so might have fresh news but the baronet was not at home and the doctor gleaned not a word.

Dr. Peter, for once, was as concerned as Dorothy. Their only surviving sister, Peabody, lived in Bath. She was their one remaining link with their old county, Somerset, and the more precious for that. Though they met rarely, the sisters and brother sent long loving letters to each other over the years. Now the post from the west was not getting through and Dorothy's nerves were stretched, ready to snap. Nellie and Hobbs, and Capel too, had left families in the old county and appeared, forever hang-dog, pleading for news she could not give. Drusilla had met her Aunt Peabody only twice in her life but she had enjoyed reading and writing her share of the letters. She hoped and prayed her dear Aunt was safe. Bernard was sick of the subject. He wished they would all get back to their card tables and he could have Drusilla to himself again.

As usual it was Nellie who caught the first crack in the silence. She got it from the old pedlar man who got it from Sir George Markham's manservant. They snatched greedily at every syllable through Nellie's tears.

"Twas terrible, Miss Dor'thy. It sounded like a great clap of thunder over the sea and then all of a sudden the waves come up with a terrible bright lightning enough to blind a body. They do say as how th'Eddystone lighthouse be under the sea, clean washed away and its keepers and all. Oh, Miss Dor'thy, Somerset beant so very far from there . . ."

Dr. Peter was dispatched once more to Sedgebrook Manor forthwith with orders not to come back without news.

"You must stay until you see Markham himself. We'll all die of suspense if we don't hear the truth. And, May, please hush your noise."

May crept back to the kitchen, and with the rest of the servants fell into the lowest of dumps at the telling and retelling of the blackest of tales.

Dr. Peter returned post haste without comfort. The Bishop

of Bath and Wells had been killed in his own bed by a falling chimney stack. People were marooned in bedrooms without shelter. The furious wind had stripped leads of roofs, rolling them up like carpets and tossing them into the filthy waters just like labourers pitching sheaves into barns. The stoutest carriages had been thrown into the air over walls and hedges as though lighter than wickerwork chairs. Great trees were bowled down as freely as ninepins.

"And it's no use you wanting to send me to Bath, my dear. The roads are impassable and travellers not welcome. In any case our sister will send us word as soon as she can, you may depend upon it."

So she did, but Dorothy's heart sank like a stone at the contents of the packet with its familiar handwriting and seal.

CHAPTER 9

The Peabodys had been rescued by boat. It had not been a pleasant experience but they had kind friends. The waters had drained off at last but left such a stink they doubted they would ever get clean again. Bristol was hit worse than Bath. The docks were choked with wrecked ships and dead bodies. There were hundreds unidentified, so battered, so bloated their own mothers would not know them; sailors most of them and dockhands and many blacks. The great warehouses stocked with the costliest goods from sugar to cotton, from silver to china were swamped and everything ruined. Salvage men were fighting with looters. Marlborough's war could not be worse. Rich merchants had become paupers overnight. The best families had been hit.

Dorothy could read no more. It made their own flood last spring look no more than a puddle but, instead of thanking God her sister was safe, she remembered that Bristol was Anthony's port. That was where he offloaded his goods. My God! It was where he berthed himself and had she not felt in her bones for months past that he would soon be at sea and on his way home?

Dr. Peter pursed his lips and reached out for his Golden Drops. How Peabody rattled on. He took a more sanguine view.

"Drink this, my dear, keep calm and use your pretty head."

That last load of Anthony's merchandise had already been sold and dispatched to London, blacks and all. The money was safe. There was not another due as far as they knew and Anthony was neither dockhand nor sailor, nor black neither.

If he had been on the High Seas they would have known it by now. Besides he had the luck of the Devil, always had.

"You can't pack me off to Virginia for news, my dear. We will have to wait for his next packet. It will come soon enough. And in the meantime we'll keep ourselves busy and so keep our heads. Don't let Drusilla see your fears either. I'll wager that child has too much imagination for her own good."

Dorothy agreed but was not convinced. Her unease did nothing to sweeten her temper and the Peabody letter did nothing to comfort Nellie and the others. There was a gloom in the house and what she would have done without Peter and his physick, both philosophick and medicinal, she daren't think. Between his Golden Drops and homilies she locked up her fears for her Anthony.

The blue of Peter's eyes, reflecting the blue of his coat, twinkled down at her from that handsome face, framed by his physician's full-bottomed wig.

"Remember this, my dear Dorothy, for years we have suffered floods in the spring, enjoyed sun and good harvests in the summer and revelled in the health giving frosts of winter. Nothing we can do will change any of that. Now what about that four for Wednesday next?"

And with that she had to be content.

The following summer of 1704 was the finest and the brightest of all, when every church bell in the land rang fit to rock both tower and steeple, let alone give Dorothy a bad head. Streamers and colours flew from every rooftop and window. Every hat was decked with red, white and blue and the words 'three cheers for Blenheim and Marlborough' heard on every man's lips.

"'Tis a wonderful victory, my dear," said the doctor as he proffered the pack for cutting. The country's heard nothing like it since Crecy."

"Agincourt," countered Dorothy with a decisive cut and the look of one who has trumped her opponent's ace.

Her brother raised his eyebrows. Was there anybody in this world as sharp as his sister, he wondered.

"Every Englishman should near burst with pride to see France in the dust. To think of Marlborough scribbling his victory note on the back of a crumpled tavern bill with naught but the stump of a plain lead pencil, only his saddle to rest on and that fool of a Marshal Tallard fast in the coach behind him. The tale's beyond belief and every word of it true." The cards fairly flew from his hands.

"Thank God for fools, then. The poor French man was never a professional soldier. You said so yourself."

They fanned out their cards, and eyed each other covertly for the tell-tale signs, a tucking in of the mouth, a greedy gleam in the eye, a turning over of carp bones in pockets for luck. With a fistful of royals the doctor could afford to be generous, but, having caught something of his sister's contrariness, he was bound to chide at her every remark.

"If we've pity to spare we should save it for the poor souls who will be paying more for their salt beef and pork to see it all through. Not to mention the thousands of good fellows dead, maimed and dying. Hm," as he laid down his cards. "Even the squires are not grudging their four shillings in the pound for once."

Dorothy's concentration was broken. She ceased wondering how to make the best of a bad hand and conceded defeat.

She let Peter rattle on. There were more hazards on the High Seas than a tempest. A foreign privateer was as much to be feared as a storm. She watched Peter rake up his winnings. She had been spending money like water lately. Perhaps the time had come to stop.

A clock chimed. She yawned. Peter pushed back his chair and was gone.

He was right of course. The longed for packet came at last. Anthony was safe in Virginia. She could breathe again. The year advanced and Christmas was as jolly as she could make it. Peter was in fine form dispensing news along with his physick.

"Did you know a retinue of French generals of the greatest distinction, all taken prisoner at Blenheim, have been confined. at Nottingham?"

"So?"

"So Marshal Tallard is lodged in high style in one of the great houses near the castle."

"Is that all?" Dorothy snapped shut her fan. "The way you came back in a lather I thought we might have captured King Louis himself at least."

"Don't be so crabbed, my dear Dorothy. How would you like to meet Marshal Tallard?"

"Meet him?" echoed Dorothy putting her fan to work at a pace. "Is he not under lock and key, this great prize?"

"He is given the freedom of the city, permission to ride within ten miles of its bounds and some of our friends have already made his acquaintance," adding, sotto voce, "and rather more than his acquaintance."

"What is he like?"

"A great favourite with the ladies!"

Dorothy snapped shut her fan and gave her brother a playful tap on the arm. Her eyes brightened.

"Peter, you've been ferreting and you've found something!"

"What I know was bought for the price of sitting with Lady Reville's old Aunt while she sucked her way through a dishful of muffins."

"Not a high price, surely? Did she enjoy them?"

"Lady Reville's old Aunt has no teeth. She slobbers and she likes her muffins dripping with butter. It was a heavy price and I can't afford to give the news for nothing. We'll cut for it."

He pulled a pack of cards from his pocket and shuffled.

"We'll cut for every tid-bit. You lose, you pay me a shilling. You win, I give you a name. I'll take you to five to start with."

She cut a deuce and paid up her shilling. She cut another

deuce and paid up another shilling. She paid out five shillings in all and threw her fan at her brother's retreating back.

By autumn the weather was still as warm as a muck heap and everybody in a bother for fear the meat should go off. She thanked the Lord a thousand times she had had the good sense to dig out an ice house.

It continued mild right through Christmas into February. She hardly held a card in her hand that month. The town and villages round about were full of agues and raging smallpox, and Peter was so run off his legs they rarely saw him. Passing bells tolled their mournful sound the whole month through. She thanked God and Anthony for their isolation on top of the hill one day and chafed at the lack of company the next. There was no visiting. People were staying at home to nurse their sick and bury their dead and pray God to send a hard frost. And she still had not got Peter to tell which of their friends had met the French general. She watched Drusilla like a hawk, not letting her out of her sight and wishing to Heaven she had not such a fear of small pox. Peter had said they were safe enough up here and he should know. Nellie had it from the pedlar man that that eccentric woman, lady Reville, had sent her Arabella to the home farm to live with the milk maids. Tish! No doubt the silly creature would be setting the child up with a stool and telling her to milk cows next. Mothers did not know which way to turn. She looked at her own pitted face and wept.

Bernard was left to his own devices. He, too, was low and miserable. Mistress Alice and her maids spent more time brewing up potent smells that were supposed to chase the fevers away than they did preparing the great meals he had become accustomed to. The stink of liquorice, balsam and rum pervaded every room. Nellie and her maids bustled about stirring pot-pourri bowls, strewing dried lavender heads, and lighting pastille burners. The combined odours were sickening. Windows and doors were shut fast, and in any case there was not a breath of wind outside. Bernard loosened his cravat. He felt more ready to die of a lack of fresh air than a fever.

He came out of his bedchamber and looked over the banisters, far down into the panelled hall. A sea of white bobbing mob-caps met his eyes, their owners still stirring, strewing and lighting. He picked out Nellie's broad back, her cap larger and whiter than the rest, but Drusilla was not there, nor was May Hobbs.

He looked up the staircase towards the attics but May was not there either, only a row of straw mattresses and neatly folded clothes, for Nellie's rule extended as far as this and she could not abide an untidiness.

His heart lightened. There was a place only a few yards beyond that belonged to nobody but birds. If there was anybody to be envied in this muck-sweat of unnatural weather it must be the birds.

Sweat poured down his face as he scrambled in darkness up the final stair and out into soft grey light. Pigeons and fantails whirred and flapped, as they had done before, showing pink and white like giant winged mushrooms. They sat invisible on the huge chimney stacks and cooed while he took in great gulps of damp air. He felt very much alone as he crossed the greasy leads to the balustrade to look between the balusters at the town beyond. He saw nothing, not even the church spire, for all was shrouded in mist. 'An unhealthy vapour' Dr. Peter had called it, and somewhere down there in that muggy pall were his father and mother and his little sisters.

Suddenly he felt afraid, along with a desire to be with his own kind. He would go home even if he had to walk every step down the hill. Neither agues nor the smallpox would keep him away.

It was clammy and wet, even up here. If he had brought Drusilla on to the roof Nellie would be chasing with scoldings of bad airs and fevers. But she did not care about him. Bad airs and fevers did not matter for him. He shivered. He wanted very much to go home.

He tumbled down the dark stair rather more quickly than he had scrambled up. He did not dwell on his family living their miserable existence in the empty draper's shop, his father using whatever charm he could muster for occasional support.

'Oh yes, Sir George. To be sure, Sir George. You are perfectly right in that matter, Sir George, and I have no doubt but His Grace will think so too.' 'Thank you, Sir Matthew, a few coals would not come amiss. My little Anne has never forgotten the sugarplums.' 'Oh yes, my Lord, Bernard is very well. The Davisons think the world of him, and with a little more help when the time comes . . .'

Oh, yes, in spite of everything, he wanted very much to go home. He made his way to the hall where a great fire blazed, as it did in each room in this opulent house.

"If the frost don't come to freeze out the fever then we'll roast him out instead," said Nellie, "Ah, Bernard, there y'are. Miss Dor'thy done been looking for you, my lad."

He wandered miserably into the little parlour where the fire roared like the furnaces down at the kilns. Mrs. Davison was seated at the little writing table and her voice was softer and kinder than usual.

He knew why when she told of the deaths of his little sisters, Anne and Elizabeth. He heard the news with the sharpest of pangs for it brought back that day he thought he had forgot when his first mother had died of an ague, but he would die himself rather than show a tear in this house.

Dorothy did her best but she was too preoccupied for sympathy. She could not get Anthony out of her mind. She feared for Drusilla. She feared for her brother down there among all that disease and death. And no, Bernard could not go home; his parents did not wish it; it was too dangerous.

Though she said she feared for them all, Bernard knew that did not include him and he must shift for himself.

His sorrow was hardly noticed at Beacon House, his hurt rarely mentioned. His grief welled inside him yet never once burst the banks of his self-control, and it was not the less terrible for that. He kept it to himself and nursed it tenderly. As though the sorrow were locked in white marble, it was the coldest, the heaviest and purest of secrets. In his heart he reproached himself for his lack of tears but lay the blame on Drusilla and her Mama.

His control was unchildlike, unnatural and unnoticed except by Nellie, whose sharp eyes missed nothing.

CHAPTER 10

Unhealthy mists dispersed at last; hard frost cleared the town of its fevers and spring blossomed early in 1705 as Dr. Peter had said it would. He had seen it all before and for more years than he cared to admit.

By April they were all of a flutter with their latest diversion. Marshal Tallard, Marlborough's prisoner from Blenheim, had become the toast and talk of the county. He held court from his house near Nottingham Castle in the most homely yet splendid fashion. They had been invited thither after meeting him at Mr. Patefield's party in Bingham, for, though the Marshal was supposed to be confined within ten miles, nobody followed him with a measuring stick and he knew it.

All the gentry for at least twenty miles around were under his French spell. Dr. Peter completely forgot the joke of Marlborough scribbling his victory note with Tallard locked in the coach behind him. No more was heard of the Marshal's stupidity or cowardice or, maybe, let's give him the benefit of the doubt and call it a desire for diplomacy, rather than battle, that had meant the slaughter of thousands of brave French soldiers as well as German and Dutch and our own grand lads at Blenheim.

In the days that followed, Drusilla and Bernard caught odd snatches of 'the merriest and liveliest little fellow you ever saw, don't you know? The drollest and prettiest English you ever heard in your life. And the scandals he'll leave behind, by Jove, when all is forgiven and forgot! Enough to keep every husband and father in the county on the hop. He's teaching the bakers of Nottingham to make real French bread since he can't abide our own. He's growing fields of liquorice and a new herb called celery down in the Meadows. He's teaching the street boys to play games of fisticuffs and running a book. He's making a mint. He's making more than a mint, he's making – sh!' And heads disappeared behind fans as they always did and "Tish!" spat Dorothy who still had not wheedled those names out of her brother.

Well, Bernard might like to hang round doorways snatching at gossip but with Drusilla it was a clear case of in one ear and out of the other. Now if they had been talking of people she knew then it might have been a different kettle of fish but Marshal Tallard and his antics could be a thousand miles away. And what was all this about trollops and visiting cards? What did they have to do with each other for Goodness sake? And wasn't bread just bread, whether English or French? And whoever heard of anybody growing liquorice when everybody knew it was that black stuff from the apothecary to be sucked for a chesty cough or stirred up by Alice in the great brass pan with Uncle Peter's other secret ingredients against the new influenza? And what made Mama so cross when Uncle Peter asked how much was she ready to bid for a name? And even though everybody agreed this new celery had the tastiest of flavours, there were far more interesting things to think about – and much closer to home too.

She looked at herself in Mama's glass. Uncle Peter was right. She was growing taller by the minute, not as tall as Bernard of course, but tall enough. She pulled down the front of her gown. There should be some shape soon, not yet, well perhaps a little gentle rounding was starting already, but one day . . .

That day could not come quick enough for Drusilla one minute and was dreaded the next. And surely her hair, thank Goodness, was not quite so red as it used to be.

Now, in the early spring of '06, the house was quiet and

still, for Mama was closeted in the little parlour checking Bolland's accounts. Bernard had taken himself off in a pique and he and May were out in the woods, looking for birds' nests and dodging Capel. Nellie was in the wash house keeping an eye on the maids with the smoothing irons. Alice had prepared enough food to feed a regiment and, having just filled a dozen raised pies with strong stock, was snoozing with her feet up before the great kitchen fire. Hobbs and his boys had mucked out the stables, groomed and doctored the horses, varnished the coaches, buffed up the brasses till their calloused hands stung with pain and the equipage shone enough to dazzle a blind man, and they, too, were dozing.

To Drusilla the stillness was unbearable, for two weeks ago today the post boy had sped up the drive with the wonderful news that Papa was in England, his ship berthed in Bristol and they were to be ready for him within the week. As Mama had broken the seal, a cry had come from her throat such as Drusilla had seldom heard in her life before.

"Anthony is home!"

Both laughing and crying, they had fallen into each other's arms and Marshal Tallard's name was heard no more from that moment.

The news had thrown the house into a frenzy of baking, brewing, cleaning and how the white down had flown as Nellie had ordered the shaking of feathered beds and quilts; how the smell of beeswax and turpentine had pervaded the house with a tingling of nostrils as maids polished floorboards and furniture with great flurries of rags and dusters. How Mama had fussed over her pot-pourri bowls, her own clothes, Drusilla's clothes, Papa's clothes and now the accounts. And whatever had happened to that frost in her eye? These days it was hardly there at all.

As for Drusilla, each surreptitious peep in Mama's glass showed a brilliance of eye, hair and cheek and, above all, a roundness of shape blooming at last.

Each morning for the past week, straight after breakfast,

she had flown up the stairs to station herself at an uppermost window, looking out over the long drive, the green sward, the red clay track winding down into Newent, whose pantile and thatch showed clear through the early spring trees, with the white spire of St. Leonard's high above all.

At first she had watched with a brightness of eye, her body on the alert ready to fly down the stairs at first sign of a horseman into the drive, and both Bernard and May too, between chores, had kept vigil with her. But the attic was as cold as Mama's new ice house and the days spent in waiting too drab, for Drusilla could not be diverted from her post at the window and was dull as ditch company. The other two took themselves off and for the past two days Drusilla had kept watch alone.

She sat now in the languor of weariness, chin resting on arms on the windowsill, humming under her breath to keep up her spirits, for it was late afternoon and the day had been long.

Would Papa ever come?

The drive remained empty as it had been for days past. The sun, moving further and further west, slanted down in the yard, deepening the sky, blackening the young cedar. The cool of the April day was ebbing into a chill, enough to make Drusilla pull up her shawl about her ears and, expectation almost gone, her humming had died away.

Would Papa ever come?

Suppose something terrible had happened on the way home. She recalled Uncle Peter's expression 'roads full of highwaymen as a buck's back with fleas'. Only the week before last a highway thief had shot old Mr Belcher clean through the chest on the Great North Road and even Uncle Peter had been unable to save him. And two days ago Mr Willoughby had taken no chances, got his aim in first and shot a coach robber stone dead not two miles from here. Well then, Papa would be safe. He could shoot as well as any Mr Willoughby.

Please God, don't let a highwayman kill Papa. Please God, make Papa shoot fast and straight. But were prayers too late? Was Papa lying already by some cold grey ditch in bright red death miles and miles from home?

She tightened her fists till the knuckles showed white, as she steadied her nerves. Please God. The evening light in the yard clouded and the young cedar blurred through the tears of her overworked imagination.

She thought she heard the sound of trotting hooves but did not look up. She had imagined that sound too often this past week, just as she had conjured his laughing voice, the opening of presents, the telling of tales. Her heart beat faster and 'don't be an addlepate, Drusilla', she told herself sternly till the hooves slowed down to a natural walk and her ears were full of a measured clip-clop on the flags. She raised herself quickly and there was a figure that must be Papa – it could be no other.

The breath went out of her body in a startled gasp of delight.

He sat straight in the saddle, even at this distance, a debonair handsome man. A dazzling cravat showed off the weathering of his dear face, his chestnut hair flaming, the brass buttons on his great coat winking in the fiery red of a dying sun. She would never chafe about her own hair again. It was just like Papa's. He came up closer, surveying the house, his house, slowly dismounting and tossing the reins expertly over the hitching post at the foot of the steps. The breath came back into Drusilla's body. She threw off her shawl and flung open the window.

"Papa!" she yelled and turned to fly down the stairs.

Her cry rang through the house and, quick though she was, as she jumped the last three steps into the hall, there was Mama already tight in his arms; Hobbs and his family fussing and patting the horse beyond the open door; Nellie beaming and bursting; May hopping about like a small scalded kitten and Bernard silently biding his time.

Papa! Oh, dear, wonderful, dearest Papa! And at last it was her turn to be hugged and kissed. He smelled of leather and horses and that men's stuff called tobacco and the smell was delicious. Drusilla wrinkled her nose in pleasure and felt she would never get enough of that smell.

The hall was filled with an electric excitement. She thought she could fairly see sparks a flying. Anthony released his daughter and grabbed at Dorothy's waist. She ducked her head and his warm mouth found her ear. He was insistent, irresistible and incorrigible, and within a moment there was a flurry of skirts and ankle as he chased his wife up the great staircase. Holding on to the newel post, Drusilla felt their rush of passion as they passed. She heard a door bang shut and sensed rather than knew there was a part of Mama and Papa that was not for her.

She put the hurtful feeling into a secret drawer at the back of her mind, turned the key and threw it away. Bernard almost watched her do it. She did not catch the gleam in his eye.

There followed such a week of showing Papa how cleverly they had managed, how well the great house ran, how beautifully kept the gardens and woods, how prosperous the wood yard, the brick kilns, the plaster pit. And what a mass of friends they had acquired, to what splendid parties they were invited and the even more splendid parties they would give now Papa was home.

And last, but not least, how proud they were of Drusilla's silver toy collection, all the way from Holland, and how she could read well in advance of any other young lady they knew.

And yes, this was Bernard Webster, the draper's son.

The ice in Mama's eyes melted forever it seemed as the old endearments of the early years of her marriage rang through the house, floating from behind doors, falling from windows, rippling down the great staircase, hovering in the hall and carrying through the gardens and down to the copse.

Leo and Lambkin and Sweet Puss were together again and Drusilla hugged herself in her own mind for sheer joy. And what was more, the corners of Mama's mouth were tucked into a permanent smile and the sparkling liquidity of her bright blue eyes quite outshone her want of complexion.

In short, she was beautiful again.

For Dorothy it was wonderful to be with her Anthony. He was so handsome, so noticeable with his great height, his flaming unpowdered hair, his laughing tawny eyes that could never be serious for two minutes on end. Oh, yes. He was her Leo again and no mistake. And since it pleased him to be admired so openly, he returned the compliment by spoiling her outrageously. She was his Lambkin to be petted and loved and encouraged to frisk and play as long as she wished.

As she sat at her glass each evening in the quiet of their great bedchamber, he would steal up from behind, gently prise the silver-backed brush from her fingers to stroke her luxuriant fair hair till the electricity crackled and snapped and a myriad shades of silver and gold shone in its fine fair strands.

"Promise me, Lambkin, you will never cut it – nor flatten it with one of those damned toupées neither."

He would kiss her in that breath-taking way she had almost forgotten, that made her toes stiffen and she thought she might burst from the pleasure. But more than anything else she wanted to show him off to her friends, this handsome, charming husband who knew how to make fortunes and did not mind spending them.

And Drusilla felt herself part of all this loving, for Anthony enjoyed his fatherhood. He called her Sweet Puss and treated her like a gambolling kitten for all her twelve years, so that she could hardly believe there was as much happiness in the world as came through Papa.

The joy of riding with this high-spirited man over the moor to Edgington, through the lanes to Barniby, where sheep nibbled the turf to a fine carpet, where tall leafless bushes were frosted with sloe blossom, where the differing yellows of goss and broom shone through the haze and larks called out their full throated song to the sky, was almost too much to bear.

As for Dr. Peter, he could not keep away and accompanied their rides more often than not, for he enjoyed a full gallop as much as Anthony, making no secret of how he admired his brother-in-law's company.

"Tish!" In spite of her new-found delight, Dorothy could not resist a comment on what were his patients doing for treatment the meantime.

"Patients, my dear Dorothy," her brother laughed, "are like the poor, they will always be with us. But Anthony, my dear, is another matter. There's a wanderlust in his blood that cannot be quenched and he'll be gone before we can say knife, you mark my words. We should enjoy him while we can – and you know what I mean by that, my dear."

She resisted the temptation to say that patients meant money and wished he had kept his last remark to himself.

Much of the joy for all of them was coming home to hear tales of other riders in far off lands where people were building houses with tree trunks, growing queer things called pine apples, fighting painted savages one minute, trading with them the next and people like themselves at that – mothers and fathers with sons and daughters of Drusilla's age and younger. They were tales of wonder, better than all the story books Drusilla had ever read to Uncle Peter for the price of a silver toy. She could not hear enough of these stories and sat on Papa's knee, asking for more, wrinkling her nose with pleasure at his manly smell of leather and horses and tobacco.

Sometimes Mama frowned and said the tales were enough to give a child nightmares.

When he started for the umpteenth time on the tale of the Deerfield Raid in America then she frowned worse than ever.

At Deerfield, near two years since, some three hundred Indians, a hundred Frenchmen and half-breeds had massacred a settlement of English. The men were boiled alive and the fate of the women and children too shocking to hear.

Nobody but Papa had such a knack of the telling. As clear as day they pictured the cabins behind their stockade with all the convivial homeliness of a new little colony and the forest beyond with its deep foreign beauty that stirred up the senses. Then hands up to mouths and eyes opened wide – was that sound a wild bird or an Indian call? The barking of dogs, gobbling of turkeys and gleam of an axe as leather-clad savages with blue-coated friends leapt down from the pales, Drusilla heard and saw them all.

She watched children scatter and men's hands grab at muskets as, protesting and pouting, she was whisked off to bed.

It was during such talks when candles wreathed and swaled, when fires were piled up, for, though days might be warm, evenings were chill, Mama silently plying her needle and thread, the two men loquacious in port and tobacco, that Drusilla felt within her the first stirrings of she knew not what. A springing joy in her breast made her heart beat so loud she thought the others must hear. New words of clearings and hunting trails and tropical islands of spices and sugar reverberating round the little parlour brought with them such hopes and desires that she could hardly contain her heartbeats. And when, half asleep, the men murmured possibilities of speeding their travels, of getting there faster with new inventions, new methods and words like knots and velocities bounced off the walls and inside her head, then the expectation that some extra-ordinary event would happen the very next minute, but never did, kept her at fever pitch.

Each day with Papa brought its own excitement and there was no doubt at all he preferred his pleasures outdoors. He enjoyed his rounds of the kilns, the wood yard and plaster pit, so keeping overseer Bolland well on the hop. What are these men paid? How many saints' days are they given? How far afield do our bricks go? How much do we pay for firing? How long will the plaster hold out?

He revelled too in his banterings with the men and women in the yards and open faced workshops and booths in the town. He discussed business and politics, gaming and horses over pots of strong ale in the Queen's Head tavern. He consulted Uncle Peter in the taproom of the White Harte where all the world could hear. He took the same corner in the Saracen' s Head as the Vicar of Newent and while the Vicar penned sermons he met Catchpole, the lawyer. He lingered in streets milling with flower girls and pie men, milkmaids and ballad mongers. He gave a silver shilling to a run away apprentice because no free born English man should suffer a cruel master. He tossed coppers to street urchins and beggars and asked after the health of Molly, the gingerbread woman.

He was lively and sociable, proud of his pretty daughter, seeing at once she carried more of his family's blood than that of her Mother. He turned a deaf ear to Dorothy's complaints that he had changed the little-used room off the dining room into something more like the saddle room of a public inn. One could hardly get into it for fowling pieces, riding boots, crops, jackets and the keg of rum at which she so wrinkled her uppity nose, not to mention the dogs with muddy paws and wet noses.

For her part, Drusilla felt she had woken as though from a dream. Her very step along the street beside Papa spelled out alacrity. It was a joyous feeling, this new found vitality, and she revelled in it, the old gripes in her stomach quite banished away. Papa jested and capered, shouted and sang, joined in rough sports, liked horse-play and hard riding and did not think, as Mama did, that one needed a ton of pomanders to venture down Dry Bridge, the shortest, narrowest and stinkiest street in Newent.

That Mama accompanied them less and less on their expeditions to Newent she did not notice. Nor did it ever occur to her she rarely sought out Bernard's company these days. She knew only that Mama hardly carped, Nellie never nagged and she could twist Papa round her little finger.

The feminine atmosphere of Beacon House was quite chased away and it was Papa she lived and breathed all day long, for he brought with him a sweet liberty and always this new found expectancy of something she wanted, just around the corner, yet always out of reach.

Chapter 11

One morning after breakfast, the dining room still full of the smells of sizzling gammon and buttered toast, Anthony chucked his pretty daughter under the chin, quizzing her with his mischievous tawny eyes.

"Now then, Sweet Puss, what day of the year is it, eh?"

"The first of May!" cried Drusilla, looking up at her handsome Papa. "Did you remember to say rabbits?"

"The first of May, and dang the rabbits, Sweet Puss, unless they be at the end of a gun barrel or tucked up in a pie." Anthony slapped his thigh in great good humour. "And what's special about today, my kitten?"

The smile on Drusilla's face quite died away. Memories of another first of May, long ago in the woods with Bernard, leapt up to torment her. How did Papa know or guess those terrible childish secrets she wanted to bury for ever and ever, amen? Her heart turned into a lump of lead as she looked at Papa.

"Don't be a goose, Drusilla," laughed Anthony, catching the look in her eyes and, thank the Lord, misreading it. "We don't burn witches on May the first any more. Today is for maypoles, is it not?"

"The dancing!" Her relief came up in a rush. "The dancing at Edgington Green! Oh, Papa, can we go?"

And though Dorothy excused herself with a sudden bad head, the pole with its ribbons, the maids and their skipping gave Anthony such a longing for all the English games he had missed for years past that he declared May the best month in God's calendar, and two weeks later was hustling them all to be ready for May Fair at Newent.

"And not on your life, Dottie, will I take no for an answer."

Dorothy sighed and if she did not approve, at least this time did not show it. She suffered herself to be bullied along with Peter and Bernard and May, for Anthony always wanted to share out his treats, and together they donned stout shoes and cloaks to go to the Fair. Lord, was there ever such a difference between two men as her husband and brother? No matter wherever he was or where he was going there was nobody so dapper or well turned out as Peter, not even General Tallard, who was generally agreed to be quite the sharpest man in the county these days. But as for Anthony, he cared not a fig for the way he looked. Whatever had made him have the tailor run up that new coat in exactly the same way as the old? Those patch pockets must be deep as sacks.

"I'll tell you why," he laughed, catching her disparaging look. "I need a loose fitting coat as'll give freedom of movement to do as I please, and I hope to God I always will. Let this popinjay here put up with a coat so tight he can hardly walk, let alone sit. And no place to put his hands withal."

He was incorrigible, always was and always would be, and a change of subject called for.

"Goodness! Will there be room enough in the carriage?"

"Carriage?" thundered Anthony. "Carriage, my dear Dorothy? Carriage be hanged. We'll ride or we'll walk."

"For shame, Anthony! What will people think?"

"Let 'em think what they like. Are we not free born Englishmen to do as we choose?"

And to Dorothy's discomfiture they walked the mile down the hill, sharing the way with Edgington maids in chintz bodices, red cloaks and straw hats, their wights in blue smocks. They took the little bridle path across Cherry Holt, past Chauntry Park and the Little Bede Houses into Barniby Gate, catching up with more sweethearts in Sunday best clothes and old people well wrapped in case of the cold.

"Tish!" she scoffed at building work going on, "A spate of new fronts being slapped on old frames I see, and none so fine as Beacon House yet. And they've all got the new sash, though we were the first . . ."

"I wish there were a dozen as fine as ours," riposted Anthony, "that way we might need to open another plaster pit and could get where we're going so much the sooner. Northgate will be the place, you'll see, Peter will have more neighbours than he can cope with."

"In that case then perhaps something will be done about the old castle. What Cromwell did not finish, the commoners seem hell bent on. There will soon be nothing left of that old ruin."

"How right you are, my dear Dorothy," Anthony laughed, "and don't forget how much we helped ourselves to for the coach house foundations."

Drusilla felt the familiar tightening of her stomach at the faint note of discord.

"You have an answer for everything," snapped Dorothy.

"Quite right again, my dear Lambkin. And I forbid you to be sour today."

Drusilla's ache in her stomach eased. "Now we must hang together in this mêlée," for they had crossed into Dry Bridge, that dark narrow street where overhanging chambers from centuries past shut out the light.

The noise was deafening. Dorothy did not know which was worse, that or the lack of air. Somewhere a band was playing that rowdy tune on everybody's lips since Blenheim.

"Some talk of Alexander and some of Hercules,
Of Hector and Lysander and such great names as these."

Lord, she would die of shame if Anthony struck up. She need not trouble herself. He might be merry enough for anything but was too busy at this moment easing them all through the throng, keeping tight hold of Drusilla with one arm and herself tucked into the other while Dr. Peter, good-naturedly, took charge of Bernard and May.

They squeezed through the dusk of Dry Bridge, under Old Roman Gate and burst into the brilliance of Market Place Square. Dorothy put up her free hand to hold off the blaze and the blare.

"But of all the world's great heroes, there's none that can compare with a tow row row row row row row to the British Grenadier."

She mopped her face with a handkerchief. Why was it noise always added to the heat? She must loosen her cloak or die.

"Look!" shouted Drusilla, making Dorothy near jump out of her skin, as she pointed to Bolland, their overseer, in front of the shambles where labourers lined up for hiring. Dorothy hardly glanced at the miserable shepherds in blue smocks, thatchers with straw in their hats, ploughboys and bird scarers all with the tools of their differing trades, but Drusilla stared hard enough for she had never lost her interest in people, be they hirelings or gentry.

"With a tow row row and a tow row row, Sweet Puss," laughed Anthony. "I shall not look at Bolland and his work today, that's for sure, and neither shall you. We don't keep dogs and do the barking ourselves."

And before Drusilla could work out whether that meant Bolland was a dog or no, she had found other interests. Anthony was recognised on all sides, for who could miss that tall, relaxed figure with the flaming red hair, his smiles and his waves? Certainly not the potboys and ostlers, milkmaids and applewoman.

"People of the commoner sort," noted Dorothy.

And Dr. Peter, too, bowed this way and that to one acquaintance after another, though Dorothy saw hardly anybody she knew and did not expect to either. It was Drusilla's squeal of recognition that proved the most significant of the day, though neither she nor anybody else at the time knew it.

"Look," she cried again, pointing to half a dozen Free School boys, obvious in their familiar dress. "Look, Bernard."

Bernard looked with distaste at his coarser contemporaries, boys pure and simple, who throve on the excitement of a battle and wilted in the ordinariness of agreement. Their cheeks bulged with humbugs, their eyes gleamed with mischief and they, in their turn, regarded their old enemy in the company of his fine benefactors. They massed for the joy of bringing down a hated bully. Having spent their last farthings, they had been looking for a sport they need not pay for and now they had found one. Bernard's heart sank. He pushed himself closer to his companions who did not catch the fall in his face.

"With a tow row row and a tow row row .... ."

Quick as a flash Anthony pulled a generous crown from his pocket.

"I'll wager you'll have more fun with your friends, Bernard. Take yourself off and don't spend it all at once."

"With a tow row row and a . . ."

Bernard turned to Drusilla, the appeal on his face as clear as day, but she had forgotten the school boys and was clinging to Uncle Peter, admiring her beautiful Papa and neither saw nor cared that Bernard was offered like a lamb to the wolves. For their part, the wolves were drooling. They snapped their teeth on the humbugs and relished the chance to savage an erstwhile tormentor.

There was nothing Bernard could do but put on a swagger, slip the coin between the fingers of a closed fist and face his adversaries.

As for the Davison family, they had already dismissed their protegé in the ravings of Black Jack, the local dissenter. Only May turned to wince at the flailing arms and kicking feet in a scrummage of boys.

"Tis not the Prayer Book you should hold in your hand, but the Bible." Thump! "The Prayer Book is the word of man." Thump! "The Bible is the word of God." Thump! "And God," thump, "will have his revenge on wicked men. The Day of Judgement is at hand. Repent! Repent! While yet there is time!" Jack thumped again on the closed bible in his other hand, sweat of passion pouring down his face, his lank black hair all over the place.

Dorothy tugged at her husband's arm as she caught the light in his eye. The last thing she needed was that Anthony should take up a verbal battle with this fellow. He was game enough for anything as they entered a prize-fighting booth. And again she kept close as a young Claypole farmer offered to take on all comers. They watched the young tough dispatch three takers in no time at all, before Anthony and Peter had finished laying their bets in fact.

By the time Peter had dragged them off to look at the quackery of bogus physicians, twisting apothecaries, tooth-pullers and the like, Dorothy was beginning to flag, but Anthony, of course, found a joy in everything from the motley band of seal woman and dwarf to learned pig and six-legged calf, and could not go past the quacks without a tilt at his brother-in-law either.

"Well, Peter, when blacks and tobacco, sugar and the rest of 'em dry up. I'll stay at home and you can go round the fairs."

"Nothing but charlatans and mountebanks," said Dorothy. "Who with any sense would believe any of them?"

"A great many by the rate their stuff changes hands," said Dr. Peter dryly. "I wish I could turn over money so fast. And if ever it comes to that I think we might starve."

"Which reminds me, I am starving," replied Anthony, "and it must be dinner time at the King's Arms. Now Peter, have you still got hold of May and where is that boy?"

That boy had had a stroke of good fortune. He had been saved from a massacre.

In the middle of a drubbing he had no hope of surviving, a team of packhorses had thrust its way. As the leathern lunged drovers whacked at the animals' rumps with their raucous 'Mind your backs! Mind your backs!', the knot of fighting boys had unravelled and scattered. Bernard had wisely put as much ground as he could between himself and his attackers.

He had turned instinctively in his misery out of Market Place Square, through stinking Dry Bridge into Appleton-gate, doubled back through the churchyard in fear of pursuit and did not stop running till he tumbled into his father's old shop, scrambling up the stairs with no breath in his body and murder in his heart.

He folded his arms on the big old table, lay down his head and sobbed until his bones ached and his eyes ran dry.

"I will never go back up there. I will stay here at home."

But it was not home without his little sisters and with his mother already breeding again. Besides, there were strangers in the house. Spare rooms, including his own, had been let to lodgers.

He had come for comfort and found none. For all his father's fine connexions, fires did not burn in these grates, this table did not groan with food, nor was there an army of minions to see to this and that.

He could not keep the resolution. He hankered after beeswax and this place had only tallow to offer. Besides, at the top of the hill there was a score to settle, and the crown safe in his pocket did not make up for that.

CHAPTER 12

No sooner had the market place been cleared of the trappings of May Fair than Anthony's restless spirit was looking for new diversions and he and Peter were off to the races at Edgington Moor. At the end of the day he resisted the temptation to ride past the end of the drive with the others and on to the fun of the Saracen's Head in Newent. He headed for home, for supper and bed and Dorothy. Next morning, he was flexing his muscles again.

His wife might groan but his daughter revelled in so much energy.

As the precious days sped by, Drusilla never noticed how silent Mama had become on these occasions, how when she spoke at last her voice was high-pitched, wound up like a too tightly wound spindle ready to snap. That lovely warm light Papa had fired in her eye had certainly changed, but whatever had given her that hurt and puzzled expression, Drusilla was too young to fathom. She never took the trouble to listen to Mama nowadays. Whatever her mother said went in one ear and out the other. Sometimes Mama complained of fatigue and spent her days on the sofa in the little parlour, and Drusilla loved those days, for then she had Papa to herself.

Well, what matter if Papa showed no taste at all for Mama's select card parties; if he preferred, as he put it, a snug little dinner for no more than a dozen or more 'up to our ears in port and punch'? Were not men always coarse-grained and did not the ladies like them the more for it? Drusilla loved her Papa to distraction.

In no time at all Anthony found what he was looking for when he remembered Oak Apple Day fell on the twenty third of May, and towards the end of the month he was stirring the household afresh.

Some few days before the twenty third he had them all, family and servants alike, up at five in the morning, cutting down branches of oak, digging great charcoal pits on the edge of the spinney beyond the garden. He laughingly swept away Dorothy's protests as he insisted on robbing her treasured beds of their evergreen herbs for the maids to twine into wreaths.

"Dorothy, my dear, if you'll not join in the fun you can go to Trent!"

He laughed his latest quip in devil may care fashion and she silenced the fears in her breast that they might be digging the pits too near the tiny graves of those unbaptised boy babies, three in all, that brought back such painful memories of happier times in her marriage.

Invitations that had put her in a flutter, for he was insistent everybody they knew should be asked, had been accepted; musicians engaged; clothes decided; an ox slaughtered; puddings stirred and tied and now there was nothing but the decking of the great house to be done.

"Goodness me, Mr. Anthony," sweated Nellie, her cheeks like hot coals. "'Tis nothing but Christmas all over again. Now Miss Drusilla, you do get from under my feet if you do please. May, you do save my old legs and run and tell your grandfather and anybody else with nothing to do as we do need some help up y'ere. And, Bernard," a fractious note coming into her voice, "what be you standing around for? You do make yourself useful, my lad. And Miss Dorothy, where . . . ?"

But Dorothy was upstairs trying to rest. Jove, Anthony and his bright ideas would be her death. And whatever the quality would think of such a show she could not imagine. They had never been invited to the like at Beacon House before. There was something so old-fashioned about Oak Apple Day. Not quite decent with the new Queen she would have thought. And not quite wise either with all this talk of Jacobites, protestant successions, risings and all that trouble brewing in Scotland and such like. Now in the old days in Somerset, in the reign of the old King when they were children, well, that was another matter entirely.

Her thoughts slowed. Such an impulsive man, Anthony. Always was and always would be. She near dreaded the morrow. She hoped she was equal to it and tried to pull her cap tighter to shut out the bustle. Sleep, dear God, sleep. Bless Peter. Didn't know what she would do without Peter. For all his hints about sons if she wanted to keep Anthony happy. Sons. She had had three. What did men know about any of all that? Still . . . Peter . . . Peter . . . was always . . . right . . .

Her chin sank on to her chest, her breath whistled through her open mouth. She was not a pretty sight.

For Drusilla, as she prepared for bed that night, it had been one of her happiest days. She hugged her blossoming body to herself in expectancy of the wonderful blessing she would find on the morrow. And best of all, it was Papa who heard her cry out in the night when, for no reason she could think of, her old nightmares returned.

She had awoke, trembling with terror, to find Papa standing over her, the bed hangings drawn back to let in the white moonlight, for she would not have shutters closed. Gently, with his great hands, he had untied the strings at her neck and raised her head to remove the restricting cap Nellie so insisted upon 'in case of a fire'.

"There, my poppet, get some sweet air to your head – that will chase away all the bad dreams in the world. And promise me when you grow up to a woman you will be like your Mama and never pin down your pretty hair with such an ugly thing as a wig."

"Oh yes, Papa, oh, yes." She would have promised him

110

the moon at that moment as, without another word, he had picked her up in his arms and cradled her like a small child till her sobbings had ceased.

"What is it, Sweet Puss?" His soft lips brushed her tear-stained face. "Tell Papa all about it."

"Oh Papa! I don't know, but there's a girl in the house who sometimes looks out for me. She hides behind curtains, in cupboards and dark corners. She comes up behind me when I look in the glass – and – and."

"And what then, Sweet Puss?"

"I don't know. I don't know, Papa. I'm too much afeared she might find me and . . . and I always wake up before she . . ."

"She never will, Sweet Puss, for I promise you there is no such girl in the house, only too much excitement today and too many of Alice's tid-bits, my Pet."

She hid her face in Anthony's nightshirt to shut out the sight of that terrible girl. And what it was that forbade her to tell of the old man who leered at her with a bagful of sugarplums, she did not know. But she could not tell that, not even to Papa, while he hugged her close and she drew in his sweet laundered masculine smell.

"Now you are safe and will stay safe all night through." He laid her gently back in her bed and sought in the pale moonbeams to light up a taper. She turned a wet face to the light.

"Papa, will you stay with us for ever and ever, Amen?"

He smiled and his russet eyes were kind as he sat on her bed, covering her small hands with his own large fists, showing their tawny mottled backs with the golden hairs.

"Now let me tell you about my own dreams, Sweet Puss. There are two girls in my dream and for them, one day, I will build a grand house with a great park such as my grand-fathers had in Somerset. And from other windows than these we will look out on to broad acres of woodlands and fields, all our own land with never a hint of brick kilns and saw mills, nor plaster pit neither. The only thing between us and

111

our neighbours, and we'll have none other but Lords for our neighbours, I promise you that, will be the prettiest village you have ever seen. 'Twill be our own village, for we'll build it ourselves for our own labourers to live in . . ."

"And when will that be, Papa? When will that be?" She wriggled with pleasure down into the lavender-scented seats as he held up her hand to his gold-warm cheek.

"Sooner than pigs might fly, Sweet Puss. Before you are seventeen in fact, and then you will marry in strawberry beds."

"What does that mean?"

He laughed softly, snuffed out the candle and kissed her lightly on the forehead.

"Remember, Mama and I are only two ticks of the clock away. Sweet dreams, Sweet Puss."

Back in his own bed, Dorothy still lay curled up in the tight little ball he had left the few minutes before. He turned to gather that roll of warm flesh into his arms. Dottie, he would have thought a good mother might have heard her own child cry in the night. Oh, Dottie. He cupped a hand under her breast, pressing her upstanding nipple softly. Daughters were all very well and he loved Drusilla with all his heart. She could have anything money could buy. But he wanted sons. He would restore the family fortunes and found a country seat and he needed sons. He thrust himself at Dorothy who moaned in her half-sleep and half turned towards him. If a bankrupt draper turned lodging house-keeper could sire a son, then surely he . . .

He slid his free hand under her nightgown up to the sweet nest between her warm soft thighs. Aah! Found it. Come on, Lambkin. There's a darling Dottie. Aah! And a seat in the commons would not come amiss either. He held his prize with a gentle pulsating pressure till her juices flowed. Though a place on the bench would do to begin with. And why not? He was as good as the next man. Better than some. And everybody knew there was as much to be got from public office as rack-renting. Don't hold back on me, Dottie. He knew how to manage these simple squires. They would be eating out of his hands before he went back to Virginie.

Come on, Dottie, come on. Good girl. It was all over in less than a minute and Dorothy dead to the world.

Anthony sighed. It was not the hottest love-making he had known but he slept sound enough for all that.

CHAPTER 13

Oak Apple Day, the twenty third of May, dawned warm as
summer, unseasonably hot for the time of year. Golden sunlight streamed brilliantly through the straw coloured dimity
of Drusilla's bed hangings and her walls glowed with the
same golden light. Pine bedroom furniture gleamed like the
silvery hay plumes of a ripe meadow, with the only brilliant
contrast of colour a patchwork quilt of new calicoes pieced
together by Nellie and May in the long evenings of last
winter.

Drusilla squirmed luxuriantly in her lavender scented
sheets. A sweet, warm air filled the room with the heady
fragrance of blossom and wood-smoke. She stretched again.
Sparrows quarrelled in the eaves, a horse neighed from the
stable, geese honked and pails clanked in the yard as servants
swung into workaday chores. Light and sound together
pierced Drusilla's sleep-ravelled brain and opened her eyes
to the day. She drew back the hangings and dangled bare
toes.

"Not raining!" she exulted.

"Rain? It won't dare rain!" Papa had thundered, as she and
Mama had expressed their fears the day before.

"And will they all manage their carriages to the top of the
hill?"

"If not, they can ride their horses instead."

And, of course, he was right. He was always right. Even
Mama said so.

And tonight she was to wear her new gown and stay up for
one hour of the ball. She had wheedled and wheedled Mama

for that favour, but it was Papa who had granted it and, since she could twist him round her little finger, surely she could stretch one hour to two or three. And who knows, she might wangle a stay to the very end?

She smiled a contented smile in that tranquil golden light, stretched up her arms, pushed down her toes, squirmed again with delight and sprang off the small, high bed. Today might be that very day when she would catch that unknown benediction, hovering so teasingly close, yet holding itself just out of reach, never keeping its promises of happy relief from the mass of physical sensations stirring her body.

She was as pretty as a picture and knew it, as she pirouetted with conceited pleasure in front of the new cheval mirror, a belated present from Papa to mark the twelfth birthday he had missed like all the others.

She danced to the window where early honeysuckle wreathed its first apricock and cream blooms on the sill, where, down below, apple blossoms were au point like Drusilla herself, where pear trees were lightly frost-sprinkled with white and, beyond the garden, hawthorns gleamed like great banks of snow. There were scents in the air good enough to eat, for over the gardens hung a haze of blue smoke, rich with its savoury odours of burning charcoal and roasting ox.

She wrinkled her nose and revelled in it.

"Only the ash, the bonny ash, burns fierce while it is green," she hummed, drumming her bare feet on the gypsum floor in anticipation of the night, as she conjured up the tap and swish of dancing feet and swirling petticoats on the wax polished drawing room boards. Of course, she would have to be content with a seat on Mama's new walnut sofa, but if only she were older . . . Well, one day she would . . . And again she felt that inexplicable stirring within.

"Miss Drusilla, you do come away from that there window in that shift or you'm be catching your death and spending your Oak Apple Day in this y'ere bed, as stiff as a board," scolded Nellie, bustling to help the young Miss as soon as she heard the thump from the bed.

Her quick eyes caught Drusilla's pout and her tone changed. She didn't need no trouble with young Miss today of all days.

"Your Mama do say you'm to be good, my chick, or no staying up for the dancing. There still be a thousand things to do, enough to bring on one of Miss Dor'thy's bad heads. Mr. Anthony's a mighty fine ideal but it makes a mountain of work for some."

She poured water from the ewcr into a bowl and laid out a clean towel.

"We're expecting everybody about noon, then, in the evening, while the quality be dancing in the drawing room, the brickies and woodmen and plasterers they do be coming up through the woods to finish the roasts and puddings and all." She chuckled. "And I do believe as how your Papa do think we be back in Somerset, my chick. He done have ordered so many barrels of dry cider that Lord knows what they be getting up to."

She bustled about, chiding Drusilla to keep still, come y'ere, wait there, and her bustle only served to feed the girl's excitement. And, truth to tell, Nellie was as near excited herself. Goodness me. The morning might drag for Miss Drusilla, who had nothing better to do but look pretty, but for some folk there bean't be enough hours in the day.

"Lord above! Keep that window tight shut do. The smell of that cooking will be all over this y'ere room," and Nellie wrinkled her nose as she pulled down the sash.

The crackle of stiffly starched petticoats exploded as Drusilla wriggled into the crisp texture of her blue India chince dress, twisting and turning to fix the new little cambrick pinafore, while Nellie's fingers, all thumbs, struggled in vain with hooks and tapes. For two pins she would have given Miss Drusilla a slap. Jove. But it was hot today. She pushed a stray curl under her cap.

116

"May! May! Come y'ere, May! Where be that dratted girl? Keep still Miss Drusilla or I'll tell your Mama. May! May!"

But May was down by the charcoal troughs that had been burning slowly for two days or more and were now long pits of bright red embers. She watched the glistening ox on a huge spit, that took two men to turn it, with the juices of beef and of men both trickling and spluttering down to the coals below. Saliva drooled into her own mouth as great iron pots of beef broth and dumplings floated their succulent odours into the air to tickle her nostrils, drowning, thank goodness, that awful wash day stink of boiling pudding cloths. Maids, standing ready with kettles so pots would not boil dry, wiped spare arms across damp foreheads and two dozen hired servants or more bustled hither and thither.

"May! You got nothing to do, May?"

"May! May! May! Come y'ere!"

Oh Lord. That was Nellie again. Goodness, it was sweltering hot. She turned back to the long boards on their trestles, spread with Miss Dorothy's best linen, in the shadiest part of the garden. She heard Nellie's voice yet again from the house. 'May! May! May!' She deliberately busied herself with shifting the cushions and stools and hassocks scattered about. Mr. Anthony had thought of everything. For sure, she must be the luckiest maid alive to live with this great family. How clever Mr. Anthony was to change the garden into such a drawing room. New grass made as fine a carpet as those inside; leafy boughs hung like the richest curtains; ladies would sit on hassocks or cushions as comfortably as on chairs or sofas; the boards and their linen were as fine as any dining table she had ever seen. Though, truth to tell, she had only seen one. Bernard might boast of other places, if he pleased, but she . . .

And where was Bernard? Come to think of it, she hadn't seen him this morning, nor yesterday neither. Surely he wouldn't be sulking, today of all days. Didn't he ever think himself lucky too? No, she didn't believe he did. There was the strangest look in his eye sometimes, if you ever caught him off guard. She remembered that time Miss Drusilla . . .

"May! May! May!"

"Coming," she called.

By noon the long drive and wide courtyard were full of saddle horses and coaches, as guests, dismounting from one or the other, greeted their friends. Stable boys, leading the animals to be unharnessed for the day, gleefully pocketed the generous vails doled out on all sides. Swarms of children leapt shrieking over the lawn into the noisy protests of defensive geese. The front door opened to the hall filling with people, their odours of all kinds mingling with the pot-pourri of Dorothy's big Chinese blue and white bowl. Young women, bright as dragonflies, laughing and chattering, leaned over the gleaming oaken handrail, looking down on young men below. One day Drusilla hoped she would laugh and lean over banisters with only her eyes peeping over a pretty fan to tease and lead on young men – blades Papa called them.

Now she ran into the yard to greet the Reville's carriage. Capital. Arabella was here and she would be good company on Mama's walnut sofa. Servants were bustling, taking over cloaks, hats and mittens. Dogs, who had somehow got loose from the stables, slobbered and wagged their pleasure at such a melee.

And whoever in the world was that droll creature leading his horse from the drive? How on earth had he ridden with three hats crowned with oak leaves on top of an old-fashioned, full-bottomed wig? It could only be Uncle Peter's friend, rummy old Mr Patefield, the apothecary-surgeon from Bingham. Papa and Uncle Peter, no doubt, would be doubled-up-tickled-pink, but Mama might turn up her fine nose if he got himself merry enough and into his repertoire of party-tricks.

Ugh! And over there was that old horror, Sir Matthew

Jenison. She would not run to greet him. And that must be the niece from Yorkshire she had heard about. Poor Elizabeth. Drusilla was glad she had kind Dr. Peter for an uncle, who smelled of verbena and leather and horses, as any man should, and not that old devil, Sir Matthew. She would not like to be obliged to spend holidays with him, thank you very much. Did he stuff Elizabeth with sugarplums and help himself to nasty wet kisses in payment? Ugh!

Oh, wonderful. There were the Hattons, the tall handsome Lord Lessington with his two girls, Biddy and Anne, and young William. How lucky to catch them. They were so often away, London, Vienna and Goodness knows where. They would be quite the prettiest family here and their gowns on a par with her own, the two girls alike as two peas in a pod and the very spit of their poor, dark-eyed Mama. And the boy, so tall for his age, and as fair as his handsome Papa. How ever did they manage without a Mama? Who arranged for their clothes, taught them their letters and ordered their servants? Her heart went out to them. Though her own Mama might often be cross as two sticks, she could not bear to think of her cold in her tomb. She would tell them how pretty they were and kiss them all soundly.

That would make four at least on Mama's best new sofa. This would be the happiest day in the whole of her life. What good fortune to have such a Papa. She tugged at Arabella, Biddy and Anne for a peep in the drawing room.

Older women were there, already seated, fanning themselves, talking of weddings, breedings and birthings, sickness and funerals, scandals and gossips. The children caught their swift oohs and ahs, their titters and gasps, well-I-nevers and upon-my-honours and at least one upon-my-mother's-death, till all heads closed ranks behind a screen of silk fans.

Through the high open windows came the voices of men out in the yard, men greeting each other with friendly oaths, lingering on this, that and t'other, that randy French general,

Brandy Nan, four shillings in the pound, the new popish plot. Heavens, thought Drusilla, the news never changes.

Anthony was in his element, hailing one guest after another.

Dorothy, well, nobody but Dorothy herself knew how much effort all this had cost her. Certainly Anthony, with his untiring exuberance, would not want to hear of it. She brushed the tiny beads of moisture off her pale forehead; as soon as she could find the moment, she must slip upstairs for a fresh powdering. In the meantime, here was Anne Belcher, looking for all the world like a . . .

"Mrs Belcher, my dear . . ."

"My dearest Mrs Davison."

Late in that sultry afternoon, when the quality could not push in another spoonful and the hovering midge-flies were taking their first nips, then the ladies retired upstairs to rest away the hours till time to change for the dancing. Drusilla, chattering with the other girls, could see from her window the men still out in the garden, coat buttons undone, legs spread wide as tight breeches allowed, still wagering, still arguing the toss and the same old issues of Good Queen Anne or Brandy Nan and dang me why ain't Marlborough satisfied, why does he have to go on wasting our men and our money? The danged French, the danged Spaniards, the danged Jacobites and these blasted flies! They moved on to the price of corn and the new ways of keeping cattle all through the winter. There were tales coming out of Norfolk, if you could believe 'em, but the flies it was that drove them indoors at last.

The older men settled to snooze off their indigestion in the drawing room, Anthony quite forgetting Dorothy's admonishment about that room, 'I don't want the drawing room used till the dancing, Anthony, remember that.'

As cards were laid out in the little parlour and guineas changed hands, Anthony got the younger ones, at last, away from their farms and off to the lands of spices and sugar, slaves and tobacco. He trotted out the old Deerfield tale with embellishments. Ha! Wait till he got his own acres, then he would settle the price of corn.

Bolder fellows hung on to the hands of young women, that perennial plea hot in their eyes. The young women either laughed and scuttled away with promises made to be broken or, with fingers on lips, foolishly tip-toed to coach house or hay loft.

Upstairs the chattering of the youngest girls changed to a gentle rhythmic breathing. Dowagers in other rooms rattled and snored.

Only Dorothy could not rest. The servants must still be clearing away the mess of the quality. Could Nellie and Alice manage without her? They had taken on enough extras, Lord knows, for Anthony would never consider the cost. The men should be coming up from the kilns, wood yard and plaster pit, wives and families as well. Anthony was so generous and there was no curbing him. What on earth was he doing? Gambling their lives away, no doubt. Oh God, would the beef hold out? Were there puddings enough?

Up the hill puffed the labourers. the woodmen wheezing and spitting the dust from their lungs, the brickies carrying the bright red dyes of their trade, the pale ghosts of the plaster men dusted over like millers and, like locusts all, they and their families fell on the remains of beef and the puddings.

The ladies in the big house hardly stirred till, faint and far away from the woods, the fiddlers started to scrape and whang. The sounds of country dance floated in the still night air and, one after another, cider barrels were broached and emptied. 'Master Anthony were a good master'e were and c'm'ere me duck, c'm'ere!' The fiddling quickened and the dancers livened, till maids and men together stumbled and rolled deeper into the woods, away from glowing lanthorns and into the dark.

From the drawing room, as the harpsichord clanged and

the viols tuned, the grand company bustled to life again and the ladies decked themselves out in toupéed head dresses, high heeled shoes with silver buckles and silken gowns in every colour of the rainbow. As the girls, too young to dance, sat together on Dorothy's best walnut sofa to watch that bright assembly, Drusilla felt again that feeling of expectancy leaping in her breast, that thirst for some untasted nectar that somehow, unaccountably, had to do with Papa.

Hoops dipped and swayed, white powdered heads bobbed, skirts and well-filled hose flew and swirled together on the high-polished floor. The younger girls' feet tapped, their eager bodies moved in unison on the walnut sofa. Their brothers and cousins stuffed themselves at the side tables on marchpane, custard tarts and tipsycake.

Drusilla felt she would never forget that day and how good it was to have Papa home. How wonderful was life with Papa at home. How lucky were those friends whose Papas were always at home. And yes, she would wind Papa round her little finger and make him stay at home for ever and ever, Amen.

Within less than a week, joyous news of another great battle fought and won had rocked the country and, once again, church bells rocked their steeples. Anthony had taken himself off at early morning to celebrate Ramillies with the cock fighting in Edgington and now, in the late afternoon, there was an unpleasant atmosphere within the house.

CHAPTER 14

In the kitchen Mistress Alice basted the geese, boxed the scullery maid's ears and sounded cross as two sticks as she sent May back to the loft for more apples. They were the remains of last season's crop, wrinkled and pock-marked, and poor May wondered how she could help that.

Nellie dozed by the huge fire in the housekeeper's room, her chin sinking lower and lower. Yes, it was wonderful to have Mr. Anthony home. Miss Drusilla had never looked better. And Miss Dor'thy, well, she didn't know about Miss Dor'thy these days. She didn't like that cold look creeping back to Miss Dor'thy's eyes. 'Twas not a look to be welcome back, that wasn't. Well, he made enough work for everybody did Mr. Anthony, that was for sure. She'd never felt so spent in her life.

Out in the stables Old Hobbs, Young Hobbs and Little Hobbs waited to rub down a tired horse, feed him his bran mash and water and hang up his harness. Dang me, they'd never worked so hard in their lives since the Master came home. And where the devil was he? The cock fighting must have finished long since. It had been dark these past two hours and more.

Inside the little parlour, where Dorothy, Drusilla and Bernard awaited both Anthony and their supper, all looked as serene and cheerful as usual.

The room was warm, almost too warm, in the combined heat of fire and candles. Shawls slipped from shoulders and Bernard asked for permission to loosen his stock. They had started the evening with a glass of malmsey wine and an eye on the clock, wondering what tales Anthony would tell of his day; had he won or lost and how much?

But the evening ticked on without him and, on her last trip to the kitchen, Dorothy had ordered Alice to take the geese from the oven or they would be burned to a frazzle. The dining table had been laid long since.

She prepared for a long wait and took up her needlework, while Drusilla and Bernard started a game of dominoes. Dorothy could not tell why, but her nerves felt tighter than viol strings ready to snap. She had been sick in the mornings for two weeks past and dreaded what Peter might say to that. Where in the name of Heaven could Anthony be at this hour? He knew well enough the roads were not safe.

"Don't bang those dominoes down like that", she ordered in a voice that crackled with high tension.

Drusilla and Bernard exchanged questioning looks. Drusilla tactfully brought out a pack of cards. What on earth was the nervousness in the room about? Papa had been away all day before, had he not? Their whispered game of beggar-my-neighbour petered out. Bernard sat twiddling the loose frogging on his second best jacket, his chair cracked like a gun shot as he leaned back and Dorothy near jumped clean out of her skin.

Silence, apart from the tick of the clock, hung like a pall over the room, its cover too thick not to notice it.

Drusilla strained her ears to catch the first sound of hooves in the yard but she heard only the rising wind in the trees. What an uneasy, unpleasant evening this was. Besides, she was hungry. They must all be hungry. Mama had made three trips to the kitchen at least. Why was she so edgy?

All three looked up at the creak of branches under the worsening wind, at each splutter of burning logs in the fireplace. There would scarce be a blossom left on the trees if this gale kept up. A hiss and a spit on the fire meant rain had started.

The clock's tick measured their discomfort, accentuated

their fear.

Something was wrong. Both Drusilla and Bernard wondered whatever it was, but Dorothy knew and they were both sure that she knew. The boy's feelings were mixed. An upset in the Davison family might not suit him at all. On the other hand, he was still smarting from the family's indifference at May fair, so somebody's come-uppance might not come amiss. He licked his lips and prepared to enjoy himself.

Drusilla started again at the sound of hooves growing louder as horses trotted at a fast pace up to the house and into the yard. Her ears pricked. There was more than one horse. Papa must have somebody with him. Before she could say so she found herself hustled along with Bernard into the dining room, Mama leaving the door full ajar in her haste.

There was the jangling of brass, the creaking of leather, the hard voices of men, Old Hobbs and his son, surely. One voice rose above the rest. Papa's voice but impossible to tell what was said. Two horses at least. Had there been an accident? Horses were now being led to the stables and their sounds clattered away. Now voices were nearer. Great Heavens. Foolish voices that jumbled their words and slurred them together. Goodness. Now the noise of unsteady feet into the hall and shrill unmanly laughter. Papa's voice again. What the deushe? What the devil? A short mumbled argument. Go to Trent. Go to Trent. Uncertain feet stumbled towards the dining room.

Drusilla braced herself.

The open doorway was suddenly filled by Papa, wearing an arrogant, spoiling-for-a-fight expression, his bright, rain-darkened hair all over the place, his long legs nearly buckling beneath him, one arm flailing the air, the other wrapped round Uncle Peter.

Uncle Peter. Thank Goodness. Drusilla breathed again. The feminine household of Beacon House was not used to sights like these, but Uncle Peter would put things right.

Anthony growled softly as he introduced his companion of the day's sport. A stranger might have thought the sound no more than a strong purr, but wife and daughter knew better. He had not earned the name Leo for nothing.

"We have a guesh for shupper", he announced, and the growl held a deep-throated menace. "Drushilla, your Uncle the physh – physh – physh – what the devil?" He leaned heavily on his brother-in-law and eyed Bernard with distaste.

Dorothy's face was ashen, her back stiff, as May set about laying an extra place.

She knew what had happened right enough. The cock fighting had finished well into the afternoon. Since then, Anthony and his cronies must have been in the King's Arms, or some other such place, spending every penny of winnings. Winnings. Drowning their losses more likely. Drowning themselves and their money as well in strong ale and claret. Tears pricked at her eyelids. Oh, Peter, how could you let him? And you must have galloped straight past the end of the drive to get down to Newent.

She tightened her lips and bade them both welcome. Anthony noticed that compression of her mouth and his look was belligerent. He eyed the two overdone geese brought to the table for carving and sniggered.

"The gooshe is a shilly bird, Dottie. Too mush for one and not enough for two. Ever'body knowshat. How many geeshe have we here? An' one, two, shree, four, five of ush to eat 'em. How the devil shall we do it, eh?"

Dorothy glanced to the door where Nellie, hot and embarrassed, staggered under the weight of a newly boiled ham. She turned to avoid the swinging arms of her drunken master as May followed with a tongue boiled and pressed for the morrow.

"Go home, Peter. Go home. There'sh a good fellow. I want to talk to my family."

"I am family," said the doctor pleasantly, while firmly leading his brother-in-law into a chair.

126

Thank Heavens, Peter was not drunk. Dorothy's eyes flashed a frantic plea to her brother. Peter, please stay. Oh, please stay.

Dr. Peter took up the carving knife and laid it against the steel. Drusilla flinched at the sound. Bernard's hands gripped the edge of his chair. This promised to.be as good as a peep show. As the doctor laid down the steel, the heavy silence returned and the ticking clock dominated the room again.

Anthony lounged back, spreading his long legs under the table. He looked at Dorothy and thought her a dried-up, po-faced bitch. He looked at Bernard and noticed for the first time that dark shadow on his upper lip. Impudent young dog with that cheeky look on his face. He regarded Drusilla's large, fear-filled eyes and struggled with his drink-addled brain to put thought into words.

"How old ish thish pup?"

He thrust a foot under the table to give the boy a sharp kick on the shins and Bernard set his face to show nothing of the pain in his leg. He looked across at Drusilla but she had hardly heard the slurred words, paralysed with fear at this open disagreement of Mama and Papa. The old gripe in her stomach tied her inside in knots as she concentrated the tears in her eyes, feeling she would die of shame if thcy should fall down her face.

"I am fourteen," said the boy evenly, staring at Drusilla.

"And high time you were gone from Newent," scowled Anthony, turning to his wife. "I thought you told me Markham would see he got into Westminster. He should be there now. Shee to it tomorrow. And straighten your cap, Madam. I'll not have any woman show me a cap on the shkew."

Dorothy could do no more than clasp and unclasp her hands, her foot swinging with nervousness under the table. Peter continued his carving. The clock ticked the seconds away. Anthony looked at his daughter.

"And how old ish Drushilla?"

"Drusilla is well past twelve, as you very well know."

"Twelve, eh? Well, ish she a woman yet?"

Drusilla gulped and could not speak. What did Papa mean? And why was he so hateful? Mama's voice was like ice, colder than ever she remembered it.

"She is still a child."

"Children should be at school, should they not? Girlsh are going to shool ash well ash boysh theshe daysh. Bear me out, Peter, bear me out. You always shink you know every damn shing!"

Peter nodded and continued carving. May handed round plates.

"Find her a shool tomorrow," and with that Anthony collapsed with head on table into a clatter of dishes and cutlery.

He remembered no more of that day for, as Peter and Young Hobbs between them got him upstairs, and before they had finished the struggle with jacket, breeches and boots and put him to bed, he was lost to the world.

That night he was haunted by dreams. Dreams that made up his mind for the morrow. There was no place, after all, like Virginie. A man could live as he pleased in Virginie. No need to bother there with stifling game laws and uppity neighbours. Nobody there complained of his roomy old coat that laid him under no other restraint but his own. A man could dress as he pleased, come to that. He could have pockets twice as big as sacks if he'd a mind to. And as to this blasted powdering and rouging of faces – pooh – he wanted none of it. And anybody who believed an Englishman still breathed sweet liberty was a fool. My God! We were taxed for the very soap that washes our hands, the tea, the coffee and anything else that slakes our thirst, the salt that savours our meat, the candles that light us to bed and even for this blasted powder to put on a nimcompoop's hair. In Virginie there were ways. Besides, in Virginie there was a young woman who had no fear of being got with child either. It was time to go back.

Within the week he was in London enjoying coffee house company and by midsummer he had forgotten Virginie when a lucky throw of the dice had won him the patronage for a commission with the East India Company.

On a particularly hot, sunny day he had boarded the East Indiaman Ponsonby and doffed his cap to Deptford, and at least two broken hearts besides, in a dazzle and blare of brass bands with bright pennants streaming. Six months later he would meet the steaming heat of Madras and in just over a year Dorothy and Drusilla would be opening packets of India silks and shawls. Poor Drusilla. The love of her life had gone and one day she would weep at the India silks cascading through her hands like sunlit waterfalls.

As for Dorothy, after her first few cries of 'oh Anthony, what have I done?', she had a practical matter to consider. Reluctantly, Peter had supplied the ingredients and Nellie had held on to her hands as the blood flowed. Though to Peter she admitted relief, the sense of loss was deep and she spent more time than Nellie thought to be good down by the little graves near the woods.

Making her way through the garden to the little white headstones, she hardly knew whether she was absolving sorrow or conscience. She had only done once, after all, what other women were doing time after time, for how else could they space their breedings? Everybody knew it. But she was a woman whose husband was away and that was another matter. How people would clack if they knew. Thank God Nellie was sound. They would look for reasons and cast aspersions. She hardly knew the reason herself. Only that she felt the whole world on her shoulders and such an agony of weariness. She could not go through 'all that' again. She had not the fortitude for it.

Bernard hugged his satisfaction secretly. Now he would have Drusilla to himself. She would be his slave again and he would not be fobbed off with May Hobbs.

But Drusilla was bereft. She missed her Papa keenly and sobbed into her pillow night after night. What was the matter and what went wrong, Papa? And yet, somewhere, she knew there was still a blessing to be taken if she could only find it; a blessing that would bring relief and quieten her sobs.

If only, if only she knew what it was.

Within a week of Papa quitting the house, she had become a woman and, though that was dramatic and frightening enough, in spite of Mama's unexpected tenderness, she was still asking inside herself why – oh – why . . . and if only . . .

CHAPTER 15

As Anthony had ridden away on that first day of June, bells all over the country were still pealing the victory of Ramillies.

In coffee houses or tap rooms, salons or servants' halls people were toasting the great soldier or groaning about taxation and the Marlborough Wars. 'We should go for another victory and bury the damned French once and for all.' And in between, an aggrieved voice would pipe, 'Mark my words, a single Scotchman is ready to give us more trouble than an army of French. '

In Beacon House such talk, along with the bells, only brought on one of Dorothy's bad heads. She had not touched a pack of cards since Anthony left. How could she, with all she had been given to do?

By the time summer was out Drusilla had waved a reluctant farewell to Bernard, for, in her misery, she had looked to him for comfort and found it. He had given his solace with a sense of superiority, for her open grief had shown his own secret the purer.

She had watched the early coach clatter down Beaumond Street and on to the Balderton Road. It had made a cheerful sound that did not match her mood. Westminster School might be a thousand miles away.

"Tish!" Dorothy had tossed her head. "The Newent gossips will be at it again, I dare say."

Well, the business was done, as Anthony had directed, and that was that. It had taken weeks of organisation, the ordering of clothes, boxes and books as well as the London coach alongside meetings with Peter, with Jenison and with Markham who had needed a few firm reminders of past promises and obligations. The whole thing had been exhausting and still there was Drusilla to settle. Worst of all had been her interview with Miss Frances Knight, Directrice of Newent's only Academy for Young Ladies of Rank, for that lady did not seem to appreciate the position of Mrs. Anthony Davison of Beacon House. Dorothy marvelled at such independence. She lost count of the number of times she had collapsed on to her daybed in the little parlour while Nellie hovered with vinegar cloths and sal-volatile phials or how many nights were broken as she turned from regret to justification.

The Hattons and Revilles, of course, had sent their daughters to uppity relations in London and on to schools in Putney and Hackney. Well, she could not do that for Drusilla. True, there was her sister, Peabody, at Bath who had married well, but some remnant of maternal instinct did not allow her to send Drusilla so far. Besides, the Peabodys did not have children of their own and might not understand Drusilla's moods.

She had carried out Anthony's instructions to the letter and could do no more. Sadly, as she kissed Drusilla goodbye, the endearments she so wanted to voice refused to come. Ah well, at least she was now free to pursue her card parties again and if she wagered cannily enough then perhaps the little entertainments could be made to pay for themselves.

When Drusilla and Nellie faced the front door of a certain large house in Appletongate, Nellie pursed up her lips as she jerked at the bell-pull.

"Surely young ladies of rank is not to be kept waiting then."

Drusilla tilted her head to stare at the painted board immediately above the eye level of this particular young lady of rank. "Miss Knight's Academy For The Education Of Young Ladies Of Rank To Improve The Opening Mind.

Satisfaction Given To So Important A Charge. Application To F. R. Knight Directrice."

Before she had read to the end of "application", Miss Knight herself had opened the door. Drusilla and her trunk were deposited together in the hallway. She felt Nellie's warm kiss on her cheek, the quick 'be good, my chick' almost drowned in the succeeding slam of front door and rattle of wheels as Hobbs bore Nellie away back up the hill to home.

Home! It might be a thousand miles away too.

She looked up at Miss Knight and marked a tall personage, dressed rather for comfort than fashion, that is to say without stays, yet of excellent carriage, shoulders pulled down, long neck erect and head held high, with the fine features and small hands and feet of a gentlewoman. Drusilla saw nothing beyond outward appearance; she was too conscious of self to do otherwise. More than anything else she wanted, needed in fact, to make a good impression, to find friends and, above all, to be loved, for the ice had returned to Mama's blue eyes since Papa had gone and, without Bernard, Beacon House had become the cold place of her early childhood.

As for Miss Knight, she approved this new pupil at least was tastefully and suitably attired and showed a pleasant manner into the bargain, but she made no judgement whatsoever beyond a feeling of satisfaction that the large blue-grey eyes that looked up to her own were not only singularly lovely but, more to the point, seemed lively and intelligent. So far she allowed only 'seemed' for she knew rather better than most how appearance is often deceptive and judgement always to be delayed for proof positive. Miss Knight was not only a business woman. She was that rare thing, a born teacher, and since a sufficient inheritance from a generous godmother had enabled her to open her school, she took the project seriously.

"Come. I will show you your room, Miss Davison."

That appellation alone took Drusilla by surprise. It was another rung on the ladder of growing up and she was not sure she liked it.

The wide passage opened into a large well housing the staircase and obviously used as a reception hall. A fire burned brightly, though it was summertime. Miss Knight was not mean with her coals, then. Some half dozen ladies, of rank presumably, twiddled with china tea bowls. They chattered incessantly, all seemingly well acquainted. Drusilla glimpsed a formidable figure managing the tea urn, another Nellie perhaps. She followed the back of the Directrice up a wide staircase; not as grand as that of Beacon House. Down a corridor they marched, through a door on the right into what she would discover the young ladies of rank called a cell. Well, it was certainly bare enough, having nothing but the necessities of a bed, wash stand with jug, bowl and pot, mule chest, table and chair, for writing presumably, all made of pine, and the only concession to comfort a cheerful rag rug between wash stand and bed.

Miss Knight inclined her head graciously and gestured an arm to make the room seen a palace.

"There is everything you need, apart from your clothes and the few personal things you know we allow. Anything else is forbidden other than that which might be used for opening the mind and gainfully exercising the hands;that is to say books, needlework and drawing materials. And, of course, you are allowed a looking glass, a small one." Not the beautiful cheval that was Papa's belated birthday present, then.

"Come down when you are ready."

Miss Knight swept out with rather more grandeur than any of Mama's fine friends, leaving Drusilla at a loss to know what 'ready' might mean beyond taking off one's cloak. In a room so bare, what could one possibly do to be ready? She opened the table drawer – empty; lifted the lid of the mule chest – empty; dipped her finger into the waterjug – empty;

peeped out of the window that looked on to a yard – empty. Slipping her cloak on the bed, expectant but apprehensive, she went down the great staircase to meet the other young ladies of rank. The next four years loomed like a lifetime.

Assembled in the hall, her new companions twittered like birds in an aviary. She saw the same shining neatly dressed hair. No powder, then. The same clear pock free faces. Like her, had they all been lucky or had their Mamas sent them to milk cows? The same upright carriage, the same tilt of the head in conversation, the same lively animation about the same seemingly earnest things. Miss Knight was not a tartar, then. The same deft little hands cupped round their dishes of tea, the same twisting and turning of neat little ankles. Did they ache to be tripping the ballroom floor?

How she envied that sameness for it spelled an affectionate companionship she did not yet share, nor felt she ever would.

Within a few days, however, she had met and weighed up, so she thought, all twenty two of them and learned that, even among so few a number, there were cliques and factions, sets that overlapped, sets that rarely met except by obligation, days that passed in tiffs and reconciliations, promises of eternal friendship broken soon after the making. In short, there was the usual mixture of kisses and quarrels of young ladies the world over, of rank or otherwise, and this was Drusilla's first experience of such a concentration of her own sex.

It had been another wonderful summer, like all the others in the first few years of Good Queen Anne. Harvests were gathered, barns were filled to the brim and yet the hot sun still lingered.

At Beacon House there might have been lazy days spent strolling the woods, pleasant enough, but lonely if May could not be spared; days riding with the grooms along old tracks to Barniby and Edgington, but grooms were dull as ditch company after that she had been used to; delightful fragrant days gathering rose petals, lavender heads and

135

bergamot sprays for the pot-pourri bowls, but only the maids for companionship as Mama was sure to be otherwise occupied. And evenings in the little parlour were no longer lively affairs without Papa and Uncle Peter who had joked he must see to his patients and their diseases, both real and hysterick. Here, on the other hand, at Miss Knight's Academy, only a stone's throw away from the market square, directly opposite the great parish church and with Bernard's old school and indeed his old home over the shop just a few yards away, one was never alone unless abed. Each hour of the day was to be used up and accounted for.

Lazy days were not in the curriculum, for idleness was a wickedness at the Academy and how Nellie feared all that orderliness for Miss Drusilla.

"Not that Miss Drusilla don't need it, mind. She do, but she'll never take to it, not in a thousand years. She done have been let too wild for it to be any use now."

But Nellie was wrong. Drusilla did take to this new orderliness. Like the garden plant properly pruned, tied in, watered and fed, she flourished and, under Miss Knight's tutelage, she blossomed. True, the Directrice still reserved judgement but after a few testing days that saw Drusilla romp through reading books, letter writing (how she blessed all those letters penned to Papa and Aunt Peabody) and simple arithmeticks, she was put into the class of the youngest elite.

This was a set who, in addition to the usual instructions in deportment, needlework, music and dancing, learned the globe and geographicks from Miss Knight herself and the scriptures and a little Latin from Schoolmaster Twells, who visited weekly from the Free School next door. As the Directrice joked privately, once a week he stuffed a little knowledge into the cream of her fine porcelain, that in turn afforded him to stuff a little cream into his own common delft.

In this superior class, Drusilla got to know her fellow pupils rather better.

Miss Elizabeth Bradford she had already met as the niece of that man-devil Sir Matthew Jenison and somehow, she knew, the girl claimed a kinship with the Hattons and Bernard too. Mama, of course, would sniff about toms and queens in backyards but Drusilla was glad of any common ground. She accepted with alacrity Elizabeth's invitation to call her Bessie. Such intimacy meant she could turn the conversation to include Bernard without embarrassment. Bessie was a softly spoken, smooth, plump girl with a clear, pale skin, dark, deep-set eyes and an even deeper intelligence. She seldom opened her mouth in class without her comments making their mark.

Miss Hester Pilbeam had a childish figure for her age and her movements, like her wits, were quick and lively. Her nut brown hair fitted her head snugly in close curls; she had the brightest of brown eyes and her olive complexion went quickly through all shades of dark red to pale green and back again. She had a nose rather larger than ordinary and the object of much teasing. With her, Drusilla found a common empathy, for Hester too had a father in foreign parts. She and Drusilla developed a friendly rivalry in tale-capping. Drusilla kept scrupulously to the letter, as far as she knew, of Papa's tall stories but Hester engaged in shameless leg-pulling, usually giving herself away in suppressed giggles. For all that, she could add up a column of figures as quick as Miss Knight herself, as quick as Mama in fact, and that was enough to ensure her a place in the highest class.

Caroline Monroe had won her place there with an ability to draw and a smattering of French, picked up, no doubt, from her young brother's tutor at home. She was a lively mimic who could turn on a voice at the drop of a hat, from the gravelly growl of Jenkins, the old retainer, who never was seen unless shifting boxes and trunks, delivering coal, hauling up water or bringing down slops, to the cultured tones of the Directrice herself.

Drusilla prepared to enjoy turning this privileged trio into a quartet.

As for Miss Knight, she breathed a vital animation into everything she touched and even the dullest pupils were affected by it; but to the intelligent and receptive she communicated a zest that enhanced the flavour and colour of their whole lives. She opened their aviary door wide to the sky as she repeated the phrase Uncle Peter so often had quoted. 'Into the bonfire with superstition and dogma and . . . ' "Let us go forward into Newton's light," snapped back Drusilla and the eyes of the Directrice glowed at her favourite pupil.

Under her encouragement Drusilla found herself back in that wonderful world of speculation, imagination and romance that she had first encountered in the little parlour, with Papa and Uncle Peter. But here at the Academy the subjects ranged wider and in all directions. Under Miss Knight's bright eye they went back in time to the older civilisations and here it was that Drusilla and her teacher found a sympathetic bond, as the eager pupil lapped up those tales of wonderful heroes and heroines – especially the heroines. Boadiceia who killed herself and her daughters rather than submit to slavery, Joan of Arc who burned at the stake rather than recant her beliefs, Margaret More who walked with her father discussing the truths of life before his cruel execution. These and many more were paraded before them.

And what had they all died for, these brave men and women? Why, Truth and Humanity, of course. Ah! Humanity! What of Humanity, then? Is there nothing but pain for Humanity? And all her old expectant feelings had rushed back to Drusilla as, stumbling at first, she had poured out to Miss Knight her feelings of pain for Mama's brickies and woodmen and plaster pit men guzzling the leftovers of Oak Apple Day.

Too much heart for your own good, Miss Davison, decided Miss Knight, but give me rather less than two years and I might remedy that.

From historick fact they turned to the philosophers and here it was Miss Knight's turn to shine as the brightest of stars, with her brilliant eyes darting from one pupil to another, her quick smile flashing encouragement, her graceful hands emphasising now this point, now that. And Drusilla's pulses raced at the mysteries of light, dynamics, gravity, electricity, as the names of Galileo, Leonardo, Boyle, Lilley and Newton whirled in her brain.

She could not understand but she could feel; how she could feel; and it was during these sessions her old sensations of expectancy thrust more strongly than ever. Somewhere, she knew, if only she could find it, was a blessing that would shake her to the very core, bringing with it joy and peace and contentment.

Just before their fifteenth birthdays, Drusilla's class became the Senior Elite and here they found days at the Academy were not always so high flown. The ordinary trivia of living was not neglected. The young ladies, especially because they were young ladies of rank, must learn the business of behaving in polite society, of rubbing along in harmony with their fellows, and then there was the importance of husbands and how to catch them to be learned. After all, that is what most of them were here for and why their fathers were paying, and grumbling at paying, such monstrously high fees.

This particular business was learned at Miss Knight's At Homes, which were an education in themselves.

Every Wednesday at two o'clock of the afternoon Miss Knight was At Home. On this day certain friends and carefully chosen young gentlemen were invited to take tea with Miss Knight and a favoured pupil or two. Later, when guests had departed and the tea board cleared, then the young ladies' behaviour was commented upon, always in public for that way they were not likely to repeat a mistake.

"Never say simply yes or no, Miss Bradford. Your reply must always lead on to the gentlemen inquiring further. You must keep the conversation going but never appear to lead. You do lead, of course, but that must never be apparent to the gentleman. They must always think of themselves as in command, whether they are or no. You must think of it as a game with rules. And remember, there are no points for full stops and silences."

Bessie, who had already discovered what really made the highest score, merely inclined her sleek head. Her deep-set brown eyes darkening to black, she intended to carry on her own game. She had more billet-doux slipped into her hand than any other young lady in the Academy, for she had developed the art of her lips saying one thing and her eyes another. So far, Miss Knight had failed to notice the eyes and, having delivered her admonishment, she turned to the others.

"You are too forward, Miss Pilbeam. Look a gentleman in the eye only for so long, then cast the eye down. It is prettier and more attractive to a gentleman than the direct gaze. Mould your voice on the flute. That is what a gentleman likes. You can smile as much as you please but never laugh. Better not to show too much teeth and gums and never, never the tongue."

And Hester, used to a lively life with six brothers at home and having no opinion whatever of the opposite sex, knowing too well the clear superiority of her own, would stuff a handkerchief into her mouth to stifle the gurgles. "Silly old goose!" Still, she was not so forward the following Wednesday.

"You have a very pretty manner, Miss Monroe."

And Caroline Monroe, smirking and preening, convinced herself, if not the others, that that dashing young lieutenant had fallen head over heels and was speaking with his own fearsome papa on that very subject at this very moment, before going off to the War.

Miss Knight would press her delicate hands together. "All young ladies should remember this: it is not seemly for young ladies, especially young ladies of rank, to make a show of enthusiasm for the gentlemen. You tread the middle path between avidity and indifference."

Strangely enough, Drusilla never received such strictures, or encouragements either. She was given full reign to exercise her views, to take the gentlemen on equal terms and, again, Miss Knight's eyes glowed at the performance of her favourite pupil. Drusilla mixed freely with the young clergymen, squires and military gentlemen every Wednesday afternoon. She alone among the young ladies scorned to play the coquette. Not for her the downcast eye, the soft answer, the blushing cheek, as she met each young man with a refreshing frankness.

With the clergy she was interested in their work, showed a lively point of view and was genuinely surprised to find they were rather more concerned with titles and glebe land, with crops and sheep than the human flock they were supposed to be shepherding.

With the young squires, she remembered something of Papa's ambitions and wondered was it the world of horses and hunting, shooting and beans and barley fields he had meant by strawberry beds? Well, she hoped Papa would not be disappointed but that would not do for her. They knew nothing at all, these heirs of landowners, beyond "rack renting" and "four shillings in the pound", unless it be the gaming tables. She did not complain of these interests, they were what she expected a man to do, but rather that they did little else. They had never even heard of Mr. Pope or Mr. Addison or Mr. Steele. Good Heavens, even when they enlisted with the militia it was more for a night out with the other young fellows and a chance to pot at a poacher or two than with any real thought it might one day be Scotchmen or Frenchies for targets.

And as for the military gentlemen, my Goodness me, she had never met such people so stiff as boards, so hard as iron, so wooden-headed, so clipped of speech. Among themselves they might be heard to comment the Tories were feeling a draught and the Whigs their muscles, that Marlborough was right and ministers wrong. We should press for another victory and, by God, if they had anything to do with it there would soon be one. A country that brooked at the cost of its army was not worth the fighting for, and as for all this fuss over a half-pint sized French Marshal in Nottingham, they could hardly believe it. We should be preparing ourselves on the home front where the Scotch were ready to eat us alive in spite of this new-fangled Union that boded no good.

So they rattled on like kettle drums before a great battle but let a young lady appear on the edge of their company and they closed ranks with a muffling of drums and a change to slow march. Did they think young ladies were not interested in such things? Well, she remembered that time at Beacon House when snatches of such talk had flown in one ear and out the other – but that was before Miss Knight had taken her in hand. Now, everything, just everything, was so vital when there was so much to learn in so little time. In fact tales of tartaned highlanders, with their plaids and claymores, dirks and trews, violating virgins and eating up babies for supper, were no worse than Papa's tales of the Deerfield Raid, and she had heard that one a hundred times, nightmares or no. In any case, no sooner did one meet these young officers than they were shipped off to fight.

She sighed as she remembered how Papa had chased her bad dreams away the night before Oak Apple Day, and how she had envied all those young girls leaning over banister rails, fluttering pretty fans along with their eyelashes, to lead on young men. Well, the day had come at last when she could do the same and she knew with some relief and some sadness that whatever it was she longed for, it was not that. In any case, all that was being saved for another.

In consequence, she attended each At Home with no hope of meeting the love of her life, no thought of either sweethearts or husbands and no inhibitions either.

CHAPTER 16

The four years that at first had seemed a life sentence were racing away. They were already into February Fill-Dyke of the third year, that month living up to its old-fashioned name.

On a certain particularly wet Wednesday the young ladies looked out into the dismal street as far as the rain-spattered landing window allowed.

"Will it ever stop?" asked Hester Pilbeam, fearing the expected visitors might prove nothing but fair weather friends.

Drat the rain! It ran wretchedly from roof and water spout, from tree and bush. It dripped damnably from men's cloaks and hats, from their noses and their horses' manes, running in streams down into their boots. It curtained off the church-yard opposite. It hissed and sizzled down the chimney as it hit the great fire in the hall below and, more to the point, it dampened the young ladies curls along with their spirits.

"Do you think anybody will come at all today?" asked Caroline Monroe, interested in nobody but her fifth handsome young lieutenant.

A pool crept under the front door. The air outside and in was dark as night and the Directrice ordered that candles be lighted.

"Heavens. Look. Somebody has come already," cried Bessie Bradford as a carriage slithered into the flood water of Appletongate and rested outside the Academy.

Drusilla's mouth made a round oh as she recognised her own family coach and oh again as she watched a dripping figure that could only be Hobbs slip down from his perch, throw the reins over the hitching post and presumably he it was who made the doorbell clang-clang through the house. Forgetting all lessons of comport and decorum, Drusilla flew along the passage and down the great staircase.

"Your Mama was passing, Miss Davison, and sent you this."

Could anybody in this world be as quick as Miss Knight? Message and packet had been delivered and carriage started away before Drusilla had reached the last step, with the bell still resounding. She flew back up the stairs with her package and straight to her cell, having seen too many such parcels not to know what it was.

Dear, wonderful, marvellous Papa. The India silks fell to the floor in a rainbow torrent. The letter she could scarcely read through her tears, a letter of love with still never a mention of that long ago unhappy day of the cock fighting, a letter full of Sweet Pusses and Darlings. Dearest Papa. She laughed through her tears.

She smiled too, she could not help it, at the thought of Mama turning out in this terrible weather. There must be a very special card party somewhere. She wondered where. Mama would not risk getting the coach stuck for me and my packet, she thought, but a game of cards and the chance to place her bets was quite another matter.

The usual Wednesday bell clanging, notwithstanding the downpour, forced her to gather up silks and missive together. A brief peep in the glass, a pat to the hair, a drying of eyes and it was a particularly bright and lively young lady of rank who tripped down the stairs to the gathering below.

"Miss Davison, my dear," the Directrice took her arm. "I would like you to meet my younger brother, Mr. William Knight."

Drusilla found her hand taken by a quick-eyed, well-dressed young man, rather slightly made, not short but most decidedly not tall, though remarkably vigorous and alert looking, his light brown hair tied into a tail resting neatly in

144

the nape of his neck. Somebody else besides Papa who does not like powder, she thought. Apart from his size, for he was a good head shorter than the Directrice, there was no doubt of him being a relation of Miss Knight. The family likeness was all too plain not to miss. He appeared to be a few years older than most of the young men present; about twenty five years guessed Drusilla. Goodness – a real man instead of a boy – no wonder the room fairly popped with excitement.

Certainly, there were a few petulant young ladies who wondered why Miss Drusilla Davison had been given the honour. After the usual pleasantries, Mr Knight fell easily into explaining his position. He was a younger son, his inheritance would be small with no fairy godmother tucked away that he knew of, but he had recently gained a degree in Divinity and now awaited ordination to a living he hoped would be in the country not far from Newent St. Leonards, for he loved his birthplace and could never be happy far away from it.

"So you see, Miss Davison, 1 am a stick in the mud, though some might call me an evangelicist. At least what I want in my church, when I get it, is simplicity."

His brown eyes smiled directly into her own and, before she knew where she was, Drusilla was discussing casily and naturally her own ideas of dissent, for she had never forgotten Papa's Mayfair when Black Jack had denounced the Prayer Book and held up the Bible.

Oh no, Mr. Knight would not go as far as that but he hoped he would be working among simple village folk and he wanted them to understand their services and relate their beliefs to their ordinary workaday lives.

"Do you think them capable of it?" flashed Miss Knight.

"Oh yes indeed," said Drusilla quickly, remembering how easily May Hobbs had taken her reading lessons; how wise, how tiresomely wise, old Nellie could be and how often Uncle Peter had said knowledge should be shared by all, as long as it was not medical knowledge, she admitted wryly.

And she gave to this young man, as artlessly as she had given to Miss Knight, her feelings for people, the bent shoulders of Mama's brickies, the coughings and spittings of sawyers and plaster pit men.

"Miss Davison," laughed the Directrice, "you are exactly like Mr. William. You would see pews full of thatchers and ploughmen, shepherds and blacksmiths and miss all the poachers and sheep stealers and cut-purses down on their knees with the best."

"Don't forget the throats as well as the purses," whispered her brother.

Drusilla laughed and in no time at all was recalling Papa and his delight in everybody around him, from Molly the gingerbread woman to milkmaids and flower girls. Miss Knight and her brother exchanged amused glances at that observation.

"Well, I shall do my damndest, begging your pardon, Miss Davison, to develop the faculties and reasoning of my simple parishioners – when I get 'em, of course – and the other things like morality and love of righteousness I shall take for granted."

"I don't think you should take those things for granted, William dear," laughed his sister. "You will have to take account of human nature, you know."

"Well, sister, I stand full square on the power of Reason while Mysticism and Miracles can go to the . . ."

"Sh! William!" Miss Knight closed her brother's lips with her fan, almost stooping to do so, "I think you had better say Trent to be on the safe side."

Drusilla breathed again. The conversation was becoming uncomfortable but 'go to Trent' was a phrase she was used to. It was Papa's own expression and before she knew it she was extolling Papa again.

Thus days at the Academy continued to pass by most pleasantly.

Mr. William Knight called into his sister's At Homes

rather more frequently than the young ladies of rank could have hoped. His lack of fortune was to be regretted rather more than his lack of height, though the tallest girls thought the one almost as bad as the other. Still, the breeding was there, they consoled themselves, though it was wondered all over the County wherever Miss Knight and her brother could have hatched their radical views, and no doubt at all that that lady turned out the most accomplished young ladies of rank. And radical views, after all, were very quickly snuffed out in the rounds of visits and balls once the young ladies were back home.

The Knights were an old family who had once owned considerable land between Newent and Maunsfielde over many generations but, rather like Drusilla's own ancestors, had been content to do nothing but live off their rents. Such lack of enterprise had been their undoing. Their estates split up among men who had made fortunes out of coal mining, sand quarrying, malting or brewing, the Knights were left with a great house and only a few acres of light land. But there were, after all, some profitable livings to be had in the diocese. Take Newent for instance. Ah. But Mr. Knight wanted a country parish where he could farm his own glebe land and feel close to his flock. Oh dear. Most of the well-laundered young ladies of rank thought he would not be the easiest of husbands and, in any case, found his lack of height the most tiresome disadvantage after all.

Drusilla thought of her Bernard who, she convinced herself, cut a handsomer figure with his winning countenance, silver-toned voice, and such a head for figures that more than made up for his lack of fortune. At any rate, he was the only man she knew that might, one day, measure up to Papa, so she was inclined to agree with her friends. Mr. William Knight was no catch at all.

Spring was warming into summer. The Academy year was almost up and already the small group was showing signs of strain as the young ladies, in spite of promises to the

147

contrary, realised that most would go their separate ways and probably rarely or never meet again.

Early one Sunday morning before St. Leonard's church bells had started their cacophony. the Academy door bell clanked through the house with an urgency that sent partly dressed young ladies in shifts and curl-papers rushing out of their cells to press noses against the landing window or, Drusilla among them, to hang over the banister rail to the hall down below. She watched the growling slow coach of a Jenkins withdraw bolt, bars and chains. Her eyes popped as round as cabuchon gems as a familiar figure was let in through the front door, none other than Draper Webster, Bernard's father.

Something must be wrong and whatever could it be? Nothing to do with Bernard, surely to Goodness.

Now Miss Knight herself, Junoesque in dressing gown and new high starched cap, appeared. There was an infuriating whispering, a retreat and a silence that went on forever. Then Miss Knight ascended the staircase alone, as the young ladies of rank scuttled back to their cells, putting eyes down to keyholes or to cracks in their doors. They all heard a firm knock at somebody's door. Whose? Oh – Bessie's. Silence again; a long, long silence. Then Bessie's door opening wide; the others a crack. Miss Knight, with a weeping Bessie beside her, descended the stairs. Draper Webster awaited and Bessie, a damp yellow handkerchief up to her face, held out a hand for his arm and was gone.

She left a dumbfounded huddle of young ladies on the landing above.

Hester Pilbeam crooked her forefinger to gather them round. With great presence of mind and a trick learned from all those brothers at home, she had been the only one to abandon keyhole or crack in laying an ear to her wall adjacent to Bessie's. Amid oohs, ohs and ahs she repeated her tale.

It was like a nightmare, she told them. Bessie's mother

and father, both of them, just think, had died of a fever. And she was to stay with the Websters who had turned their old draper's shop to a lodging house. With the Websters? Well, I declare! And why not Sir Matthew Jenison? He is her uncle, is he not? Oh, have you not heard? He has troubles enough of his own. Oh dear. Poor Bessie. Upon my honour. It was too much to bear. In a lodging house. We should call it a guest house – that sounds so much the better. Let me finish. You haven't heard all. The family home to be sold and it will give her a portion of twelve hundred pounds. Well, it might be a portion, but is it a fortune? What do you think? Well, somebody's brother had once said he couldn't manage a gentleman's life on less than five thousand a year. Poor Bessie. Now you know that place, Drusilla, what can it be like?

Drusilla's heart pounded so she could scarcely speak. She remembered only a particular visit to that shop so long ago when Mama had taken her to buy bonnet ribbons. A torrent of bright silks flashed before her, richer even in that dark hole of a shop than Papa's India silks. Shining motes hung like miniscule stars in the air. She heard a weeping woman, a tearful small child peeping half round a door, the hectoring voices of coarse men. She saw the steady gaze of a boy at the back of that shop she had not visited once since that extraordinary day.

It was where her Bernard had come from, but that was something else she had chosen to secrete away in her mind's darkest corner.

Since then, she had heard of that shop and its changes only through Nellie's tittle tattle and she certainly had not liked what she heard. Poor Bessie. What could she do? She would take the beautiful dove-grey India silk from Papa and a bottle of lavender water round to the market place for Bessie. Mama could not possibly object to that.

And if that old reprobate, Sir Matthew Jenison, was in trouble, then it was no more than he deserved and no more sugarplums either and, best of all, no more of his powdery dry face and wet lips.

Miss Knight's lustrous eyes sweeping from one young lady to another, her warm smile, her vibrant voice and graceful hands were in vain. The fire had gone out of the last few weeks of this year's Academy and the final At Home was a subdued affair.

The ladies of rank had returned to their cells. Miss Knight was taking leave of her brother in the hall below.

"Well, William, what do you think?"

"A most admirable young lady of rank, dear sister."

"You would not say there is still too much heart?"

"Oh, undoubtedly I do. I do. But a young lady without too much heart now would not be an attractive proposition in two or three years' time, I think. Do you want a verdict?"

"Indeed, William, yes."

"The best yet, my dear Fanny. She is malleable. She could be transplanted, cultivated, trained, in short, all I could wish for the purpose. She has already had access to informed opinion. Dr. Fletcher has obviously had some influence, and her incorrigible Papa – we must guard against him – but you, my dear Fanny, so very much more. I thank you for it."

He turned to gaze up the stairs and smiled an indulgent smile. Was she, at this moment, taking up a little needle-work? Was her pretty head bent over Mr. Addison or Mr. Steele? Were her dainty feet practising a minuet? For, though he stood four square on the power of Reason, he understood young ladies of rank must be allowed their frivolities.

He thought he caught the sound of feminine laughter as he opened the front door to the street and his indulgence deepened.

In fact most of the young ladies of rank, all clutching their pillows, were making their way to Caroline Monroe's cell. They crammed themselves into her tiny space, looking to this comedienne naturelle to lighten the end of their last At Home. Soon enough somebody's pillow knocked poor

Caroline down to the floor, her cap up in the air. One pillow followed another till feathers flew in all directions as a desperate Amazonian fight got underway.

One of the elite, a certain Miss Drusilla Davison, took no part in the battle for she was not there.

That particular young lady of rank was seated at her own little writing table her usual position after four o'clock on a Wednesday afternoon. She was penning yet another letter to Mr. Bernard Webster and if he ever read these epistles then he was better acquainted than Mr. William Knight with the regime of the Academy. She was engaged in a labour of love and she was perfectly aware that Bernard could not reciprocate these outpourings of the heart since Westminster School was a very different establishment from Miss Knight's Academy. It was for boys for one thing. It turned out young men, and important young men at that. Bernard was a busy fellow, Captain of Garnes, Head of the School, Protector of Thomas Pelham who might one day be heir to the great Duke of Newcastle and whom he had taken under his wing. My Goodness, what high society, I do declare. Higher even than the Revilles or the Hattons and certainly two or three cuts above the squires, the military and the clergy she met every Wednesday afternoon at Miss Knight's At Homes.

She folded the letter and fixed her seal. It would be the last to that address since, within a few weeks, Bernard would be up at Trinity College, Cambridge. Mr. William Knight and his longed for parishioners could be a thousand miles away but Bernard Webster and his school fellows were locked in her heart.

They had been eventful years, those spent at the Academy. So many battles fought and won. So many favours streaming from hats and bosoms, posts and windows. So many full peals of bells with, no doubt, the usual complaints of bad heads from Beacon House. So many rousing cheers for Marlborough, though not loud enough to drown the jeers against him. And hardly a single officer, handsome or otherwise, left in Newent. Only the youngest of greenstick cornets so that Caroline Monroe agreed wholeheartedly Marlborough the Hero deserved his new title of Marlborough the Butcher.

Drusilla's mind was on other things. She was remembering her Mama's disparaging remarks about Bessie Bradford's parentage. Now that Bessie was lodging in the Webster household, Drusilla was rather more than keen to keep that acquaintance warm. After all, there would be no need in that establishment to look round corners to avoid Sir Matthew Jenison. He, the old horror, was nicely rotting away in his great mansion, The Friary, if rumour be right.

Mama must be got round somehow.

CHAPTER 17

A lively congestion of carriages, servants and baggage, not to mention young ladies of rank, blocked the Appletongate road opposite the churchyard. Its rowdy chorus of iron on cobble, jangling brass and grunts of box-heaving coachmen, all but drowning the lighter tones of the young ladies, told every frustrated passer by this was the end of the school year for Miss Knight's Academy. It was the privilege of her elite sixteen year olds to be the first to leave and, between fluttering handkerchieves and blown kisses, the young ladies made the usual protestations of love and friendship, almost certain to be forgot in the rounds of routs and balls and eligible young men most of them were hoping to meet, once they were miles away and safely home.

That august personage, Miss Knight herself, no less, singled out her favourite pupil. She stood in her elegant doorway and clasped Drusilla's hands, warm in her own.

"Promise me, Miss Davison, you will not neglect your reading. And please tell your dear Mama that we are still At Home every Wednesday afternoon and the both of you most welcome."

Drusilla bobbed and smiled, accepted the hand of old Hobbs into the Davison carriage and, with more waves and blown kisses, her school days were over at last.

She was not in the least surprised at her dear Mama's disdain for Miss Knight's pressing invitation and very much surprised at her concurrence that Bessie Bradford should be invited to spend the day at Beacon House.

How Drusilla looked forward to that day and what plans

she made for Bessie's comfort and delight. They would feed the ponies and ride them, too, if that would please Bessie. They would walk in the gardens, chase each other through the shrubbery as she and Bernard had used to do; then seek out Mama's new garden house in the copse and, more than that, oh, very much more than that, they would talk of Bernard.

Drusilla was ready to welcome Bessie Bradford with all her heart.

The disappointment of Bessie's tight-shut response stung like a slap in the face. That young lady simply could not remember how often letters from Cambridge had been delivered to the Websters and, really, she had no notion at all of Bernard's progress, intentions or ambitions. She was as close as a clam and Drusilla's winning ways of no consequence.

When they left the garden for the dining room, where Mistress Alice had prepared the kind of delicacies a young lady, especially a young lady of rank but not much fortune, might relish, she hardly opened her mouth other than to put food into it. Everybody guessed that Sir Matthew Jenison, her rogue of an uncle, was in some sort of money trouble but, no matter how Dorothy prodded or Drusilla hinted, nothing could be got out of her on that score either.

Dorothy soon lost interest and Drusilla found that any future suggestions that the carriage be sent for 'poor Bessie' fell on ears deaf as posts.

"There is something out of the ordinary about that girl I don't like," said Dorothy, "and that is that." Drusilla could only bide her time.

The years of her girlhood passed like those of her child-hood, tumbling over each other in the pleated layers of time, so that years later it was hard to remember the sequence. She pulled at one fold and two or three fell apart. One day there would be children, fascinated by the warmest of smiles and kindest of eyes, the expressive hands and beautifully clear

154

voice, hanging upon every word of her recollections.

She would remember how she had danced at the wedding of her oldest school friend, Caroline Monroe, with Colonel John Hardcastle of the Grenadiers and how her heart had danced in tune with the jigs, 'this will not do for me, for me, this will not do for me'. Poor little Caroline, still only sixteen, she had married a man of forty five to please her Papa and, in fear, if she waited one minute longer for her seventeenth birthday, both face and figure were bound to go off. Within a week of their marriage her husband was called to the field and Caroline left behind, a new matron, three years off twenty, with her husband's elderly sisters to see her through her subsequent breeding.

Girls of seventeen, sixteen and even fifteen could not rustle themselves into their wedding gowns fast enough.

Drusilla thanked the good Lord above she was not pressed to do the same. Mama was too otherwise occupied and Papa too far away to act as marriage broker, in spite of the broadest of hints from Uncle Peter and old Nellie. As for Bernard, she thanked the good Lord again, he was secure in nothing but masculine company at Cambridge, so she thought, and bound to be safe from wedding bells.

Tilting her head, wrinkling her brow to the tiniest crease and laying a forefinger against the smoothest of cheeks, she would one day remember how all those wonderful summers of drying soft coloured petals for Mama's pot-pourri bowls, the packing of baskets for meals out of doors, the gathering of fruits for Alice to boil up into preserves or distil into wines had deteriorated towards the end of the good Queen's reign into a run of cold, wet harvests and bitterly cold winters.

How the farmers had grumbled as they always did.

"Tish!" snorted Dorothy, counting her blessings. "It's an ill wind. Poor harvest or no, that plague in the Baltic has sent the price of our corn sky-high. They should be rubbing their hands, not wringing 'em."

She was remembering her own good luck out of the

Buckford fire when she had sold every pantile hot from the kiln. She did her own grumbling, however, that even the yeomen farmers' wives could afford the new craze for blue and white china coming in by the ship load as ballast for tea. Everybody's old-fashioned earthenware was being relegated to kitchen or scullery and even pewter hardly used except in taverns and servants' halls.

"You should be as pleased as Punch, my dear Dorothy," counselled her brother. "Whatever Anthony sends home sells as soon as unloaded and all but the poorest can now pay the price of their medicine and the same goes for their plaster, their wood and their bricks. It's no use berating the farmer, my dear, if we're tarred with the same brush ourselves."

Dr. Peter had come home from one of his London trips to regale them with a tale of four great Mohawk Chiefs paraded down the Strand to St. Paul's and how he had paid out a crown for a seat in a window on Ludgate Hill. That tale did nothing but bring the tears to their eyes for it brought back memories of Anthony and his spirited telling of the Deerfield Raid. How far away those warm loving evenings in the little parlour now seemed, when Dorothy had quietly plied her needle and thread and Drusilla, all ears, had revelled in that masculine smell of leather and horses and tobacco with the faintest whiff of verbena from fresh laundered linen. Lavender for the bed linen, Nellie ordered her maids, verbena for small clothes and bergamot for the rest.

And how horrifying were the tales coming out of India, though not as fast and frequent as out of Virginia. They were terrible tales of exploitation, pestilence and death that made them want to stuff up their ears. How they wished Anthony were safe at home.

"Come, come, my dears," chided the doctor, refilling their glasses, "Take no account of 'em. Have I not always said our Anthony has the luck of the devil? He'll be home, you mark my words, as fit as a flea and as rich as a nabob. We shall get our family estate yet, never fear, bigger and better than ever our great grandfathers had in Somerset. We'll not only live like Lords in a year or two, we'll be Lords ourselves." He drained his glass with a satisfied smack. "You'll be a Lady, Dorothy, and we'll make our Drusilla a Duchess, or at least her husband will. They're now floating this new South Sea Company and as fast as Anthony makes it we'll quadruple it. Then a little greasing of the right palm at the right time and you'll see!"

"Tish!" snorted Dorothy again, her sound common sense not deserting her.

A little cold fear nagged at her heart. She had been spending money like water again, carried away in an orgy of alterations to house and garden. It was worse than the gambling. She could not stop. As fast as one room was turned over she sent the decorators into another. As fast as one plot was improved she pushed landscapers and gardeners to do even more.

Drusilla knew nothing of Dorothy's fears. She took everything for granted. All Peter did was to chafe there was neither room to eat nor sleep at Beacon House for the banging of labour. He wondered how the household stood up to it and did they marvel he went up to London at every verse end to get away from it all? It was quieter in Northgate even with all the traffic rolling straight past his front door.

"My dear brother," said Dorothy, handing over her glass for more. "I wonder you know anything at all about Northgate. You are up here as much as you are there. And very welcome you are too, my dear brother, in spite of your crack-brained ideas, though I wonder your patients don't think you've deserted 'em."

"You can say that with truth the first time I miss a Wednesday at the White Harte and not until."

She had caught him on a raw nerve and knew she had overstepped the mark. She busied herself with her latest correspondence for there were invitations to Miss Knight's

At Home, among others, rarely accepted since there was rarely the time to go. Once or twice William Knight had called at the house, only for a few moments in passing, on his way to visit an elderly cousin in Edgington.

"I do believe that young man is keeping an eye on you, Drusilla," chaffed the doctor.

"Then he'd best cast his eye elsewhere for I am not interested in him."

"Well done, Drusilla. You keep him on hot toast at the end of a long fork, my dear. Every man knows the value of a rare chick."

"And before he can keep one," said Dorothy, her ribbonny cap all of a quiver and her petticoats on the flounce, "he needs a cage to put it in."

"Don't be a slow-coach my dear Dorothy. Who on earth goes on tiresome visits to elderly cousins if there is nothing to be got out of 'em? I daresay James Knight Esquire of Edgington has the wherewithal under his mattress to provide a better cage than you or Drusilla ever dreamed of."

"You were talking of duchesses only a few weeks past. And what do you know of such things anyway, you old bachelor?" And to close his chatter Dorothy buried her head in the latest copy of the Female Tatler, passing the new Weekly Courant to Drusilla. Both let such talk, along with much else, drift in one ear and out of the other.

If the Queen mourned the death of her dear Prince George from an asthma and dropsy then, apart from that confounded passing bell, they hardly noticed it. If the local gentry petitioned their sorrowing monarch against damage to crops from the Queen's own deer, they cared not a jot.

"And much good it will do them," laughed the doctor. "These grumblers' tenants suffer the very devil from our pernicious game-laws and yet have to pay rack-rent at that. These complainers pay not a penn'orth of rent themselves and are only getting a dose of their own physick. I hope it chokes 'em. Let the good Queen keep her deer and good luck to her."

"And will you say the same when we get our acres?"

Beyond that, Dorothy could not be bothered to pursue the argument. Why was it Peter had to get so involved with every buzz he picked up?

That first September of Drusilla's homecoming was as cold and wet as a February Filldyke. When Dr. Peter tried to lighten the air neither she nor Dorothy chose to listen to his umpteenth telling of 'that most shocking slaughter when the brave Duke of Argyle escaped with a brace of musket balls lodged in his periwig'. Dorothy was too busy adding up pounds, shillings and pence and Drusilla was too busy penning letters to Mr. Bernard Webster at Trinity College, Cambridge.

Whatever life and feeling Miss Knight had aroused in her breast was reserved for him. Uncle Peter's tales were never anything else but the thinnest of gruels beside Papa's tale of the Deerfield Raid, until he came home with the account of his visit to the Bridewell House of Correction.

It was close to Michaelmas, the days growing shorter and colder. He had spent the morning at a coffee house near Westminster picking up buzzes of this and that. He had dined rather well in the gayest of company. A new acquaintance and he fell into the singing of songs and reciting of verses. They tried a hand of cards but could not finish it, they discussed going to the theatre but made no effort to shift till the friend said he knew where there was the drollest sport in town and was the doctor game? Oh yes, indeed. The doctor was game enough for anything though he doubted the cock pits here were to be compared with his own at home. His friend sniggered. Oh! The cocks here were very fine cocks indeed.

They had taken a chair to Tottlefields and were set down outside a great court ahead of a crowd of other would-be revellers. They made as free and easy an entrance as though to a peep show. On the right of the yard was a long low building where, at first glance, a great number of villainous-looking men were seated on rough planks, so many in front of huge blocks of wood like butchers' boards. Each held a heavy wooden mallet for beating out flax on the block.

Peter's heart sank that he had been such a fool to be so foxed. There was no retreat for the press of that revolting audience behind. He and his friend had a clear view at the front so they got the full blast of the stench as well as the din.

"That should cure 'em," gloated his companion, "if they were not beating that flax they'd most like be beating our heads and filching our purses."

But Peter took a closer look with his physician's eye. It was their rags and chains and nothing but common hunger gave that villainous look to the longstanding inhabitants of that dreadful place. Newcomers still wore their good clothes, though dirty, for there were no means of washing, and still had some flesh on their bones. It made his own flesh creep to see how these wretches cringed under the whip of their cruel overseer. He did not agree with his friend and, on enquiry, though he could scarce open his mouth for the stink, discovered some so-called villains were there for the most trivial offences, albeit repeated. Somebody in the crowd guffawed. Peter's friend gave him a nudge.

"I said you would see some fine cocks."

He pointed to the rags of one poor fellow dropping about him and Peter wondered if those rags were due to the wear and tear of a whip. He felt sick but could do nothing more than go with the crowd.

Bedlam could not be worse.

On the other side of the court was a shed full of women, some of the genteeler sort, who were beating out hemp. Here the overseer was a woman, but no less a tyrant than her brother in charge of the flax beaters. Her prisoners' arms were bright red from the raps of her cane.

Peter shut his ears to the crowd's coarse remarks on the faces and figures of the women. His physician's eye was more concerned with their festering wounds. He made

160

allowances for those who hurled lewd remarks at their tormentors and wished with all his heart he had not come.

He wished it all the more when, at one side of the shed, they found a number of children engaged in pin making. His heart was so smitten that he procured the release of the youngest for the price of a crown and, on hearing the sobs of her neighbour, put his hand straight back in his pocket for another and was dragged off by his so-called friend before he be bankrupt.

"Have we crowns then to throw away on robbers and thieves?" Dorothy's voice was tart.

"The creature put me in mind of our Drusilla." The doctor looked ashamed. "She had the same hair and eyes . . ."

"And is our Drusilla a criminal, then?"

"Oh, Uncle Peter, what happened to the poor little mites, once they were free?"

"Don't you bother your pretty little head about 'em, my dear. It's an episode I'm ashamed of and don't relish the telling of it. Come here and I'll teach you how to play solo. 'Twas a great fault in Miss Knight's Academy that radical woman never taught you to play a good hand of cards."

He pulled a new pack from the little drawer in the card table and shuffled the cards in the deftest and neatest of ways.

"Now, my dear, you do the same and let's see how you handle the pack."

Poor Drusilla, her fingers were all thumbs. Her heart was not in it. She was fretting over two little girls wandering the streets of London. Did they get home safe and was there a kind Mama to welcome them? Next time Uncle Peter went to London she would give him all the crowns she could muster to procure the release of more of the poor little things.

"If there be crowns to spare," snapped Dorothy, reading her thoughts, "Newent and half the villages round about have their gaols. But you'll surely not be cracked enough to release vagabonds and ruffians on our own doorstep."

161

The doctor shifted uncomfortably. If there be another woman in this world as sharp as his sister, he would not like to meet her. What she needed was a dose of her own Anthony. He wished to High Heaven his brother-in-law would make his way home, nabob or no.

Within a few months, he had earned Dorothy's displeasure yet again.

It was just past Christmas into the following year. He had settled himself in the snug of the White Harte Inn in the corner of the market square. It was a dull enough day and the old panelling dark with smoke from pipe and candle, hearth and spit did nothing but add to the gloom, though it was close and warm. He called for a wench to mop up the dirty table. It was hard enough to keep one's linen clean in this place without trailing one's cuffs in slops of ale.

He had just finished prescribing for old Mrs. Belcher's granddaughter. The girl was pale and translucent as a moonstone and as thin as a rail. If it wasn't consumption then it must be a worm. Both conditions, he said, brought on a cough, loss of appetite and a fever. Judging by the stink of the little girl's breath, he inclined to the latter and recommended a small piece of chewing tobacco rolled up to a pellet, coated with sugar and swallowed whole first thing in the morning. He guaranteed she would spew up the worm and her trouble all over. Before the old lady could get out her purse for the half-guinea he reckoned she was well enough breeched to afford, there was some sort of stir at the far end of the room.

"Dr. Fletcher! Dr. Fletcher! I come in the Queen's name for Dr Fletcher!"

"Here Sir," the doctor held up an arm, leaving old Mrs Belcher to owe him his money, neglecting to ask after the old lady's twice-bereaved son, both wives dying in child birth, herself and her gout.

He recognised the fellow pushing his way towards him as a sergeant-at-arms from the Queen's Bench in Nottingham and wondered what the devil was amiss. It was a Wednesday market day, the day he set aside for seeing those country patients come into Newent. They paid on the nail, though it might be a basket of eggs or a dish of brawn and the day was sacrosanct in his calendar.

His irritability increased soon enough as he heard what had brought the fellow to seek him out. It was his old friend Patefield, the surgeon-apothecary from Bingham, in the gravest of trouble and arraigned to appear at the Nottingham Assize.

"And what the devil for? I'll guarantee this county has no finer surgeon apothecary than my old friend."

"I'll take a seat, if I may, and a quart of ale," said the sergeant seating himself opposite the doctor. "It's been a rough ride here and might be a rougher ride back by the look of the weather."

"I asked you a question Sir, and made you a statement."

"So you did." The man wiped his mouth with the back of a hand. "And to be topsy-turvy, we'll take the statement first. I don't deny it. But the finest surgeon apothecary in the country, let alone in the county, is not to be allowed to get up around midnight and, still in his nightshirt, set fire to Bingham market place in three places." He leaned back with a fat smile on his face to see the effect of that.

"I'll not believe it," the doctor was thunder-struck.

"You've no choice," the man slurped at his ale, small eyes winking over a pewter rim. "He was seen by a neighbour who had got himself up to look at the moon from a top window. As well as the moon he saw the gentleman in question, your friend I believe, going about his incendiary business."

"And what do you want from me?"

"Nay, I want nothing at all. It's on account of the prisoner I'm come. He wants you to speak for him and I come out of goodness of heart on account of what he once did for my sister. Queen has nothing to do with it. But I needed your

163

attention among that halt and lame crowd."

"I thank you for it. Any damage done?"

"To him or the market place?"

"Devil take it man. Don't talk like a lawyer. I gave you a plain enough question."

"When you come into court you will find His Honour the Judge requires you to be plainer than that. Damage to him? None, unless it be inside his noddle. Damage to market place? None neither, for said witness raised up the neighbourhood afore the three fires took a hold."

"What is the trouble, then?"

"Maybe the people of Bingham don't fancy a pyromaniac in their town and no more would I. At any rate, good doctor, you have no choice. You are required to come. Justice demands somebody speak for the prisoner. My sister is still alive and only Patefield to thank for it."

"I'll come with all possible haste to speak for my old friend."

"Haste will not be needed. The trial is six weeks off."

The time of the Assize was given and the man took his leave. Peter left off his physicking that day. He had no stomach for it and his patients had to take their half guineas and crowns, their eggs or their brawn back to wherever they came from.

Six weeks later the thud of a stave against a solid oaken floor thumped through the court at Shire Hall. The formalities were called and the court hushed its mouth, shuffled and creaked to its feet. Judge and jury progressed to the chamber. There was a solemn bowing and bobbing. The court reshuffled and sat. The prisoner was brought up from the cells. Poor Patefield stared about him at such a fine show of grey wigs, white stocks and black gowns on his account.

Mr. Learned Prosecutor rose to his feet clutching a great ream of papers. He said it was 'a serious matter, m'Lud.'

The judge scratched his nose and stared at the prisoner. The prisoner was sworn. That done, his attention was lost.

164

His eye caught the bright colours of the Queen's Arms directly above and behind the head of His Honour the Judge and held them fast.

"Patefield, you have heard the charge, how do you plead?"

Still Patefield stared at 'Dieu et mon droit' and 'Honi soit qui mal y pense'.

"I ask you again, Mr Patefield. How do you plead? Are you guilty or not guilty?"

The defendant found his voice and it did not waver.

"I give you the first verse of the fifty-eighth psalm: Are your minds set upon righteousness ye congregation; and do ye judge the thing that is right, ye sons of men?"

Witnesses testified to his strange habit of walking abroad wearing a wig with three hats one on top of the other and more little harmless eccentricities. Dr. Peter testified to his competency as surgeon-apothecary. Mr. Patefield continued to stare about him, reciting the psalm.

Neither judge nor jury needed the wisdom of Solomon. Poor Patefield was led away to be 'detained at Her Majesty's pleasure till a proper place of safety could be provided for him at home'. The court crossed his name off its list and moved on to the next.

Dr. Peter walked his colt up the hill to bring Dorothy and Drusilla the news. In spite of a huge fire in the grate, an abundance of candles, a gleam on the furniture and silver in the little parlour, it was a melancholy trio that sat after supper mulling over the case.

Drusilla remembered how amused she had been as a child at the antics of dear Mr. Patefield.

"Do you remember, Mama, how he would take a card from the pack – always an ace – rub it between both hands, lean back his head and balance the long edge of the card upstanding along the line of his beautiful aquiline nose and walk round the room with the card still in place?"

'Lord, yes," agreed Dorothy, wiping an eye, "And how long he managed to keep it there was no more than a miracle. His thin legs were so bowed I always wondered they didn't crack up beneath him."

"And do you mind that time he took Papa's walking cane, twirled it between his hands, point on the floor, let go and jumped clean over the stick that continued to twirl all by itself like something bewitched?"

"Will we ever forget Anthony's Oak Apple Day when he came with three hats balanced on top of his wig and a great bough of oak across the lot. Peter, you must see they make him the most comfortable den and as soon as can be."

The doctor was quiet. He had no confidence in his ability to influence events as far as the law was concerned. He could not get out of his mind the poor wretches at Bridewell, their leg irons and chains, their hunger and rags, their whippings and beatings.

His fears were well-founded. Some weeks later he took Dorothy and Drusilla with him to Bingham to visit his old friend who he had heard was now snug in a new little den built by the parish.

"It will do him the world of good to see his old friends have not forgotten him. And Drusilla will be the best physick of all. He was always so fond of you, Drusilla . . ."

"And sent me funny presents now and then. Do you remember the book in which he drew such comical pictures of himself?"

"It's a rough enough drive," said Dorothy. "I hope the outcome is worth the pain."

What a sight met their eyes when they pulled up in the little square of Bingham. Mr. Patefield's 'snug den' was no more than a miserable two-roomed shed they could hardly see for the press of a motley crowd around it – and not all of them from Bingham, either. The doctor's mouth saddened. The ghouls. They had come to mock and jeer at his dear old friend. He remembered his own visit to Bridewell and felt ashamed. No crown pulled out of a pocket could help poor Patefield.

166

Dorothy chafed to get back to Newent before Peter's kind heart got the better of him.

Drusilla was shocked to the core. The bewildered look of the one-time surgeon apothecary with the sniggers of the gawping crowd she folded neatly away like a piece of laying out linen, never dreaming that one day she would be forced to shake it out for an airing.

She turned her back on the year 1710 with few regrets and looked forward to 1711 with all her heart.

CHAPTER 18

Now seventeen and a half years old and an acknowledged belle, Drusilla stood in the wide hall of Beacon House.

He is coming. He is coming!

The shining surface of the great oaken chest reflected the blue and white of Mama's pot pourri bowl and, as she moved, it caught too the sheen of her green silk panniered gown.

She stared into the looking glass above the great fireplace and could not help but admire what she saw. The hated red hair of childhood had deepened to a rich chestnut shade that could only have come from Papa – whatever Nellie and Mama might say about juniper rinses at new moon. She put up a hand to pat the faultless ringlets.

He is coming. He is coming!

Her heart raced as she stroked the fine lace at her sleeve, such quality and stylish too. Would he never come and had he altered as much as she? They had not seen each other for so long. He had been hard at work on his thesis and was now capped and gowned Dr. Bernard Webster. Dr. of Divinity. Uncle Peter knew one of his tutors who said he was a brilliant young man set to rise in the world.

Soon. Soon! He would surely come soon. She had waited all day in a fever of impatience that was nigh on unbearable. She turned to the window and peered out at the empty yard. She sped back to the looking glass and again a hand went up to the perfectly dressed hair. Suddenly the sound of a coach and shouts of the grooms sounded without. The bang of a door, then a brisk tread across the flags. She turned to the light and there he was.

How tall he had grown, how good-looking, how worldly and self-assured and how beautifully his travelling dress suited him. Her loving eyes looked up to the strong face, tanned and handsome against the creamy stock at his throat and the white of a superbly powdered wig. How that wig turned the boy into a man. How she longed for a toupée of her own. Whatever was it made Mama so perverse? All the fine ladies were wearing them. In London, Uncle Peter said, there was hardly a wigless head in sight.

A sudden shyness made her lower her lids, an action she would have despised at Miss Knight's Academy. She caught the cut and sleek polish of his immaculate boots. Her name was whispered softly, and her eyes lifted past smooth breeches up to the cloak he let slide to the floor. He was striding towards her, arms outstretched. She put her hands into his and thrilled at the touch, innocent of the effect she had upon him. He whispered her name again and she caught that well remembered faint medicinal-sweet smell of his breath. His dark eyes glinted at the sight of her as he let fall her hands and stepped back to admire.

"Green, my favourite colour."

He studied her searchingly, scanning the silken gown down to the little matched slippers and back to her face. He noted the curling hair, smooth and shining, the large blue-grey eyes, exceptionally lovely. There was nothing of the fashionable beauty about her; no dustings of chalk or rouge on the cheeks, no darkening of eyebrows or painting of lips, no spots or patches and she excited him the more because of it.

From a little pocket in his long vest he took out a tiny silver box and popped a rose-coloured comfit into his mouth. At the elegant crook of his finger Drusilla's heart beat so she could scarcely breathe, let alone speak.

"Welcome home, Bernard."

They both turned. There was Dorothy, sailing in like a

golden galleon and as near pleased as Drusilla herself. The hall filled with servants, some struggling with boxes, others with bags, but it was little May Hobbs who retrieved the dropped cloak, holding it close to a rosy cheek as she dawdled her way to the linen room to press, to brush and to dream.

Dorothy proffered her hand to be kissed, only Nellie noticing his sly look at May's tender back.

"Welcome home again, Bernard. We have so much to show, have we not, Drusilla?"

She drew her daughter close with her free hand as, laughing and chattering, they tap-tapped their high heels into the drawing room. Not until they were in the middle of that vast room did Dorothy release her hold on either side to spread out her butter coloured skirts and spin round, like an actress, thought Bernard, feeling a familiar surge inside his tight breeches.

"Well, my dear boy, what do you think? Have you ever seen anything quite so splendid at Cambridge or anywhere else for that matter? Her eyes sparkled with triumph. She was almost flirtatious, he thought. He relished her skittishness and looked about him.

The great room had been completely redecorated and its once plain walls now brilliantly coloured. On every side rosy Venuses and gauze-draped nymphs were chased by hairy satyrs and vine-clothed gods. The teasing figures hid among trees, behind Grecian columns, or peeped between garlands of flowers, all exquisitely painted in natural colour. He gazed up at the ceiling, now a rich pattern of cherub heads with rosy arms and wings lost in pink and blue and fleecy white luminous clouds. The cornice, which had once been tipped with gold, was now as fully painted as the rest, each plaster flower made to look as real as its natural counterpart. He looked to the floor where new needlepoint had been laid only a week before. What magnificence, his heart whispered, what richness, and the thought of it all sent his pulse racing the faster. He turned to the woman awaiting his answer and had some difficulty controlling the husk in his voice.

"It is splendid," he pronounced. "I have never in my life seen anything so perfect," fixing his bold eye on Dorothy's neckline.

Dorothy preened while Drusilla clapped her hands and almost skipped from one dainty silk slippered foot to the other.

"And there is more, so much more to see, Bernard. I'll wager you . . ."

"But no more at this moment," interrupted Dorothy, missing the uplift of Bernard's brow at Drusilla's remark. "Some things have not changed a jot. Mistress Alice and her maids are still the best cooks in the shire so we hope you have bon appetit. They have been busy for weeks. We take dinner now, just the three of us, and tonight a cold collation with friends, a little conversazzione and a hand at this and that, a little music . . ."

They tapped into the dining room where, over mounds of food, the sheen of new blue and white china, the glitter of silver and the fussing of minions, they prattled their news. Bernard listened with apparent interest to Drusilla's progress at Miss Knight's Academy and how she and her mother still had invitations to Miss Knight's At Homes, though never the time to go. He could hardly take his eyes off the two necklines opposite as he listened with rather more interest to Dorothy tell how she had stolen the idea of the murals from Lord Lessington's summer pavilion at Park Lodge. She chattered on how superior were the Beacon House painters who had a far better eye for colour than his Lordship's artists. And, if he listened to all of it with half a mind busily weighing up other things, then neither Drusilla nor Dorothy noticed the lapse.

His own family had had a stroke of good fortune, he reminded them. The Jenison bubble that had trembled for years had burst at last. Sir Matthew had near ruined himself,

171

like many another, with his dabblings in politics. He had been forced to mortgage his great house, The Friary, and the Webster family were now living there and running a select Boarding House for Young Ladies.

"You know one of the young ladies, I believe, Drusilla; my cousin, Miss Elizabeth Bradford, and I understand she has received some kindness from you. I thank you for it."

Drusilla glowed at the slight praise. In spite of Mama, she would find ways to be kinder than ever for Bernard's approbation. He noticed the glow and smiled to himself. He did not feel at such a disadvantage now. There was nothing to be ashamed of in his father living at The Friary. It was an address that could be dropped out to acquaintances with some pride, and no mention of young ladies boarding.

They chatted of honours and preferments. Twelve new Tory peers had been created to balance the strength of the Whigs. Nottinghamshire's own Sir Thomas Willoughby had become the new Lord Middleton to the accompaniment of clarion peals all over the county as Dorothy's poor head could very well testify. The Queen had appointed Lord Lessington of Park Lodge, their old friend Robert Hatton don't you know, her new Ambassador to Spain and his family were in the throes of packing up for their duty in Madrid. Park Lodge was not to be shut up as it had been during their time at the Court of Vienna. It was to be let to relations and Dorothy had high hopes of visits and parties.

Dishes were offered, tasted or rejected and whisked away, the diners becoming more and more loquacious under the influence of food and wine. Drusilla's cheeks were pink and shining. Dorothy giggled foolishly. Bernard sipped a little more wine. The time he had been waiting for had come and he meant to press his advantage. He leaned back in a way he would not have dared to do if the master were home. He stretched out his long legs to give Drusilla's foot a conspiratal tap under the table as he had done years before in their childhood.

"You have heard the news of Newcastle, I take it?"

"We are not buried alive up here in the Shires." Dorothy's foolishness ceased immediately.

"One forgets," drawled Bernard. "One thinks of him still at Westminster bustling about offices and palaces. They say certain people were terrified of him."

"And might be more terrified of his heir." Dorothy's voice was crisp.

"You know, then?"

"My dear Bernard, the Newcastles own almost the whole of Nottinghamshire, are related to nearly all our quality, have fingers in Lord knows how many local pies their affairs are not likely to go unnoticed here. Without sons, the title is bound to go to that nephew of his – though nothing is settled yet."

"Thomas Pelham," breathed Drusilla, eyes fixed upon Bernard.

"The very same, my dear Dru. My old school friend, Tommy P. It's an ill wind, is it not? If my father had not wasted his talent electioneering for Markham, he might never have lost his business . . ."

"If Drusilla and I had not driven in for bonnet ribbons . . ."

"Markham might never have sent me to Westminster," Bernard's eyes snapped wickedly.

'If I had not pushed him . . ."

"That was where I met Tommy P. you know."

"And Markham allowed you enough change in your pockets, – you were not at a disadvantage . . ."

"Lord!" Bernard ignored the interruption. "What an ugly little beast Tommy P. was, to be sure, and still is for that matter. I was a senior when he first came to the school, not long after me, a little sniveller who daren't say boo to a goose. I rather made it my business to look out for him. He rather fell for me – didn't know his own worth. Still doesn't. You never saw such a sight with that great spread of a nose, complexion as swarthy as a gypsy, shuffling gait, dress all of

173

a shambles and as for that full-bottomed black wig . . . But he had what I hadn't got, the young dog, and still has . . ."

"Oh, Bernard!" protested Drusilla. "You had so much. You were top of the class, Captain of Games, Head of the School and handsome too."

"Ha!" Bernard's laugh was a sneer. "Handsome is as handsome does should sound who handsome knows. Top o' the class, Captain o' Games, Head o' the School, nothing without influence, any of 'em."

"You knew how to play your cards though, did you not? You have not gone short?" Dorothy eyed his good clothes.

"I was still at Trinity when he came up to Clare in my last year. We had mutual friends in both colleges. We met now and then. I made it my business to help him along. There were games I taught him, there are tales I could tell." His eyes glinted again and he showed his white teeth, while Drusilla's cheeks burned redder, as she remembered Bernard's games. He groped under the table towards Drusilla's knee, thought better of it and slid his hand to his own thigh instead.

"You are to be ordained, are you not?" Dorothy reminded him.

"Yes. I got my degree. I can call myself Dr. Bernard Webster. I shall soon be wearing the cloth . . ."

"And pretty good cloth it will be too, if it's as good as this." Dorothy eyed his attire again.

"H'm. Through Tommy Pelham's recommendation I can expect to be wasting my life in an obscure parish in the backside of Lincolnshire while he tries on the dead Duke's shoes in Westminster." His voice grew sulky. "Already they tell me he does little but add to his empire – all honours, preferments, monopolies, commissions and what else pass through his hands while I . . ."

"He is not the son of a draper," Dorothy hesitated to use the 'broken' but he is not the Duke yet. He has to take the name of Holles first and settle the estate with the old Duke's daughter. It may be years before he gets title, unless she consents to marry him. That might smooth the way."

Bernard shrugged. The wine had made him bold. A woman with a husband across the High Seas might be hotter than any virgin. His voice was drowsy.

"You have connexions I know – I believe you could help if you would . . .

Dorothy cut him short with the scrape of her chair.

"I am weary and need to rest for an hour or two. There is so much to see to. You are still young enough to be lively all day and half the night as well. Show Bernard the garden, Drusilla, but don't stay too long. Take a hat and put on your pattens. Remember we have company tonight and must look our best."

She gathered her golden skirts about her. Let young Bernard wait for her favours. She had done enough, Lord knows. He could cool his heels a little and consider who put best butter on his bread. His father still did nothing more than eke out a poor living, though it was at the Friary. A Select Boarding House for Young Ladies. Tish! It was not such an advancement, if any, on the draper's shop in Newent Market Square. She yawned as she climbed up to her bed chamber. One thing was sure, it was easier to do one's entertaining with Anthony away. Though she missed him, that was for certain. And how the money was pouring in. Another ship load carrying their share due any day now, so Peter said. Enough to spend and store as well. Though there were such tempting offers of speculation nowadays. She used to be so cautious in such matters but now everybody was dabbling in this or that and it was the dickens of a job to know where to place one's bets. But no denying the excitement.

Down below in the panelled hall Drusilla folded a silk shawl round her shoulders, tied the velvet ribbons of a wide brimmed straw hat under her chin and quite forgot the ugly pattens. There leapt up all her old feelings of expectancy.

Goodness, it was like Papa coming home, as she took Bernard's arm and pulled him outside into the yard.

Across the back terrace, with its ornamental figures and urns, she drew him and could not get through the budding rose garden and shrubbery fast enough. Her eagerness delighted him. There was something to be said for breaching virgin territory, after all, nothing quite like that final break of resistance, nothing quite as sweet as the sobbing afterwards. He gave her a tender look that made her heart lurch.

They sped through the arched gateway and she indicated what lay before them as triumphantly as Dorothy had earlier displayed her splendid drawing room. She watched eagerly to catch his reaction.

The young man drew in his breath as he took in the change. Surely, thousands of tons of earth had been shifted and Jove knows how many gallons of water pumped and made to run wherever Mrs. Davison directed. 'Struth. Rustic bridges had been artfully sited, rare bushes planted, all kinds of natural flora and stone fauna, both domestic and exotic, scattered about. And beyond all this, the copse he remembered so well, where he and Drusilla had romped and played to dodge Capel the woodkeeper, had been thinned yet let to stay in an assumed naturalness.

The air was heavy with Maytime scents. Bees busied themselves in the hawthorn snowed under with blossom and birds chattered and flapped everywhere. Fern fronds uncurled and the finger-like leaves of horse chestnut expanded. By Jupiter! You could almost see and hear their crackle of growth. The place throbbed with life.

Together they sniffed the bosky air and laughed as though drunk with the scent of it.

Bernard moved away from the girl and looked about him while she stood there, her face, above the emerald green of her gown, shining like the first rose. She was alight with pleasure at his open amazement. The magnificence of it all astounded him. A whole army of workmen must have laboured here. Anthony Davison Esquire was obviously amassing a great fortune beyond the High Seas and his wife at home was just as obviously spending it. He faced Drusilla and his voice was rich.

"Drusilla, you look like a wood-nymph."

"Come to the garden house," she said and shyly reached for his hand.

Her touch was electric and he stifled as best he could, a desire to hold her tight and near crush the life out of her body. It was a familiar urge that gave him no rest in feminine company. It maddened him beyond endurance, but curb it, this time, he would for his mother's sake.

Unheeding, Drusilla led him to the middle of the newly thinned copse and there, on the familiar flat glade, like a great green shelf in the slope, stood an amusing little hexagonal structure. From a six-sided base rose an equal number of slender columns surmounted by a decorative cornice supporting a domed roof. Seats were arranged round a hexagonal stone on the central base and above the seats sprang plaster vaults that disappeared into the dome. Atop the whole little edifice poised a fine figurine of the Greek God of Love.

Still fighting his passion, Bernard studied every detail and then looked down at Drusilla.

"I like it," he said not missing the flush of pleasure his slight praise brought to her face. He stooped to examine the bas-relief on the seats and looked down at the wood-nymph below.

"Have you noticed anything in particular, Drusilla?"

"Oh yes. Indeed I do." She felt his voice like a caress and ran to meet it. "One sees almost a different view from each side. If the garden palls one can look to the copse and if the copse is dull one can look over the field to Clay Lane down below. Sometimes I bring my sketch book down here and imagine the brickies in blue smocks after their day at the kilns, heads bowed, shoulders slouched. They plod so . . ."

She caught the impatience in his eyes and smiled.

"Now you are going to be like Mama and Uncle Peter and say I have plebian tastes. I like people better than trees and urns and plots, that's all. Do you remember you once said I never see a fine piece of lace without thinking of the poor hands that made it?"

"It is not that, Drusilla," his voice like silk. "This place is the exact spot of the coven meet." He stroked one of the pretty columns and gave her a meaningful look. "It would be a perfect place for the game."

His torment mounted again as he spoke but for all that he was quick enough to catch the alarm that leapt to her eyes.

"Drusilla, tell me you have not forgotten how to play the game, our game, Drusilla."

She had no armour against that voice and her alarm fled, giving way to excitement that showed in her face.

"Yes, my dear wood-nymph, it would be a perfect place for the game." His voice quickened. "And today is the first day of May, is it not? Do you remember that other Maytime, Drusilla? You do, I know you do."

Her heart beat painfully against her ribs and she closed her eyes against memories so hurtful. How could she ever forget that other first of May with its feelings of mingled excitement and fear as she had blabbed out those words to describe her foreknowledge?

Deliberately she recalled Papa's Maytime to shut out that other. With a conscious effort she hung on to the laughing way Papa had brushed off her fears. It had been one of those beautiful days when she had kept Papa all to herself, as she had bathed in the golden light of his unashamed joy in the maids at their dancing on Edgington Green. But the image faded away and she was left with that scene of Capel's green glade transformed to a coven meet. The smell of crushed herbage and wood-ash pricked at her nostrils as she remembered the dead crows suspended like some awesome warning.

"I am glad you are wearing green, little wood-nymph." Bernard broke into her thoughts. "Do you know 'tis the mystical colour of good fortune – a pagan colour if ever there was one?"

He leapt down from the dais and held her hands warm in his own, turning them over to caress her open palms with the tip of his tongue. She never knew the rein he kept on himself, nor the effort it cost, but she knew the effect it had upon her.

"Meet me here tonight, Drusilla."

"Oh Bernard, there's a party here tonight. Mama – she – ." She made a desperate effort to resist.

"All the better, little wood-nymph. We will not be missed. Here, Drusilla, tonight. Your Green Man commands it."

She could not trust herself to speak but he knew she would come.

CHAPTER 19

Evening fell at last. She thought it never would.

Outside in the courtyard carriages waited, horses' heads thrust into nosebag or trough as men clumped off to stables or kitchens.

Inside the great house dozens of guests, gay in brocaded satins and silks, chattered and quizzed, all puffed and powdered, rouged and ruffled. My Goodness, how fashions had changed since Mama's first select card parties of years ago. How comfortable the ladies must have been in their simple saques, the men, too, in their roomy breeches and coats. Still, if the only way to push up a bosom was to suffer the excruciating agony of too-tight stays, what else was a young woman to do? Drusilla looked proudly down at her own round white breasts, their nipples just decently covered, and smiled a self-satisfied smile at Biddy Hatton's ruffles hiding her lack.

She would miss Biddy, she thought, when her important Papa took her over the water to the court in Madrid. And Mama would miss the card parties at Park Lodge even more. Perhaps she might never again see Biddy who would grow up as high and mighty as a Spanish Grandee. Oh, no, surely not. She could not imagine for all the world that little Biddy Hatton would ever – tish! There was no time to think of that now.

Men were clearing thick heads with pinches of snuff and on every side little flat boxes, plain or bejewelled, were slipped out of sprigged satin pockets. A pinch of fine green to one nostril, a pinch of coarse black to the other and a

violent sneeze spelled out relief, while silken hand
kerchieves flew like flags. But my Bernard has not caught
the habit, she purred, though he sweetens his breath with
floral cachoux. The covert smile broke free. At any rate,
flower scented comfits were rather better than the garlick
and honey lozenges used by Lady Reville and her friends.
She giggled aloud and was forced to cover her face with her
fan.

Never had Mama had such a gathering. All the quality of
the county was here and more besides. Even more than on
Papa's Oak Apple Day. A myriad candles burned in all the
rooms, hired servants, (how Nellie and the others hated
them) for all the world like tropical birds, flew silently up
and down the long passages, loaded trays expertly poised
like flying crests. No expenditure spared. It was a splendid
assembly and she was excited by it.

She caught sight of her own reflection in an ornamental
pier glass nearby. Her white wig shimmered like new spun
silk and set off her clear skin and luminous eyes. Her hands
went up to touch the unfamiliar texture of this unexpected
present from Uncle Peter, so Mama could not possibly voice
an objection. Somehow she could not get used to the hot,
tight feel of it, worse than the stays. She held her head high
for fear it would tilt, keeping a watchful eye on the candle-
filled sconces and catching the flash of her low-bodiced silk
gown, worn especially for Bernard.

From the depths of the glass the throng of bright colours
glittered and shone and suddenly she was aware of Lady
Reville's reflection quizzing her fixedly. She coloured,
discomforted at being caught out in her vanity. The old tabby
cat. Jealous because her own Arabella had no shape at all
worth the looking at. Even less than poor little Biddy.

She turned to catch sight of Bernard on the arm of his old
benefactor, Sir George Markham, still Member of Parliament
for Newent. What a dodderer the old gentleman looked.
Could it be true what the gossips clacked about him and his

reason, that there was not much wick left to his candle? Uncle Peter always said there was the smell of madness in that family and he should know.

The old man's shuffling gait showed up her Bernard's elegance. Surely Bernard was that benediction she longed for every day of her life. She watched the young man bend towards Markham's ear and she smiled at the sight. Now, was that good manners or just plain flattery that made Bernard so attentive? No wonder that ugly fellow, Thomas Pelham, had worshipped him, heir to the Newcastle estate or no. Why, even Mama had warmed towards Bernard. Though one could never be sure of Mama; she blew hot and cold about so many things, like Miss Knight's At Homes, like poor Bessie Bradford, like the spending of money and, in any case, it would be Papa's authority that would count in the end. Dear Papa, she must not think of Papa now.

Bernard looked up, the leap in his eye catching the response of her own. He guided the old man towards her and she held out a hand, suppressing a shudder at the unwelcome touch of an old man's lips.

"My dear, Drusilla," wheezed the old rogue, "when shall we see you young people at Sedgebrook? We've stables full of the prettiest little fillies just waiting for you to try 'em. When are you coming, eh? My dear, eh?"

She smiled prettily and nodded, for he was as deaf as a post.

"Eh? Eh, my dear?" He cocked his old head and laid a rheumy ear close to her mouth.

"Yes, Sir George. Yes," she shouted, looking away in controlled disgust.

Bernard slipped round the old man to her other side to give her elbow a sly squeeze in the passing. She wished he wouldn't. She felt uncomfortable at the attention and common politeness made her attend to Sir George.

"And another thing, my dear," the old man coughed and spluttered, "My god children, two nephews and a niece, are coming over from Ireland this year. They're a merry crowd and I should like you to meet 'em. My heirs, you know. Would you . . ." But the rest was lost in a barking fit while his purple face looked like bursting a vein or two.

Bernard pressed her elbow the harder and his warm lips brushed her cheek. "Meet me in half and hour, you-know-where."

She felt her legs weaken and almost grasped at Sir George for support. Bells rang in her head, till she felt the whole room might hear. 'Meet-me-in-half-an-hour-you-know-where.' Surely soon would come that delight, that satisfaction, that joy she longed to drown in over her chin and up to her ears, from the toes of her feet to. the very top of her head in fact. Don't think of it, Drusilla, not now, but she could not help it and thanked the Lord she had been left to cope with Markham alone.

She searched the little dorothy bag that perfectly matched her green silken gown and slippers and handed an inadequate snippet of lace to the baronet.

"Do take this, Sir George, I'll get you a . . ."

"Drusilla, my dear," a high-pitched imperious voice bore down upon her. "I do so want to introduce you to my niece from Somerset. She knows a kinswoman of yours," and she was swept away, leaving a hired footman to attend to Sir George.

She suffered herself to be drawn into the hall and, for Heaven's sake, it seemed an age before she could disengage the giantess of a woman and her simpering niece chattering about people she had never seen and hardly heard of, though the clock in the hall showed only a few minutes had passed. How Mama would have frowned at such a lapse of good manners.

As soon as she decently could, she slipped into Papa's room where he had been used to take off his boots and hang up his fowling pieces so long ago. It was quieter here and she needed to collect her thoughts. She avoided, though she

183

hardly knew why, the smiling portrait of a youthful Dorothy and peered out into the dark night. Servants had forgotten to close the shutters against several commodes scattered about the room. She dared not stay. Supposing somebody came to use one. Somebody like old Markham. In any case, this room was enough to draw Uncle Peter mumbling about closets and close stools, privies and cess-pits. He had the most objectionable hobby-horses for all his popinjay ways. And if poor Mr Patefield were not safely tucked up at Bingham, the pair of them would be here exchanging their crack pot ideas.

From the hall she had seen Bernard step out boldly through the front door and, though sure no other had noticed, she herself could not be so brave.

She saw nothing outside for black night and the brilliance indoors changed the window's clear glass to a verre-glise that threw back the room into her face. She knew that in itself would conceal her secret trip to the garden, yet still she hung back to gather her courage. A backward glance to the hall showed nimble servants and leisurely guests still passing this way and that in lively jigs of light and shade. Like those brilliant butterflies in Papa's tales of the Islands, she thought. Dear, dear Papa. For a moment she hesitated. Then Anthony's blood came up through her veins in a rush, drowning both good sense and caution, and she slipped swiftly down the hall to the back of the house and into the yard.

On one side sounded the voices of men from the coach houses and stables, the whinny and snicker of horses, on the other the chatter of maids in the brewhouse and dairies. She threaded her way between lines of carriages and strange servants and on between pots and urns on the terrace. She shivered in the moving shadows. Foliage rustled and whispered in a small, damp wind and she wished she had brought a shawl. A ground mist had risen and the full moon was veiled by vapours that cast near as much shadow as shine. Her heart lurched as a bird flew out of the shrubbery and she remembered those other frightening woodland sounds on that other first of May.

"Bernard. Bernard," she whispered aloud for comfort. Swish sh. Swish sh. Her silk skirts rustled as she hastened along, fearing that all the world might hear.

"Bernard. Bernard." Swish sh. Swish sh. On through the shrubbery, down to the copse, she flitted like will o' the wisp topped with the ghostly light of her white toupee, heedless of silken gown and slippers.

"Bernard. Bernard." Swishsh. Swishsh. Thank Heaven. The garden house loomed at last before her. She could neither hear nor see him but she felt and knew him to be there.

He held out his hand and her quick light spring hardly needed its help. As her feet touched the stone floor she felt in the air that hush that Papa had so often spoke of when a beast crouches for that final and fatal spring. Whatever was coming she dreaded as much as she longed for it. She ought to turn back. There was still time. Yet she was drawn irresistibly on.

The dark of the night hung between the lighter columns of the garden house where small golden lanthorns served only to augment the mystery and accentuate her fear. She thought she saw a small stand or table before her. He must have bribed one of the servants to help him. She wondered which one? It was a niggling question and she suppressed it, blotting out the picture of May Hobbs staggering beneath a weight of laden trays up at the house. She put out a hand to steady herself. Yes, it was one of Mama's kettle stands from the little parlour and it held a small cast iron chafing dish.

She drew in her breath. There was a strong smell of incense about the place.

Bernard released her hand with a slight pressure on her trembling fingers and before she knew it she was on one side of the stand and he on the other. Between them rose a blue spiral of scented smoke from the iron dish with the charcoal beneath glowing darkly red. His body melted into the shadows behind, yet his eyes remained fixed upon her and she caught the faint smile of his lips, the cream-coloured sheen of the linen bands at his throat but no halo of spun silk above, only his own dark hair nearly as black as the night beyond. He had removed his toupée.

The place was full of shadows, thick with the scents of burning spices and the silence weighed heavily as she stared into the chafing dish and up at the wreathes of smoke, twisting, curling, intertwining like her own thoughts and Bernard's, like their very minds, inseparable, identical. The columns of the little edifice dissolved into the night and she stood there breathing the air that was different, feeling strange emotions and trembling with fear as she had done years before in that very place.

At last he broke the silence that had brooded for two full minutes.

"You are perfect, Drusilla."

She raised her eyes to his and in the mysterious half-light her feelings were plain.

"Drusilla, if you were a man, I could take you with me to Trinity and you would be the toast of the Tempus Club."

"Tempus Club? What is that?"

His mocking voice took on an eager tone. "The Tempus Club, my dear Dru, is composed of some of the best and foremost philosophers of the day. We talk and experiment and write up our findings and talk again . . ."

"Tempus? Tempus fugit?" She knit her brows and wished she had paid more attention to Mr. Twells, the schoolmaster.

"Ha!" He laughed and jolted the kettle stand so the chafing dish rattled upon it. The smoke spread about and an extra rush of pungent scent pervaded the air. It stuck to her clothes, her wig, got into her throat and almost sickened her. Her head swam yet she stifled her revulsion along with her conscience.

"Time flies, Drusilla. Indeed it does. Once upon a time

you were a pale faced miss and I was a broken draper's son. And look at us now."

He cocked his head to one side.

"But which way does it fly, Drusilla? Come you little witch, you know how to make time fly whither you choose."

He reached forward to snatch at her hands and again the draught made the odours rise. He forced her hands over the chafing dish till they smarted with pain.

"Come, Drusilla, make Time turn around," and he pressed her hands ever closer to that blistering dish. She caught her breath and bit her lip. Tears welled in her eyes.

"Which way do you want it to turn, Bernard?"

"The Future, of course, you little witch. Come, show me the Future. And get off the ground this time. No more stuff about short-skirted women and girls at school."

His voice was insistent and immediately she was pulled into that hidden timeless world, elated and burning with curiosity. He felt her acquiescence, released the pressure on her smarting hands and drew her round the stand towards him. More than that, he felt her leap at the promise of some unknown delight and in a trice he had pulled off her shimmering toupée to tousle her flattened curls with trembling hands.

Time died away and its passing was unaccountable. Clouds shaded the moon and darkness swooped like a gigantic snuffer to block the soft glow of the lanthorns. She sensed again that curious feeling of time folding back and forth upon itself. She saw the long thread of her future fixed in the tangled skein of Bernard's present and she could neither understand nor unravel the complexity.

Alien, yet familiar, words tumbled out of her mouth to reverberate between the columns, among the trees and back again like so many echoes, her voice high pitched and full of a strange excitement. She could not help herself. In that excruciating thrill she crossed endless oceans and fought in terrible wars; she whirled through an infinite and beautiful

187

space rocketing twixt moon and stars; she watched horrifying experiments and suffered painful agonies as she saw dead men brought back to life. She rushed headlong over a crazy world, meeting with bold men and even bolder women.

She felt gloriously free. Her spirit flew through swirls of brilliant colour to the beat of amplified sound.

The colours shone brighter, lights flashed ever more fiercely and sounds beat out louder till freedom was lost and there was scarcely room to move or air to breathe. She was crushed in a vice that forced her to arch up her hips as strong hands pressed at the small of her back, shifting her hoops, seeking their way to the front of her body.

Suddenly she was struggling for breath, fighting for life. She plummeted from God knows where with rushing ears and thumping chest in her too-tight stays. She fought like a wild thing against an unwanted embrace. Bernard, more in remembered intent than fear of discovery, let her go.

"Drusilla!" he whispered and her breathing eased.

Blessed name! She was back. Thank God, she was back. Whatever it was she longed for, it was not this. A cold draught eddied about her feet. She shivered and raised her head. The lanthorns shone low and the chafing dish died. The mist fled and the moon shone high and bright. And, as though from yet another time and another place, she remembered Papa. "And promise me when you grow up to a woman you will be like your Mama and never pin down your pretty hair under such an ugly thing as a wig." She put a hand to her head.

Someone called from the house.

The quivering possibility of another world breaking into this receded. She stared at Bernard. There was complete silence between the two, neither venturing to disturb that other fearsome world in its own fold in the natural layers of Time. The realities of Present crowded out all else. Had they been missed? Was Mama searching the house? Had servants been sent to look? Was Nellie suspicious? Again she was fearful and afraid. What in the world would they say to the state of her dress?

Without another word she turned and fled through the moonlit garden, terrified lest she be seen, forgetting her discarded toupée and her smarting hands as she gathered up her voluminous skirts. Never, she vowed silently. Never will I play that game again.

Panting, she reached the stone flags near the house. It was as bright as day. She blinked and looked down on a short skirt cut well above bare knees. Weeds had sprung up at her feet. The house was shabby and in need of repair. Mummy was calling.

"Lucy! Lucy! Come along darling. Time to go home now." Flo Beresford stepped briskly out of the front door, across the courtyard to the car.

"Well, I suppose Daddy will call this a wasted afternoon – but it isn't. I now have it absolutely clear what I want to do and get. What have you been doing, darling?"

Lucy turned away to hide her confusion. She flicked back her head to feel the comforting weight of her long, thick, straight, brown hair. She nearly wept for joy to find her hands perfectly normal, unmarked and unblistered.

'Never again,' her heart whispered. 'Never. Never. Never. I'll never play that game again.'

CHAPTER 20

But she did. Both she and Drusilla continued to play that dangerous sport of living in one age with the personal knowledge and experience of another.

In her dreams, day and night, Lucy roamed the grounds of Beacon House, sat in her garden house, slipped through hidden arches in shadowy walls, tip-toed along passages into rooms thick with scents of unhouselled ghosts. She stared out of bricked up windows into a courtyard alive with the sounds of horses and carriages, the bustle of servants.

Her real world faded away, like an old snap shot, to reform as another with the dazzling clarity of a fresh exposure.

Once, in the little parlour, she had caught the sound of a sob and No! No! They were heart-rending sounds that made her stretch out a hand to succour the crier. She could have sworn she saw the unhappy face of a grown girl with large fear-filled eyes looking through one of the high sash windows. Her unease did not abate when she realised that face was her own, reflected against the blackness of night outside.

But it was the odd room that beckoned her more than any other. There was a tranquillity about that room, a feeling that here was a blessing if only she could reach it. She lingered there often to catch the sounds of sibilant whispers, muffled giggles, shufflings and, sometimes, a faint rhythmical chant of da-da-di-da, da-da-di-da, da da-di-da. She caught only the cadence and could make no sense of it. And there were always the squeaks. No matter how many traps were put down, the squeaking continued.

And always there must be time for the sneaky bike rides to Edgington that she hugged to herself along with her dreams.

Drusilla was plagued by a similar fertile imagination. She, in her time, saw the Beacon House of another century filled with strange tenants in outlandish garb. They were noisy and quarrelsome but, in some unaccountable way, seemed happier than she had ever been. It was their freedom she envied. She longed to know them and join in their lack of restraint. Once in the hall, she had come close to a girl whose large blue-grey eyes were bright in a shining face. Drusilla moved quickly to greet a friend. "Stay! Oh, please stay," she had breathed, but the girl swung long, straight, brown hair about her shoulders and sped up the stairs in a trice, a ridiculously short skirt showing long, thin legs in gay-patterned hose, looking for all the world like a mediaeval page. Before Drusilla could reach the bottom stair, the shade had vanished into the thin air of the upper landing, taking her old dread with it. She now longed to know.

In short, reality had broken their dreams and their dreams had become realities.

All over the house lights begged to be shed, shadows demanded to be chased and, at Bernard's insistence, Drusilla obliged them all. Each revelation closeted the pair of them closer and closer in shrubbery, garden house or parlour. Yet the first time he moved to slip a searching hand under her bodice she shrank like a frightened kitten which only excited him the more. As his persistence grew so did her courage in fighting him off, till an unnatural control checked his ardour to gentle persuasion. She trembled with fear lest Mama should surprise them but it was a fear tempered by an excruciating thrill as his practised hand caressed her warm bosom.

She need not have fretted on that account. Dorothy was busy with new projects. Having got her house to perfection, the exhilaration of the stock market now vied with the thrill

191

of the card table and between one and the other she had hardly time to turn round. She noticed nothing other than Drusilla now had a companion again and was kept agreeably amused whenever Bernard chose to stay away from his Lincolnshire Parishes.

That Bernard neglected his parishes, as he had once neglected his schooling, Drusilla took as the greatest of compliments. He could not bear to be out of her company.

As for Dorothy, between her cards and her share jobbing she still chafed, as she always had, at the clanging of bells. They clanged fit to burst towers and steeples when peace was declared, especially since their own Lord Lessington, to give Robert Hatton his proper title, had had a hand in the negotiations.

"And a wonderful job he helped make of 'em", said Dr. Peter. "Though there'll be some give neither him nor Bolingbroke credit. When all's said and done, France is humbled but not humiliated and the balance of power is steady. What more can you want? By my reckoning, our friend Robert deserves recognition. I hope they send him back to us and let's have Park Lodge lively again."

Bells clanged even louder when the greatest public holiday in living memory ensued. What a fuss Anthony would have made of that had he been home. They clanged when the dapper little Marshal Tallard was returned to France leaving behind a litter of broken hearts and their offspring, along with flourishing liquorice and celery fields down in the Nottingham Meadows; a number of bakers hoping the fashion for French bread would not go off along with the Marshal and numerous street urchins missing their lessons of fisticuffs and the Frenchie's generous vails.

They clanged when Bernard's old friend, Thomas Pelham, was made Earl of Clare and sounded louder than ever when that young man came of age.

Sadly, the passing bells tolled their grief to the town and beyond when Lord Lessington's young son, William, died in

Madrid. In Newent St. Leonards they felt the loss keenly. Robert Hatton had doted on his sixteen year old son, the very spit of himself.

Shocked matrons whispered behind their spread fans. Such a pride and joy. And have you heard of the trouble our poor Lord Lessington had to get the boy's body home? Trouble? Oh no! Do please tell. Well, the Spanish papists, the most bigoted lot that ever drew breath, won't leave a protestant body in peace. For shame! And to call themselves Christians indeed! When one of m'lord's servants died they not only desecrated the grave, they did the most unspeakable things to . . . Sh! My dear! So m'lord wrapped up his son in a bale of cloth and smuggled him home for a decent protestant burial. And if any folk wonder why the Stuarts are not welcome back, they should be in Bedlam. Then fans had closed ranks and heads closeted together for more tales of terrible papist atrocities. Sh! When the time comes there'll be more Jacobites crawling from under our beds than ever we thought on.

And the bells tolled yet again when Good Queen Anne of Great Britain rested at last. In the high summer of August 1714 up on the hill at Beacon House they had heard the slow solemn ring.

Dr. Peter had come as he always did when there was news to dispense. For a full day, so he had heard, messengers were galloping in and out of the Queen's Palace as the poor woman lay a-dying. All her garrisons had been strengthened and in some places the militia called out. All her ports were sealed to keep out the Stuarts. Newent's Mayor, John Cooke, along with others all over the country, had been commanded to prepare for the Elector's succession. No longer were people saying they cared not a fig who ruled as long as they were let well alone. Most of them cared very much it should not be the Stuarts with their troublesome ways, their catholicism and their hobnobbing with France. Though a minor hotbed of Stuart support bubbled under the surface.

No sooner had the passing bells ceased than a full peal was clanging for the new King of Hanover. Mr Cooke, the Mayor, cut a fine figure in his red and black robes standing high on the proclamation stool in front of the King's Hall with his ringing Oyez! Oyez! Dorothy stopped up her ears and said those wretched bells rang louder than ever she remembered. And Brigadier Hatton, Lord Lessington's cousin, had done her no service at all when he ordered the recasting of the six old bells and, not content with that, added two more to make eight in all – the old fool. She felt her whole life was being lived through those tiresome bells.

In the months that followed, Drusilla caught odd snatches of Hanoverian George, George the Dunce, don't you know? Never a word of English they say and the scandals left behind in Germany, my dear, enough to make the blood run cold. Better left there than brought here, don't you think? That's all you know! A pair of frowsty foreign trollops. Elephant and Maypole! Did you ever hear the like? I've said it afore and I'll say it again, there'll be a rising afore we're finished. Did I tell you what Lord Middleton's footman told my Betsy? The servants are arguing the toss more than we. And it's not puddings nor dish clouts they're worked up about neither. No. It's Jacobites and Dissenters they're cooking our goose with. Tish! The damned French, the damned Scotch and Devil take the King Over The Water!

The bells continued to clang despite Dorothy's complaining. They clanged on Coronation Day, on the new King's birthday and the day after that to celebrate Restoration Day. Nowhere was the irony of that seen more clearly than in Nottinghamshire. After all, it was at Nottingham the first Charles Stuart had raised his standard. Newent itself had remained true to his cause and been the last of all the King's strongholds to surrender. And was still proud, nearly seventy years later, that it had never given up of its own volition. It was even rumoured the new Lord Middleton and some of his friends were not averse to James

Stuart, the Pretender. Put that in your churchwarden and smoke it!

Dorothy kept her head bent over her cards and heard hardly a word of this gossip. Drusilla and Bernard were forever seeking out places to linger unheeded. Dr. Peter was attending his old friend, Mr. Patefield, sick of an ague as well as that lunatick malady. There was an epidemic at Bingham and he was run off his feet and no time at all for the climb up Beacon Hill to dispense either advice or news.

"'Tis no wonder neither," Nellie said. "Miss Dor'thy do have no time for nothing but gambling these days."

And if the old housekeeper, with her eyes at the back of her head, had suspicions of Drusilla and Bernard, she might fume about the young man's long absences from his poor parish but for the rest she kept her own counsel. Drusilla slyly hid her stays to facilitate Bernard's caresses and, with his iron self control unbroken, he kept her at fever pitch, getting his own satisfaction elsewhere. That is to say anywhere and everywhere and Nellie had plenty to say about that.

"Hm. They do say as how there bean't be a virgin left at the Friary. Boarding house for young ladies indeed."

"Tish!" Drusilla's reply was pert. "They must be as bad as an old Queen's Maids of Honour."

"And what do you mean by that, Miss Drusilla?" Nellie turned round sharply.

"Ready to change titles at first chance."

"You'm be so keen, Miss Drusilla, you'm be cutting your own self one of these fine days."

But Drusilla hardly heard. She was already on her way to the garden house where Bernard was waiting, and when his desire mounted extra strong as he teased her quick pulse, he fixed the picture of his weeping mother between himself and the girl and cruelly pinched her flesh till she winced with pain.

Between the perversion of one and the frustration of the

other Time hurried along. These years of Drusilla's young womanhood slipped by as others had done before and, again, she hardly noticed their order of passing. She skipped by that milestone dreaded by all unmarried girls, her twentieth birthday, without admitting a care in the world. She felt herself standing still as events rushed by. They hardly touched her. She was still beautiful. People commented on her beauty. She, herself, was amazed by it. She did not trouble, as other girls did, to unpick the dates of her childhood samplers. That subterfuge never entered her head. She still hugged to herself that Mama did not concern herself with the question of husbands. And her distant Papa was no bogeyman to force her into a marriage not of her own choosing.

The tenor of the house was like that of the country. Underneath that dull Hanoverian calm, though it was said often enough that Hanover George attracted his own rats, all scratching for place and pension, growing so bold they would soon have the neck to expect pension without place, there was a racing current ready to burst banks and flood the land with rebellion. It was the greatest good fortune the man elected to open the sluice gates had hardly the strength to do it.

On the sixth day of December 1715 at the great summer hunt at Braemar the standard of insurrection was raised by the Earl of Mar. He was eloquent against the English, against the cursed Act of Union he had had a hand in the shaping and against Hanoverian George. He spoke right heartily for the Chevalier, the old religion, the love of France and 'our brothers in England waiting to rise up to join us'. By October most of Scotland had declared for the Stuarts and on the first day of November a combined Highland-Lowland force crossed the border to England. If they met small opposition, they met even smaller support and from Preston in Lancashire were beaten back to the border.

Revolutionary fervour was quite spent and sighs of relief

heard all over England.

Drusilla trembled. Though she had hardly heard of Lancashire and of Preston never, she certainly remembered her eavesdropping on the military gentlemen at Miss Knight's Academy. Didn't the Scots go in for violating virgins and gobbling up babies for dinner? And was Preston so very far away, after all, for an army of rapacious toughs on the march? And was not Newent always known as the Key to the North and likely to be a great prize on their way to the South? The thought of the Scots in Newent was not to be borne.

"Tish!" snapped Dorothy. "Doesn't everybody know the Scots be mighty brave enough in battle but when 'tis done they can't get back to their heaths and heathers fast enough? Though, Lord knows why. When Lord Middleton's cousin travelled up there he said 'twas the dreariest place on God's earth."

She had gotten herself into a nice little school of players and begrudged a single hour given to anything else. They were people after her own heart. No time was wasted on great dinners and feasts, just the daintiest, quickly prepared and more quickly despatched morsels, then on with the next game. The stakes were high, the winnings enormous. The losses, well, the losses, she shrugged. One just bore them and hoped to recoup at the next meeting. Just one little whiff of a win was enough to set the pulses racing. There was nothing nowadays made her heart beat so fast as fanning her cards, not even a packet from Anthony.

"Pooh!" said Dr. Bernard Webster. He was translating a tract of sermons from the French and it was a task he could accomplish more cheaply and comfortably at Beacon House than at either Frisby or Great Steeping whose livings had fallen into his lap, or even the Friary where his parents still eked out a precarious living from their boarding house for young ladies. Besides, here at Beacon House he could keep an eye on Drusilla. It did not suit him to let her alone for some other fine fellow to snap up. There was a decided thrill to be had from keeping such a beauty at fever pitch. No, like Dorothy, he had no time for rebellious Scots. He had had the brilliant notion of dedicating his translations to Sir George Markham of Sedgebrook. His lip curled. He knew what the world would say to that. It would call him a sycophant. Let it. He owed the old baronet something and the more fulsome he made the dedication, the more the old fool would lap it up as a propitiation for all his sins. He smiled to himself at the prayer-book touch.

The Scots and their rebellion could go to the devil as far as he was concerned.

The year advanced. Christmas had come and gone and on Twelfth Night 1716 Bernard sat snug in his bedchamber at Beacon House. A fire blazed in his grate and a full bucket of coals beside it had not been hauled up by him. A half bottle of brandy and a full glass sat at his elbow. Paper, pens and ink all belonging to Beacon House were spread out before him. Drusilla was somewhere about the house. He had only to call out her name to make her come running.

As for Drusilla, she too was snug. She kept company with Nellie and May in the little parlour and between them they pieced together a patchwork counterpane out of the India chintz from Papa. The government could please itself at how many laws it passed to forbid the import of cotton. Uncle Peter said there never had been any way of beating the ladies. He believed the new fashion would double the life of the poor. They could now wash their clothes and bed covers as easily as the rich and, once in a while, get some air to their bodies. Papa's India cottons were now his latest hobby horse and what were the fortunes of a few sheep farmers when set against the health of the nation? And for once Drusilla and Dorothy heartily agreed with him.

"I do declare," said Drusilla, "this is the prettiest we have done yet. May, pass me the pink with the little red dots."

The fire blazed and candles flickered. Walnut furniture

and silver dishes fought together to make the brightest shine but the glace chintz it was that won the day. Drusilla sent May to the kitchen for hot chocolate. She caught sight of herself in the glass. She was still beautiful, especially in this light. She had nothing to fear and everything to hope for. It was the cosiest of evenings. The Scots and their terrors might be a thousand miles away.

Dorothy was up in her own bedchamber snug in her new Turkish dressing gown and turban. Hanover George's Turkish servants, Mustapha and Mahomet, had started the fashion and she blessed them for it. Nothing in this world was so comfortable. She had opened out her little fold-over table and laid out cards, paper and inkstand. She sat alone dealing two hands. There was a little trickery she was working out, a system that, if one did this or that, one could not possibly lose. The difficulty was remembering the sequence. She had nearly got it, she was sure she had. She picked up a pen to scribble the last step.

A bell clanged through the house. Lord above us, whatever was that? She had been concentrating so she had heard no sign of a horse in the yard.

She knew soon enough when her brother burst into her room, looking as stern as ever she'd seen him in the whole of her life. He closed the door behind him and there he stood, looking across at her from his great height, as she laid down the pen. Her heart near stopped. It must be Anthony. Nothing else could make him look like that.

"Dorothy, I come to ask you a question and I want a truthful answer."

She heaved a sigh of relief. Whatever he wanted to know she would tell. In all her life she had never been a liar.

"Of course, Peter, do sit down. You are come just right. I can try out my new theory . . ."

He preferred to stand and he cast a scornful look at the cards.

"Dorothy, have you gotten yourself into that school at

Chauntry House?"

"And what if I have?" She was on the defensive. If he had come to chide her about last night's losses then he could hold his tongue. It was Anthony's money she played with, not his.

"And have you also been to Lady Leake's place in Kirkgate?"

"Yes, and a more uncomfortable, poky place I never played in all my life." She clapped a hand to her mouth at the admission. Something in her brother's stiffness told her she was being inquisitioned and there was the rack and thumbscrew to come.

"So I'm told." He left the door and sat down heavily beside her. "You are to go to neither place no more. I forbid it."

"Forbid?"

"Yes. You have been a fool," he said roughly. "Do you never listen to the state of things in the country? By Jupiter! 'Tis easy to see I have not had time to come trotting up here with every snippet."

"What in the world . . . ?"

"Dottie, my dear, whatever would you do without me to look after you?" His voice softened. His eyes were kind again, as she had always known them. "The sooner your Anthony comes home the better. Do you hear nothing up here at the top of this hill?"

A great surge of loving warmth swept over her. She had not heard that pet name for so long. She was sick and tired of being a woman alone. More than anything else in the world she wanted to pass the reins to somebody else. He patted her hand.

"I know, Dottie, I know. Pour out a glass and listen to your old brother. Now take a sip like a good girl. I have come straight from a meeting at John Cooke's house."

"The Mayor? What in the world has a little card-playing at Chauntry House to do with him? Is it against the law to have . . . ?"

200

"The Pretender has landed," he was quick to see the change in her face. "Don't fret, Dottie. He won't get as far as this. He is no more enamoured of Scotland and the Scots than they of him. King George's red coats will chase him back where he came from quicker than a dose of rhubarb through gut. But it's put us all in a ferment. Mayor Cooke has had his orders from London. We are to start up a posse of trained bands. Some are taking it to the extreme and suggest calling up every man and boy over fourteen. We'd not have the officers to handle so many, nor the weapons to give 'em. It's like a hysteria . . ."

"But what . . . ?"

"I'm coming to that. Somebody mentioned comings and goings at Chauntry House and at Kirkgate. Somebody else imagined they were both safe papist houses."

"Tish!"

The doctor drained his glass and poured another. The fire had burned low along with the candles. The gleam of silver and furniture was not so bright.

"Somebody else raked up that old tale of Sir Francis Leake after King Charles was beheaded."

"I've never heard of it. What is it?"

"He was a committed royalist . . . "

"So were they all in these parts. And we're talking about seventy years ago in Heaven's name. Peter, what has this to do with me?" She started to tremble again.

"Will you listen? And take another drink. They were digging up all those half remembered historick tales which meant nothing to me. After the death of the King, this Sir Francis Leake had a fit of the melancolicks. He took off his good clothes and went into sackcloth. And that wasn't the end of it. He had his own grave dug and coffin made and laid himself down in it every Friday fast day. If that isn't the extreme, Dorothy, I don't know what is. Then some addle-pate said there were rumours of a ghost in that house and that led to a calling up spirits and Lord knows what other rubbish.

201

I tell you, some of these people's minds are still in the Middle Ages."

The whole thing was so ridiculous Dorothy stopped her trembling and showed some mettle.

"What about Kirkgate?"

"They raked up God knows what about that too. After all there is that chapel for all to see in that back room. Queen Henrietta Maria stopped there. Prince Rupert visited. That most certainly must have been a safe papist house, if ever there was one."

"But Peter, all that was nearly seventy years ago."

"It's all very well you talking about seventy years back, my dear. In London they're probably thinking the same. But up here in Newent they're remembering their great grand-father's tales of a siege and the Scots camped only a mile off at Kelham. I tell you both houses are being watched and I don't want you to be seen there. Anthony would not wish it either. Now, have I your promise?"

"Yes." It was a very small reply.

"Good girl, Dottie." He kissed her warmly on both cheeks. "Now one thing more. In all the time you were in either house, was there any sign of a toast to the King over the Water?"

"None."

"No shrines to the virgin? No paintings of saints? No tables set up like altars?"

"No," she said, too afeared to say anything else.

"Dottie, I believe you, but you're incorrigible," he laughed. "I'll wager you never saw anything at either place but the cards in your hand, your opponent's face and whatever was thrown down on the table. But you haven't heard everything yet. The Mayor of Nottingham is at this moment in his own House of Correction."

"Whatever for?"

"For getting down on his knees in his own home and pledging a toast to the Pretender."

202

"Whoever saw him?"

"There are spies everywhere. The town' s in a ferment about it and some of our gentry visiting him openly and applauding his sentiments. Dorothy, no more games at Chauntry House or Kirkgate."

He stood up to stir the dying fire to life and throw on another log. "Now, my dear, ring the bell for Nellie. I'll stay overnight. I need an early start for Bingham tomorrow to see poor old Patefield and back again before dark. We'll have a snug little sup up here for the two of us.

We must never forget, my dear, London was the place people ran to for cover in the war but up here in Newent they fought it out. And the aftermath was worse than the fight. Half the people dead of a plague and thistles waist high in the market place. And if there'd been dandelions, they'd have eaten 'em. People remember their grandfather's tales and are afeared. Makes 'em nervous."

He lifted the buckram stiffened skirts of his new blue coat and settled himself into a chair.

"Bye the bye, the eldest Hatton girl is dead of an ague in Vienna. Whatever has poor Robert done to deserve such a blow? First wife, then son, now daughter. And he's soon to lose the other, I hear. Little Biddy is to marry the Marquis of Welby. A fine match but her father will take it hard. I don't see us enjoying a hand at Park Lodge for long enough, though he and Biddy are home again I am told."

Dorothy felt a cold chill in spite of the fire blazing again. How depressing the evening had been. If only Anthony were home. She shook a little hand bell, wishing with all her heart he would come home soon, and such a yearning for her Anthony swept over her she could scarce hold her tears.

As Nellie heard the bell she signalled her helpers to pack away their bits and pieces. For Miss Drusilla it might be time for bed but she and May would be up and astir for long enough. Lord, she was tired.

Bernard sanded his last page, tidied his newspapers and

203

waited for Drusilla's step on the stair. He intended to snatch a kiss as she passed and so send her restless to bed. He speculated on the thrill of offering the same medicine to the high and mighty Miss Dorothy. To keep both mother and daughter on the hop might prove the sweetest folly. It would be a dangerous excitement he rather cared for. His eyes snapped at the wicked thought – though she might well show him the door before anything else.

The house was so full of frustration you could very near smell it and so it continued till that dreadful day, months later, when they were brought news of Anthony's death from the India sickness.

CHAPTER 21

Drusilla would never forget that day; Mama's stony face, Lawyer Catchpole's dry hacking cough, the breakings of seals and rustlings of vellum and papers.

Anthony had been dead for months before they had heard of it and the hope there had been some hideous mistake, that it was a nightmare to be banished next daylight, did not last long. The settling of Anthony's affairs, in spite of old Catchpole's concern, lingered interminably, while Dorothy fretted for more news from India and chafed that her brother was away in Amsterdam.

"Never here when needed," she sniffed to a white-faced Drusilla.

Bernard removed himself to the Friary. He left with the manner of one bestowing a benediction. They needed to nurse their grief in private, he said, though he would be in Newent for some time. The Newcastles were in Nottingham and he hoped very much to see his old friend, Tommy P.H., who had taken the name Holles to get him his Dukedom. But if there was ever anything he could do, they had only to send. Meanwhile, he gave them God's Blessing and left Beacon House amid a clatter of boxes and trunks and a cloud of scented cachoux. Yet the house was full of him. He was in the air, having left his traces in all manner of ways; an empty pill box in the drawing room, a long black hair on Mama's sofa, a lacy stock in May's work basket and that unmistakable odour that was all his own. How these things added to Drusilla's misery.

Dr. Peter returned to Newent at last and Dorothy thankfully looked to him for support but Drusilla was desolate. She found no comfort anywhere.

She and her mother sat now in the little parlour with a young attorney they hardly knew, instead of old Mr. Catchpole they were used to. Shutters fast closed and candles lighted in daytime gave the place an unnatural air. Through odd chinks in the shutters, streams of high summer sun showed up the dust settling on the worn colours of this unhappy room. Dorothy sat stiff-backed in her mourning dress that did nothing for her pitted complexion, her face barely altered since that first terrible communication, when the colour had seemed to drain even from the dark blue of her beautiful eyes.

The young man, ill at ease in such company, nervously untying the pink waxed strings and tapes, shuffled through endless papers and cleared his throat. Drusilla, herself in unbecoming black, was bewildered and afraid. She avoided, though she hardly knew why, the smiling portrait of her handsome Papa though, truth to tell, she could hardly see it for tears.

"Mama," she faltered. "Uncle Peter should be here, I know he should – why – ?"

Dorothy made no reply and the young attorney cleared his throat yet again.

"The burial was immediate – ahem – the heat you know and the fear of contagion it would have been impossible to get the body home. Ahem. A Christian burial, of course. Everything was done as you would have wished. There are details here you might like to peruse later."

He nervously shuffled a few papers and Drusilla wanted to scream as the mention of burial opened her wounds afresh. She looked across the round table to her mask like Mama. Dear Papa. Dear, dear Papa. No more letters, Papa, no more presents! I wish l had written oftener, dear Papa. I wish I had written by every post. Why don't you cry, Mama? Why don't you speak? Don't just sit there like a graven image, Mama.

Don't you know how plain and unfeeling you look with that set look on your face? You should weep, Mama, I know you should weep —.

She reached out a hand and moaned. The young man shuffled more busily than ever, having no notion whatsoever how to cope with hysterick young ladies. A noise from without saved him the experience. The barking of dogs, servants' voices properly hushed, hurrying footsteps, scattered their mood.

The little parlour door burst open and there stood Uncle Peter. Relief flooded Drusilla's heart and as quickly subsided as she stared at the figure in the doorway. The man was distraught, breath laboured, stock half-tied, waistcoat buttons undone, wig awry. Even allowing for the obvious hard riding, he did not look like Uncle Peter.

"My God! I need a drink. Port and brandy for all of us – we all need it."

Drusilla's hopes crumpled at the coarseness of these words. She remembered that maxim of poor Papa. 'You mark my words, Drusilla, wigs or white caps askew are indicative of stormy weather and that's why I never wear either!'

"Peter," Dorothy opened her mouth at last.

"My God! I know why Catchpole has sent this pup up here." The doctor tossed off his liquor and eyed the young lawyer. There were more rustlings of papers.

"What is it, Uncle Peter? What is it?" Drusilla was beside herself.

The doctor steadied himself, discarded his ridiculous physician's wig and regarded sister and niece helplessly.

"We're ruined. That's what. We're ruined. That's all, my dears."

It was Drusilla's turn to sit like a statue but Dorothy came to life with alacrity.

"Ruined? What do you mean ruined?" and if her white cap was not askew before, it was most certainly on the waver now.

"It was a wild speculation," Dr. Peter mopped his brow with the back of his hand. "My instincts were against it at the time. We should have listened to Walpole after all but I trusted Anthony's judgement. The town's full of it. They say Squire Gordon's hanged himself . . ."

"You have not told us the trouble yet." Dorothy's voice was as cold as only she could make it.

"I'm sorry, my dears, I never felt so wretched in my life. First Anthony – then this . . ."

Dorothy thrust a handkerchief into his hand and he mopped his face again.

"They fetched me out to Dr. Atterton this morning. Heart failure. Shock. Nothing I could do. His widow hasn't a penny, nor old Mrs. Belcher neither. And God knows how many more. I rode straight out here as soon as I could. The South Sea Company's crashed." He gave his sister a look of resigned futility. "Those damned Spaniards . . ."

"Is everything gone?" Dorothy's voice was sharp as a surgeon's knife.

"Our all, I should think. Those devils of directors are naught but artful knaves and we are naught but fools to have lent them our money."

Drusilla looked from one to the other. She wanted to shut out both sight and sound. How could Mama be so dull about poor Papa and yet so keen about his fortune? And whatever had happened to Uncle Peter, so strong and kind? How could he go to pieces over nothing but money? And why should they be putting up with this young attorney, shuffling, helpless, inadequate? Where was dear old Mr. Catchpole who Papa had always met in the White Harte Inn and who could take care of everything? This room was dark enough at the best of times, but to have the shutters closed and candles lighted in the daytime . . .

Dorothy poured out more brandy and tossed it back with wrist and elbow poised like a man. Drusilla felt sick, her legs weak beneath her, as she slipped from the room, thinking how they did not even notice her going.

Out in the hall, Nellie, her face puckered with anxiety, hovered near the parlour door.

"Oh, Miss Drusilla. Be there anything your Mama do want?"

"No. Nothing, Nellie, but fetch me a shawl and tell Hobbs I need the little closed carriage straight away."

She twisted a limp curl, rubbed her pale face with a handkerchief till the blood came and was glad when Nellie, with an unusual lapse, had forgotten about mourning and brought down the rose-coloured India shawl that suited her so well.

"Take me to the Friary", she whispered to Young Hobbs and settled herself into the darkening air of the carriage, for the bright sun had slipped behind cloud and would come out no more that day.

She was rushing to Bernard, not as a sweetheart to a lover, but as a child to its father. She remembered that night when Papa had cradled her in his arms, the soft, warm feel of his nightshirt, his wonderful masculine smell and the tender brush of his lips to quieten her fears. The gentle warmth of that night wrapped her round, as she remembered how he had chased her nightmares away. No strawberry beds, Papa, whatever they are; no acres of land, no village we will build for ourselves with never a trace of plaster-pit, brick-kiln nor woodyard, neither. And worst of all, oh, much the worst of all, no more Papa.

At her urgent knock a young maidservant opened the old Friary door.

"Is Dr. Webster at home?"

"In the drawing room, Miss Davison. Please to come in and I'll tell the Dr. you're here, Miss."

"Please don't," and Drusilla, impatient of formalities and, noticing neither the girl's hesitation nor the slight shrug of her shoulder, made her own way to the drawing room, totally unprepared for the shock to come.

It was the end of a bright day turned dull and a dull fire was struggling in the large old grate of the Friary drawing room. Beside the fire, one hand resting on the marble mantle shelf stood Elizabeth Bradford. Drusilla's stomach churned. She felt sick at the sight of that sleek figure dressed in a saque of shining grey silk, unbuttoned at the bodice, almost beyond the bosom. And no stays – most definitely no stays! And unkindest cut of all, it was her own silk and part of her very first India present from Papa all those years ago, that had changed Bessie Bradford into this sleek grey seal. Drusilla had never seen a seal but she had seen pictures, heard numerous stories and could still remember the seal woman at Papa's May Fair who had hidden her flippers beneath a grey silken coat and had poured tea and dealt cards with her toes.

She caught Bessie's tilt of the head, the glossy black hair scraped away from the smooth round face and what looked like a hastily replaced white cap most decidedly on the skew-whiff; the deep-set, glittering black eyes and the lop-sided,triumphant smile on the small, tightly shut mouth. She caught, too, the soft, plump hand stroking the unbuttoned grey silk and it was the silk that cut her to the quick – Papa's grey India silk she had so impulsively given away. And it must have lain unused in a drawer till now. She could tell the dress was new, for Bessie gave off such a strong smell of orris root.

How that silk, covering and sleeking the curves of Bessie Bradford's body, put Drusilla in mind of Nellie's tale of the Somerset seal woman who had sirened the fishermen. Yes, she thought, Bessie Bradford has sirened my Bernard. And this was the same girl who had once, and not so long ago, either, been glad of her friendship, welcomed her visits and presents, who once had been too overcome to speak when first invited to Beacon House.

Mama had been right after all. There was nothing of the matter-of-course about Bessie Bradford and Drusilla feared her from that moment.

Elizabeth inclined her head towards a high-backed chair beside the fire from where Bernard extended his long legs into the hearth. With pain, Drusilla noted the disordered stock, the wig removed to a table nearby, the flushed cheeks, the thick lock of dark hair falling over the high handsome brow, the eyes shining like a cat's sated with cream. She could not check the notion. His whole indolent attitude reminded her of a handsome black cat with white bib at the throat. She almost expected a raised paw to be licked, a tail to twitch, sharp claws to show.

These pictures of the pair of them lasted no more than a fleeting second, taking longer to tell than to see, but they would haunt Drusilla for long enough.

"My dear Dru," even Bernard's voice was the sleepy purr of a contented cat. Drusilla could not get the metaphor out of her head. She plucked at the rose coloured shawl to disguise her ugly mourning dress and looked questioningly at Elizabeth who inclined her head while the tight,smug smile still played infuriatingly about her lips.

There was a stuffy smell in the room of dying coals, orris root, scented comfits and something else unpleasant like overwarm bodies. Bernard stretched lazily to his feet and Drusilla smarted under the insult.

"Come, Drusilla. You can talk in front of Elizabeth. She is an old school friend of yours and a cousin of mine."

"Oh, Bernard! A distant cousin by marriage only." Bessie's lips smiled through her words and Drusilla remembered Mama's scorn of cats in backyards.

"You are part of the family, my dear," Bernard patted the plump little hand, noting the effect that had on Drusilla. "Have I not proved it?"

Darts of jealousy pierced Drusilla' heart and her eyes were full of questions she dared not give tongue to, while his desires for both women mounted and his voice thickened.

"Drusilla, you will be the first outside the family to know.

I am about to learn the arts of political management and jobbery." He enjoyed the look of incomprehension on her face. "I intend to revel in borough mongering, in pulling hidden wires, in back stair control." Still she looked amazed. "Tommy Pelham-Holles has come up trumps since he was made Duke of Newcastle. He has dealt me an ace. I am to have the living of the Parish Church of Newent St. Leonards." He took out the familiar little box and popped a comfit into his mouth. "Yes, my father will say good riddance to the Friary and the young lady boarders. All except Elizabeth, of course. You will come to the Vicarage, my dear, for how could we manage without you?" And again he patted that odious white hand. "You are like another daughter to my father, and pray don't trouble to deny it."

His voice was a caress and Elizabeth smirked while pride came to Drusilla's rescue.

"I congratulate you, Bernard. Mama will be pleased." She forced the words out of a stiff mouth, struggling to normalise her voice. "I have been into Newent for bonnet ribbons. We were passing the Friary and . . ."

Pride deserted and her misery came out in a rush.

"We had bad news today – and it was a chance to tell you. There has been a crash on the market – something to do with stock in the South Sea Company – the Spaniards are responsible I think – I don't understand it all – but we've lost everything – Uncle Peter, Mama, Squire Gordon, Dr Atterton, old Mrs. Belcher – and so many others . . ."

Her voice broke at last, furious at herself for coming out with the daft bonnet ribbons, hating herself for blurting this out in front of that minx. She could hardly believe her ears at Bernard's callous reply.

"We know, my dear Dru. We heard the news this morning. The town, the whole country, no doubt, is full of it. You are upset, naturally, my dear. Please sit down. And come along, Elizabeth, you will have to do rather better than this at the Vicarage. We will be receiving Society there, you know.

Ring for tea for Drusilla. The poor child is all in. Bonnet ribbons can be an exhausting business!"

His eyes gleamed wickedly on the ribbons and again she could almost see the extended claws, let alone feel them.

She nearly choked to see how her rival performed at the tea board. Miss Knight would have been proud of her old pupil, as the plump white hand delicately unlocked the caddy; the soft whisper of India or China; that same odious hand turning the urn and passing the Newhall cup; though she might have frowned at the leaning forward to show a soft curve of round breast from the indecent opening of the smooth, silken gown. Drusilla missed nothing, not even how Bernard had obviously started to spend on his future. Things like tea caddies and Newhall china had never before been part of the Webster furnishings, nor fires neither on such a warm day.

Bernard and Bessie were like characters in a play such as Miss Knight had once taken her to see in the Saracen's Head Yard, but their act was a charade without the relief of a final curtain and blessed reality thereafter. She had discovered a great wrong in the man she loved. The evidence was not much but she felt his guilt in her bones. She had been robbed and, though Bessie Bradford was the robber, he had been her willing accomplice. In her heart of hearts she knew this play was being acted for her alone and, though she blamed the one as much as the other, she struggled to deceive herself with excuses for him.

She sat hurt and stiff-backed throughout the ceremony, drank her tea like a young lady of rank and listened to Bernard's heartless prattle of the generosity of Tom Pelham-Holles and his agreement to the necessary alterations to the Vicarage. His constant referrals to Bessie showed Drusilla that minx had obviously been invited to see the Vicarage and its need of repair.

It was a dark, lowering, half-timbered structure of a previous century that harboured a warren of small rooms, as

Drusilla well knew, but it had, at this moment, become a highly desirable residence she would give her right arm to move into. Dr. Bernard Webster of the Parish Church Newent St. Leonard's. There was nothing to be ashamed of in such a match. Neither Mama nor Uncle Peter could possibly object to it. Not now, most especially not now. Besides, he was already Prebend of Frisby and Great Steeping. No wonder then that tea caddies and Newhall china were part of his furnishings. Memories of a school friend's brother who had said that nobody could live like a gentleman with less than five thousand a year she pushed to the back of her mind along with Bessie Bradford's twelve hundred and felt a deep sense of shame to be thinking of money when her heart was breaking.

She crumbled a little plum cake, her remaining tea standing cold in its cup. Conversation had died away along with the fire and no effort was made, either, to light up the candles. The gloom in the room matched her low spirits. The man spoke at last, his looks roving from one young woman to the other. There were just a few more words, given time, that he hoped to hear from his old friend, Tommy P.H., he said. The women were silent.

"My dear Bernard," he imitated the new Duke's mincing tones, "I shall not fail to represent you to the King himself in your true light, who I am sure will own his obligation to you for it."

Bessie's eyes glowed as she reached for the bell, summoning a maid to clear up the tea things.

Drusilla searched for a handkerchief as she bravely forced unwelcome tears into her nose. She suppressed a sigh, her eyes now upon that strumpet's cap. Had Bernard himself removed that cap as he had once removed her own toupee? Had he ruffled that smooth black hair as he had once ruffled her own chestnut curls? How hopefully she had rushed out of the carriage to rest her head upon Bernard's breast, to blurt out the pain of Mama's hard heart, expecting the comfort

Papa would have given, only to reel as from a slap to the face.

There was nothing to stay for. She suffered the uppity maidservant to shepherd her out to the carriage and, as Hobbs opened the door, she turned back to look at the drawing room window. She thought she caught Bernard's handsome shadow leaning towards Elizabeth Bradford. She thought she saw that minx slip a seductive hand under his arm. Oh, yes! This play had all the signs of being well rehearsed. They had spoken these words before, lounged in this chair, leaned on this mantle shelf, moved towards each other in exactly this way. She saw their shadows plainly despite the poor illumination of the room and the scene raised a feeling of deep and infinite sadness in Drusilla. She remembered once more her own penniless state and her rival's small fortune. She tightened the rose-coloured shawl about her, feeling mortally cold, bruised and out of breath. She was alone and afraid, the dam within her at bursting point.

That feeling was compounded soon enough as she confronted the reproachful gaze of Nellie waiting for her at home.

"For shame, Miss Drusilla. I don't know what wc bc coming to, I don't. The lies I've had to tell your Mama. Come y'ere, my chick. She do think you be in bed with a bad head, she do." And Nellie shook the rose-coloured cashmere shawl as, no doubt, she would have liked to shake Drusilla, who was saved explanation and argument by the sight of May Hobbs lingering near the stairs.

"May! Don't you hang around there, my girl. You do know where Miss Drusilla done have been and she haven't got no news for the likes of you. For shame, Miss." Nellie shooed May away with the shawl as Drusilla, with heavy heart, climbed the stair.

She went straight to the looking glass and pulled down the hated mourning dress till her bosom showed, blurred through

215

her tears, like Mama's white peaches ripening on the south facing garden wall.

"I am prettier than Elizabeth Bradford. I know I am. Sniff. Sniff. Even in this hateful black dress I am prettier than she. Sniff. And I will get him back. I will. I will. I will."

But for all that she took her sense of bewilderment to bed where hope rose and fell a dozen times that night.

He does love me. I know he does. Why was he so hateful today? And what is Elizabeth Bradford to him? She is a cousin, a distant cousin, by marriage only. Do people marry such cousins then? Uncle Peter says cousins ought not to marry. She has twelve hundred pounds and I have nothing. Why should he care about that now he is Vicar of Newent? She does not, she cannot love him like I do. I would live like a peasant for his sake. I would. Oh! If only Papa were here. Papa! If only . . .

And so she tossed and turned till the early hours brought with them a return of bad dreams.

CHAPTER 22

She awoke, late next morning, to a wet pillow, an aching throat and the knowledge it would be no use looking to Mama for comfort. Dorothy had troubles enough of her own and, with Peter gone to pieces, only herself to solve them.

Drusilla opened the little parlour door a crack. There was May staggering across the room with a huge ledger and there was her elegant Mama seated at the little secretaire with the usual sheaves of paper.

As long as ever Drusilla could remember, she had never seen her mother other than beautifully turned out. Whether enjoying a party, managing the household, walking the garden or, even now, when mourning Papa, Dorothy's luxuriant fair hair was always tidily tucked under a clean muslin cap, the faint scents of verbena and bergamot coming from her rustling skirts. Sometimes, when Drusilla looked at the perfection of her mother's toilette, she wondered if Mama had ever once been young, silly and vulnerable. Had she ever romped in the woods, kissed in dark corners, thought wicked thoughts like wishing Elizabeth Bradford would be spotted with smallpox or, better still, drop dead of a fever? Had Mama ever done bad deeds because she was head over heels in love and could not help herself?

Oh no, surely not. Mama could never have been anything else but perfectly good, her hair never rumpled, her thoughts ever under control, her actions well calculated. Still, she had had her moments, had she not? Look at her impetuosity in bringing Bernard home all those years ago. Think how skittishly she behaved at parties sometimes. Think of her joy when Papa had come home. If only Papa could come home again. And such a longing for Papa welled up inside Drusilla that she could scarcely bear the pain of it. If only . . .

She closed the parlour door and crept silently and sadly away. There was nobody in the whole world to whom she mattered first now Papa was gone and the thought laid on her heart like lead.

Dorothy shifted her position on her straight-backed, hard chair. She had fibres of steel under her veneer of quality but there were limits even to her ability to juggle with figures when her head was full of other things. She rested her quill for a moment, sent May off to the kitchen for hot chocolate and, with chin on hands, stared at Anthony's portrait on the opposite wall. She was forty two years old and had buried three new born sons and lost her husband besides. She remembered how once she had been considered the belle of the Somerset County Ball and how that attack of smallpox within the first year of marriage had robbed her of her lovely complexion as well as her baby. Still, Anthony had comforted her, the disease had done nothing to dim the brilliance of the bluest of blue eyes. A tear fell. She knew in her heart of hearts it was the most piercing, cold light in the world that shone there as often as not.

Anthony's portrait – it was as though he were alive in the room and smiling directly towards her – had been painted, along with her own, soon after their marriage, and the peripatetic artist who had knocked at their door one bright June day must have been a man of some talent for he had caught her young husband's likeness remarkably.

The vigour and alertness of a man living all his life in the open, troubling his head very little with dull things like books, having been expelled from school and sent down from Oxford, were all there on the canvas. Yet the artist had not missed the lively intelligence of the sitter, either. He had painted a man smart enough at many things, like riding well, shooting straight, dancing lightly, carrying his liquor, driving a bargain, dreaming sweet dreams.

Dorothy felt a catch in her throat as a burst of sunlight into the room, for she had allowed the shutters to be opened at last, showed up her Anthony's long legs, thick with saddle muscles. The elegant, devil-may-care thrust of the back of a hand to the side of his coat high-lighted the fine quality of cream coloured linen that lit up the sun-burned face, the deep chestnut coloured hair, for he never was nor never could be a slave to fashion, and the tawny eyes merry with devilment. The warmest eyes Dorothy had ever seen.

How those vital russet eyes, spirited and dangerous, looked into her own. Leo. Dear Leo. The very name was apt. But Leo, My Dear Heart, you threw your life away and left me bereft. She dabbed at her tears as she recalled the foolish, girlish self who had fallen hotly in love, when only fifteen years old, with a man her high nosed, land-owning family from Frome abhorred.

"He's a red headed rascallion and gamester and I'll not trust my daughter's life and happiness to such a fellow." her father had thundered.

Anthony Davison came from an old enough family but he was a younger son and a dreamer of wild dreams at that. His family had objected as much as Dorothy's for she was not an heiress and however would they manage to live? But she was constant as well as foolish and would look at no other. When plans of an elopement were discovered, the Davisons packed off their troublesome son, poste haste, to a cousin who was planting sugar in the West Indies. From there Anthony had made his way to Virginia and five years later he came back to claim the twenty year old bride who had waited for him like a faithful Penelope in spite of a father's threats and mother's pleas.

To the surprise of both families, he had come back with a small fortune made out of trading sugar and slaves and tobacco, omitting to mention the little matter of a lucky streak at cards that had won him his first shipment. He had come home, as well, with the title deeds to a parcel of land in Nottinghamshire safe in his pocket, won from a young member of the Willoughby family idling and gambling life and fortune away in the taverns of Bristol.

"Nottinghamshire? Nottinghamshire? snorted Dorothy's father, "Sounds an outlandish place to me. Who lives there?"

"All the great families you can think of, Sir. The Kingtons, the Newcastles, Pierrepoints, Hattons, Suttons, Willoughbys . . ." Anthony had an answer for everything.

"All right. All right. And this Newent St. Leonards whatever you call it – never heard of it – what goes on there?"

"Plenty of gusto, pluck and bottom!"

"What the devil does that mean in plain English?"

"It's a market town, Sir, on the River Trent where the Fosse crosses the Great North Road and it trafficks in timber, grain, hides, hops, flax, madder, malt, saffron, hoof'n horn for glue, plaster and . .

"All right. All right. That don't signify much unless you've a part in it."

"I have got me a hill – a hill with a plaster pit on one side, a wood yard at the foot and I have built us a fine house on the summit. It's a perfect site for a perfect wife. And I tell you this, Sir, our future looks rosier than your own."

That remark did nothing to endear the young man to the older who very well knew there were few bidders for unmarried, penniless daughters over twenty. If either family had reservations they held their peace and the wedding was celebrated in great style.

Dorothy could not dwell on that day. She sipped at the pretty little cup of hot chocolate. Oh, Anthony you chose to leave me. You could, you should, have stayed. She gulped the rich sweetness down.

Her parents, after all, had been rather more generous than they intended with a fine wedding and trousseau, if only a modest dowry of two hundred a year along with Nellie, a strong, healthy young woman of her own age to maid her.

They had included, as well, two useful men servants, Jacob Hobbs and his son, James, who could turn a hand to almost anything. She had felt herself rich indeed as she and her handsome husband headed the little cavalcade riding to the unknown north.

She became a girl again as she wiped a forefinger round the inside of the chocolate rich cup and licked it clean. How eagerly she had taken up her new role of bride and house-keeper. What sport it had all been to begin with. She was delighted with the two little blackamoors, along with jewels too numerous to count, Anthony had showered upon her as home-coming presents. And in no time at all he had added the brick kilns in Clay Lane and a field called Appleton Close, pronounced cluss in these strange parts. "To keep the wolf from the door, dear Lambkin," he had laughed. Such presents were quickly followed by introductions to all the great county families. How he had enjoyed introducing to her the diplomat Lord Lessington and his Lady from Park Lodge as his great friends, Robert and Margaret Hatton. Hm! Not that he cared a fig for a Lord or a Lady either but he knew how to please his Dorothy.

And if there were disappointments Dorothy forgot them in all this loving spoiling.

She remembered how he had once swept her up in his arms, carried her to the top of the house, right out on to the leads, when she had complained he had not warned her theirs was the only hill in the district.

"My dear Lambkin, if you look in that direction four miles straight as the crow flies is Mickelborough Hill close to Park Lodge; over there lies Oxton Hill and further to the south-west the Fosse is called Six Hills Road. How many hills do you need, devil take it? You have only to say the word and I'll find you another."

His tawny eyes had smiled into her own with that tender look that had caught at her heart-strings so. He held her light as a feather back to their own bedchamber to ease her gently on the great eider-down bed. One arm had cradled her head as he lowered the length of his eager body on to her own no less ardent than his. Together they had sunk into enfolding warmth and bliss.

But for all that, the land remained flat as a pancake compared with North Somerset and nothing could ever make Newent as attractive, in her eyes, as the growing, golden town of Bath. The smug River Trent, heavy with craft all shapes and sizes, was quite unlike the cascading streams she was used to but, if the people had flatter voices and sharper elbows than those she once knew, all that was nothing if she was with her Anthony.

She sighed. How grateful she was for her parents' foresight in giving her Nellie and the others. Now she was doubly thankful to have Somerset folk about her.

She sucked at a sticky finger, remembering those bitter-sweet years of early marriage. As soon as her parents had heard of her first breeding, they had sent up their second son, Peter, newly qualified physician and surgeon. Dorothy knew she owed him her life and, though he had not saved the baby, she could not bear to let him go. Dr. Peter, for his part, took to the Vale of Trent like a swan to the river and in no time at all had carved out a niche for himself among the ailments, whether real or hysterick, of the local gentry. Neither Dorothy nor Anthony wanted him to leave and he was more than happy to stay.

Soon there was another baby on the way and if they were disappointed when the child, to be baptised Drusilla Mary, bawled her way into the world, then nobody showed it – certainly not Nellie who vented all her own frustrated maternal instincts on the squalling bundle. They all knew there would be other babies and so there were, but they died with regular monotony in spite of Dr. Peter. Dorothy became listless and Anthony restless. At the rate they were spending their fortune the time had come to make another and off he went.

In twenty two years of marriage, apart from those first few happy years, Dorothy had known him for only a few months at a time on no more than a half-dozen separate occasions.

She wiped her fingers on a snippet of lace and sighed again. Somehow, along the years, that girl from Somerset had slipped away to become this woman, now a widow, who counted money as speedily as any man; a woman whose pulse quickened at the sight of a pack of cards as though of a lover; who acted as she generalissimo over all her affairs; a woman who felt the whole world on her shoulders. She knew in her heart that she had managed for so long alone that Anthony's death, apart from his money, would have little effect on her life. Her one fear was that Peter, in his present foolishness, would do something stupid like taking a wife. She might miss him rather more, for all his tiresome hobby-horses, than she would miss her Anthony.

As for the pressing matter of money – well . . .

She shifted on the hard chair tucked up to the little secretaire that had once been her mother's. It was the place where she had always cast her accounts, decided menus, answered letters. Now she looked down at the clean double pages, blank except for the two headings: Assets and Liabilities, in her clear hand.

She scratched the side of her stippled cheek with a new quill and considered.

The first blow to be got over was that her small dowry was lost, for all Anthony's fine words that that was her very own and never to be used in speculation. In fact the only cash not touched was the little settled on Drusilla at her baptism. And it was very little. Anthony always meant to do more. There had seemed plenty of time. Poor Drusilla.

She looked at the two headings again. On which side should she put down the house? It cost a fortune to run and she must start pruning somewhere. The servants. Should she start with the servants? Well, this job was too big and this desk too small.

"Come along, May. Help me to move this stuff to the dining room. We can spread ourselves there."

Whatever is the matter with the girl, she thought, as May struggled with heavy ledgers, looking fit to faint. Why did she look so washed out these days? She must ask Peter for a tonic for the child and wasted not another thought in that direction. Her own problems were too pressing.

I must shift for myself, she thought, perusing her papers, underlining assets, subtracting debits. She was surprised to find her heart lifting. She was not beaten. She could manage. With Anthony's restless ways, she could see now, her life had never been anything but precarious. No doubt after each fall he would have picked himself up, dusted himself down and laboured up to the top again as he always did. But she was getting too old for such capers. Now she realised how for years she had hidden her sharp intelligence from the world, hidden it behind such foolishness as dropped eyelids, swaying hoops, fluttering fans and false pleasantries. Only occasionally had her ancestors' plain common sense come to the fore, as when she had managed her own brick kilns and managed them well.

A triumphant smile cushioned her cheeks. She would enjoy scraping the barrel, putting her resources to work, building things up, as her own parents had had to do. Not so high as Anthony, of course, but high enough. Retrench was a word she had heard her own father use and she was equal to it.

First she would keep up appearances, in fact she must, for Drusilla's sake. If the house could not go, then other things must. She would sell the field called Appleton Close. The income from it was negligible, a little grazing and prize fighting booths once a year was all it was ever used for. Perhaps it could go for building. That devil, Jenison, was borrowing money to buy up all the odd parcels of land that he could lay hands on but whether he paid a fair price was another matter. Peter must pull himself together and make some inquiries for her. The money that made she would put into the brick kilns and wood yard. She thought hard over the plaster pit. It was so profitable. It would clear her debts though reduce her income. And it was on the other side of the hill across the Boston Road. Yes. She should get a good price for that.

A knife turned in her heart. How proud Anthony had been of owning the entire hill and here she was proposing to get rid of near half of it. Well, needs must . . .

She would keep up the gardens immediately surrounding the house but the rest could go over to scrub. And Capel had better earn his keep. Their land was not much but they must live off it if they could, conveniently forgetting the game laws in her enthusiasm. And as for the army of gardeners, she wondered whatever they did with themselves all day long. Well, she would offer them work in the extended kilns and wood yard and if that did not suit them they could go. The King's new plans to force unemployed hands into the army would do them, nor her neither, no harm at all. And those that stayed must work harder. She wanted that ice house kept full to its roof.

And inside the big house the maids could spend less time with polishing cloths and beeswax and more with needle and thread. Both she and Drusilla, and servants too, must take better care of their clothes. There must be more turning, retrimming and dyeing. Not enough for anyone to notice, of course, though that jumped up sister of Matthew Jenison had eyes like gimlets. And if the servants used their heads, they would keep their mouths shut - the first to clack would be the first to go. She could rely on Nellie for that.

The carriages? Oh no, not the carriages. Not when she thought how many hours Peter and Anthony and the old coach builder had consulted together over wheel size and axle width on account of the hill. Nobody else had carriages like the Davison carriages, not even the Hattons and their hill was nearly as big. Old Hobbs, Young Hobbs and Little James could pull their hose up. There was plenty to do with paint-brush and varnish. She would let them know there was to be no more extravagance and she would expect better maintenance for less expenditure. Though there was no doubt this hill played the very devil with axles and wheels and horses as well. She might sell a horse or two. She would ask Peter about that.

Peter. Oh, Lord. He had to be got out of his hole somehow. Well, he could sell Mulberry House and come to live up Beacon Hill. That would be a saving if ever there was one. He wouldn't like it of course, but would have to lump it if he were to pay off his debts. That way she could keep an eye on him and curb his popinjay ways. And he could get rid of the blackamoor. Nothing but an extra useless mouth to feed. They had been fetching a good price, though that was bound to drop now. Still, she might persuade that old fool Markham. If not, they could advertise in the Weekly Courant.

And Drusilla? She made up her mind. As soon as they decently could they must have a party, a gathering or assembly of some sort. Not lavish. Nobody would expect it while they were still in mourning. Pity Drusilla did not look too well in black. She had been neglecting her duty towards Drusilla. Goodness, she had been married and buried three babies at Drusilla's age. Well, one thing was for sure, that muffin-guzzling old aunt of Lady Reville's was quite right when she said the misery of marriage was worth enduring for the pleasure of widowhood. To be one's own mistress – that was the thing. Certainly, Drusilla must marry.

She sat bolt upright and quite still, struck by the gradual realisation she could manage everything perfectly – better than Anthony in fact. With Anthony at home she had no doubt things would soon be chaotic again as one project was left undone to make way for another. Now she would have everything ordered and orderly as her father had done in Somerset so long ago.

Bolland the overseer could go. She would be her own man and she would be damned before she changed her silver tea kettle for a tin pot.

With the idea she was capable came a sudden rush of pride and a desire to prove it, to make money and to make that make more. But tish! No wild dreams now. No talk of estates and villages and strawberry beds. Nothing but plain common sense and hard work. Never, never, never – she would never have to ask for or account to somebody else for money.

The pen scraped on until her wrist ached and fingers cramped, her mouth set hard in concentration. A draught of cool air hit the room as Nellie came in.

"Miss Dor'thy, you'm been at it for long enough," only Nellie would have dared to say that, "and May is tired fit to drop. Dinner is ready and Lord Lessington's man has called with this." She held out the familiar stiff cream coloured card of Lessington stationery.

Dorothy opened the folded sheet. She and Drusilla were invited to a reception at Park Lodge. There would be supper and dancing. Those rumours flying all round the county, they must be true. Robert Hatton had come out of retirement at last. He was offering himself for parliament. It would be an electioneering party. Everybody would be there. She would not miss it for the world. There was a deal of comfort in the invitation that brought a gleam to the eye. Society had not forgotten her. She still counted for something. After all, there was nothing to be got out of a widow at election time, and a widow of no fortune, at that.

She raised her eyes to Anthony's portrait and almost smiled. She dipped her quill in the pot and scored through her notes on party costs. No need to spend a penny. Let Robert Hatton do it all. He could afford it more than she.

CHAPTER 23

At last the unbecoming mourning clothes were folded away, laid to rest between layers of dried verbena and bergamot, fond memories of husband and father alongside.

All Dorothy's waking hours went into the management of her affairs, the paying of debts, the pruning of extravagance, the slow steady mounting of assets. She now settled her own mind and her own life and more than anything else she struggled to hide her shame in the keeping up of appearances. What was it Peter had said, though whether he were in his cups or no she could not remember, "We're in a modern world, my dear, a world of banks, cheques, budgets, Friendly Societies, share-jobbing – though devil take that after what it's done to us – newspapers, coffee houses, clubs, magazines, microscopes and these new fangled contraptions called parasols Lord Middleton's cousin brought back from China – not to mention water-closets!"

Tish! The world was going forward and she determined to go with it, dragging her family after.

As for Drusilla, she thought of nothing but how she could win back her Bernard, but whereas Dorothy's sound Somerset Fletcher genes conspired to her advantage, Drusilla had the drawback of her father's blood. Forgotten memories locked away with old mourning clothes could not get away from that.

Now, in her bedroom on a late summer afternoon, she held up the peacock silk she would wear tonight at the Park Lodge ball. It was not new, to be sure, but she had worn it only once before; Bernard had not seen it and nothing suited her better.

She smiled in satisfaction. The brilliant mixture of blue shot with green was exactly right. Blue was her favourite colour and did wonders for her eyes and the green, she knew, would have its effect upon Bernard. She lowered her lids and prayed for good fortune. "Please God . . ."

Before her Amen was out Nellie was in the room to shake out crisp petticoats, brush up a pair of green velvet slippers, search the drawers for clean hose.

"'Twill do you and your Mama a power of good," she prattled. "'Tis time you did have some enjoyment after what you done have been through. And mayhap you'm be meeting new friends, Miss Drusilla . . ."

And Drusilla, holding a looking glass to the window to see her complexion the better, could not help another smile. A month ago that remark would have provoked an angry flush to her cheeks for she knew what lay behind it. But not today. Today she was happy, light-hearted almost. No wonder Bernard had been cool of late. Neither black stuff nor wishy-washy lavender had ever suited her and who in his right senses would want the drab, peaky girl she had been lately? Certainly not a beau as handsome and eligible as Bernard. She swung back the chestnut coloured hair that tugged at Nellie's heart-strings so. Begone dull care! Tonight she would be gay at all costs, flirt a little with Markham's Irish nephews if they were worth the bother, make Bernard jealous, sweep him off his feet with this new Drusilla.

Nellie rattled on. Nobody knew Drusilla better than she. 'I can read you like a book, Miss Drusilla,' she would say, a remark that infuriated the girl, knowing full well poor Nellie could scarce spell out the alphabet. 'I'd like to see you try, you old addle-pate,' she would mutter between tight white teeth. Now, without preamble, Nellie launched into attack to prove her point.

"They do say as how he done have over-reached himself this time. Not a wench can they get to stay at the Vicarage. There be many a father and sweetheart and husband and all

229

as wouldn't mind getting transported to the plantations to get at him. But clever as a cart-load of monkeys he be. And how he do keep in the Duke's good books be the biggest mystery in Christendom."

She was in full spate.

"'Tis just amazing as how living after living, appointment after appointment do keep dropping his way. Just like apples to orchards and more coming every day. They do say as how Sir George Markham might make him Steward of all his lands in Lincolnshire. And that must be worth a pretty penny on top of . . ."

"Tish, Nellie!" Dorothy's expression was forever on Drusilla's lips these days. She shook out her long hair and brushed till the red-gold strands shone among the gleam of rich brown, knowing full well what effect the candlelight and thumb cut glass would have tonight. She remembered how, like Papa, Bernard had hated to see a woman's natural hair hidden beneath a toupée, how once he had rumpled her own hair with the softest yet strongest of fingers. A thrill stirred her body.

"Nellie! That's only Newent gossip."

But it's true her heart sang. He is Vicar of here, Prebend of there, Steward of this, Treasurer of that and he has published his translations of French sermons and had the wit to dedicate them to Sir George Markham, a master stroke if ever there was one. With both Newcastle and Markham behind him there would be no stopping his climb up the ladder. Why, his income must be sky high. Her own lack could no longer matter and by the same token Bessie Bradford's twelve hundred was of no consequence either.

Nellie pursed her lips as she near brushed the nap off the little green velvet slippers and proved her ability at thought reading whether she could make head or tail of the alphabet or no.

"And as for that Miss Bessie Bradford, she do think her body every self and all over Newent people do call her Dr.

Webster's tally woman, the hussy. And I was talking to Sir Matthew Jenison's man only yesterday and you just listen to what he did say, Miss Drusilla. He said Bessie was a good girl till that, that Bernard Webster," she spat out the name like a bite from an unripe plum, "that Vicar of Newent did get his cloven hoof over her! There's a thing to say now. He b'eant good enough for you, Miss Drusilla, and there be the truth if it now. Huh! Shining his lanthorn at every maid in the county! And none so deaf as them that won't y'ear, nor so blind as won't see neither."

Drusilla's mouth tightened at the mention of Sir Matthew Jenison as she remembered that old man and his nasty kisses.

"Pot calling kettle black." The words were out before she could stop them. Just when she wanted to be carefree and light-hearted, Nellie had to start this fuss.

"Huh!" snorted Nellie with a look that overstepped frontiers. "I don't know about no black kettle but if he went for a chimney sweep, he'd come out a miller."

Drusilla picked up her glass again to admire what she saw. She would gamble everything on her own beauty tonight. She thought of her rival's sleek, plump face and smiled as she pulled down her ruffled modesty vest to show off more of her round white bosom. It's the best part about me, she thought, so why should I hide it? Not too much like the hated and hateful Bessie Bradford who would look like a pouter pigeon tonight, if she is there, which I hope not; nor too little like Arabella Reville who, no doubt, at this very moment is stuffing lambswool into her bodice.

Nellie watched her shrewdly. Really, the child's Mama should make her to see sense. But there was no understanding Miss Dor'thy these days. The shocks must have been too much for her. Heaven forbid she do end the same way as Dr. Peter. But no, she didn't think so, for Dr. Peter be too soft and Miss Dor'thy too hard. She sighed. What wouldn't she give to be under Somerset skies again?

231

To see the sweep of they hills, the lush meadows and the golden stone houses.

She glanced out of the window, wishing hope to reality, but what caught her eye was the yard at the back of the house where maids drew water from the black iron pumps. She watched May Hobbs put down two heavy buckets and awkwardly straighten her back, her face creased with pain. Poor May, looking for all the world as if her heart had been put through the mangle. Nellie noted the contours of the maid's full figure and turned back to Drusilla.

"'Tis a pity our poor little May's brothers are so much the younger," shooting a sharp glance at her charge as she put down the slippers. But Drusilla threw back her long hair and brushed harder than ever to fill up her ears with the sweep of the brush.

"They do say as how . . ."

"Tish! Pooh! Pish!" exploded Drusilla. "They say, they say, they say! Who are 'they', in Heaven's name? Now, Nellie, you are not to spoil my evening. Let us talk about Bernard's good points. Is he not generous?"

"I dare say as how he do be generous when it do suit him, Miss Drusilla. I y'eard tell as how he did give May Hobbs a new white petticoat . . ."

"Can he help it if every wench throws herself at him?" Drusilla's colour rose.

"Not only wenches neither. They say . . ."

"If I hear you say 'they say' once more, Nellie, I shall scream." She threw the hairbrush down on to her bed. "Now tell the maids to bring up gallons of hot water, lots and lots, for I mean to be really beautiful tonight. Where are the rags to do up my hair? And don't pull this time or I'll tell Mama how I caught you sampling her eau de toilette this morning."

"Miss Drusilla, you wouldn't do no such thing. You'm a mischievous monkey. Come y'ere my chick," Nellie's voice took on a wheedling tone. "Next full moon, my chick, I'll cut your hair and you shall have a Duffy's Elexir and a Dr.

232

Peter's Powder. And if you do want to look beautiful tonight, so you shall."

And so she did. The silk peacock gown shimmered in the candlelight, its sheen rivalled only by that of her red-gold hair and her luminous blue eyes. She wore no jewels out of deference to Papa but neither did she need them.

The Hatton residence at Park Lodge was not large enough for company to assemble and be announced in orderly fashion so that by the time Drusilla and her mother arrived there was an exciting confusion of thronging guests in the outer hall leading off the main salon. Yes, the whole county must be here, she thought. The house seemed fit to burst with the old and the grey, the portly middle-aged and the beautiful young. Oh, the young, so many handsome young men and women, Lord! She had not seen so many in a hundred years, not since before Papa died and that must be an age since.

Surely that was Biddy Hatton with her new husband.

How fine she looked. She was pleased for Biddy. An odd thought crossed her mind briefly. How might she herself have fared if, like the Hattons, she had lost a mother instead of a father? She used to feel such pangs for poor Biddy. No Mama and a Papa quite broken up by the death of his only boy. But look at her now. Still, though the man at her side was the future Duke of Denston he was as bald as a coot and could not compare with her Bernard. And where was Bernard?

Old Mrs. Henry Belcher bore down upon Mama leading her off to a group of matrons gathering for gossip. Drusilla was left standing alone, yet jostled on each side, under the arched entrance to the salon where, on a clear day, it was said, you could look from the west door straight through the house to see the spire of Newent's Parish Church, now Bernard's church, framed in the opposite doorway. And straight as the crow flies, just four miles away, was that other hill – Beacon Hill – where Beacon House stood in perfect alignment with church and Park. Beacon House, Beacon Hill, Bernard had so often said it was an ancient site. The thought lifted her spirits as she felt herself part of this exclusive assembly of exclusive company.

She was happy, confident, expectant and where was Bernard?

Tinkles of glass, rustles of silk, clatterings of heels, harmless chattering and spiteful gossiping buzzed and floated through hall and salon. Occasionally an odd word pierced her brain but most went unheeded. She was too busy searching the throng for Bernard to notice the tall stately girl partnered by a proud-looking young man.

"Who is she, dear brother?"

"Nobody you need trouble yourself about, my dear Liza."

"Oh?" The girl's eyebrows arched in surprise. "Let me be the judge of that, Winchelsea. She's beautiful and her gown the finest so far."

"There are rumours about her and the Vicar of Newent," came the short reply.

"Another one?" The girl laughed softly. "That's the third tonight. You must introduce me to this amorous cleric, my dear brother."

"I will not."

She tilted her head towards him and was almost flirtatious for there was barely fifteen months between them; they had been constant companions as children and still enjoyed each other's company.

"Come, Beau," she teased, "I'll practise my ice-house act upon him, just to show we maids don't all of us melt under his hot breath."

Lord Winchelsea scowled and led his sister into the salon to seek out Tommy Pelham-Holles who had got his dukedom at last along with a grand daughter of the great Marlborough for wife.

Had Drusilla heard those words how her cheeks would have burned. But her mind was on Bernard and unluckily she

234

did not. They might have done more than all Nellie's heavy-handed admonishments to warn her of the dangerous path she was treading.

She caught sight of the Duke of Newcastle almost as soon as the Winchelseas. One could hardly miss such an oddity in that grand assembly, with his full-bottomed black wig, that must be out of date by at least twenty years, near hiding his ugly face. Certainly the biggest wig here in more ways than one. Still, what a catch for Lord Lessingham. 'Congratulations, my dear Robert, you have hooked a big one,' would have been Papa's mischievous comment. No wonder there were rumours about the Duke being the bete-noir of the Hanoverians, frightening them all to death, shuffling about their palaces, eyes at every keyhole, ears on every whisper, redealing the cards to suit himself, manipulating every event, fattening himself on monopolies, preferments and commissions as his uncle had done before him. He was in the county to oversee the refurbishing of his inheritance, Nottingham Castle, and it was whispered he wrote by every post to his dearest Henrietta who had gone back to Sussex.

It was even said the King supported him against his own son, the Prince of Wales. Whatever had happened to that old maxim about blood being thicker than water? It was one the Hanoverians had never heard of if gossip be true. No wonder 'go to Hanover' had replaced the old quip 'go to Trent'. And that there could ever be a close friendship between the new Duke and Bernard, one could not imagine. The attraction of opposites she supposed. Her eyes still raked the crowd for that handsome figure, inches taller than most other gentlemen now Papa was gone, that winning countenance, that silver voice, that quick perception with its lively imagination, to say nothing of the head for figures that brought apples to orchards as Nellie so often complained.

She could recite his achievements by heart and often did: Vicar of Newent, Rector of Frisby and Great Steeping and

235

Winthorpe, Prebend of Lincoln, Master of St. Leonard's Hospital, Chaplain to a regiment. There was no stopping him.

All the while she greeted this guest or that with the most radiant of smiles, the most charming of nods and the prettiest use of her fan to disguise the search for. her lover. Tonight she determined to be gay at all costs, to win Bernard's heart and keep it. Would he introduce her and Mama to the great Duke? Where was Mama? And where, oh where was Bernard?

Her heart leapt at the sight of him. Yes, that was he, that tall handsome one over there, leaning against a pillar, his long vest finer, his cravat crisper . . . Remember your resolutions, Drusilla, don't stare too hard. Make him seek you out. Will him to look your way. Her heart sank as easily as it had arisen a moment before. Surely, that was Bessie Bradford beside him and, surely, he did not need to smile so amiably in her direction. Her eyes filled with fear as that – that woman – that strumpet looked straight at her. She tilted her head, summoning all her superior feelings of breeding and beauty to bolster her courage so that Bessie's eyes were the first to slide.

She noted the soft, plump hand playing with earrings, with necklace, now resting possessively on Bernard's arm. A flame of jealousy flicked through her body. Now Bernard was introducing the Duke, bowing and scraping, Bessie curtseying. Drusilla's heart bled with pain. Oh, yes, there was no doubt his eyes flashed. But not for her. How could he smile like that? Why did he not come to her? They belonged to each other, surely he knew that. But nobody else knew, certainly not Bessie Bradford. Nor all these people, talking, laughing, fluttering, quizzing. Now he was turning to Sir George Markham. It should be me. It should be me her heart cried.

She set her teeth behind her fan and willed him to look her way, but before her power had time to work she heard her name called by Mama.

She turned obediently as she always did. Mama was near the great staircase with a group of strangers – and a strange group, at that, she thought. Wherever had Mama found such oddities? A girl of her own age and two young men appeared hanging on Mama's every word. The girl was the oddest of the three creatures, surely. The poor thing had no notion what to do with her fan, dropped her dorothy bag, clutched at her skirts, everything about her in confusion from the wisp of dark hair peeping grotesquely from a toupée askew to a buckleless slipper. The deep red cheeks, the bright brown eyes and big white teeth reminded Drusilla of she could not say what. Something about the girl's appearance, not her awkwardness or lack of fashion, but rather her complete lack of self-consciousness made Drusilla want to laugh, when she least felt like laughing.

The girl was a horse, she decided, a filly not yet broken in. And the two young men like peas in a pod must be of the same family. Colts, thought Drusilla, amended to dolts as Mama made the formal introductions to the Ogle family, Markham's Irish connexions. Ah, now she understood Mama's interest in the trio.

Miss Bridget Ogle dropped her fan yet again, her two brothers cracked heads as they bent to retrieve it. The young filly blushed puce with pleasure, showed her large teeth and whinnied. Her brothers, Edmund and Thomas, neighed, tossed heads, stamped feet and flicked tails.

From a far corner of the salon came the scrape of fiddles tuning up for a dance. A sudden flurry to find partners ensued with much laughing, protestations, delights and disappointments. The Duke turned to Miss Ogle who dropped her fan for the hundred and first time at least. Sir George Markham took Bessie Bradford's arm. She could scarce refuse that honour scoffed Drusilla to herself, thanking her good fortune she had not caught the old roué's eye.

Both Ogle brothers turned towards her. They did everything together, these two. She smiled prettily without favour. She might be merry with malmsey wine but not merry enough to forget her resolution. She cocked her head prettily to catch the sound of the fiddlers.

"It's a jig they're calling," she said, thanking the Lord the evening would be a country romp with neither minuet nor gavotte to be seen nor heard.

If Bernard was in line for the stewardship of the Markham estates and if it be true that Markham's Irish relatives had been named as his heirs – well then! She proffered an arm to one Ogle, though whether Thomas or Edmund she neither knew nor cared, while Mama took the other. With a certain amount of triumph she met Bernard's eye.

"You will promise me Haste to the Wedding," he said.

"It depends," she replied craftily, "whether that comes before or after supper."

"In that case, Drusilla, I must take the first dance after supper."

"Oh, that pleasure has already been given to Mr. Ogle." She turned her brightest smile in the Ogles' direction.

"Your Grace, Milords and Gentlemen – take your partners," and away they whirled. Amazing, the Ogle fellow, whichever he was, could dance! He was neither colt nor dolt as he led her easily through the sets, commanding the leading fiddler to keep things flying. One more round and another and another. Floor and shoes together were polished like ice, everyone, even the most elegant of ladies, in danger of a slide and a fall. Her hand was taken so many times she lost count and was almost giddy as wide-hooped gowns dipped and swayed like sails at sea and toupéed heads bobbed up and down like porpoises riding a heavy swell. Like most other young women on the floor she had never seen the sea but she had heard so many tales from Papa and had a lively imagination.

She resolved neither to look in Bernard's direction nor to

be available if he approached. Let him stew with his Bessie Bradford. That minx had not had so many partners after all. She knew she herself was beautiful and the filly and two colts were awkward and odd only in each other's company. Apart, there seemed nothing she need be ashamed of. They were Markham's relatives, after all, and of higher rank than any broken draper's son, Vicar of Newent, or no.

One call followed another. Mama had danced three times with the great Duke himself, and was in high good humour.

"I love a mob," he called out, leading the gallopede. "I've always wanted to head one meself," and whirled Dorothy round the faster.

"And now you can say that you have, Your Grace," laughed Dorothy, almost breathless.

It was during the lull after supper that Drusilla heard her mother make yet another introduction, not so much an introduction as the renewal of an old acquaintance. She extended her hands with genuine pleasure to her old school mistress, Miss Knight. And what a pleasure, too, to meet Mr. William Knight again. Oh, yes, she knew he had called at Beacon House now and then but she was so rarely at home nowadays. There was so much to do. Visiting and so forth, you know, though they had been in mourning these past months. Was he still being coerced to Miss Knight's At Homes? Oh no, now he had been given the living of North Heskham and was too busy by far. Did she remember their many earnest conversations on Wednesday afternoons? Yes. Most certainly she did. And what a long time ago it seemed, to be sure. Oh yes, she still had opinions of many things, but they were not so easily practised now. With Papa gone and Uncle Peter – well, Uncle Peter, perhaps you have heard, is not quite himself yet. There was the crash, you know . . .

"Not that that made so much difference," Dorothy hastily cut in. "We have pretty well recovered."

Drusilla smiled her prettiest smile again. Oh yes, most certainly you may call. We are out of mourning now and are at home always on a Tuesday. The Ogle family were pleased to hear that too. Could they call? Bridget would be staying with Uncle Markham for several months, though Tommy and Eddie would be returning to Ireland within a few weeks. Oh yes, you can all call.

It was an age since Dorothy and Drusilla had felt so lively. Fiddlers fiddled, hoops swayed, periwigged heads dipped and rose till at last clocks chimed a late hour and candles burned low. Musicians flagged. Gentlemen yawned. Their feet ached and they were shooting or coursing or hunting tomorrow. The ladies might hanker to dance until dawn but servants, cloaks and carriages were called for. It was time to depart.

They hardly needed the wraps and foot warmers so solicitously prepared by Young Hobbs, forty five if he were a day, as they rolled back to Beacon Hill.

Dorothy mulled over the evening, admitting Robert Hatton's ability at giving a ball. The excellence of all the arrangements was commented upon. She could not have done better herself. He must have gotten over his sorrows at last and was quite the handsomest man there, though they had seen little enough of him. She smiled a wry smile. She must remember. A widow, after all, was no great prize at election time. Still, as far as great parties go, Margaret Hatton, had she been alive, could have done no better. They had stayed to the end for Drusilla's sake. She hoped Drusilla appreciated that. It could have been a trial but they had carried it off. And she must have a new cap. They seemed to be growing larger every week and lappets quite passe. She could certainly afford to do that since nobody, she was sure, had noticed her retrimmed gown. She smiled a satisfied smile. Nobody in this world, apart from Nellie, was as useful as little May Hobbs.

Drusilla herself was leaning back, very still, eyes closed. She was mentally underlining her resolution. She would ignore Bernard. She could afford that risk now she had made

240

new friends. The Ogles would be more than useful and, in any case, she liked them. And Mr. William Knight too. She had been much admired, there was no doubt of it. The new Duke of Newcastle had even told her she had a voice as beautiful as good old Queen Anne. Still, her resolution was a risk after all and one she braced herself to take. With both body and soul compromised she must take it, if that would force the issue and get her a declaration.

How Mama rattled on.

Dorothy was arranging a party, on a smaller scale than before, naturally. She still had a well-stocked cellar. Food would not be a problem either. They were still pretty well self-sufficient and tradesmen could always wait, at least until Drusilla was settled.

Drusilla wriggled her toes against the foot warmer as she had always done since a child, at least since her legs were long enough, when recalling the pleasurable. She was ready and willing to be deceived.

Bernard had noticed her popularity – he must have done. She had him where she wanted him. Come the end of October she might even be Mrs. Bernard Webster in the new house he had started to build in Baldertongate. And quite right too. That old Vicarage on the Mount was nowhere near good enough. By Christmas she and Bernard could be giving their first party. What bliss not to have to think of money, nor to have Mama forever carping about this or that, though she had been cheerful enough tonight, had she not? To be one's own mistress in one's own home, that was what every woman wanted. She hugged herself inside at that happy thought.

"How the Marquis of Welby reminded me of Papa. Upon my honour he did." said Mama. "With hardly a hair on his head he scorned to wear such a thing as a wig. Though your father had a fine head of hair, to be sure. And as for Miss Ogle . . ."

"Mama, when one gets to the bottom of her, Miss Bridget

Ogle is . . ."

"I never got to the bottom," laughed Dorothy with a rare flash of humour. "The top was enough."

Drusilla smiled. Mama had enjoyed the evening as much as she.

Their content fled as soon as the carriage turned up the drive for home. Why so many lights about the place? The corners of Dorothy's mouth turned down. Tish! When the cat's away . . .

Cold air hit their feet as soon as they touched the ground. They looked up at the house, sensing a trouble there. Dr. Peter met them in the hall and both of them caught something of his old air of authority. Drusilla's gaze was riveted upon his shirt splashed with red. Red what? Not blood, surely not. Whatever was happening?

"Go straight to bed, Drusilla." Dorothy's voice was as strong as steel. She had shaken off one mood into another.

"What's amiss, brother?"

"Damn that Parson, sister. He nearly cost one of your maids her life. Young May Hobbs will never draw another bucket of water nor do any other heavy work either. Now she needs all her strength to last the night. The child, a boy it was, is dead. Well, poor lass, she's saved herself the trouble of a bastardy summons or us the bother of a knobstick wedding. I . . ."

"Sh! Don't let Drusilla hear of it."

"Come to your senses, Dorothy. I'd as lief see my niece wed to a footman as to that serpent we nourished in our bosoms. Mark my words – he'll be the ruin of our Drusilla."

"Peter, you're drunk."

"And so might you be if you'd seen what I've seen tonight." He helped himself to more brandy and invited her to do the same.

"Without a dowry worth speaking of, Drusilla has no great hopes. Webster's intentions are not honourable, any fool can see that, Anthony would have seen it. He's a lustful maniac and the only things that interest him are sex and money and power, and in that order too. And I would not see her married to a fool like either Tom or Eddie Ogle for all their promise of Markham's money.

Oh, don't be so flabbergasted," as Dorothy's jaw dropped. "I know they were at the Hatton's tonight. Markham himself told me. Seems he has a taking for Drusilla and would welcome her into the family. I should just think he would too. Well, let me tell you, what that family needs is a little blood letting to reduce their mangy corpuscles and I'll not be a party to Drusilla providing them with our good fresh blood."

"Tish!" Dorothy was too stunned to find another word.

"The Vicar of North Heskham, is looking for a wife. Consider him."

"The Vicar of North Heskham, the brother of the school mistress!" Dorothy's voice was scornful.

"The Vicar of North Heskham. The younger son of Thomas Knight. No money, of course, but breeding, and, more to the point, as I told you years ago, scholarship too. I recommend him. You don't want an old maid on your hands do you? We must get her married before she marries herself. Leave it to me, Dorothy." His voice softened. "I will see Drusilla is safely wed before the year is out, upon my honour, I will."

Dorothy stared at the blood on Peter's shirt and felt sick.

"I must go to May," she said. "Is Nellie there?"

She thanked God Peter had not been well enough to attend the Park Lodge ball and thanked Him again he was well enough to shift in a crisis.

CHAPTER 24

Dr. Peter did not stick by his promise made on the night of the Park Lodge ball and Drusilla did not keep her brave resolution either.

Within weeks she was meeting Bernard in strange places by design, or by accident, in St. Leonard's vestry, in the woods at home, in the little parlour when Dorothy was not there, even in carriages. Once they met in a deserted corner of the church yard where a funnelling wind had whirled under her cloak and through her skirts, cutting her ankles, biting at mitten-clad fingers, nipping her nose till she was forced to cling to a headstone for support, her hair all over the place. He, in his turn, had to hold fast to both hat and coat and whatever he mouthed at her she could not hear. That gale matched her feeling that lifted her off her feet and forced open her mouth to snatch her very breath away. His feeling for her was altogether another matter, a calculation as strong and cold as steel.

There followed two or more years of torture for Drusilla. She was on the rack, pulled both ways at once.

As far as the world could see, so she thought, her social life had settled into a round of visiting and being visited. She met young men by the dozen, and eligible men at that, openly attracted by her beauty and even to her own true self. On closer acquaintance some of them were afraid of her. They labelled her 'bookish' and cantered off to dip their toes in shallower waters. Even the bravest replaced one another with rapidity as soon as Drusilla's name was mentioned to their formidable Mamas. Their fickleness, which she did not notice anyway, was tempered by the constancy of her three stalwarts; Tommy and Eddie Ogle whenever they were in England and not to be considered apart, Mr. William Knight whenever he could be spared from the serious business of parochial duties and Bernard Webster whenever he chose to take himself from other engagements.

"You'm wishing your life away, Miss Drusilla," counselled Nellie but Drusilla was in no mood to listen.

She had the sense of feeling deeply and living dangerously in hiding things from Mama, from Uncle Peter and Nellie, especially from Nellie, since she, the old spinster, was the most watchful. She became a practised liar but she was not happy. Her social rounds, her life at home, her meetings with Bernard she struggled to keep in separate compartments, like teas in a caddy, but, at any time, when discussing earnestly with Mr. William Knight, giggling foolishly with Bridget Ogle, being falsely flirtatious with Tom and Eddie or especially when suffering from Nellie's carping and Dorothy's indifference, then forbidden recollections of his fingers expertly unleashing her clothing, searching out her secret places would leap up to torment her. Meetings that enlivened the plain fare of her life had become an addiction she craved to conquer.

She danced at the wedding of her old school friend, Hester Pilbeam, and looked forward to her own, still in a fog of self-deception.

Dorothy, discovering that keeping their heads above water without Anthony's regular shipments was a wearisome business, never settled, was still closeted in the little parlour. Day after day she spent with ledgers and quill, face screwed up with effort, tongue between teeth, pondering this, pruning that. She troubled herself sick whether to apply for the proposed new turnpike rights of the Boston Road – she would kick herself if somebody else beat her to it and made a fortune. Whether to sell her jewels or pawn them and even whether to pack up and return to Somerset, nagged at her day and night.

She would think about Drusilla tomorrow. In the meantime she was fighting off as big a temptation as her daughter's. The card table offered such a chance of solving all problems.

As for Dr. Peter, he had acquiesced to the suggestion of selling Mulberry House to live with his sister and niece with alacrity and a thankfulness that quickly evaporated as he realised they were dull as ditch company. Drusilla had her own life and friends and no time at all for the companionable talks he had so looked forward to, the mulling over of magazines, periodicals, lampoons and libels. Dorothy was forever tucked up to that damnable desk, scheming how to cut off a piddling farthing here or trim a farting ha'penny there. She even turned up her nose at a pack of cards and threatened him with the workhouse if he as much as laid a single penny. He marvelled at her resistance.

It was easier to stay at home with the Weekly Courier and a brandy bottle than to ride into Newent each day to the White Harte Inn waiting for patients that rarely came. Dammit, a man needed some excitement in life and it was while he was pouring out this and that to cure himself of a brandy head he found his cure-all for boredom. Now he spent as much time as Dorothy behind a closed door, measuring here, topping up there and if the smell of juniper berries, eucalyptus drops, liquorice and balsam that seeped under his door kept him happy and sober then what did it matter? And if now and then he left home at dawn, with saddle bags bulging, to trot back at dusk with the jingle jangle of golden guineas in his pockets then Dorothy never mentioned it – for, indeed, she hardly noticed. Though Anthony, wherever he was, might have turned over and smiled a 'told you so' smile.

When Drusilla heard of the wedding of Arabella Reville she set about planning her own. Her self-delusion was complete.

Only Nellie sucked in her cheeks, pursed up her lips and shook her head at how far the family had fallen as, one early morning in late summer, she busied herself in Drusilla's bedchamber. Dear – dear. If only Miss Dor'thy had time for accounts and Miss Drusilla as well. Though nobody do know of the struggle she done have had to keep things together, Lord knows. She tossed nightgowns and shifts on to a pile of mending for May. Still, any caring Mama would watch such a chick like a good hen and get her safely married off before gossip and no fortune together do muck up her chances.

"May, May, come up y'ere sharp!"

Miss Drusilla do have that dangerous Davison blood in her veins, she do, and what she do need is a little loving chastening now and then to keep her on a proper path.

"May, May, come y'ere. Where be that dratted girl?"

It was the inherent weakness of Anthony's blood that Nellie feared, a negligence or carelessness, not so much of others, for Mr. Anthony was always too kind by far, God knows, but of self. Yes, that be it. Miss Drusilla did not have a proper regard for herself. Nellie's eyes were keener than Dorothy's, nor had she lost the teaching of that countrified Somerset upbringing with its old feelings of decency and honour that Dorothy had allowed these sharp-boned northerners to elbow away. Well, if the mother would not sound warning bells, then she would, and she had become ever more clamorous with her advancing years.

"Hm!" With a shake of her mob-capped head and a tidying up of this and that. "And what do you think now, Miss Drusilla? Everybody knows he be harping on to His Grace about a Bishopric, though he haven't been a Vicar no more than five minutes, and the Duke don't listen to him – and I should think not indeed." She shook out Drusilla's petticoats as though she were shaking the Vicar himself. "Well, if he can't be no Bishop it seems he be determined to get as close to any old title as he can. And he done have the cheek to pay court to Lady Elizabeth Finch indeed, did you ever y'ear the like?"

She plumped out Drusilla's pillows with double vigour.

"But lucky for her, Lady Elizabeth that is, she done have a brother. And th'Earl of Winchelsea got no more time for our Bernard than done have the Duke of Newcastle. And when he called at Sussex House, Sussex House, would you believe it, he was bundled down they steps and up into his carriage as if he were no more nor a tradesman dunning for bills. And the servants done have orders not never to let him show his face there again!"

Drusilla swilled her face in the basin to shut out the sound of Nellie in full spate, the cold water stinging her eyes and whipping the blood to her cheeks.

"Lady Elizabeth be a proper-born lady, Miss Drusilla, and Lord Middleton's Betsy did tell me as how she disdained him, she did. Disdained!" Nellie repeated the word with another flourish of curls from under her cap as she feather dusted the top of Drusilla's dressing table cluttered with brushes and combs, paints and pastes, her rheumaticky fingers shifting bottles of lavender and rose water.

Drusilla lifted her face from the snowy white turkish towel.

"Tish! Get my stays ready please." She shut her ears to unpalatable gossip and rushed to defend her lover. "What about his sermons, Nellie? He has the finest voice and best delivery in the diocese. Everybody says that too, but you don't care to tell me truths like that."

"Truths, Miss Drusilla! Truths!" How Nellie rolled her tongue round that word. "Pity the people of Newent don't y'ear his fine voice more oftener then. Nearly every week he be spending a couple of days in London while his own parish can go to the devil. Going on church business, he says. And funny business 'tis too, I reckon. And has more to do with loins nor temples. Hm! There's more than me thinking as how our Bernard Webster's church business should be down there in Newent." She picked up Drusilla's stays. "Drat these y'ere laces, they be as weak as cobwebs they be," and she set about relacing the offending stays.

Drusilla hid her feelings in insisting on replacing the lace herself, as the sound of Bernard's name threw up, with a

248

rush, the excitement and danger of his presence, the odour of his scented cachoux, the pure soft creaminess of his stock, the depth of his voice and that spark in his eyes that she had ever hoped and believed was reserved for her alone.

"Miss Drusilla, keep still, please do, while I do fix your hair."

"Ouch, Nellie! Please don't pull so."

That cry struck a chord in Nellie's memory. So Miss Dor'thy had squealed the first time she had tried to alert her to that man's baseness – when he was only a boy, at that.

Drusilla sighed. Would she never know peace? Fear and love of danger fought together in her breast and filled her with emotion but it was an unsatisfying substitute for the fulfillment she craved. If she was honest with herself, her snatched times with him were times of frustration for her, at least. In spite of his skilful undoing of buttons and tapes, then the warm searching fingers and insistent beating of her own pulse, there was a point beyond which she would not go, nor did he ever seek to take her beyond it. She had given him her heart, not knowing that was more precious than her body, her dearest treasure in fact. But he knew it and held that treasure fast. Nobody else could reach her. She was as constant as her mother had been before her. She could not get rid of his claim upon her and her excitement, whenever she was aware of that faintly floral-medicinal smell, did not abate.

"Now, Miss Drusilla, you'm be needing a shawl. Today be as different from yesterday as good Cheddar cheese from this y'ere curdish wet-tasting Trent Valley stuff."

Drusilla's heart came up to her mouth as she thought how she had persuaded Mama to take communion at St. Leonard's instead of St. Wilfred's at Edgington. The shameful thrills she had felt at that silken voice and the sweet smell of his breath as she accepted the sacrament or caught sight, through her prayers, of the handsome robed figure processing past her deliberately chosen seat next the aisle. From the recesses of high windows and between arched columns a diffused light would float through air thickened with candle and incense smoke. Though it touched and hung around marble effigies, gilt frames, brass and bronze, and though it mingled with splendid chants, it served only to accentuate the presence of her lover. How the stained glass and candlelight, the swell of organ and choir heightened her senses, stifled her conscience.

"Don't fuss so, Nellie, please."

Of Bernard's sternly kept control she did not wonder. She took it as an expression of his love and shut her ears to Nellie's gossip. The confusion of it all was beyond her. In spite of parties and balls, meetings and waitings, dashings to windows at every sign of a horse or a carriage, rushings to doors at every rat-a-tat-la she was no nearer a declaration. The longed for proposal was never uttered.

She sighed again as she looked in the glass. Her hair was still bright, her complexion still clear. She smiled. Her teeth were still white. Only her age was against her and, like other unpalatable truths, she pushed that fact into the drawer at the back of her mind.

Nellie was still rattling on as May limped into the room.

"Ah, there y'are, May. Have you done finished Miss Dor'thy's room and collected her mending? Good girl. Now see if Dr. Peter be astir and open they windows. The stink up there be enough to blind a body. What he be doing lately, Lord knows. Such a stench of burning or summat."

Drusilla studied her forehead for the first sign of a wrinkle and found none. His fine house in Baldertongate – rumour said it had all but ruined him, though she did not believe that, – was very near finished. And the old-fashioned Vicarage on Parson's Mount almost packed up to the last tea bowl and saucer. He must surely declare himself soon. She could find neither wrinkle nor freckle, no blemish of any kind. She sighed again. Yet he had fulfilled himself with that Elizabeth Bradford, she was sure of it, and the knowledge was like a sharp physical pain in her breast. Elizabeth Bradford had done with her Bernard what she had not. Well, he was a man, after all, and how could he help it if that strumpet threw herself at him? How had she herself managed to hold back? Was it fear of Mama? Her own niceness? An innate sense of right from wrong? Nellie's carpings and warnings? Well, whatever it was had sullied their love and made it less joyous. He was hot-blooded and needed more than she could give, for to yield entirely she would not, nor could not. Yet she had been more daring than she ever meant to be. There were liberties he had taken – no, had been given – and still between them her virginity was respected, like an unread book. Her own respect she understood but not his.

"Don't dawdle so, Miss Drusilla. You'm as pretty as a picture, my chick and I y'eard your Mama go down to breakfast some minutes past. May, May, come down y'ere and take these slops y'ere."

Drusilla got up from her dressing table. Why, oh why, did he not force her if it were not out of love to keep her intact for the marriage bed? There had been times when he could have, when her resistance hung by a weakling thread. She longed for strength to throw off his hold over her. But resolution was wanting. She could no more cast him aside than she could throw out her old favourite iridescent peacock silk gown now worn thin at the edges. She longed for that lack of restraint she had been used to see in her unhouselled ghosts. She longed for marriage. Would she never have that unknown benefice both heart and body cried out for at all hours of day and night? She had been her teacher's top and favourite pupil. She had discussed Plato and Galileo, Pope and Newton but she could not understand the complexity of all this. She had to admit his control hurt her more than it hurt him. He took his pleasure elsewhere. But not with me, not with me her body cried. Why am I so special then?

So she made her excuses as she went down for breakfast, heart breaking inside, face smiling without.

It was not until that meal was nearly over that Dorothy's

insistence struck her with the force of a canon ball, for she had not been listening.

She and Dorothy faced each other across the breakfast table like protagonists in a fighting booth, the table and all its appurtenances, the urn, the china, the silver, the bread and meat all silent and stock still witnesses to the fight on hand. Dorothy's eyes glinted like frost but the blaze of her cheeks showed up the fire within. Tears spurted from Drusilla's eyes as water from an overflow pipe in a rainstorm, her force of feeling was so great.

"Mama, you would not, could not, be so cruel!"

"Cruel!" The room rang, the cups and saucers fairly rattled and jumped at Dorothy's pronunciation of that word. "Cruel! If I had the strength and sense I would box your ears for that."

"Not now, Mama. Not now. Please don't take me away now, not when I know everything is about to turn out as I wish. I know it is. I do. I do. I do." Drusilla's anger gave way to self-pity as she sobbed through her tears. "If you take me away now I stand to lose everything I want. Everything I have ever wanted."

Such deep sobs coming from the very depths of her being must surely move Mama to pity.

"Tish!" Dorothy exploded, throwing a scrap of lace at her daughter's breaking heart. "Dry your eyes, child. We are going to Bath to my sister Peabody. I am determined on it. We must go."

She felt like shaking Drusilla till the girl's teeth rattled when she thought of the hours she had worked at stitching her jewels into her voluminous skirts, for had not Peter once laughed about roads being full of highwaymen as a buck's back with fleas? And not to mention the heartache beforehand. They were treasured jewels given to her by Anthony and the few even more precious stones that had come from her own very dearest Mama. Well, the time had come to trade them in. She needed the money. Drusilla needed the money, if only she knew it, but Dorothy had resolved to keep that pain to herself and it was a transaction she could do more discreetly in Bath than in Newent.

"I hate my Aunt Peabody!" Drusilla clutched at any straw.

"Hate your Aunt Peabody!" Dorothy was incredulous. "You have only met her the twice and that was an age since."

"I don't care. I don't like her. She was unpleasant to me," lied Drusilla, maligning her poor Aunt, so she thought, for Bernard's sake.

"If you stay here, then Nellie must stay too." Dorothy paid her back in kind. "And she would like to see the old county and her own family as much as I. You are a selfish puss . . ."

"Mama, please . . ."

"Please me no pleases, Miss, my mind's made up."

A door opened.

"Then, my dear sister, allow me to unmake it."

CHAPTER 25

Uncle Peter! Drusilla's thankful sigh was scarcely audible between her sobs. She quietened her cries but did not dry up her tears altogether. Mama would not be persuaded in a matter of minutes. But persuaded she was, though against her better judgement, as she would repeat often enough later on.

Summer had drawn to a close, harvests were gathered and the yellowing woods, raided by schoolboys for unripe nuts and by old women for kindling, kept Old Capel on a stiff-knee'd rickety hop. Dorothy was anxious to be off before early nights and bad weather set in. She and Nellie, well buttoned up against highwaymen rather than cold, left for Bath by the early coach on a particularly sunny day in mid-September with so many instructions and admonishments those left behind could scarce take them all in.

Don't do this and remember that.

May was to keep an eye on the maids, the linen and silver and brewing but not get under the feet of the bad tempered cook. Dr. Peter was to watch over Capel, Young Hobbs, brick kilns and wood yard. As for Drusilla, she was to do nothing at all but keep out of mischief and be a good chick. And, for Heavens sake, yes, she could have Bridget Ogle to stay, if that would please her. After all, they had promised Tom and Eddie to keep an eye on their sister and, Lord knows, it must be as dull as fog in November at Sedgebrook with only old Markham for company.

Drusilla's face was crimped into a sly little smile. She would wind Uncle Peter round her little finger as she had once wound Papa and with both Mama and Nellie away . . .

Dr. Peter breathed a silent sigh of relief. That was Drusilla taken care of, thank the Lord, and he could get up on his latest hobby-horse and ride off to fame and fortune.

By the time Dorothy had been away for a week he was up in his bedchamber wrestling with a technical problem and if only he could get it right he might get his reward this side of Heaven. He had abandoned the tiresome business of fire-eating to advertise his infallible pills and elixirs. It had very near frightened a couple of maids to death. At the last Bawtry Fair he had overheard half a tale of how to do away with the nuisance of stinking chamber pots, yet another subject after his own heart. It only needed the application of a scientific-cum-imaginative mind, such as his own, to turn a close stool into a water closet.

Just one simple trick eluded him. His water closet still stank to high Heaven. He scratched his head and blew his nose and set about dismantling his apparatus for yet another try.

Drusilla and Bridget sat in the little parlour idly turning pages of the new Weekly Courier till Hobbs should trot round with the carriage. Drusilla and her Mama had been invited to spend the day with Mr. William Knight at North Heskham and, in Dorothy's absence, Dr. Peter was only too pleased to give the two girls his blessing to go. A whole day to himself with his new set up at this crucial stage of his calculations was not to be missed. His working model did not work yet, but, by Jupiter, it would if effort was anything to do with it. And, if Drusilla would only use her head, she might well come back with a proposal that would save him, and Dorothy too, if only she knew it, a deal of pain and trouble.

For all Dorothy's past hints to Bridget about a little powdering to tone down one's high colour, a little sugar water or diluted gum arabic to control one's unruly hair, a little stitch here and there to keep one's clothes from falling apart (May is very good, my dear), a little reselection of garments to stop the frightful clashings of colour, dear Bridget remained obstinately and exactly the same. She was as unselfconscious as she had been the night she and Drusilla first met at the Park Lodge Ball. She cared not a fig for fashion, propriety nor anything else and Drusilla loved her the more, for it put her in mind of Papa. Bridget Ogle was a warm and genial Irish colleen with the kindest heart in the world and a droll turn of phrase that made her such an amiable companion. Now she let out a peel of unfettered laughter such as Miss Knight would have disapproved mightily and jabbed a forefinger at the open newspaper.

"By the Great Horn Spoon, Drusilla, will you not be listening to this? 'An able bodied young man, looks no matter, but extra strong in the back and furnished with a good carnal yard and all its parts intact and in a clean-kept condition, can have a guinea a week with best linen to perform nocturnal practice on one Mary Ferrars, Bridlesmith Gate, whose impotent husband agrees he hath forced his wife to this desperation.'"

Two young faces stared at each other, mouthed their round Ohs and fell upon the paragraph like wasps upon a ripe pear. Neither believing ears nor eyes, the two heads, one with hair neat and shining, the other with ribbony cap askew, together bent over the column of personal advertisements.

"Should we be taking this to Mr. William knight would you believe?" Bridget giggled.

"Whatever for?" Drusilla's own giggles ceased at the question. Her sense of humour did not stretch as far as Bridget's.

"Sure, and all the world knows he is looking for a wife. Perhaps Mrs. Mary Ferrars might suit the wee fellow."

"But she is married already."

"Sure and all, so she is. I meant for the wee man to do a little practising on. She mentions the word practice, does she not? Oh no. I think not after all. He would not suit her, he

256

would not, for sure and all, there's nothing carnal about him."

"However do you know that?"

"Sure, I can smell it on a man, can you not?"

"He's a poor man." Drusilla primly ignored the question. "If he needs an heiress he would rather have you."

"And if it's beauty he's looking for then he'd rather have you. In any case, he would not do for me at all, I can tell you that, I know better."

Drusilla gave her friend a sharp look. What on earth did Bridget mean by that? But the carriage was at the front door and Bridget already dropping her gloves. They settled into their seats, still tickled by Mary Ferrars' predicament. Bridget's laughter threatened to get rather more out of hand than out of mouth and Drusilla decided to change the subject.

She took Mr. William Knight's letter of invitation out of her pocket.

"Miss Davison, it would do me the greatest Honour if You and Your Dear Mama would Condescend to spend a Day at The Vicarage Nth. Heskham. There is Something I am Desirous to Show You and would value Your Opinion thereon. My Sister, Miss Fanny Knight, stays here. She has these past 3 mths Retired here till such time as is not Convenient to me or to Her. May I Suggest You arrive on the afternoon of Last Day of Sept. when My Sister will be Happy to Receive you? Yours Respectfully, William Knight.

"Well," said Bridget, deaf to Drusilla's wishes for a change of subject. "Whatever he wants to show you and values your opinion thereon will not be anything to interest one Mary Ferrars, I'm thinking. For sure, he would not be likely to show you anything that lady might be interested in in front of his worthy sister and especially not in front of your dear Mama."

Drusilla blushed at her friend's outspokenness.

"And that's an odd phrase, is it not, Drusilla – 'until such time as is not convenient to me or to her'? What in the world

257

would you be thinking he means by that? Sure and all, the wee man wraps up his intentions. Myself, I like a man whose meaning is plain."

Drusilla smiled. As far as she was aware, Bridget, heiress or no, had never been paid court by any man, whether his intentions were plain or fancy, so how on earth did she know what she liked?

There was no time to pose the question for there at the entrance to North Heskham Vicarage off the Great North Road stood William Knight ready with a warmth of welcome given equally, without favour, to both young ladies. In her usual fashion, Bridget whinnied and pawed, dropped her dorothy bag, caught her skirt on the catch of the wrought iron gate, caring not a jot for the horrid sound of tearing cloth.

As for Drusilla, she had as keen an eye and interest for the house as for its incumbent. It was a place of some antiquity and incongruity. She faced a pretentious facade that had been added these past five years or less, pulling the house forward, almost to the roadside. Behind that new brick, Mama's bricks no doubt, with its typically well balanced pattern of windows and door, Drusilla knew would hide the original priest's house, not unlike the Vicarage on Parson's Mount; oak beamed, thick-walled with higgledy-piggledy small low rooms and uneven stone floors. It was not the new facade that caught and held her attention. All that was ordinary enough for nearly every old place in the country had been given a new front like a layer of pink paint on an old woman's grey face.

It was what had been tacked on to the south side of the house that made Drusilla stare.

There was an obvious recent addition, almost ludicrous in its lack of proportion, looking nearly as big as the house itself. Her questioning eye took in the mock crenellation of its roof, the church-like windows of leaded lights, the massive gothic door. Surely, Mr. William Knight was not responsible for this monster. Certainly, Mama's bricks were

258

not or she would have heard of it.

"Ah, you have noticed?" The clergyman clasped her mittened hand warmly as he led her indoors. "It is my pride and joy and could not have been done without my sister's help – and is a great surprise for you."

For me? For me? thought Drusilla, arching her brows, pursing her lips.

She smiled prettily, though not flirtatiously, as she and Bridget were led into the drawing room, which answered her expectations well enough. They sat comfortably with their glasses of cowslip wine, this year's brew, for Mr. William Knight served nothing but that he produced himself from his own glebe land. True enough, Bridget sat on the cat, knocked over a glass, whinnied louder than ever but that was only to be expected and of no consequence.

Drusilla marked the change in the young man since she had first met him at Miss Knight's Academy. And where was Miss Knight, by the way? There was no sign of her here,in spite of the promise in the invitation.

Bridget was wondering the same thing and, perceiving no answer to the silent question, her mind leapt back to the Weekly Courier and Mary Ferrars' advertisement. She dribbled her wine. Her teeth glistened. A wicked gleam shone in her eye. She stared hard at whatever there might be between Mr. William Knight's breeched legs and stifled a giggle into a hiccup.

Drusilla remembered the young man as she had first met him; the quick-eyed, well-dressed young man, slightly built; the smooth brown hair tied into a tail that hung tidily at the nape of his neck. Good Heavens. What a difference the two or three years of living at North Heskham had made and why had she not noticed it before? He had cut his hair, and not very well at that. That was the most noticeable thing about him. And there were other things too. He was not so dapper. His clothes had a – a – she searched for the right word – a workaday look and not the workaday look of a parson either.

What was it Papa had once said when Uncle Peter had demurred about taking that practice near Bath that Mama was always rattling on about? You're a fool, Peter, don't our clergy, and doctors too, tally ho, farm and guzzle with the squires? Well, this clergyman had more the look of a yeoman farmer than a squire, with his weather-beaten ruddiness and his hands. Jove. Best not look at his hands.

She thought of Bernard's hands, soft, warm, pressing and a familiar flame shot the length of her body. She concentrated hard on Mr. William Knight's eyes for they had not changed after all. They were still quick, lively and kind, the skin rather more wrinkled against wind and sun but that spark of lively intelligence glowed as bright as ever and she grabbed at that spark to extinguish the other.

There was, as well, a certain sobering of voice, though she had hardly heard a single word of his conversation. In any case, her ears were cocked for other sounds coming from somewhere in the house and not servants' voices either. Sing-song sounds she had never heard in her life before.

They sat down to dinner, with Bridget's usual fidgeting, dropping and knocking over, until the missing sister made her appearance. She had been at North Heskham these past three months, had she not? Well, in that three months Drusilla saw nearly as big a change as she had seen in the brother after three years. What was it about North Heskham that wreaked such a havoc?

Miss Knight was dressed in the simplest way, more like a housekeeper than anything else. The grand manner that Drusilla had once thought more stylish than any of Mama's friends was quite gone and in its place was this plain but still authoritarian body. And the conversation! Whatever had happened to those burning deserts and blinding snows? Those wonderful heroines? Those ancient and new philosophers whose thoughts and theories would so alter our lives? They had become pigs and chickens to be fed, eggs collected, fruit gathered, cow milked and ale brewed.

260

And all these things were said or implied with long meaning looks at Drusilla who remained obstinately in the dark of the reason for it all. As for Bridget, between dropping a spoon and spilling the cream, she still concentrated on her interesting speculation of what there might be between Mr. William Knight's legs and wondering whatever Drusilla would say if she opened her mouth and let out her secret. The familiar flame that had shot the length of Drusilla's body now licked away at poor Bridget too.

After the last of the puddings was offered and declined, Miss Knight was more obtuse than ever and if her brother had not kept the spark in his eye he would have looked positively smug.

"You have been wondering, my dear Drusilla, just where I have been all this morning. Not with chickens or brewhouse, I assure you, but with something William will show you himself." Again Bridget stifled a giggle into a hiccup. "We are only more than sorry your dear Mama is not here, though we welcome dear Miss Ogle, of course. We would have liked so much to show our pride and joy to your Mama."

Once more Bridget's giggle was smothered by yet another hiccup while Drusilla's face was pure consternation.

"You will forgive me, my dear Drusilla, the liberty of using your Christian name. Since we are no longer Directrice and pupil and since I am so much the elder, you will gratify my wish to think of you as a friend, if not a sister, and one day perhaps you may bring yourself to call me Fanny."

Drusilla's mouth crimped to a smile that might or might not be taken for agreement.

"And my brother has a good, sound Christian name too."

"My dear sister. Pray don't make such heavy weather of a name. But you are quite right and now we shall be all the more comfortable. Drusilla, can I not persuade you to take a little more of this excellent pudding?"

"No thankyou, William." She met his eyes and smiled

again at the new informality.

Bernard, of course, was always Bernard and she had hardly ever called Bridget's brothers any other than Tom and Eddie or how could one distinguish between them? She was happy to call Mr. Knight William but could not imagine for all the world she would ever call Miss Knight Fanny. And as for thinking of her as a sister – tish!

That formidable lady took her leave. The others lingered at table. They were offered tea and a bedchamber nicely laid out for their needs. The sing-song sounds increased with a regular cadence she could not identify. The two girls tripped down the old oaken staircase and at last William was ready to show his secret.

They were led to the new addition at the side of the house. It was a huge room, quite as large, if not larger, than the drawing room at Beacon House. There, Miss Knight, with something of the old light in her face, confronted some thirty or more children seated on benches as she took them through the familiar counting rhymes. Ah, these were the sounds she had heard and wondered at. Two, four, six, eight. At each number the children struggled to put up the required fingers. Mary at the cottage gate. It was a laborious process, Miss Knight losing neither patience nor dignity as she held her own fingers high.

The children were at sixes and sevens. Fingers did not want to work while tongues mouthed the figures. Tongues could not work for concentration on the fingers. They were in a comical fix but Drusilla did not laugh. She noted the children were all shapes and sizes, of both sexes, roughly but warmly clad, well nourished and totally under Miss Knight's spell as she herself had been in her schooldays.

At a signal from their teacher's once elegant hands the children rose in an uneven body, dropped their mixed curtsies and bobs, muttered their Sirs and their Ma'ms and reseated themselves with a shuffling of boots on the sanded floor and a shifting of bottoms on benches. At another nod and a wave of a hand, two older girls picked up a pile of slates in wooden frames and what looked like, as far as Drusilla could make out, rough knobs of gypsum rock. With occasional meaning looks at Drusilla, Miss Knight instructed the children in the writing of the figures they had just finished reciting. Using the same two girls as helpers, monitors she called them, her old teacher went up and down the rows, instructing here, admonishing there.

Drusilla was astounded. So this was William's pride and joy. He had built a school for his sister to work in. She could not help herself. She thought back to Miss Knight's classes at the Academy for Young Ladies of Rank. She remembered that lady's quick smile flashing encouragement and her graceful hands expressing this point and that. She recalled how her own pulses had raced at the mysteries of light, dynamics, gravity, electricity, at the names of Galileo, Leonardo and Newton. And how they raced now.

She walked up and down between the benches feeling for these children that same feeling she had always had for Mama's brickies and woodmen and all her old sensations of expectancy that somewhere there was a blessing if only she could reach it, welled up inside her. She looked at these children and loved them. She did not see the wooden-headed villagers that Bridget saw. She felt an empathy with them, poor and low as they were,and was reminded of Bernard's sneer. 'Pooh! Drusilla, you never see a piece of fine lace without translating it into the coarse hands that made it.' She knew both William and Miss Knight regarded her closely. She did her best to stifle her emotion.

Bridget was gritting her teeth and shutting her ears against the squeaks of white rock on blue slate.

Drusilla hardly heard Miss Knight's suggestion that dear Miss Ogle should visit the stables while William showed Drusilla the gardens. Neither did she notice how Bridget was out of the schoolroom in a flash to catch the whinnies of horses instead of those frightful squeaks. The children rose again with a respectful shuffling of boots and mumblings of Sirs and Ma'ms as William and Drusilla took their leave.

The gardens he led her to were not like those of Beacon House, even allowing for their alteration since Papa's death, nor did she expect them to be. Pleasure and leisure were incidental not paramount in these vegetable plots, orchards, grass fields and chicken runs that came right close to the house.

Their feet scrunched along gravel paths. It was William's own gravel dug from the river bank, and how proud he was of every economy. Drusilla smiled. Mama would approve of that. He did not take her hand, nor even her arm and she knew he would not. They walked separate and apart, heads never turning towards each other. He was not like Bernard, then. How Bernard rose up before her and how she concentrated on driving that spectre away.

They came to a seat made in that curious new fashion of allowing logs to keep their natural twists and curves. Oh, yes, he had made it himself. Oh no, he never sat upon it. There was not the time. How that seat invited her to slip off her shawl for a cushion that they might sit down together. She could have lodged there comfortably, hands in lap. His hands he might have clasped behind his head, for he would never have touched her; she knew he would not.

A kitten following at their feet grew tired of Drusilla's skirts and gambolled away after a falling leaf. Before them a peacock trailed its long feathers as iridescent as the blue-green silk gown she had worn on the night of the Park Lodge Ball but she knew William would not remember that. Sheep grazed on the green and beyond lay the shining river, limpid in the last September sunlight. The sights were homely and comfortable; she enjoyed them but it was the sounds that caught and held her fancy.

The country was not a quiet place after all. There were farm noises like the hard voices of men, the clanking of pails, the jangle of harness and creaking of leathers, the lowing of cows and bleating of sheep and, overall, like a chorus, the rhythmical sound of rote rising and falling from the schoolroom, like her own breathing and muffled heartbeat under her tight stays. His voice droned and she hardly heard it. His words of an orderly and useful life that had in it the means of doing so much good in the village were lost in the more natural sounds of the garden.

She did not listen to his tales of kindling to be cut, snares to be set, fishing to be done, seed planted, stock cared for. She heard the children but her thoughts were far off and between them the shadow of Bernard Webster was rising again.

William led her towards the farm buildings and, at last, out of all the everyday sounds there, he made his own voice heard. His repeated use of her own name forced itself upon her, driving off that spectre of the Vicar of Newent. Now he spoke of himself, his love of his church and his parishioners, his village and his glebe land and his school. His tone was that of a man laying his words on canvas like colours from a brush. He wanted her to see the picture of his future, a true picture neither highlighted nor shaded. His words made sense at last.

"You see, Drusilla, I would rather convince and persuade than frighten my people into piety. For God, I believe, as I am sure you do, my dear Drusilla, if that is what I may call you, is a benevolent deity who loves all men. And within my church I want a freedom for debate with a liberty of thought and expression in all theological matters. I want no stupid blind-folded sheep in my flock, Drusilla. There are some, I know, who would call these dangerous, even seditious, sentiments – but they are wrong. And I am not afraid of Bishops, Drusilla, no, nor of Dukes neither."

He was eloquent but prosaic in his eloquence and she had been used to a silken tongue.

His school would take up to sixty scholars, he thought. Yes, he knew The Free School in Newent catered for the sons

265

of shopkeepers and farmers but he wanted a school for girls as well as boys, and the children of labourers at that. And, of course, it would be a completely different place from his sister's establishment. Did she know his sister had sold her old school to help him with-his?

"What I want, Drusilla, is a congregation of intelligent men and women who can understand their God. I'll not believe my people are to be taught only to know their station in life so that they be always diligent, honest, humble and submissive for the benefit of their superiors. Nor do I accept, Drusilla, that vice will flourish along with learning. If that is not so with us, why should it be so with them? No, Drusilla, I'll not accept they should be ignorant as well as poor."

Still he did not look at her nor she at him but he had gotten her attention and held it fast.

"My school, Drusilla, is conducted upon the new Parish System and is open, free of charge, to all the poor of North Heskham and the neighbouring parishes on application to me, the Vicar. They shall be taught Reading, Writing, Arithmeticks and Geographicks and the girls, Sewing. I know at times the numbers will fall, for I hope to take up to sixty children. I have no illusions, Drusilla, the labourers will still need their children to turn out for bird scaring, stone-picking, harvesting and the like. That is why there will be no charge. I have expectations, as you know, from our old cousin in Edgington. We will be comfortable enough."

How she longed to be comfortable enough. Still not looking at each other, they had come round to the pigs housed close to the schoolroom and he turned towards the first sty. Together they looked over the gate, neither touching nor looking at each other, but simply staring into the pen. The sow had farrowed only a few days before. He was enthusiastic. It was a litter of nine, only one runt and the sow a good mother.

Drusilla allowed a small smile. He might be sick of sucking pig for dinner before he got through so many.

He turned the conversation, but not his face, towards her and she thought there should be more excitement in her breast.

He told her how she had appeared to him when they first met at his sister's At Homes, so young. How she appeared at the end of her schooling, so much improved and how she appeared to him now, so very much improved, but wasted. She tucked the doubtful compliment away as she might have tucked a crumpled handkerchief.

The sow grunted. Her piglets snuzzled and squealed. The runt ran this way and that.

"I want you to know, Drusilla. I care not a fig for gossip nor slanders and I do not boast when I call myself a reasonable man. At least I can forgive a mistake easier than most men."

Hush, oh hush, William dear. You are raising that spectre between us again. You are a clergyman, her heart very near shouted aloud at these words meant only in kindness and understanding, yet piercing her breast like a knife. There have been intimacies you could forgive as a man, but there have been practices forced upon me, even the most liberal cleric might blench at. Practices that you, with the kindest of eyes and noblest of thoughts, could not even guess at. You have not the imagination for it.

"You must by now, Drusilla, be more than ready to leave your Mama. And for you and me together, my dear, there is work to be done. Do I make myself plain, Drusilla?"

Her cheeks burned at these words and at last, at long last, he turned to face her.

"Oh yes, William, you make yourself very plain indeed."

She could barely understand her racing pulse, her clammy hands; this blowing hot one minute, cold the next. Was this, then, the benediction she had waited for? She looked at William Knight full in the face and what she saw there was simple honesty. She thought of Bernard Webster and his proud new mansion in Baldertongate. She thought of the homely Vicarage here in North Heskham and knew which of the two pleased her most. There was no comparison between one pretentious, one so homespun. But when William touched her hand, as he did now, where was that excruciating thrill she had become used to at a lover's touch? When William's voice opened up his heart where was that timbre that affected her so when that other used his powers of persuasion? Besides, there were still, in spite of William's protestation, those experiences that bound her as strong as any wedding ring to Bernard as a wife. Why then, this excitement in her breast? If William did not thrill her, what was it?

The sounds from the schoolroom changed. 'Curly Locks, Curly Locks wilt thou be mine?'

She was of average height for a woman and he was short for a man. As they stood, eyes, noses, lips, perfectly level, before he could diminish the distance between them, the scrunching of gravel tore them apart as Bridget cantered down the path, her high colour enough to set a blind man's teeth on edge, as Nellie would say.

'Thou shalt not wash dishes nor yet feed the swine.' The children's voices carolled sweetly.

They took their leave. The carriage slowed to a walk up Beacon Hill. Drusilla mulled over the children's song, heart too full to speak. 'Sit on a cushion and sew a fine seam and feed upon strawberries, sugar and cream.' Was that what Papa had meant by strawberry beds? William Knight would grow strawberries by the bushel, she was sure of that. But there would be more of the hard work of picking and turning them into strawberry preserve than simply eating them up with sugar and cream – she was sure of that too.

If only he had said, just once, 'into the bonfire with superstition and dogma and let's go forward into Newton's light!' She sighed. If only he had said just once, 'Drusilla, I love you.'

Bridget squirmed in her seat. Her big teeth glistened. Her

brown eyes shone. Her bonnet had slipped to one side of her head. She could contain herself no longer.

"Drusilla, cross your heart and hope to die you'll not tell a soul so you will not."

"What?"

"I've been bursting to tell you, so I have, God forgive me. Bernard has asked me to be his wife! Oh, Drusilla, my darling, we are bundled, so we are, and 'tis a great secret, so it is. Bernard will skin me alive, so he will, for the telling of it. We are engaged, so we are, and when Tom and Eddie come back – though they know nothing about it – nothing at all – 'tis me will be living in the new house in Baldertongate with Bernard. We're to be married, so we are, and the priest fetched from Grantham . . ."

It came out in a rush till the look on Drusilla's face made Bridget shut her mouth tight.

CHAPTER 26

Drusilla thanked the Lord for Uncle Peter's snores coming from the dining room as she pulled the protesting Bridget upstairs in her madness to hear more. Poor Bridget was reduced to a garbled gibbering.

"Take no notice, Drusilla! 'Tis not true, I promise you that. I'm sworn to secrecy, so I am. On my mother's death, so I am. Please don't, Drusilla, I'll be telling you nothing at all, so I will not. Bernard will murder me alive, so he will. Please, Drusilla, please," her voice reaching higher.

And Drusilla might press and stamp and shake as much as she could, there was no more to be got out of Bridget that night, nor next day neither. The girl had gathered her wits, insisted her visit was at an end, thanked them all kindly, so she did, but her Uncle was expecting her back at Sedgebrook that very day, so he was.

The carriage was called and off she went. Dr. Peter could make nothing of it at all. Young ladies were the very devil and he must get back to his water closet. He was nearly there, damnit. He would think about Drusilla tomorrow. There was plenty of time for her but Dr. Fletcher's New Water Closet Perfect and Unrivalled in the Country could not wait another minute. He did not doubt there were others with pipes and pails, ropes and pulleys racing against time to beat him to the demise of the chamber pot.

How wretchedly Drusilla got through the next few days. She gave William Knight and his school not a single thought. How could she when both heart and mind took her back and forth between Sedgebrook and Parson's Mount, Parson's

Mount and Baldertongate and back to Sedgebrook again? Not knowing, not being sure, that was the misery of her days and nights.

Forbidden recollections of that man – she could not name him – rose up to disgust and terrify her. His hands, his odour, his voice, the exhilaration and danger of his imagined presence stayed to torment her. She thought of that time, after Papa's death, when she had shrugged off her pride to rush to Parson's Mount and the scene that awaited her there. She felt the hot flush of shame on her face. She had the physical sensation of her heart filling her mouth. She could not eat. She could scarcely breathe.

There was nobody to notice and thank God there was not.

She hovered outside doors for snippets of news, as he had been wont to do. Remembering a school-friend's trick at Miss Knight's Academy when that Bessie Bradford's parents had died, she laid an ear to the kitchen walls, for servants always knew everything and what they knew they clacked, but she heard nothing other than Mistress Alice scolding her maids and the usual chat of the King over the water, the damned Scots and twice-damned French. His engagement to Bridget was either a close kept secret or nothing but a figment of her own and Bridget's imagination.

She remembered Uncle Peter's diagnosis of the Ogles' eccentricity, 'the taint of insanity' he called it, and tortured herself the more. So she troubled herself for over a week until Uncle Peter placed a sealed note in her hand.

"Markham's man brought this. It was Miss Bridget's letter of thanks, he said and was gone before I could send him to the kitchen for a bite or a sup. Servants are always as daft as their masters." He regarded her sharply. "You're looking peaky, Drusilla. Wait till I've worked out my water closet – we should all feel the better for it."

She broke open the letter's seal almost before it left Uncle Peter's hand to be enclosed by her own trembling fingers. She had a job to decipher the words from the blotches but she recognised the hand immediately.

"Drucilla, Kepe this Secrete. The Saromony I spoke you of took place this last nigte. My Uncle and that from Gantham I told you of as Witnesse. B. to London Today Church Busyness. I waite till He Come and Hope He Come Soon. I Wait in Joy as am Bid. My Uncle to Bath. No Servants still I Spare one for this. Pray on Yr. Honour Send No Word Now. B.W. (B.O.).

B.W.! Those initials hit her like a blow to the face. Bridget Webster. The thing was done then. The end of dreams and hopes, like a rush of cold water shocking her back to reality. She had lost him. And to such a one. To Bridget who looked like a filly and behaved like a donkey. Pride wrestled with hurt. Was it possible? She had hardly believed Bridget's hints that day they went to North Heskham but she did not doubt the veracity of this letter still fast in her hand. She guessed how foolish Bridget would have tumbled for him but could not fathom his feelings. He did not love anybody but himself. Now she knew he did not. What was it, then, that pushed him? Money! It must be money.

So she comforted herself. Bridget was, after all, more bearable than Elizabeth Bradford.

She was in the dark and she longed for light. She walked the length of the drawing room, up and down, as she tried to tease out the facts. She went through the letter line by line and between. There was an excitement in the few words and an innocent honesty. In her own heart there was nothing but cold pain for herself but she did not dwell upon that. What she combed from the ravel was bedevilled by questions she could not answer.

Her legs trembled beneath her as she sank on to Mama's sofa.

Why was the ceremony so secret with no family other than Old Markham there? What about Tom and Eddie? Why a priest fetched from Grantham? Why late at night? And a cleric's wedding too. She would have thought he would have

272

wanted a bishop, no less. What on earth did Bridget mean by 'no servants'? Everybody knew Sir George had an army of them, though they be the most ill-disciplined troops in the shire. Why had a new husband chosen to go on church business instead of a honeymoon? What was it Nellie had said about his church business – more to do with loins than temples! And why had Sir George, who had been abed these two months past, taken the long journey to Bath? How could either of those men consider leaving Bridget alone in that miserable old house?

And as for her own self, how could she have been so ill-used, so betrayed? She shuddered as her fertile imagination warmed to life.

She saw the decaying mansion of Sedgebrook by moonlight, one of those great half-timbered buildings of a previous century that was gloomy without and even more gloomy within. A coach rattled up the neglected drive. Black horses, they were bound to be black, slithered to a standstill. A figure, too clad in black, apart from the clerical bands at his throat, alighted. The moon was bright, no lanthorns needed, and she saw the scene as clear as day, as though from a play, exactly as she had once seen him and his strumpet in The Friary drawing room. Another figure entered the stage from the front door to greet the visitor and it had that sly look on its face that Nellie had forever carped about but that she, Drusilla, poor stupid fool, had never seen till now. There was a shaking of hands, a muttered word or two she could not catch and a nod of assent. Pushed ajar, the great oaken door creaked and complained like a rheumaticky old man. The scene shifted and opened into the old great hall. A candelabra was picked up. Moving shadows played on the old fashioned room, thick with old portraits on the panelling, dirty with age and neglect. There was no doubt Sir George's servants took advantage. The light moved and fell upon uneven patches of deep shadow, on the rich gildings of heavy frames encrusted with dirt, it made a dull sheen on unpolished floor and furniture; it licked at dusty cobwebs hanging down from the old ceiling like ropes from an old Spanish galleon. Where was Bridget and where in the world would the ceremony take place? Markham had been confined to bed these two months past, all of Newent knew that. She knew better than anybody that all the doctors in the county had tried one remedy after another without success.

The two near identical figures slipped from the hall up the great, dark, oaken staircase. Markham's bedchamber – that was to be the wedding chapel then! She refused to be left behind and in her mind's eye followed the sinister pair through a labyrinth of long galleries to the old man's room. Her mouth turned down in disgust as the old roué showed up in a flickering display of light from fire and candle. The dingy bed hangings were drawn back, their occupant propped by pillows that were not too clean, along with his other linen, if what Nellie had been told had any truth in it at all. The moving shadows enhanced the mystery, underlined her fear. An awful sick room smell pervaded the air.

Bridget was already there, waiting, unbridelike, the shifting lights catching her shining eyes, her glistening teeth and the sheen of her best silk dress, an awful concoction of too many frills and furbelows and an unnatural fighting of colours. There had not been time for special dress-making then, nor would this curious need for secrecy have allowed it. Somewhere there should be documents and inkstand. Ah, beside the bed was the heavy oaken table supporting lotions and potions and from where Uncle Peter had done his blood-letting, cupping and blistering, none of which had ever done the old man any good.

Words would have to be said and written. She shut her ears against the actual ceremony. She could not bear to hear him say those words to another. But she heard the shuffle of papers, the scrape of a quill, the shake of a sander. It took an age. The old man's hand shook. He was in his cups and all of a fuddle – never out of them if gossip be right. That was his trouble, Uncle Peter had said, a surfeit of loose women in youth and strong liquor in old age and there was nothing any honest medical man could do about it.

Bridget dropped the quill, blotched the page, smudged her signature and whinnied as she was bound to do.

They were husband and wife then. The deed was done; the priest paid off and sent home and they to the bridal chamber. She would not follow them there and the scene closed.

Drusilla's knuckles showed white on the edge of the sofa. Did Bridget come as a virgin to that room? She was innocent enough, Drusilla was sure of that, but she had hinted on that day at North Heskham, ah yes, she had more than hinted of indiscretions. Where had she been meeting him? At Parson's Mount? At Sedgebrook? In coaches? In woods, as she herself had done? Drusilla blushed as she thought of her own indiscretions with that man. What was it Nellie had said, Bessie was a good girl till the Vicar of Newent threw his cloven hoof over her? Well, now he had his cloven hoof over Bridget and a wedding ceremony, however secret, would not turn a devil into a man. And he was a fiend, she had no doubt of it.

She remembered those childish games in the woods, in the little parlour and their secrets of the garden-house. She knew, more than any other, how softly persuasive he could be. Poor Bridget would have collapsed like butter in a thunderstorm. Yes, now at last she could admit it. It was true. All the young ladies at the Friary had succumbed and not a wench could they get to stay at the Vicarage. The whole of Newent knew it. And in this very house there had been May Hobbs and perhaps others for all she knew. Had they all played at Wood Nymph to his Green Man? How he must have laughed between each conquest.

What a fool she had been. Lady Elizabeth Finch had shown a deal more sense.

Well, she would be a fool no longer. Scorn, hurt, anger and jealousy fought in her breast and scorn it was that won the

275

day. He was not worthy and she despised him. She would not stoop to hate him but she would have her revenge, she determined on it. A sound in the room opened her eyes. May Hobbs limped through the door and on seeing Drusilla thrust an arm quickly behind her back.

"May, what have you there?" Drusilla's voice was sterner than she meant, for her thoughts were elsewhere.

"Nothing, Miss Drusilla."

"Come, May, you know you do not need to be afraid of me. What are you hiding?" She held out her hand and stared at the offering of a small pile of magazines.

"May," her voice softened. "You have kept up your reading, then?"

"Oh yes, Miss Drusilla. Please forgive me."

"Forgive you, May? Whatever for? Do you think I have forgotten how Uncle Peter always said in teaching you I would teach myself?" She patted the spare seat on the sofa. "Come and sit here beside me. Let me hear you read as we used to do."

Somewhere in her breast a sluice gate opened a crack and a trickle of Pity crept through. Scorn got its toes wet.

"What shall I read, Miss Drusilla?"

Drusilla picked up the top of the pile, opened the book at random and stuck out a forefinger.

"Read this," she said.

May shifted to settle her bad hip, using her own finger as marker.

"It is well known that the women of China have deformed feet from bracing and binding them hard from infancy. It is also known the Chinese women do not grow as they should and are short-lived. It is this unreasonable binding of feet that affects the free flow of blood making the health and growth of the whole body to suffer."

May paused. The sluice in Drusilla' breast opened wider and Pity's trickle became a stream that lapped at Scorn's ankles.

276

"You read well, May. Is there more from this interesting subscriber?"

May pushed out her forefinger again.

"My next observation regards the dress of new born children in our own country. It is a barbarous custom to make living mummies of them by confining their legs and arms and depriving them of that liberty they enjoyed in the womb. Much misery arises from the heat and weight of swaddling bands that bowels are injured by their pressure and the flow of blood restricted by compression."

Again May paused and the stream filled to a river where Scorn struggled to keep its balance.

"Carry on, May." Drusilla's voice was low. She could hardly trust herself to speak.

"Can we now consider the position of our women whose hearts and lungs are similarly bound. Can the consequences be less disastrous? Let us, too, consider the education of our women. Are our daughters' minds not tied up with stays in like manner as their chests? Are their minds and brains not stifled with their inferior schooling? Are their . . ."

"Enough," whispered Drusilla. The dam crumbled, the river swelled to a rushing torrent and Scorn was all but carried away on the tide of Pity. She could scarcely get the words out, asking May to leave her be. As soon as she heard the drawing room door open and close, she threw herself down on the vacated sofa, buried her face in a cushion and wept until she thought her stays might break, her gown split.

She wept for Papa who had thrown his life away; for Mama who had lost all but one of her children and who now struggled to keep their home about them. She wept for May who had been so dreadfully wronged; she wept for herself who had been such a weak addle-pate but most of all, she wept for poor Bridget.

Scorn struggled for Life and Pity weakened. She must not let Scorn drown. He was her one ally in the fight for Bridget.

Her heart went out to Bridget alone in that terrible house,

277

waiting, longing for that man, her husband, to return. Oh. He had a cruel streak, that man. She had felt it herself, remembering how he had pressed her hands to that red hot chafing dish on the night of Mama's great party. How she had acquiesced to unmentionable things under such torture. Oh, if only Uncle Peter's tales were true she would fly over to Sedgebrook and back again and no-one the wiser. Sedgebrook, after all, was not so very far away down the steep hill behind the house, past Balderton, on to the Grantham Road, south to Allington Lane End and across the bog. The way was engraved on her heart.

She dried her tears, tucked Bridget's letter into her bodice and pulled herself together. The realisation of his treachery now filled her with an unexpected calm. At last she knew, finally and irrevocably, where she was with him. She no longer reproached herself for having been so ready to be deceived. Instead she rallied her forces. She would right the wrong done to Bridget if she could. She felt responsible for it. She must save Bridget. She would save her. Her own peace of mind depended on it and this time she would stay strong and not weaken. To be independent, that was the thing. Great Heavens Above, in spite of Mama being forever at her accounts and Uncle Peter closeted upstairs with Goodness knows what contraption, she could do nothing without justifying each piffling little action to either of them, and to Nellie even. The falsehoods she had told, the subterfuge she had endured in her struggle for freedom.

However did one cut these apron strings without marriage? That word brought William Knight to mind.

Was it only nigh on two weeks since that day at North Heskham when he had asked if he made himself plain? Was she prepared to make that sacrifice? Was that, then, what it would be, a sacrifice? She did not know, but she knew she would try all other avenues first, if only she could find them. She thought of William's sister. That lady had once done it, had broken free and independent. Ah. But she had been a

278

woman of means. There had been a godmother behind her. Money; was that the answer then? Yes, if it came down to money she was done for. She and Bridget both done for. What could a woman do to get money, other than marry? Was she prepared to live a lie to be 'comfortable enough'? That did not seem such a sin after all she had done. But live a lie with a man who might find her nothing but useful? No, there must be something better than that, not withstanding the old cousin from Edgington.

Miss Knight's changed condition presented itself. Even she, after all, in the end, had subjected herself to a man, though not a husband. No doubt she had done it for love. If only William Knight had just said once 'I love you, Drusilla'. There were many kinds of love, were there not? Once she had been thrilled by a love of Humanity and that wretch had been right when he said she never saw a thing of beauty without thinking of the poor hands that made it.

A noise sounded without. She was drawn to the window. Great Heavens. Here was Mama returned home. She put a hand to her bodice. The letter was safe. She walked slowly out into the courtyard, struggling to maintain her calm.

She could not see her future and was afraid.

CHAPTER 27

Dorothy had returned from Bath in high humour. She had been most comfortably lodged in the Peabody household. The whole family had put themselves out, even the most distant cousins. She had met up with old friends and acquaintances, taken the waters, joined in the assemblies and entered into the most favourable of transactions over her jewellery with not a highwayman in sight, either coming or going. But glad to be home again after such a ricketty-racketty journey, she thought, sinking gratefully into her own eider-down bed for an early night, dreams of moving to Somerset quite squashed flat.

Bath was a noisy place after all, building and rebuilding going on in every part, and stone dust flying everywhere. There was something to be said for the peace and quiet of the top of the hill and plaster dust not such a trial as one had thought. One thing was sure, she would never grumble about church bells ever again.

Next morning found her facing Peter and Drusilla across the gleaming breakfast table, appetites for news and food crossing each other like fighting cocks.

"And now what's new in Newent?" she asked between mouthfuls of ham baked in cider the Somerset way especially for the mistress' homecoming.

"Oh, very little happens here, as you know, Mama," said Drusilla evasively, thanking the Lord that letter that had never ceased to occupy her thoughts had been delivered without Mama's and Nellie's prying eyes, especially Nellie's who missed nothing and grew ever more fearless of speaking her mind.

"Well, did you and the Ogle girl enjoy your day with Mr. William Knight, only a few days after we left, if I recall from Peter's letter? And where is the Ogle girl, come to that?"

"Upon my honour, I have hardly thought a word about that day," said Drusilla, almost truthfully, choosing to ignore the second question and turning to take a piece of hot toast from May kneeling in front of the great hearth.

She buttered her slice absent-mindedly. Did he propose to me on that day? He said did he make his meaning plain. Well, I thought he did. Surely it was marriage he meant. He is unconventional in many things but . . . Well, if so, it was a very plainly wrapped proposal. No ribbons nor bows, no kneelings, nor protestations of undying love. So yes. I suppose he made himself very plain indeed. Curly Locks, Curly Locks, wilt thou be mine?

"Did you hear what I said, Drusilla?" Dorothy stabbed at another piece of ham. "Come back to earth, do. I thought we had gotten you out of that tiresome day dreaming habit. But when the cat's away . . ." The rest was lost in another mouthful.

"Oh yes, Mama. Oh yes. It was a pleasant enough day. William Knight has started a school." Thou shalt not wash dishes nor yet feed the swine.

"A school!" echoed Dorothy. "We shall be as bad as Bath next. The place is full of them. Young ladies and gentlemen visiting here, visiting there, taking up road space, crowding the pavements – wherever there are any. Do we need any more schools for Goodness sake?"

She cut up the ham on her plate as no doubt she would have liked to cut up the young people of Bath.

"But not that kind of school, Mama. A school for children of all ages. And labouring children at that." Drusilla's breath quickened as she spoke, deciding to say nothing of events at the end of that day. But sit on a cushion and sew a fine seam and feed upon . . .

"Tish!" Dorothy laid down both knife and fork. "If that's all that happened here, then you had best listen to my news . . . May, that's quite enough toast - go and help Nellie sort out my linen." She gave a significant look at the door, May enough time to limp out of the room and the others her undivided attention.

"In the middle of our stay Sir George Markham arrived at his house in Bath, only a few doors from your Aunt Peabody, who, by the way, sent you much love and a very fine present which, no doubt, you might give to May on account of your deep hatred of your poor Aunt who I found still to be the most loving and caring of sisters I have always known her to be . . ."

"Get on, sister, get on." Dr. Peter was impatient for the tid bit to come and it took Drusilla all her time not to put a hand to the bosom keeping Bridget's letter safe.

"He died three days later." Dorothy relished those few words almost as much as she had relished the ham.

Drusilla stared, as one struck dumb. The doctor poised in mid air before the next forkful reached his mouth.

"Well, sister, the devil only knows how you managed to keep this warm till morning. It knocks any Jacobite gossip into a cocked hat."

"Well, brother, by all accounts he was half dead when he arrived and his coachman in a pretty bad state too. Though whether of drink or a fever, there are differing opinions about that. Our Sister Peabody's housekeeper had it from Markham's housekeeper it was six of one and half a dozen of the other. The town was agog, I can tell you that. For such an old man to come such a long way and in such a weak condition and unaccompanied too, nobody but the coachman, whoever could have let him do it?"

Drusilla's hand went straight to her bosom. She could not help it. Dr. Peter rested his knife and fork.

"Well, that puts the cat among the pigeons. It will bring Tom and Eddie Ogle home from Ireland to claim their own sure enough. And I wonder where all this leaves our Webster friend? I declare the Ogles might not be as well disposed towards him as that old libertine of an uncle of theirs."

"And you have not told me yet where Bridget – Drusilla, my dear – ." For Drusilla had stuffed a handkerchief into her mouth, pretending to choke on her toast, and as the others turned their full attention upon her she fled to the safety of her own room, straight to the wash stand to splash her face with cold water and swill out her mouth.

With a trembling hand she brought out the letter.

That fiend, that devil, that serpent. His plan was as clear as the wart on Old Noll's face. His idea it must have been to send Sir George off to Bath for the good of his health, knowing the old man would never withstand the journey. And his idea it would have been to send the servants away. What bit of common sense poor Bridget possessed would have melted away at the first mention of marriage. Now she would come into her share of Markham money and her husband's fingers would itch to get a hold of that. Tom and Eddie had best watch out. It would be a race between them in Ireland and him with his church business to get to Sedgebrook first. She read the letter again. There were still questions that had no answers. If only Papa were still here . . .

A call up the stairs made her stuff the letter back into her bodice.

"Drusilla! Whatever's amiss?"

"Nothing, Mama, only a little toast gone the wrong way."

"Come down immediately, we have made a decision."

Mama was ringing her bell, ordering the carriage and sending for cloaks. Uncle Peter was still wiping his mouth and getting up from the table with rather more haste than usual. His voice had new vigour in it. He was on his mettle. It wasn't every day he flushed a mystery.

"We're going a-hunting Drusilla, my dear. Hunting for news. Not vermin nor game neither. I shall ride the taverns while you and your Mama take the shops. Though you might get a better sight if you drive out to the Jenisons. That family's as good as a pack of hounds any day."

Still mumbling, he stomped off to search for a hat.

"There's some devilment afoot here, I am sure of it. Seems a rum thing to me the way Bridget took herself off in a rush saying she was expected at home that very day."

"Are you suggesting that ninny packed her Uncle off to Bath in order to kill him off so she and those daft brothers of hers could get their hands on his money?"

"Well, sister, she may not be such a ninny as we had thought and if her brothers are in the plot, they're not so daft neither." Dr. Peter adjusted the hat of his choice. "Come, Drusilla. Make haste . . ."

Drusilla summoned her courage in defence of poor Bridget. She, too, made a decision.

"I shall not come with you, Mama. My courses are running strong today and I would rather not." For the first time in her life she thought of herself as a woman. She was no longer a child.

"Tish!" Dorothy pulled on a pair of gloves and discarded them straight away. "In that case you would be no help at all and had best stay behind. Come, Peter."

The sound of hooves in the yard stopped Dorothy in her tracks to the door, sending her, still gloveless, to the window.

"Mr. William Knight, as I'm alive," she said. "I would have thought this house might have had its fill of clerical gentlemen."

"Not this one, sister. Not this one," with a significant look at Drusilla. "You see to your bonnet and things, Dorothy, I have a little something to check upstairs and then we'll be off."

"One thing's for sure, he won't have heard a word shut up with that sister of his in a place like North Heskham. Now, where is May with the rest of my things?"

Drusilla's heart leapt as she rushed out into the yard. Thank God. Here was help at last and she was holding the bridle before William had time to dismount, if indeed that had been his intention, though not before he had taken a nosegay from inside his coat, his eyes smiling down into hers.

"My sister sends this to you, Drusilla, along with her love, the very last of this year's blooms. She allows me two minutes only as I am on my way to Edgington . . .

"Oh, William. Thank God you have come," her upturned face shone into his own. "Please will you ride over to Sedgebrook for me? It's Bridget, she . . ."

"To Sedgebrook?" His own face dropped. "But that's in another direction, my dear. I must make Edgington within the next half hour or Fanny will never forgive me. We have just got word our cousin is dying . . ."

She could hear a bustling within, Mama calling for May as she hunted for this or that, Uncle Peter coming heavily down the stairs. She put her whole heart in her face.

"Oh, William, please. If you value my good opinion, if you care anything at all for me, or for Bridget either, please ride over to Sedgebrook."

He looked down at the rose-flushed countenance and, in spite of the tear-filled eyes, he missed the urgency there, sensing only a maid anxious to get a girlish note off to a friend she had seen but a two-week before.

"But, Drusilla, a man's peace of mind and his soul are at stake at Edgington."

"Please, William, please," she sniffed to keep the tears off her face.

"We cannot afford that luxury, neither you nor I, Drusilla. It's as well you should know a parson's lot, my dear. Our own wishes are nothing to the duty of office."

Her heart sank at the untidily cropped hair, the weather-beaten face, the work-a-day clothes, yet rose again at the kindest of eyes looking into her own.

"Come, Drusilla. I will most certainly be expected to stay the night at my cousin's. There are family matters to settle

285

that might be to our advantage and my allotted two minutes with you are well past. I promise we shall ride over to Sedgebrook together before the month is out. Now give me your hand and your love for Fanny, if not for me."

Tears that before had vexed her voice now wetted her cheeks but he turned and was gone. The nosegay, a delight-fully nimble arrangement of roses and greenery, dropped unnoticed to her feet. If only she were a man she would ride over to Sedgebrook in a trice, excuses neither given nor expected. And there again, if she were a man she would take a gun or a sword to that villain and call him out. Smarting under William's rebuff she looked up at the sky and sniffed at the weather. It was one of those grey, rain-beckoning days that might turn fine after all. She returned to the house where Mama and Uncle Peter flurried about the hall.

"You would learn nothing there," said Dorothy, not waiting for any reply.

Pleas and counter pleas rallied themselves in Drusilla's heart and in her head. They battled and stuck in her throat, a barrier as strong as a stone wall holding them back. Don't go, Mama. Please don't go. Poor Bridget, she . . .. For God's sake go. The both of you go. I will save Bridget myself. Oh, Mama, if only you knew. Poor Bridget. That man . . .

Speechless she watched Dorothy's unusual flustered searchings for gloves, bonnet strings, shawl, handkerchief, walking cane; caught a screech from upstairs from one of the maids; eyed a steady drip – drip of water down from the ceiling and into the hall; heard a gasp from the doctor; a bundling of Mama through the front door; the roll of wheels down the drive; the heavy puffing of Nellie up the front stairs and a 'Lord above us, what be going on y'ere, then?' and a veritable cascade of water from heaven knows where soaking her through.

Whatever domestic catastrophe was afoot she thanked the Lord for it as she raced to the stable block, unheedful of dripping hair and wet clothes, for added to her anxiety was the exultation that today, at least, she was her own mistress.

How silently she cursed Mama forcing the Hobbs into extra work in the wood yard, as she struggled to harness her uncle's colt, a wild thing if ever there was one, but he would fly wherever she wanted, near as quick as one of those contraptions imagined by Papa and Uncle Peter so long ago. She ignored the slobbering dogs and the soft whinny of her own little mare, too gentle by far for this morning's work. Anybody who could sit a sedan could ride her and at the speed of a chair, too, she'd no doubt. It took all her strength to force the curb between the colt's teeth as he flung back his head, showing whites of eye at her unpractised hand. She heaved down a saddle that weighed near a ton, abandoned the struggle to lift it on to the animal's back and, in desperation, leapt up and rode him into the yard bestraddled like a man, not forgetting in passing to grab hold of a whip.

The colt kicked back with his hooves and flew off the way she willed him to go. Down the steep hill on the far side of the house he slithered, never faltering, knowing every hump, every hollow, caring not a jot for the spectacle, light as a feather, upon his back. The spectacle herself thanked God there was nobody to see her uncovered hair that trailed in the wind set up by the speed of the colt, for there was no other, her loose hose hanging at heel, the flutterings of wide under-petticoats, the show of white legs near up to the knee.

She kept the rein loose and the colt flew like a demon across the tough terrain, skirting Balderton village and on to the Grantham Road. Faster, Boy! Faster! The whip thrashed on his neck as he took the old track to Allington and the heavy going through bog that threw up great clods as far as her face. Good Boy! Good Boy! He neither slipped nor stumbled till Sedgebrook Church caught her eye, holding it fast. She tugged at the rein to turn the colt up the long drive to the Manor. Good Boy. She held the rein steady and breathed easy at last. Whoa, Boy. Whoa. She slid down to bang at the great oaken door and at that moment the promised rain began to fall.

How she persuaded the haggard young bride to give up her vigil and get up on the colt in front of her she never would know. Drenched to the skin, caked with mud, they trotted back to Beacon Hill the long way round by road. What might be the outcome of her morning's work Drusilla had no way of knowing. She knew only that she had promised Tom and Eddie to look after their sister, that poor Bridget seemed more than usually half out of her wits and was not to be left unattended at Sedgebrook to wait for that – that murderer.

There! The word was out at last, for that was what she believed and knew him to be.

CHAPTER 28

Somebody was hammering at Death's door that night but it was certainly not William Knight's cousin at Edgington. That elderly gentleman was sitting up, hale and hearty, demanding roast beef and parsnips for dinner by the time William reached his bedside.

At Beacon House was a different story.

Here fires were lighted, warming pans filled, flannels heated, water boiled, possets and poultices prepared and, all over the house, could be heard the terrible sound of stentorian breathing. Thank God, in this house, at least, there was no need to fetch a doctor. Peter was in his element and those who expected Death's door to yield would be disappointed. The doctor with his maids turned into nurses, running upstairs and down from bedchamber to kitchen and back again, had that door firmly bolted and barred. In spite of poor Bridget's desperate efforts it would not budge.

When, on his way home, William called to repay his respects to Drusilla, to say he would be only too pleased to ride over to Sedgebrook, if that be her wish, the need was long past. He left slowly and thoughtfully, the sickening combination of gruel, pastille burners and rum still in his nostrils.

Dorothy was at her wit's end. Not a word of sense could be got out of Drusilla. Whatever had she been thinking of to land them with such a responsibility? Neither she nor Peter had had a moment to consider their foraging expedition for news. Neither Jenison gossip nor that pertinent report in the Weekly Courier picked up from the White Harte were of any consequence with a life in one's hands.

When, after weeks of careful nursing, the patient's bodily health improved, though her reason not a jot, then Drusilla was forced to reveal that incriminating letter.

An early frost and bitter wind had hastened the year's advance. Together they conspired to strip the last brown leaves from the oak and encrust the holly white with hoar. There was no work done in rimy fields and woods; brick works and saw mill were at a standstill and indoors folk were hard at it to keep themselves warm. Blazing fires scorched knees and faces while draughty doors chilled backs to the marrow and Dorothy much too preoccupied to chide Drusilla about scorch marks and pole screens.

Bridget's was the only room in the house where they had managed to stop all draughts, to keep an even temperature and hang the cost. Drusilla sat up there now, her role to amuse the patient and try to bring some order to her muddled brain, otherwise, she was grateful to be let alone.

"But on no account," Dr. Peter was firm, "on no account at all, introduce any subject that might raise another brainstorm."

That left the nurse with precious little to say except are you warm enough, Bridget dear; is there anything you need; do you wish to sew, to play cards, to read? She dare not add to write for that was all Bridget had wanted to do when she first came out of her fever. She had worked endlessly with pen and paper practising the letters of her name, never getting further than the first syllable, Brid – Brid – Brid. And when Drusilla had told her to 'dot the is, Bridget dear,' the poor girl had turned the pen upon herself till her eyelids and forehead were a mass of inky freckles. The ink spilled everywhere, upon cap, face, hands and bodice till Dr. Peter had ordered the writing materials to be put away.

"Sure, 'twas a lovely document so it was, Drusilla. We both signed it, man and wife, so we did. And the priest and Uncle Markham and all. 'Twas a lovely document so it was."

There was nothing Drusilla could do but repeat her questions and at each one poor Bridget, rail thin in her cast-offs, shook her head, smiled, teeth larger than ever in her wan face, wept, dried her eyes and whinnied. In short she behaved no differently from the day her breathing had eased and her fever abated.

Drusilla's heart went out to her. That man she must not, nor could not, mention by name was forever on her mind. Her anger that was near to tears almost took control and, suddenly, she could stand the sickroom heat no longer. At least if she could not let the frosty air in she could look out upon it and imagine the delight of great gulps of it.

A door opened and closed immediately behind Nellie.

"Miss Drusilla, don't you be opening that there window, mind. Dr. Peter be . . ."

Drusilla smiled in spite of herself. It was quite true, Nellie could read her like a book whether she knew a single letter of the alphabet or no.

"I'm to stay up y'ere with Miss Bridget, Miss Drusilla. Your Mama and Dr. Peter do be waiting for you in the little parlour, if you do please."

Dorothy and Dr. Peter sat up to the round table there, a great fire crackling behind them, Anthony's portrait smiling down on them and an old copy of the Weekly Courier between them. It was obvious their patience was at an end. Drusilla carried her apprehension tight within her like the crumpled, much read letter she still concealed in her bodice. Dr. Peter's face creased to a forced smile as he drew up a chair.

"Come, Drusilla, my poppet, now tell us how our patient improves."

She did not wish to reply. She knew the request was not innocent. She had noticed the drawstring pursing of Dorothy's mouth, the falseness of her uncle's affability. She guessed there had been some discussion beforehand and knew she was to be inquisitioned. She had always been nervous of discovery of any little wrong or misdemeanor and now a great feeling of guilt weighed like a leaden shawl on her shoulders. She looked at her would-be interrogators and tried to keep her own feelings at arm's length but the note in her bodice, as well as her fear, almost shouted aloud. She looked to Papa's portrait for support and found none. Her uncle's voice resumed its heartiness.

"If you young ladies were well enough, my dear, we would have you outside, well wrapped up for the sliding and skating, with cheeks as red as Beauties of Bath instead of cooped up here, pale and thin."

She smiled bleakly, tremulously.

"This frost is the very devil – and no sign of it yielding yet. Everything's slowed to a standstill, news included."

Dorothy put out a hand to catch at Drusilla's cold fingers.

"Drusilla, my dear, there are things you must know now you are strong enough and if you can throw any light on Bridget's trouble then you must let us have it." Drusilla shifted her shoulders uncomfortably as far as the lump of lead would allow. "She has a family of her own, my dear, and cannot stay with us for ever, to say nothing of her state of mind which does not improve at all. Uncle Peter can do no more, surely you see . . ."

"Drusilla, you know Markham is dead." Dr. Peter decided to grasp the nettle. "Do you know that he left nothing at all to the Ogles? Not a penny to either Tom or Eddie or Bridget? Do you know that his entire fortune goes to Bernard Webster and that the new will was made not too long since, as Sir Matthew Jenison told us. And he had it from his own attorney who says the Inns of Court are full of it. And with Sir Matthew's bankruptcy case coming up any day he is better informed than anybody else in Newent. You can imagine how he enjoyed the telling of it. Nothing like somebody else's troubles to dispel one's own."

Drusilla was speechless. The shawl felt heavier. Her shoulders drooped.

"And Tom and Eddie Ogle are so hell-bent on getting their money back they seen to have forgotten they have a sister, except to blame her for their misfortune."

His voice softened. He knew she still had to hear the worst.

"And to cap it all, Webster has left his father at the Vicarage, moved into his new house on Baldertongate and taken Bessie Bradford with him, the trollop."

Still no sound came from Drusilla. She could do nothing but shake her head and let Dorothy keep hold of her hand. The leaden shawl weighed heavier than ever. She would have given anything to lay her head somewhere, the table even, but dare not.

"Newent is full of it," Dorothy's voice was crisp. "Everybody is bringing up those old rumours of Markham being his natural father and I'm damned if I don't think there might be some truth . . ."

Drusilla withdrew her hand as though from a wasp's nest. Don't swear, Mama, she prayed, please don't swear. Dorothy's coarseness suddenly brought home that day when Uncle Peter had broken the news of their own lost fortune. It was not a happy memory and she tried to shut her mind against it. If only there were somewhere to lay her head and shift the weight from her shoulders.

Dorothy looked at her empty hand with regret. Once she would have been irritated by that sharp withdrawal and wondered whatever it was made that child so prickly and difficult and was there any other mother in this world with so much trouble? But not now. Now she knew only the deepest sorrow that she and Drusilla should be at such odds. If only she could bridge the gulf between them she would. She sighed. To be met half way would be something.

"Read this, my dear," Dr. Peter thrust the newspaper into Drusilla's hand.

"Her eyes caught the title words. 'Bernard Webster D.D. Vicar of Newent St. Leonards in the County of Nottingham-

shire Offers this Vindication of his Mother a Virtuous Woman.'
She read as commanded and, though the words shimmered and
blurred through her tears, she got the gist of them.

'It has come to the notice of this Reverend Gentleman that
the Good Name of his Dead Mother is Slandered not only in
this County but in the Metropolis and Country Places. He
States and Confirms his Mother's Virtue was and Remains
Spotless. His Parents' only Relationship with Sir George
Markham Bt. of Sedgebrook in the County of Lincolnshire
now Deceased was to Aid him Electioneer for the Seat of
Newent St. Leonards. Sir George Markham was Ever
Grateful and Repaid by Finding the Tenancy of the Friary in
Appletongate to Conduct their Business. He supported their
Son, Bernard Webster, at Westminster School and With
Other Benefactors Supported his Candidature for Cambridge
and the living of Newent St. Leonards. Bernard Webster
D.D. was his Steward and Friend and Dedicated his Great
Work of Translations from the French to his Benefactor thus
Claiming his Protection. Articles of the King's Peace will be
Exhibited in the King's Bench Against Any who Outrage
Name or Person of Bernard Webster D.D. '

"And what is more," said Dorothy, "he has had bills
printed to that effect and posted all over Newent and in the
London coffee houses. The country's agog and Matthew
Jenison has it there have been questions asked in high places
and all the periodicals. But he is as clever and devious . . ."

"And impudent," interrupted her brother.

Drusilla's hand went straight to her bodice. She laid
Bridget's letter upon the table where Dorothy's quick fingers
made the first snatch.

"Tish! I make neither head nor tail of this," she handed the
torn and crumpled thing, splodged with Bridget's blots and
Drusilla's tears, to the doctor.

"It's plain enough, as I read it. They are married."

"Married!" Dorothy shrieked. She stood so quickly her
chair crashed to the floor, her ribbony cap, the lace at her

neck and her wrists all of a quiver. "Is that a married woman we are harbouring upstairs?"

"I'll lay odds married but not consummated – and nothing better than a Fleet Marriage at that. The country's full of marriage criers and Grantham will have its share of unfrocked villains who'll do anything for a fee – no questions asked, no answers given. And, by Jove, there's a certain priest in Newent would join 'em if I had my way. The man's not worthy to wear the cloth."

He took advantage of his sister's speechlessness and gathered spate.

"It must be forty years since the law required a registry of marriages as well as births and deaths and no more notice taken of it than a dose of physick. There's no protection for a woman at all till we get some proper marriage laws. And how the devil we'll do it when the Chancellor himself is a blatant bigamist and all the world knows it . . ."

Dorothy picked up her chair and sat down again to shut him up. He'd gotten his teeth into a subject and before long it would be another hobby-horse and they'd never hear the last of it. He'd be drawing up marriage laws of his own and presenting them to parliament and they'd be no more effective than his useless water closet. The sooner he got back to physicking and pill-making the better.

"What do you know, Drusilla?" She asked sharply.

Drusilla could only shake her head while the doctor forgot his marriage laws, or lack of them, and gathered his wits.

"Here's a pretty kettle of fish, my dears. Markham dead. Webster married. To an Ogle, though not acknowledged. Webster inherits. The Ogles don't get a penny. Though they are rightful heirs, remember that. And Webster takes Bessie Bradford to live with him as bold as brass. There is only one place for this letter and that is the fire for it won't do this family any good to be mixed up in this dung heap. And the sooner Tom or Edmund Ogle come to claim their sister the better."

"No! No! No!" Drusilla shouted, not knowing where her strength came from. "It is my letter and I'll not give it up. It could be the saving of poor Bridget."

"And our downfall."

"And perhaps not," said Dorothy, suddenly calm. "Drusilla is right. It is her letter till we need it. Keep it safe." She folded the missive thoughtfully, handed it back and felt herself in command. "We have got to get word to the Ogle brothers as quick as we can."

"Tish!" Peter borrowed Dorothy's expression. "As mad as hatters, the pair of 'em. The whole family alike."

"And tish to you!" Dorothy's pock-marked face had on that calculating look. Drusilla knew so well. "If that is what you think then keep it to yourself. That's the excuse Webster will give to make them and Bridget look like a trio of crazy liars. It's his only defence."

"Against what?"

"Against what he's done. It's as plain as a pikestaff and you too blind to see it. Now, do we pay another visit to Matthew Jenison or do we send you up to London?"

A violent ringing of the doorbell saved them the answer. They almost held their breath, it seemed, till Nellie appeared.

"Miss Dor'thy, Mr. William Knight be y'ere and begs leave to see you alone. Miss Dor'thy, I done have taken the liberty of showing him in to the drawing room and done have told May to light up the fire in there."

A strange wailing sound floated from upstairs, hung in the air, died away and started up again. Nellie cocked her head and turned an alarmed expression to her mistress.

"That must be Miss Bridget, Miss Dor'thy."

The wailing increased but Dorothy decided William Knight could not wait, while Drusilla followed Uncle Peter and Nellie swiftly upstairs.

The heat in the bedchamber was intense. Bridget was stripped to her shift. Unashamedly she held up the hem of that garment and presented her thin body for them all to see.

The neighing quality of her voice subdued, she ran her spare hand over her loins.

"He said I had the loveliest, softest, sweetest little nest he had ever seen and the duckiest little bird in there he had ever felt. And I will go to him. I will. I will. It should be me so it should, in that new house in Baldertongate. By the Great Horn Spoon. He built it for me, Drusilla, so he did, and not for anybody else at all, at all. So he did. So he did." Still that spare hand caressed her poor bones.

Drusilla caught her breath. Whoever could have been so careless as to tell her about Bessie Bradford? Not May. Surely not May. Nor Nellie neither.

"Take no notice, Drusilla," said the doctor, already making preparations. "It's nothing more than the extraordinary intuition of a mad woman"

"What is Bradford to him? He is mine, so he is. And the softest, the sweetest, the loveliest little duck I'll be having!"

Dr. Peter got the laudanum between her teeth. Nellie laid her upon the bed. Drusilla held her hand and wept. The heat in the room was enough to make the strongest feel faint but she hung on to herself for Bridget's sake.

Downstairs, in a different temperature, Dorothy braced herself to meet her visitor. She sat now on her best walnut sofa and William Knight stood before the smoking fire, the room as cold as an icehouse. It had not been used since her return from Bath and had a neglected air of gathering dust and tarnishing silver. Well, there had been other things to think of, no time for entertaining, and she knew their trouble was not finished yet. How untidily William Knight dressed nowadays, more like a common yeoman than a clergyman. She sniffed. But that don't signify much. He looked mighty serious.

"Mrs. Davison, I have come with the most unfortunate news and I want you to hear the full truth of it, not half truths and gossips and rumours."

His eyes smiled kindly down at her as if to ease the pain of what was to come.

"There has been a deputation to the Bishop complaining of your old protegé, Bernard Webster. The charges against him are prodigious. He has misappropriated to his own use funds of the St. Leonard's Hospital. He has sold coloured glass from the church windows and pocketed the money. He has accepted bribes from tradesmen that they be given repair work to do and they have done it badly. Some of the church windows are stuffed up with broken bottles and mortar. He has given gross and drunken dinners as political bribes and paid for them out of church funds. He has increased the salaries of choristers and bell-ringers beyond that which is permitted only to have his hold over them. The people are incensed and he has been called a liar in his own church . . ."

But what in the world has this to do with me? This is tedious stuff, thought Dorothy. And whatever is happening upstairs? This room is not just neglected – it is dirty. Nellie is getting old.

William Knight looked sternly down.

"His ruling passions are Lust, Avarice, Ambition and Impudence," he gave each vice a capital letter.

Impudence; she had heard that word already this morning. Peter had used it. She raised her head to look her informant full in the face.

"He means to build more houses for his own advantage as close to the church as he can get. And he is planning to annex church land to do it."

Dorothy was listening but not to William. Her ears were strained to catch any sound from upstairs. The deathly quiet increased her apprehension. She could not see the fire for her unwelcome visitor and could not feel it either. This room was not only dirty, it was as cold as a vault. She shivered and wished she was wearing a thicker gown.

"He has published a further vindication of his conduct. He states Sir George Markham made his will freely and the Ogles are mad and not to be believed."

Her ears pricked at last. She had thought as much herself.

That was what she had expected Bernard Webster to say. William Knight's next words brought her back to the drawing room and kept her there, hands and feet freezing but eyes warming.

"Nevertheless, the Ogle affair is at an end. They have settled out of court. Webster has handed over thirty thousand pounds of Markham's money, though that leaves him with one hundred thousand for his own use. The man is an embezzler, a thief. The two brothers, Thomas and Edmund, are deranged over the sad affair, conveniently so, for that helps his case."

She stopped her ears. Then where does that leave Bridget? What in the world are we to do about Bridget? But she said nothing and his voice forced itself upon her as though he did not expect her to say anything either.

"This, Mrs. Davison, you will not know. He has been frequently absent from his own parishes, supposedly on church business."

Dorothy's ears pricked again. 'On church business.' Where had she heard that phrase before and not so long since, either?

"He has, in reality, been visiting a young woman in the village of Holborn near London. And not one belonging to the notorious houses of that place, but a respectable young woman who has sued him for breach of promise. She has been awarded seven thousand pounds in damages."

Oh Drusilla! My poor Drusilla. Dorothy closed her eyes. She sensed there was more to come and squared her shoulders, lifted her chin.

"His shame is in all the newspapers and magazines, even the best of them. You are bound to hear of it. Early yesterday morning he took a closed carriage to Claypole with Miss Elizabeth Bradford well tucked up inside and married her there. They were followed by a curious servant who watched through a church window and saw it all. I will not repeat the gossip about Miss Bradford, Mrs. Davison. But she, no

299

doubt, has a hold over him and he may have met his match at last.

You don't believe me, Mrs. Davison?" He smiled.

"Oh yes, I believe you. Every word." She rose from the sofa where she had felt at a disadvantage and now faced him on level ground. "You have just confirmed what I saw but the others did not. The priest was a notary; The document was a will."

"I do not follow, Mrs Davison." William Knight was puzzled. This affair was enough to derange other minds than the Ogles'.

"It matters not." She felt unaccountably strong and light-hearted, as though a great weight had gone from her back. Her blue eyes shone kindly as they had not done for years. William Knight was encouraged.

"Mrs. Davison, you must know I have admired Miss Drusilla for many years, too many by far, but could not declare myself without something to offer. I have already made plain my intentions to the young lady herself and she did not rebuff me, so I am full of expectation."

Not too plain, I hope, Mr. Knight, thought Dorothy, remembering her own Anthony's ardent wooing.

"I am asking you for your blessing and her hand."

"I can give you the one but not the other. Drusilla must speak for herself." She knew now that her many years of bitterness had, after all, not been too high a price for her few of the sweetest bliss. She looked up and was relieved to meet the kindest and warmest of brown eyes, a darker shade of Anthony's own but without his dangerous devilment. "Be patient, Drusilla is a good girl and I will send her down to you."

"I will never give up. She is the only woman I will ever take. And I am a patient man, Mrs. Davison."

Bridget was sound into her laudanum-drenched sleep. Drusilla was resigned. There could only be a lunatick asylum for her friend. She shuddered at the thought of old Mr.

Patefield at Bingham in his hut in the market square with its staring, stupid, hostile crowds.

"But let it be a good one, Uncle Peter, where she will know only kindness, some small private place, some family perhaps where there will be no cruel audience as at a circus. Whatever money I still have from Papa, she can have it."

Dorothy led her gently from the bedside, directed Nellie to spend a few moments' repair to hair and face and sent her down to the drawing room. Drusilla descended the stairs slowly. She liked William Knight well enough. And rather more than well enough. She admitted that freely. She had enjoyed that day at North Heskham immeasurably until poor Bridget had demolished the walls of her airy castles. Her face hardened. No, she would not risk another turning herself into a doll over a man. Decisively, straight backed, shoulders squared and head high, she crossed the hall and turned the knob of the drawing room door.

Dorothy and Dr. Peter sat in the little parlour snugly waiting. Peter rubbed his hands and helped them both to brandy.

"I never thought there could be such a satisfactory conclusion to this hornet's nest, my dear Dorothy. But now 'tis done, I hear Mulberry House is on the market again, so let us sell this place, brick kilns, wood yard and all, and go back to town. I promise I'll build up my practice again. We'll live as snug and comfortable as anybody. For remember this, shrouds don't come like your best dresses with pockets made to match, my dear." He swilled his mouth with liquor and swallowed noisily.

Dorothy held up a warning finger. "You are counting chickens, my dear Peter."

The door opened into the room, letting in a blast of cold air. There stood Drusilla dressed, surprisingly, in a coat and bonnet, her head high, and bright spots of colour returned to her cheeks. Both Peter and Dorothy, mouths open, rose to their feet. Drusilla held up in her hand the cryptic note.

"The fire?" the doctor suggested, head on one side, wondering why ever in the world she was dressed like that and where was William Knight?

"A young woman from Holborn got seven thousand pounds for breach of promise," Drusilla's voice was hard and high. "What would be the price for bigamy? I want my own school."

"And it won't be necessary for you to go extortioning to get it. It would be useless anyway for that's the only crime he's not guilty of."

"Oh Dottie, my dear, be kind. Be very kind."

"You shall have your school, my child, even though we have to turn the copse into a plaster pit to pay for it." Dorothy opened her arms.

The leaden shawl slipped and was gone. Drusilla was across the room in a moment to lay her head upon Dorothy's bosom.

"Oh, Mama. Oh, my dearest Mama."

Relief swept over her like the comfort of a warm bath. She would get what she now knew wanted more than anything else in the world. To be a free woman, to be an influence for good under nobody's tyranny but her own and to be at peace with Mama. These things were within her reach at last. She would not let them slip.

1968

CHAPTER 29

The Beresford family had been working on the wreck of Beacon House from Easter to September. As soon as the roof was finished and the Newton paraphernalia shifted, they had thrown themselves into an orgy of plastering, painting. tiling and every kind of do-it-yourselfing they could think of.

Lucy and Emily laboured like beavers on their adjoining rooms and, though Emily and her rickety sewing machine had turned out a rushing torrent of curtains, bedspreads, cushions and chair covers, she was well and truly finished before Lucy had as much as started.

Lucy was too particular to have everything exactly right. She used up time and energy insisting nobody should see her efforts till all was done, which made her a luckless target for the Nibs' teasing. She was forever slamming her door shut fast; enough to bring the house down, said Flo, let alone chop the twins' fingers off. She made trial sketch after sketch, worrying about width of hoops, lowness of necklines, depths of cuffs, lengths of hemlines, full wigs and half wigs, hats and caps. Her waste basket overflowed with discarded efforts and she hysterically accused the boys of sifting through them to find out her secrets.

"Daddy's the history expert, why don't you save yourself all this bother and ask his advice?" Flo queried.

"I don't want to ask him," came the vehement reply. "Can't you understand I'd like to do something all by myself without somebody else butting in?"

Poor Flo wondered whatever it was made that child so prickly and difficult and did any other mother have the same problem?

Sam and Robert half-tiled the vast kitchen, hampered by the Nibs who covered miles between one do-it-yourselfer and another.

"Don't be in too much of a rush, you two. When it's all done you'll find we're not so happy to have you dim wits tearing all over the place, upstairs and downstairs and in my lady's . . . DON'T DO THAT and KEEP O U T O F THERE."

But even Lucy's caustic comments could not wipe the grins from the Nibs' faces. Smiles ran from ear to ear like a couple of Devonshire splits. They were in their element, enjoying picnics, bonfires and the general atmosphere of dirt and chaos. On rainy days they chased up bare stairs and landings, bashing each other with whatever broom and dustpan they could lay their hands on. There were deafening shouts of 'No Quarter' until Edward pushed a shield-wielding elbow through the glass of the kitchen dresser and Henry's pikestaff sent a light fitting flying. Accused of vandalism, they avoided Flo's fury with sudden and violent fits of coughing that, with much practice, developed galloping consumptive proportions.

Their culminating joy was a friendly, old-fashioned chimney sweep till Sam stepped in, forcing him to refuse their sincere, but doubtful, offers of help.

Between them, Sam and Flo restored the lovely main staircase, broken steps remoulded, balusters repaired and gilded, oaken handrail gleaming richly brown, just as Flo had imagined it would. Wall niches were painted, shelved and lighted and already she had tried out her best glass and china in one combination after another. Sam had relaid stone flags in the courtyard and spent pounds they could not afford in sale rooms on garden urns and furniture; money that might have been better spent on replacing that old boundary fence, thought Flo, though not for the world would she dampen Sam's enthusiasm.

She said for years they had been struggling underwater, near suffocating in a sea of ordinariness. Now, at last, they were coming up for light and air of the rarest quality.

"Don't get carried away, old girl," Sam had grinned. His outward calm optimism hid an obsession with interest rates, loans and accounts, and a perverse wish to give Flo whatever she wanted. It never occurred to her he saw the hazards so much more clearly than she, and now and then his guard slipped.

He had come across the Nibs engaged in a furious battle of fisticuffs over possession of a hose-pipe and, by the way Edward seemed to be getting the worst of it, not the mock variety either. Sam rounded on the victor who, seeing the thunderous look on his father's face, dropped his trophy and, careless whether Sam got a dowsing or no, showed a clean pair of heels across the courtyard.

Flo watched the comical sight of a nimble ten year old shinning at breakneck speed up the coach house wall while the corpulent fifty year old Sam huffed and puffed in sweaty pursuit. The boy scrambled to safety over the coach house roof; the cursing Sam admitted defeat and stamped off to change his wet clothes. Flo could not fail to notice he took the whole trivial incident rather more seriously than he should.

When a white-faced Henry reappeared, obviously still smarting from a mistaken sense of injustice, forgetting all family rules, her heart went out to him.

"Come here to me, Henry," she said, arms wide. "There's a Mars bar in my pocket."

"What?" spat Henry, his smouldering temper springing to life in a flash. "Accept a Mars bar from the wife of Cassius Clay? Never!" And, at the sight of Edward peering round a corner, he ran off to pummel the life out of him.

As the thirsty man guzzles his ale so the Beresfords

opened their mouths for great gulps of Flo's rarified atmosphere, almost to the point of intoxication. And, of course, the word 'ghost' hung in the air like a cobweb, high up and out of reach, in spite of Flo's matter of fact efforts to brush it away.

When Lucy vowed they would discover the most exquisitely painted murals on the drawing room walls, Flo was quick to rub home that all they got for their pains were broken nails and sore fingers. When a scream like a Dervish jerked all their terrified heads upwards, she smartly proved the hideous row was no more than Robert putting his big feet through a wooden floor where somebody, Sam of course, had made a rotten job of floor board replacement. As she said, anybody who has lived in a house with four males was well used to people screaming before they were even tickled. Odd creaks and groans were put down to the old house complaining about the discomfort of Sam's do-it-yourself central heating. Creepers that tapped at window panes inviting Robert to croak, "Cathy, for God's sake come home!", sending the Nibs into paroxysms of half-pretended fear, Flo ordered to be cut to the ground. Squeaks from the odd room she put down to mice, though the baited traps remained infuriatingly unsprung.

"Pooh!" Flo said on the last day of the holiday. "It's hot. I'll be glad when . . .

"What did you say?" Lucy demanded with a sharp, watchful look on her face.

"I said 'Pooh – it's hot . . .'."

"No you didn't. You said 'Tish!'"

"I certainly did not, I've never said 'Tish' in my life."

"Yes you have. You're always saying it. You said it just now."

"Lucy, I did not."

"You did. You did. Why did you say Tish if you meant Pooh?"

Flo held on to herself to stay both hand and tongue

lashing out. "For Heaven' s sake, what does it matter? Go outside all of you and get some fresh air while I finish the clearing up. See if the blackberries are ripe. Then we'll go home. There are a thousand things to do there, let alone here, Heaven knows."

She turned to clean the last of the paintbrushes. Emily gathered up the remains of the picnic. Sam picked up a broom. He couldn't understand what the row was about. Women were the very devil.

Robert chased the Nibs whooping it down to the old quarry. Lucy followed at a slower pace. There was no need to push one's way through the shrubbery since the boys had done a mammoth pruning job. The top of the copse was in view but she turned to look back at the house.

"I love it," she said aloud, shielding her eyes from the sun. "And I can't wait to live in it."

She took in every detail of their repair and restoration not yet finished. Daddy still had not made up his mind whether to remove the stucco or not. The bank manager would decide in the end, he laughed, whenever Mummy pressed. It was on occasions like these, after a tiring day, that the stucco so often had faded away, the rose red of new brick glowing warm in the sunlight. Now the scene stayed obstinately and normally in the present and she was glad of that.

She left Daddy's half finished boundary fence that Mummy was always nagging about and continued down the side of the old quarry to the copse beyond. The day was warm and bright but there were no ripe blackberries as far as she could see. Her face tucked into a smile. She had conquered it. She was sure she had. That feeling she never wanted to feel again. Should she put herself to the test? She dared herself to go down to the garden house. She would think of other things. The copse was as lovely in September as it had been in spring and early summer. Fluffy seed heads of willow herb parachuted softly in the balmy air.

Her project was nearly finished now. Nobody, she was

sure, would produce anything so original or in such detail. She was bound to be the winner. It might even get her the School Prize. She would die if it didn't. She'd worked a hundred times harder than anybody else. It wouldn't be fair. Em had dashed hers off in next to no time. She noticed the hazelnuts were ripening and, if only those little devils would leave them alone, they should get a good crop, choosing to forget they were all trespassers once they got beyond the shrubbery.

The thing was, what to call it? Was just Webster's Place too ordinary? The magical, enigmatic words she wanted refused to come. Good old Daddy, it was his suggestion had started her off. Or was it that day the Rector called? A combination of the two really.

She could hear the boys somewhere near the trees and could do without their crappy company, thankyou very much.

All this hoo-ha about whether the street should be demolished or not gave such a sharp point to the whole thing. The more she thought of it, just plain Webster's Place was exactly right. Built by that Dr. Bernard Webster, a pluralist if ever there was one. He'd pinched half the Vicarage garden, all the churchwarden's garden and even part of the graveyard to do it. Cheek! What was it his bailiff had said to the poor widow who wanted to rent one of his new houses? 'Widows! The Dr. has no houses for widows. Widows don't vote.' That was when he was dabbling in politics against the Duke of Newcastle, in a pique because the Duke wouldn't get him a bishopric. Could all those tales she had unearthed possibly be true? She could write reams about him and had done.

Well, it was finished now. She needn't go to Edgington again, thank Goodness. That man gave her the creeps. Mummy would have a fit if she knew. She daren't even tell Em. Mummy would be bound to think the worst. Mothers always did. Why was it she found her own Mother so irritating but could get on with everybody else's? She didn't want to be at loggerheads. She wanted to be kind and loving but Mummy always said something to set her teeth on edge. But it wasn't always Mummy's fault. She must try harder. She did try . . .

A spray of blackberries hung before her like devil's fruit. Absentmindedly she crammed the purple globules into her mouth. They were the first food she had taken that day and once started she could not stop.

The ground flattened beneath her feet and here were the columns.

She felt unaccountably weary, her body a leaden weight. She dragged her feet up the stone base, sat down on the ivy-covered hexagonal block and closed her eyes as that familiar feeling, as cold as stone, crept up her back. Wishing she had not gobbled all those blackberries, she leaned back against the rounded niche of polished stone that wasn't there. She ought to put her head between her knees. That was the remedy for nausea, but her back held fast to the stone as though by force. Time died away as it had done before.

She opened her eyes and it was dark, pitch dark. I am asleep she told herself and closed her eyes again. A familiar smell filled her nostrils, that floral-apothecary odour that excited, frightened and disgusted her. She felt sick. She moved her hand, brushing her clothing as she did so and flinched. She felt a smoothness she had not known these past months. She had become used to hands, roughened and cracked through hard work, pricking and grating unpleasantly, snagging threads and laddering tights. Now her hands were unusually soft and moved smoothly over her light cotton skirt. The touch, the smell, the dark were all new yet familiar. She had sensed them all before but could not remember where or when.

A long forgotten dream stirred in the convoluted depths of her consciousness as she struggled against the passing of Time. An ache started up in her stomach.

There was the sound of a quick, light tread through the

309

undergrowth nearby. She wanted desperately to get up but could not. Tiredness still lay like a ton weight on her body. The brisk step closed in, then she heard a man's quiet voice.

"Are you awake?"

It was a pleasant voice, attractive, resonant, smooth, seductive; she ran the gamut of all the adjectives she could think of. It was a voice for winning hearts and breaking them. It terrified her. Her own voice inside her head was urgent.

"No. No. I am not awake. I am asleep."

She hoped, she wished, she willed that to be true. She was afraid he could be real and not a dream. She knew him. She had seen him before and wished never to see him again. I must wake up, she told herself, yet perversely she closed her eyes and longed for sleep, the oblivion of dead sleep.

"Are you awake?" The man's voice was insistent.

She shook her head. She must not speak. To speak was to admit the presence of the man, the man she never wanted to see again, the combination of dark charged with smell she never wanted to sense again. She made one last gigantic effort to push this unhouselled ghost away. Let him keep to his own world and she to hers.

There were echoes of dreams ringing inside her head and she knew they were dreams but was uncertain where she was and why and could not be sure whether she was dreaming and remembering reality or awake and remembering dreams. She held on grimly to the taut thread of her bare consciousness of being, deliberately forgetting sharp and definite identities. A shapeless shadow moved round her, over her, through her, as though she were not there. Perhaps it was no more than her own invention. She hoped it was that and shuddered in her unnatural sleep. So tired she was, she could hold on no longer. The taut thread snapped beneath her desperate grip and that shadow broke into her world, sharp and clearly cut, the once blurred features of the man now well defined as she slipped helplessly down the aeons of Time.

She opened her eyes to see the rounded arches of the garden house and between them and beyond was that pleasant greenery she knew and loved. A pheasant clacked hard by. A rabbit scuttled. A pigeon cooed. The September air was soft and warm like silk.

She pressed her back harder into the rounded stone niche as the man bent over her. She winced as he picked up her hand and held on to it. His own hand was no dream. It was real and warm and pressing, a loathsome hand and she was disgusted by it. A current shot up her arm from the press of his lips on her palm. Did he know she felt that thrill of revulsion? She would die of shame if he misinterpreted it.

In spite of herself she whispered his name. It was an odious name and she shuddered at her own pronouncement. The man pressed closer. His breath sickened her.

"You must not tell. There is no truth in the tales you might hear. Promise to say nothing. Do you understand me?"

He squeezed her hand cruelly as he had squeezed it so many times before. "Promise!"

"Yes," she whispered and shivered in her thin clothes.

I know this place, her heart cried out. I know this man. Yet who is he and who am I?

She suffered the torture of not knowing whether to extricate her mind from an alien body or that other body from her own sane mind. Suddenly she remembered Edward with his chalk-white face when they had first found this place and his later disgust at the mention of that street. 'I don't like it' he had said of the one and 'I hate it' of the other.

"I must get away," she moaned inside her head. "I must get away now while I can." She tried desperately to take her leave but her body was still like lead and that man pressed closer. "I can't. I can't," she moaned to herself.

"Why can't you?" His voice roughened. "You must keep quiet about everything between us. I could bring down a terrible punishment upon you."

"How?" her eyes pleaded, for no sound would come.

"Witch!" He mouthed at her. "You could be burned and worse for what you have said and done." Her tongue clove to the roof of her mouth as his voice took on its pulpit tone.

"You have made damnable prophecies. You have conjured up Demons that fly to the Heavens and dive to the Depths. You have communed with those worse than our own Body Snatchers, Devils which deal in Stolen Hearts and Sacred Parts of the Body. You have given yourself to the Prince of Darkness and are Damned to all Eternity."

Her chest was bursting as though from over tight stays but at last brain and vocal chords pulled together. She screamed aloud and jolted herself into wakefulness, wet with the sweat of fear. Robert came running from the copse.

"Lord!" he panted. "What's up, Lucy?"

Lucy! Blessed name!

"I fell asleep," she gulped.

"You look terrible."

"I'm whacked, that's all." She lay a cramped arm across her forehead.

"Come on," he croaked tenderly, "I'll give you a push back to the house."

They spoke no more all the way up the steep slope, past the old quarry, straight through the shrubbery and the old rose garden but she felt the strength of his arm and was glad of it. He held open the iron gate and they could see Sam and Flo on the back terrace. Voices, argumentative, loud and angry hit them. They watched Flo go round towards the front of the house and they heard the fierce slam of a car door. Sam winced.

"What's up, Dad?" Robert asked.

"Nothing really. We're all tired I expect. That fellow from Edgington called and your Mother was rather rude to him, I thought. More than rude. Unkind really. Come on. Let's go home. Lucy looks all in."

They went round to the car. The engine was running with Flo in the driving seat, Emily behind her, an empty blackberry basket on her knee, purple stains round mouth and chin. The Nibs, trying to see their blue-black tongues in the mirror, were squashed in their usual corner. Sam got in the front, Lucy and Robert tucked into the back with the Nibs.

Flo had that set look on her face they knew so well. She released the brake and tore down the drive. She could see in the mirror her children's pale faces and felt more furious than ever.

"If that wretched man calls again . . ."

"My dear, you needn't worry about that," Sam's laugh was short. "After the way you . . ."

"And a good thing too. I never want to see or hear him again. The man's a lunatic and ought to be locked up – and his breath stinks! Early beds tonight, everybody, you look whacked."

The car nosed down the drive, a slight pause in the gateway, a sharp left turn and then, whoosh, down Beacon Hill.

"Steady on, old girl," said Sam mildly.

"My mind's made up," said Flo, her face still tight. "We definitely move in at the end of the month. We can easily do it. The sooner the better. It won't be so tiring doing all the work on the spot. Daddy can keep the office in Fair Promise Road till it's sold."

The children's glumness did not escape her.

"Cheer up. We'll have our first party at Beacon House by Michaelmas. And it's time somebody finished the boundary fence."

CHAPTER 30

Flo and the two girls were on their knees in the drawing room of Beacon House where cardboard boxes, tissue paper, luggage labels and a tangle of clothing littered the floor.

"Just look at this lot," said Lucy bitterly. "Em put all her things in a tidy heap and the louts have just left theirs like a jumble sale."

Flo, resigned to male untidiness, continued fastening and folding.

"Why do you let them get away with it? Why should we have to do it all?" Lucy insisted.

"Because it's quicker and less tiresome," said Emily, quietly helping her mother.

"You mean it's just pandering to them and their sloppy ways. I pity their wives if they ever get any. Where's the breeches for these?" She held up a blue satin waistcoat and Emily passed over the matching garment.

"Thanks," snapped Lucy. "That's Daddy's regency buck all found, though what an aging regency buck would be doing at a Queen Anne-cum-Georgian house party I don't know. Now for the two blackamoors."

"Why is it that things coming neatly out of boxes never go back the same way?" Flo sighed, straightening her back and pushed a stray curl out of her eyes.

"Oh, Mummy," Lucy was contrite. "You're tired. Let's not bother. It was a super party and there are still the glasses to do."

"We must bother. They'll charge extra for this lot if we don't get them off today. And the glasses can wait. You're sitting on Mrs. Fitzherbert's wig. Be careful, we don't want to have to buy another."

"No, we jolly well don't," Lucy was irritable again. "You're all hopeless and that should have been Queen Anne's or Sarah Churchill's wig, not Mrs. Fitzherbert's. But nobody in this place knows any better."

"Blow Mrs. Fitzherbert," unnoticed Sam had slipped into the room. He looked kindly at their industry. "I bet Newent's never seen a party like ours. It was a triumph, my dears. Congratulations."

"And didn't everybody come up trumps?" Flo asked, trying to cram the regency buck into a box too small to hold it. "Who do you think looked the best?"

"Well, outside the family I think old Bill Naylor in his clerical rig looked as good as anybody," said Sam.

Lucy closed her eyes, leaning back on her heels. "To think that over two hundred years ago such people – apart from regency bucks and Mrs. Fitzherberts – really walked through these rooms when they were new. Sat down to eat and play cards, stood up to dance and gossip and . . ."

Emily giggled. "Think of the palaver in all that gear every time they went to the privy."

"No problem at all," countered Lucy. "It was mostly commodes and chamber pots anyway and our drawers didn't have any gussets – they were wide open between the legs and we just lifted our skirts and sat – ouch!" Her father caught the side of her head with a bushy white wig.

"Stop day-dreaming," he grinned. "Come on, let me help or Mummy will never be ready for the Appleby's tonight. Two parties on the trot . . ." His big hands busied among the boxes, tying on labels, writing addresses. "I think our Lucy looked the best, but I didn't notice her join in the fun. She seemed to be a spectator most of the time. Aren't you very well, Lucy?"

Lucy flushed. "Of course I am," she snapped. "Belt up."

Flo stared at the child. Goodness, how thin she was and

315

ghostly looking with eyes too large in a too small face. They'd all had a hectic year, but on Lucy it really showed. She had worked harder than any of them with all that decorating, sewing and Lord knows what. And she'd thrown herself, heart and soul, into this Regency party, making her own green silk panniered dress, little silk slippers and dorothy bag, going to infinite pains to find exactly the right toupée and fan. lashing out with precious savings instead of hiring with the rest. As if it mattered. And all those endless arguments about calling it a Georgian party and her scathing comments about addle-pates and nincompoops when Regency had won the family vote. And, on top of everything, staying up till all hours on that darned school project that obsessed her so – as if any school prize was worth it. Girls' schools were the limit. Everybody said so. The boys were not made to work half as hard but they got there in the end. Emily had had the sense to abandon her non-conformists for something simpler.

One thing, Lucy had not been sneaking off to Edgington lately and a good thing too after what she had heard last night. In any case, it wasn't safe for a girl to be cycling along country lanes these days. And whatever did she mean by our drawers?

"Put a finger on here for me, Flo dear," Sam interrupted.

She obliged. Thank Heaven. The last knot. Together they piled up the boxes and Sam took a teetering load into the hall.

"I say, Mummy," Emily stretched. "That was an interesting bit of news I heard Mrs. Appleby come out with last night. About the Rector of Edgington. Does Lucy know?"

"Oh – him." Flo's voice was casual.

"What about him?" Lucy snapped.

"He's been carted off to the loony bin," laughed Emily.

"Don't be so coarse." Flo felt her mouth tighten. "And we needn't talk about him."

"And why not?" Lucy was in a belligerent mood again.

"Why are you always pushing things under the carpet? What about him, Em?"

Flo made as much noise as she could, stacking the remaining boxes.

"Apparently he went off his rocker in the middle of a sermon about S.I.N." Emily cupped her hands round her mouth and reduced her voice to a whisper. "Sin: If we don't believe in S.I N. we're atheists and damned to all eternity. Dr. Frazier had to help get him down from the pulpit and get him back to the Rectory." She giggled again. "It's quite spooky, really. Do you remember that time he came to see us at Fair Promise Road?"

"No we don't," said Flo firmly, relieved to see Sam picking up the last parcel.

"Come on, all of you," he said, "into the little parlour. Put your feet up and watch television while I make a cup of tea. Then Mummy can have a bath and freshen up for tonight. And you girls go to bed early and see the boys do the same." He turned to Flo and his voice was tender.

"Or would you rather not go, Flo? Let's pretend we've got colds or I've got some drawing to catch up on or something."

"Of course you must go," shouted Lucy. "You wanted everybody to come to your party, didn't you? Just like a man to be so bloody selfish."

"Lucy!"

But Lucy was past caring. She slouched into the little parlour, switched on television and sat looking at the screen, one leg hanging over the chair arm, her foot tapping against the coal scuttle, knowing and pleased that she was annoying Emily.

She looked at the screen as though from a distance, the square box receding and shrinking, not shadowy but in the sharpest detail, like the view from the wrong end of a telescope. It was not only the television set that was receding, the room itself and everything in it was leaving her, but still sharply defined. She no longer knew the real size of anything.

She had that familiar feeling of her mind detaching itself from reality and she too tired to resist. From another world a hundred little men with long noses tapped with tiny hammers against her eardrums. The tappings crescendoed through beatings to thumpings for the little men with long noses determined on a hearing, their voices worse than their hammering.

Don't do it. Don't do it. Don't do it. Don't do. Don't do. Don't do. Do. Do. Do. The voice of conscience was neither still nor small.

"Don't wake her," said Sam as an hour later he and Flo left for the Appleby party, and, "Let's not stay too long," as he manoeuvred the car to make sure they would not be boxed in.

"Good grief. You say that every time we go anywhere. Be sociable for a change." Oh Lord, she thought, what's happening to us?

"We'll stay as long as you like, my dear," said Sam peaceably, taking her arm.

"Sam and Flo," called their hostess from the front door, "Lovely to see you again so soon. Aren't you exhausted after last night? Come on. Everybody's still talking about your party." She led them into the drawing room full of people, alcohol, smoke and chat. They were given the usual Appleby punch and separated immediately.

"Sam, come over here," commanded a loud voice out of a brick red face. "We want your opinion on this. Have you seen what they've done to Webster's Place?"

But Sam couldn't get a word in.

"They've shoved a bulldozer straight through the middle of one side of it. You never saw such a bloody mess in all your life. Poor old Jane Shaw will go off her head."

Flo groaned. She was listening to half a dozen conversations at once. Sam had kept his promise to keep that useless client away from Beacon House and the last thing they needed was a resurgence of interest from that quarter.

Let the old girl go somewhere else for her free consultations.

"But what can we do about it?" wailed an emaciated woman in a dress like a dishcloth.

"And they reckon the demolishers have gone bankrupt and can't even finish the job," shouted the brick red face.

"Pity," said a dark-suited solicitor. "It should have been done years ago. The place is nothing but eighteenth century slum with a rotten history. I'd like to hear what Bill Naylor says about it."

Flo was now talking with Bill Naylor, the very guest she had been trying to avoid, but he was available and everybody else seemed engaged. He was chairman of the music club and bound to go on at her about that last set of minutes she had not managed to get out yet. He had been too polite to mention them last night. If only he knew how packed her days were.

"Did I hear your name taken in vain, Bill?" she asked. That should keep him clear of the music club.

"They can say what they like," laughed Naylor. "I don't want to get involved in that argument. Though I don't agree with the word 'slum. Let me refill your glass, Flo dear. Now tell me about that daughter of yours. Is she still writing her history of Webster's Place?"

"Thankyou, Bill. That's finished now. She didn't get the school prize. Her sister beat her to it with an amusing thing on Newent's smells."

"Poor Lucy. How did she take it?"

"Not too well inside. She's still besotted. Spends all her spare time by a ruin in that copse just below us. She says its a Georgian garden house but . . ."

"Do you mean those two or three tatty old columns near the old gypsum quarry?"

"Yes."

"Oh no, my dear. You know what they are, surely? When some of the colonnades in the market place were removed, many years ago of course, an eccentric old chap who lived in

319

your house, long before the Newtons, had 'em erected as a kind of folly in that little wood."

Flo laughed a gurgly laugh as a great weight left her shoulders.

"You really mean it? That's all they are? Columns from the market place? Lucy was so positive she even had the rest of us almost believing her tales. And as for that daft Rector from Edgington, the way he encouraged her – I could . . ."

"Oh, him. There are rumours about him and his last living. Dr. Frazier has known him for years, says he's as mad as a hatter. If this hadn't happened it might have been the Court House instead of a hospital. We might have had to . . ."

"Flo, my dear, what a lovely party you gave us last night!" A woman she hardly knew interrupted. She was a newcomer mutual friends had asked if they could bring along. Flo hated familiarity too soon. Whatever was the woman's name? Unable to introduce properly, she felt awkward.

"Oh, hello. Yes, the children let us have our way last night, now we'll have to do something for them." What the dickens was the woman's name?

"My dear, haven't they let you know? The gang's been planning it for weeks."

"Do tell me," Flo's voice was faint.

"It's those superb vaulted cellars of yours. They want lots of dark corners, a few candles in bottles and a group."

Flo caught on immediately and her imagination ran riot. She felt light-headed. It must be the wine, or the noise. Or the loss of that weight she'd felt on her shoulders for months past.

"We'll have a gypsy evening. A Spanish gypsy evening. Bull fighting posters on the walls. A Spanish cave party. They can dress up . . ."

"No, my dear," screamed the unidentified woman. "You're making a thing of it again. They just want candles in bottles. Simple food. A group. Nothing else. You'll spoil it. It's the 'in' thing. Candles in bottles. I've got five children too. We're all terribly envious of you and your cellars."

There was no point in reply. The din was too much. Flo caught sight of their hostess looking determined. She was clapping her hands. Dear old Meg, you could tell she had once been a schoolteacher.

"Food, everybody," Meg called and everybody carried on with alcohol, smoke and chat. The name suddenly came, Molly Carpenter, but before she could make the introduction Bill Naylor had been whisked away and a little Scottish body had taken his place. Oh Lord! What was the Scotswoman's name? She couldn't hear herself think and why had it suddenly got so hot?

"Talking of the 'in thing', have you heard what the Lamberts have got?"

"Is there anything left for them to get? I thought they had the lot."

"My dear, they've got a sauna . .

Meg Appleby was looking even more determined. "Supper time," she interrupted. "Flo dear, are you all right? Everything's in the dining room. Be a pal and lead the way."

People started to move at last. Somebody jogged at Flo's elbow. She dabbed at a stream of punch down her best dress. Sam appeared, gently taking away her glass. Dear old Sam. He always looked after her. She must be nicer to him. He didn't say much but she knew he was worried sick about the Ashfield project. She thought people were looking at them.

"We'll go home soon, Sam," she whispered. "Straight after supper."

Sam busied himself with plates while she looked at the wonderful Appleby spread. Two whole Scotch salmon beautifully glazed and garnished, as done up for a sacrifice. Chicken galantines, a game pie. Bowls of green salad, nut salad, potato salad. Tiny home-made rolls, piping hot, and curls of butter. Bettter be careful of those and this new dress. Various soft puddings, one lemon, one chocolate, one raspberry and the Appleby speciality flavoured with nutmeg.

She hoped Sam wouldn't make his usual stale joke about aphrodisiacs. A whole Stilton. Massive fruit bowl, highly coloured and polished like a Carmen Miranda head-dress. Lots of gleaming napery and shining silver. Little posy pots of miniature Michaelmas daisies.

Meg must have been busy for a week or more. Everywhere we go, thought Flo, it's the same thing. Same well upholstered drawing rooms, same people, same food with the odd variation like nutmeg mousse, and same chat. But Beacon House is different. And suddenly she wanted to go home. People were definitely looking, and whispering too.

They slipped away as soon as they decently could, fresh air hitting them like a blow from Skegness.

"It's a damned shame about Webster's Place," said Sam as he turned the car up Beacon Hill Road. "What the hell is our town council thinking of? Most of them haven't got any aesthetic sense at all. It's wicked the way Newent's architecture has been allowed to . . ."

"Well, at least while they're leaving most of it alone, apart from Webster's Place and Naylor's Yard, of course, they're not doing anything terrible to it. You ought to be pleased. Most of it's intact, only shabby. And Sam, talking of architecture, I can't wait to tell Lucy. That ruin in the spinney is just a few old columns out of the market place. Did you . . .?"

"Yes. I heard Bill Naylor going on about them and he should know. I should have sussed that out myself really. What with one thing and another there's hardly time to breathe nowadays." He turned the car towards their drive at the top of the hill. It was an awkward turn.

"Oh! Sam!"

"I wish you wouldn't shriek like that when I'm driving."

"Sorry, darling. But guess what? I know exactly what we're going to do with the odd room. And it won't cost us anything like the Lambert set up. We'll do it all ourselves. I can't wait to get started."

"On what?"

"Well, they've got a sauna. But we'll have an indoor swimming pool."

"Then you'd better start cutting down on electricity bills," said Sam shortly. "Look at the drawing room lights full on. I told you to switch them off."

"I did. Oh, Sam," Flo's heart sank.

Sam picked up her altered mood immediately. They scrambled out of the car, through the hall towards the lights.

CHAPTER 31

A pair of steps leaned against a drawing room wall, two buckets of dirty water slopped on to their best carpet and Lucy was attacking another wall with a wallpaper scraper. Sam and Flo watched their specially chosen handmade French wallpaper hang down in wet curls from the scraper to fall in a soggy mound round Lucy's feet. The child stepped back, a messy squelch sticking to the soles of her slippers. Sam and Flo stared first at the uneven patch of splodged plaster and the gooey liquid trickling to the wainscot below and then at Lucy.

"I know we shouldn't have put paper here," said Lucy excitedly. "We've covered up the Davison murals. If only we can find them there are beautifully painted murals under this lot."

My God! They stared at their daughter. How excessively thin she was in that skimpy nightie. Shoulder blades and elbows looked ready to break through the skin.

Together they remembered, and faced at last, her increasing irritability, her hands forever on the move, twisting her broken-ended hair, screwing up a handkerchief, playing the piano for no more than a few minutes, endlessly writing in a script that had become too tiny to read, drumming a chair arm, never still, and now forcing the scraper up and down the wall again, digging into the plaster, knuckles showing white through her skin.

Flo took her arm gently. It was like taking hold of a stick. "It's all right, Lucy," she said kindly.

Sam went to the bathroom in search of a sedative. He

would ring the surgery first thing.

Oh, my God! They both had the same thought. What have we done?

Incredibly, by eight-thirty next morning Lucy was on her way to school looking like a lost soul nobody loved. Sam was already on the Ashfield site after a desperate phone call in the early hours. His worst fears were confirmed, bloody great cracks everywhere, one corner slipped completely, two men in Kingsmill Hospital and one dead. Flo sat at the great kitchen table, head in hands, the world on her shoulders.

She had never felt so wretched in her life or so ill-equipped. She did not know where to turn, nor had the energy to make the move if she did. She had the coldest feeling that Lucy was all but lost. She got up to pace round the room, her mouth dry, stomach churning. She couldn't concentrate. Her legs trembled beneath her. She sat down again, knowing she was close to panic, and it wasn't Sam and the Ashfield site she was thinking of.

This was worse than that time when Lucy was on the way and there had been all that bother with Sam's mother. The old woman would have broken things up, if she could, and very nearly did. "I shall call you Florence," she had said in her superior voice and always had.

Worse than the death of her own parents who had died too young, one quickly following the other. Then she had been too busy with babies to mourn and, like a too-short convalescence, had felt the pain for too long.

Worse than that time when Robert was hurled over the handlebars into a dry clay field set hard as concrete. He lay in hospital concussed for days on end. Then she had prayed as never before in her life. Dear God, bring him round and I'll never go on at him again. And as soon as he was up and about the nagging had restarted; his appearance, his school work, his pop records, his friends. She tried to pray now but couldn't get the words together.

Worse than that time Sam had decided to chuck in his job

and go it alone. All he had done was to stick up his plate and wait. He would have waited forever as the bills piled higher. It was she who had done all the urging to join this and that to get himself known. Was there a single club or society in this town they didn't pay subs to? And it was always she who got on with their orgy of entertaining. Did he know the effort it cost? She didn't believe he did, forgetting the times he came back from a job, tired and worn. He was too kind, always had been. He attracted clients like batty old Jane Shaw and her mythical cottage instead of jobs with any meat. Though the Ashfield project was an exception and look where it had landed them. But even that didn't matter as much as Lucy.

This, whatever it was that was wrong with Lucy, was different. She could neither comprehend nor get to grips with it. Life was a long drag uphill and she was bone tired of hauling the others behind her. If she wasn't pulling she was pushing.

Every holiday they had ever taken she'd had to arrange. Every school the five had attended had been vetted and chosen by her. Every successful exam had been won by her. Every personal letter, apart from the children's, written in this house had been written by her. And if only Sam had finished the boundary fence Lucy might never have . . . And if she'd not been so cruel about Jane Shaw, Lucy might . . .

The tears started, she couldn't stop them. She felt ashamed. How could she harbour such thoughts with poor Lucy so ill and poor Sam in such trouble? She was a child and she desperately wanted her mother.

She heard the coroner's voice, slow and clear, "Mr. Beresford, I see from the schedule here, you missed three important site meetings at Ashford." A pause almost too long to bear. "Why was that?"

Poor Sam. If only she'd not pressed him so. Poor Lucy.

Lucy had always been the odd one out of the five. She didn't know why. She had been a knowing child from her

326

earliest days, a demanding child, an exasperating child, a loving child, a giving child. If only Lucy had got rheumatic fever or consumption or even polio she felt she could cope. But this was something beyond her ken and something she felt in the depths of her heart more dangerous than any of those. And more than anything, she had to admit it, she felt ashamed such a thing had happened to them. She thought she caught some funny looks last night. People were whispering.

What could she do and where could she go? There was reorganisation at school and new doctors in the surgery; no grannies, no aunts, no experience. Apart from old Bill Naylor, most of the people she spoke to last night, she hardly knew. The rest had avoided her. They must have done.

She was alone. Sam sorting the debacle at Ashford. The children at school. Time crawled one minute and raced the next. She longed to lay down her head on the massive scrub-top table she and Sam had so joyfully, fetched all the way from Hertfordshire in the Appleby's big pickup. But how was she to help her family if she couldn't help herself?

She looked round her vast kitchen with its original pine cupboards, the glazed dresser taking up the whole of one wall, the overhead clothes rack, now drying out bunches of herbs, the renovated old Aga, the black and white old stone tiles that had taken the skin off her hands in payment for her scouring all those coats of Cardinal Red.

Her gaze rested on the room's only new addition, a huge stainless steel unit of sinks and drainers hiding innumerable gadgets.

How could something that had once given her so much pride now turn to ash in her mouth?

It was true what that wretched cleric had said in Fair Promise Road. This was an unhappy house. Look what it was doing to them and God knows what it had done to others. If ever there was a millstone round their necks, this was it.

She knew there were things she should do, if it were only chivvying the family along. But she'd had enough of all that.

Somehow, the words came at last. She prayed to God for strength to cope and already felt better for it. She and Sam didn't talk about God. Or go to church either unless it be weddings, funerals, Christmas Eve or the odd civic service it might be politic to be seen at. But the children were all Christened, the older three confirmed and they'd all been to Sunday School on and off for two or three years. She believed in God. She willed the others to do the same.

She heard the back door open and footsteps along the passage and did not look up. Any other time she would have leapt to her feet to a mirror, a pat to her hair and a dab to her face. But not this time with the stuffing all but knocked out of her.

She heard a voice. Good grief! It was Meg Appleby. She couldn't get up, not even for her oldest friend.

Meg came purposefully, calmly, kindly into the room. Her face, her walk were all of these things. The two women looked at each other. Flo felt naked. She was past pretending and glad of it. It crossed her mind for no more than a second, how on earth had Meg managed to get here so early with all she must have to do at home? Meg smiled and sat down beside her. She was decisive and her voice brooked no nonsense.

"Flo, dear, we can see what's happening to Lucy and we want to help."

Flo opened her mouth, said nothing and felt the tears well again in her eyes. Meg put out her hand. It was the strongest hand Flo had felt in years. She clutched at it like a drowning woman grabbing a rope to the lifeboat.

"We've been through all this with my sister's girl, Flo, and we're going to help you get out of it. Don't, for Heaven's sake, get yourselves mixed up with psychiatrists – they'll lay the blame at your door or Sam's and neither of you will have the strength to shift."

"Oh, Meg!" There was nothing else to say and nothing else needed.

"Now the day after tomorrow we're going to Wales. It will be our last stay at the cottage before packing it away for the winter. I want you to let Lucy come with us and I promise we'll bring her back on the road to recovery. Flo, this has been brewing for months but I could see something must be done straight away on the night of your party."

Words stuck in Flo's throat. She wanted to say but I can't let her go. It was at one of your parties we first met that wretched man. And Meg knew that was what she wanted to say.

"Flo, dear, you need time to get your strength back. And Lucy needs it too. Believe me, Flo, I know what I'm saying. Now where's the kettle?"

The world slipped from Flo's shoulders. Meg Appleby understood. She understood more than Sam. She understood because she was a woman. And because she was a woman Flo put her whole trust there. She knew she ought to be weighed down by the Ashfield job. One man dead. Others in hospital. All those families. But Ashfield seemed a thousand miles away and Lucy was here at home. Between them, she and Meg, with God's help, would get lucy better. She knew they would. Sam must get himself out of his own hole and she didn't doubt that he would. She drank her coffee, every drop.

The two women hugged each other long and tight. Meg picked up her car keys.

"Must dash, Flo dear. We'll pick Lucy up about ten tomorrow morning and bring her back as soon as she's turned the corner. Only casual things, mind. And don't forget wellingtons and a mac."

A kiss on Flo's cheek, an extra hug and Meg has gone.

Flo was left staring at her state of the art sinks. Suddenly and inexplicably, as if the very taps had turned themselves on to gush out the notion with all the force of Niagara close to her ear, she knew her family's future.

This house would continue whether they loved it, or not.

Without love, there was nothing to keep them here, so why should they stay? Nobody but the Applebys would miss them and dear old Meg was rich enough to visit them any time, anywhere. A whole world was waiting outside Newent. Canada, Australia, New Zealand. Sam could practise there as well as here. She felt equal to any of them and she'd always been charmed by pictures of their colonial weatherboard houses. Sam must be got round somehow.

She tucked the brilliant idea away to bring out when the time was right. She got up from the table, suddenly confident, buoyant, strong enough to carry the family along as she always had. They would begin again. Wiser perhaps. No impossible dreams. But plenty of plain common sense.

Thankyou, Meg. Thankyou, God. Her prayer had been answered. She was sure of that.

Early this afternoon, she would walk down Beacon Hill into Newent, her eyes fixed on the pale spire of St. Leonard's. She would enter the calm gloom of that hallowed place and let its peace creep into her bones. Through the dark rood screen, beyond the gilded reredos above the high altar she would look up at the jewelled lights of the great east window and thank God for her new found will.

And then she would meet the girls on their way from school.

She would tell Lucy she loved her. Lucy would respond, she knew she would. They would talk and talk as they had not talked for months. Not even Emily had been able to cut through Lucy's irritability. Now Flo felt equal to it.

She blew her nose, long and hard.

And she would welcome Sam home, no matter how late, with tenderness and understanding. No recriminations.

She stacked up the coffee things and picked up the local paper delivered that morning. A headline on the front page caught her eye. The Reverend John Clements of Edginton had been given an unexpected sabbatical. He was in retreat at Betham Hall. And if not there, she thought grimly, it might

330

have been a penitentiary. He had been the cause of their trouble and she was glad at his confinement. She threw the paper into the bin and hoped never to hear his name again.

Her face lightened as she ran briskly up her once beautiful staircase, that was now only a set of stairs like any other. She must look out a suitcase for Lucy who'd always loved going to Meg's cottage and then check over her clothes.

Sunshine streamed through the big landing window. Her leaden morning was magically changing into golden afternoon.

EPILOGUE

Our Dad's birthday bike was a godsend. Throughout that enchanted summer of '68, I stalked Lucy Beresford. Don't ask me why. Out of an unnatural curiosity, perhaps. Because I'd fallen for a pair of blue eyes. I can't tell what made me do it.

I was obsessed.

From Easter till summer's end I biked round the streets near Fair Promise Road to keep an eye out for that girl, dodging behind trees and gate ways so she never caught sound or sight of me. I knew when she went to play tennis, to music lessons, to the shops or the public library.

She and her sister usually strode out of the High School gate with a gaggle of other girls, all flicking their hair, flashing their eyes, sporting their legs. But when Lucy went to the library she was always alone and always quiet. That's when I liked her best.

I made a grab for her returned books and flicked through pages like flashes of film. They were a rum collection of old diaries, letters, accounts and engravings of Nottinghamshire. I was in clover when she left her own notes behind in one of them. The same names cropped up again and again. And the tricks they got up to – I could hardly understand the half of it. No wonder Lucy was so secretive with her brown paper covers and plastic bags.

I knew when she started those early bike rides to Edgington Rectory and once I left my own bike at that gate to creep up some way behind her. I thought I saw something she wouldn't like her mother to see, as I wouldn't like Great Aunt Jane to see what I was up to, either.

I never let on to the old girl that I was finding out more about Webster's Place than she'd ever dreamed of and I'll never forget that time we took her cat, Ginger, to the vet in that street either.

He was an old tom and his halitosis was poisonous. He spent most of his life on a soft cushioned chair near the Aga in our old fashioned kitchen. Waking, he would stretch and yawn, then sitting up with an air of 'cook – is – the – dinner – ready' he'd mark time with his off-white front paws.

He woke up regularly at meal times.

This particular day he yawned right across the apple-pie-on-a-plate just out of the oven and none of us would eat a crumb. Not even when Great Aunt Jane offered to ease off the light as thistledown top crust and throw it away. Poor Ginger didn't know her bête noir was waste. She couldn't abide it. Anyway from the moment she threw that pie away, and we all watched her do it to make sure that it wouldn't turn up as a crumble next day, old Ginger's number was up.

"You get your blazer on, you," she said pointing to me with one hand and picking up Ginger with the other. "You know where we're going." So we turned into her favourite street, totally unprepared for the shock to come.

"Look, oh look," she cried in anguish, dropping her jaw along with the cat who landed light as a feather and bounded off like a lion.

There, where her accusing finger pointed was a great hole and a bulldozer through one side of her precious street. Three jolly workmen like friends from Hell, in a pile of rubble, were stoking a roaring fire with her beautiful eighteenth century doors and shutters.

"Vandals," she shouted, as sparks flew around us like a bonfire night party and the men laughed louder as the bright flames shot higher.

The dickens of a row ensued with letters to the local paper, for and against. But the damage was done and there was no point in crying over burnt wood said Great Aunt Jane. After

333

all, one side of the street was still intact and the gap in the other showed up the old graveyard converted to gardens. And somebody must have been looking out for the street when a little matter of the demolisher's bankruptcy put paid to further activity.

We never saw Ginger again after his terrified dash from Webster's Place, though we put an advert in Lost and Found, offered a reward and I cried a bit. Soon afterwards we were adopted by a stray black wisp of a kitten, a scratching, biting creature only at peace near Great Aunt Jane. He was nobody's cat but her own and she called him Grim.

By the middle of September when evenings were darkening and I wasn't allowed out on my bike after tea, I was already getting fed up with Lucy Beresford. She didn't come out to play tennis or go to music lessons, not even to the library any more. Even those sneaky bike rides to Edgington stopped. I caught a glimpse, now and then, of the family squashed up in that big old car of theirs, Lucy no more than a pinched up white face at a window. She'd lost her good looks, though her eyes were still brilliant. Besides I was getting into fishing. Our Dad had left his tackle behind and nobody packed a better picnic than Great Aunt Jane. And since Mr Beresford moved his office to the town she didn't bring back tales of his family any more.

Though I always wondered if he was on the other end of that mysterious phone call of hers one late afternoon in October.

The others were playing football. I was in the kitchen struggling with a letter to our Dad. It's difficult when you never see who you're writing to and you can't tell him you want your mother back. Our black lab called Fred was yelping to be let in on the game.

Suddenly the back door burst open and Great Aunt Jane rushed in like a tornado. Fred shot straight between her legs and out, nearly up-ending her. There were wild shrieks from the garden. Goody gum drops. He must have stopped somebody's goal. Great Aunt Jane didn't hear a thing. Her face was set. She cocked an eye at the clock and made straight for the phone.

"It looks as though we're going to lose the other side of Webster's Place," was all she said. She replaced the receiver without her usual bang and I knew I had witnessed a secret.

It was three minutes to five and she'd run all the way from the municipal buildings where she'd heard a couple of aldermen coming out of a Public Health and Watch Committee meeting.

"I saw a family moving into Webster's Place the other day," whispered one.

"We'd better get another bulldozer down there quick," whispered the other.

If the machine ever got there it found a preservation order placed on what remained of that street which caused the aldermanic remark that with a bit of luck a certain lady might walk down there and catch a fever.

The rest of Great Aunt Jane's houses might be safe but the chaotic mess they were in stayed with us for years. I'd be nearly at the school leaving stage by the time we set off to see how their renovation was coming on.

"Fools," she shouted, pointing to basement kitchens now filled in with rubble. "Don't they know every cubic inch of space matters?"

She examined the windows and bemoaned the loss of shutters, noted some boot-scrapers gone and only three lampholders left so who'd made a mint from the others? "Still," she sniffed on the way home through the old graveyard, "It's better than nowt."

We turned, as we always did, to admire the striking roofline and she let out a yell loud enough to wake the dead beneath our feet.

"Look," she shouted "They're knocking down the bloody chimney stacks!"

She grabbed my arm and our heels hardly touched ground

as we raced home for the phone. Her terse message got the same result as before. No more chimneys came down and there was another municipal row about putting them back again. To this day half the houses in Webster's Place are without chimney stacks.

By this time my siblings had left home, I was asking for a year off before university and our Dad was still too far away to put up a stiff enough resistance. I picked grapes in Italy, had a brush with the law in Spain, got involved with a nurse in Germany and came back with a small debt, a well developed taste for older girls, this novel inside me bursting to get out and thoughts of further education quite squashed flat. Great Aunt Jane was more than pleased to see me and we celebrated the prodigal's return in style with one of her slap-up dinners.

She should have built that bungalow at the bottom of the garden but she'd left it too late. Mr Beresford had emigrated to New Zealand long since after he was cleared of negligence. His practice was swallowed up by a giant who'd have flicked off a mythical bungalow like a crumb from his Sunday best suit.

Before they left, the local paper gave the Beresfords quite a splash with a photograph of the family. I could see the girl with the remarkable blue eyes had got her looks back. Her hair was no longer ragged and her clothes didn't hang like sacks. I'd imagined her standing on the porch of one of those old colonial weatherboard houses. She'd be leaning against a pretty cast iron stanchion, one hand restraining her skirt in that stiff New Zealand breeze, the other shielding her lovely eyes against that strong New Zealand light. I knew those eyes to be just like our mother's. I knew her voice too, for I had often imagined her speaking my name as she might have spoken it.

I thought I wanted to starve in a garret and get on with my writing but by the time I was pushing twenty two in '81 I was still in my old room with Great Aunt Jane's cooking instead and the novel still struggling. She was wrapped up in family history, usually with old letters and diaries spread over the kitchen table. I was used to her Yorkshire voice, breaking my thread, summoning me down to hear this or that family tidbit.

When her voice was no more than a hoarse whisper outside my door I knew it meant something worth coming down for.

She settled herself in an old windsor with Grim on her knee. I sat beside her, both our backs to the Aga. She had that excited sheen on her face that she used to bring back from her Beresford sessions and that mole over her left eye brow was definitely getting bigger.

"Listen to this, you," she said, her voice still soft, "We're going back a hundred years. There's no date on the letter so we can't be exact. Your Great Grandfather didn't want to farm like the rest of 'em and you'll never guess what." She gave one of her wicked grins. "He wanted to be a window dresser."

I made no comment. I wanted her to get on with it.

"When he was a lad they apprenticed him to that draper's shop in the Olde White Harte in the Market Place. Used to sleep with all the other lads up in that top room where they keep the towels and bed linen and such like."

I'd never been up there so, again, no comment.

"Imagine it," she whispered, "early morning Christmas Eve and a hard frost the night before. Shop windows gummed up with Jack Frost. Young Joe, your Great Grandfather, was given a taper and ordered to light up the candles in the window bottoms. No use having a brilliant display if nobody can see it."

It seemed appropriate to agree with a nod of the head.

"As soon as the frost melted he could see the other side of the square where another lad in a draper's shop was doing the same thing. But that cakey-soft lad held his taper above his head. Paper chains and other Christmassy stuff caught light and before he could shout fire the whole shop was ablaze. The lad and the draper ran out of the shop dancing about in a panic. The man's wife showed a sight more bottom. She ran upstairs to the stockroom to chuck what she could out the window. Christmas shoppers had a field day. They were catching hold of stuff before it hit the cobbles and then running off like the clappers."

Again, I nodded, wondering where all this was taking us.

"A fish shop, a tripe shop and a chandlers close by all got a good dowsing else it might have been pobs for the church. Any road up, all that old property was pulled down. And guess what?"

I knew in a flash.

"The columns," I said.

"You're right," she said, "somebody got hold of the columns from that spot and had 'em erected in that little wood."

"And you want to see them again."

She pushed Grim off her knee and gave me another grin.

"We're usually on the same wavelength, you and me," she said. "Pity about poor Fred."

Her dog had been killed on the road ages ago so it was just the two of us, this time.

It was a long enough walk for such an old woman, up Clay Lane and over the bridge. We found the rubbish tip levelled and gone, landscaped and tidied up. The atmosphere was different. More normal, if you like, though not another soul in sight. No swings, no mountain slide but the old fence around our secret place had been repaired and fortified. "Damned cheek," she muttered as she valiantly fought her way through, getting off lightly with torn tights and pulled jacket but no blood drawn.

It was autumn, the copse floor dappled yellow and brown. Sun filtered through thinning foliage and an aura of golden light filled the little wood. We rested by the columns she had called her folly. It was now so obvious what they were. I took hold of her hand.

"Had enough?" I asked.

"Nay lad, let's see the lot now we're here. It's a magical place is this."

We passed alongside the columns till stopped by an old wall. She cast a brief look at the narrow red brick of centuries past but said nothing. We turned uphill along a narrow path, scratched by wall on one side, thorns on the other, her tights in ribbons by this time. She seemed not to care, she who had carried on darning long after others had sent their equipment to charity shops. She couldn't stand an unmended hole. Showers at school had been a nightmare for us with vest and pants more darn than anything else.

We kept close in single file. She led and I followed. Falling leaves had turned her into some kind of primeval creature of the forest. It was tough going. The hill was steep. Brambles lay like gin traps across our path.

I remembered how she had once talked of Time like a scotch kilt. I'd known for long enough how the tenses fold back and forth upon themselves yet I'd always puzzled over her 'and summat else, lad'. Now I recalled how my sisters would adjust their plaid skirts, the ends overlapping the beginning.

I felt light headed.

Suddenly she stopped, indicating to the left where the wooded hill gave way to an enormous ivy clad hole, terrifying in the lessening light.

"Keep well in," I said, knowing she would neither relinquish her lead nor turn back.

We passed what could only have been an old quarry and skirted a half finished fence. The slope continued through neglected shrubbery and old-roses. There were paths and low walls with an iron gate. It had taken longer than I thought. The light was fading, the air damp.

"Keep going," she said, her breath coming quick but shallow.

Beyond the gate was the house.

A little sigh escaped her mouth. Beads of sweat glistened on her whiskery upper lip.

"I always knew there'd be summat here, lad. And it's All Souls Day, don't forget."

And I knew then, whatever it was, this empathy with the past, she was passing it over to me. I felt a surge of love and regret at so much unsaid. I reached for the gift like a relay runner taking the baton, poised to race like the wind for the next changeover, my stride suspended in a false start as a voice called from the house.

"Bern-ard! Ber-nard!"

Four clear notes sounded so bold and piercing I could all but see them like flashes of light in the mist.

"Bern-ard! Ber-nard!"

I knew that name and the voice that called it. A thousand genii loci drummed their heels around me and with all my strength I fought a pull as strong as a magnet to get me into that house. A house I no longer wanted to see.

I looked down at Great Aunt Jane and caught hold of her hand to get a grip on myself.

"There's talk of building up here," she said, matter of fact. "It's pobs, is that. Mechanical diggers and a lass in a silk frock and white wig won't mix."

Nor one with warm arms, soft voice and speaking eyes, I say to myself.

I faced up to it, at last. Our mother wasn't coming back, Lucy Beresford would be knocking thirty and that other was no more than a phantom. The local paper was advertising for a junior reporter. It was time to knuckle down. That stubborn last chapter could wait. The mist was clearing. I squeezed Great Aunt Jane's warm hand.

"We're going back, old lady."

"Ready when you are, kind sir," she said. "Now, Bernard lad, what do you want for your tea?"